# ESCAPE FROM
# EDEN

## ELISA NADER

MeritPress
Avon, Massachusetts

Published by Merit Press
an imprint of F+W Media, Inc.
10151 Carver Road, Suite 200
Blue Ash, OH 45242. U.S.A.
*www.meritpressbooks.com*

Trade Paperback ISBN 10: 1-4405-8284-X
Trade Paperback ISBN 13: 978-1-4405-8284-4
Hardcover ISBN 10: 1-4405-6392-6
Hardcover ISBN 13: 978-1-4405-6392-8
eISBN 10: 1-4405-6393-4
eISBN 13: 978-1-4405-6393-5

Printed in the United States of America.

10 9 8 7 6 5 4 3 2 1

Cover design by Elisa Nader.
Cover image © Corbis.com.

*This book is available at quantity discounts for bulk purchases.*
*For information, please call 1-800-289-0963.*

*For Brent and Cici*

# Acknowledgments

First, it's crazy that I'm writing acknowledgements for a novel I wrote. Crazypants crazy. This book couldn't have been written without the advice and support from the following people:

Brent Canfield, my voice of reason, my best friend, and B$ husband (thanks for loving me when I had scary, unwashed writer hair).

My parents, German and Mary Nader, who love and support me, even when they think my ideas are weird.

My sister, Susan Nader, who hung out with the monster so I could write.

My sister, Carolyn Nader, who would have loved this book.

My brilliant crit partner, Nina Berry, who deleted the darlings when I was too afraid to do it myself.

My unshakable agent, Danielle Chiotti, who deleted the darlings Nina did not.

My BFF Kami Greene, who has read almost everything I've ever written, including all the dirty fan fiction in high school.

My parents-in-law, Jane and Tom Canfield, who were enthusiastic about everything, from the writing process to the book cover.

The "Edenton" Beta Readers: Erin Bush, Suzanne Lago, Marjorie Lee, Sue McCarthy, Claudia Osmond, Lori Parsons, Milissa Tarquini, Kim White, and Juliet White.

The team at Merit Press, particularly Jackie Mitchard, Meredith O'Hayre, Skye Alexander, and Sylvia McArdle.

And Cici, the center of my little universe.

*"A fool's paradise is a wise man's hell!"*
Thomas Fuller, 1608–1661

# Chapter One

"False prophets!" the Reverend Elias Eden yelled into the dented microphone. "False witnesses! False apostles!" With every furious word, sweat flew from his brow, disappearing into the blinding fluorescent lights overhead.

He'd begun tonight's prayer service as he did every evening, scowling down at the congregation as we sat on hard wooden benches under the protection of God and a sloped tin roof. Beyond the pavilion's pillars, the sounds of the jungle at night came to life: the chirping of frogs, croaking of toucans, and the incessant buzz of insects.

"Move over," Juanita whispered to me, placing her hand on my shoulder.

Her skin was cold. A welcome shock in the soupy heat. I glanced up at the Reverend. His eyes were now squeezed shut in passion, arms thrown out from his sides, momentarily blind to his Flock below.

"Deceitful workers," the Reverend said in a low voice. "Deceitful accusers of true faith . . . "

"Mia, move," Juanita said, eyes flicking around the pavilion, and to the stage.

As I scooted to my left, a splinter lodged in my thigh. I swallowed down a yelp. The last thing I wanted was the Reverend's full and pious attention on me during evening prayer. With a wince, I lifted the hem of my skirt, plucked the splinter out, and threw it on the wooden floor. A bead of red blood formed.

Aliyah plopped down between Juanita and me, out of breath, and bowed her head. She smelled of thick grease and bleach. She was late because of dinner cleanup duty.

"False brethren," the Reverend said and opened his eyes. "And even false worshippers. How do we detect a truth from a falsehood? How do we avoid deception and lies and allow the true light to shine on us?"

I resisted the urge to roll my eyes. I had endured six years of sermons and preaching. Six years of being told what was right and what was wrong, and the Reverend was never in the wrong. Under the harsh lights, the

Reverend's doughy face looked even paler than usual, highlighting the broken capillaries that spidered across his nose and cheeks like a web. A perpetual sheen of sweat slicked his brow. Why he had a full beard—a wiry ginger beard—in the middle of the jungle I couldn't guess. Although I'd imagined countless times how I'd draw him, mapping the page in slivers of intricate lines, I never did. My sketchbook was sacred.

And I suspected the Reverend Elias Eden wasn't as sacred as he believed he was.

"Mia," Aliyah whispered to me, "I got the call."

I turned to her. Her black hair was pulled into a series of ponytails with colorful holders like gum balls placed at the base and end of each. We'd known each other since we were little girls, and in the six years we'd been friends she still had her nine-year-old hairstyle. She peeked at me through her braids. Her brown eyes were alight with excitement.

Because getting the call only meant one thing.

"The Reverend invited you to Prayer Circle?" I asked.

Juanita's head whipped toward us, a flurry of dark curls falling across her face. "What?" she whispered.

"In ancient times," the Reverend boomed, "in the great city of Ephesus, the people were tempted to worship Diana, the goddess whose temple was one of the wonders of the ancient world . . . "

Aliyah bit down a smile and nodded. "My dad got the invitation right after dinner."

"But there were all sorts of dark things in the shadows of this temple. Magic, sorcery, astrology! Sexual immorality and crime . . . "

Juanita met my gaze over Aliyah's head. For the Flock, it was a coveted invitation, an invitation neither Juanita nor I had received yet, even though we were a year older than Aliyah. Secretly, though, I was relieved. Initiation into Prayer Circle opened up a new chapter in life at Edenton: courting with a person chosen by the Reverend, which would end in marriage and proliferation of the Flock. I didn't want to be with anyone, though. I only wanted one thing, and an attachment to another person would get in the way.

The Reverend raised his hands, as if fighting off invisible forces. "False idols tempt us—they are present in everything. Money is idolized. Beauty is idolized. Churches themselves can become idols! A church is a gift—a means to an end, but churches become idolatrous when made ends in themselves . . . "

"When do you go?" Juanita whispered. Her eyes, the color of the blackest peppercorns in the Edenton kitchen, expressed a mix of envy and concern.

"Thursday night." Aliyah grinned, her teeth white against her ebony-pink lips. "Will you help me make something pretty to wear?" she asked me.

"Uh, sure—"

"Ssssh," Bridgette hissed from behind us. Loud enough for the Reverend to tear his divine focus from the rafters and skate his eyes in our direction.

We dropped our heads.

The Reverend continued as if we hadn't disrupted him. "Edenton was created to shelter us from these temptations and keep our focus on the worship of our true God. Now let's bow our heads in a silent prayer of thanksgiving."

"Silent prayer of thanksgiving, Mia," Bridgette hissed.

I half-turned my head and gave her a sneer. Bridgette glared at me from beneath her perfectly blunt-cut golden bangs. As I turned back, I caught Juanita shaking her head at me, a definite *don't stoop to her level* in her eyes. It was hard not to. Bridgette was so—so Bridgette.

I kept my head down, mind wandering off as I let it do during silent prayer. The Reverend didn't control my thoughts. They were my own. But most times I couldn't help the guilt and the fear that weighed on me. If anyone knew—if Reverend Eden knew—that I wasn't spending this time praying, I didn't want to think about the consequences.

After our prayers, the Reverend spoke. "My children," he said in a low voice, perched on the edge of his wooden throne.

It was painted an iron gray. The color, and the gold-painted emblem on the chair back—a majestic tree surrounded by a gilded fence—symbolized Edenton. My uniform dress was the same serviceable gray, starched so stiff at the collar it itched. The Edenton emblem was stitched in white over my left breast, ever-present over my heart. But the Reverend didn't want control of just our hearts. He wanted our minds as well.

The Reverend's shock of bright ginger hair danced against the dull color of the chair. "Tonight we welcome more sheep into our Flock with open arms and open hearts. Edenton is about leading an honest life, a peaceful life, one that we devote to God and each other. And it is indeed a pleasure to welcome new members into the Flock of the Promised Land."

He outstretched his hand. A dark ring of sweat circled the underarm of his blue shirt. He always wore shades of blue.

Three people climbed the stage steps at the right and stood next to the throne. The Reverend pushed himself up and waved a thick-fingered hand at the woman first. She came forward. Her hair was the color of sand. She was tall, and eyed the Reverend down her long, pointed nose.

The Reverend was a big man, overweight in a community of people who tended to be lean and strong. Food was plentiful, but we worked and trained hard. We attended physical training classes, daily. We ate fruits and vegetables from the gardens. Jake the Chicken Man watched over the coops like a tyrant; Enrique and his brother Angél oversaw the fishing nets at the shore. Every week, a shipment of grains, water, medical supplies, and other necessities came in from a nearby city. Like all the teenage girls in the compound, I worked in the kitchen, cooking and serving meals. The Reverend, though, rarely ate with the congregation. He was usually served meals in his cottage.

Reverend Eden shook hands with the woman. Her grip seemed sturdy. The man next to her, whom I assumed was her husband, wore expensive but disheveled clothing. His shirt was rumpled, shorts crooked, one hem higher on the knee than the other. He shoved his glasses up on his nose, then greeted the Reverend with a friendly enough smile.

The Reverend moved to shake hands with their son, but the boy jerked away. I smirked with mild satisfaction. Reverend Eden's bushy brows furrowed at the snub, but he covered it up with a hearty laugh. The congregation laughed too, because that's what the Reverend wanted; emotion shared, even if it was forced.

"Ah," Reverend Eden smiled, his teeth the color of fishbone. "What a gift it is for us, to welcome into our family one of God's strong sons. Isn't it?" The congregation agreed with hollered yeses. "How old are you, my child?"

"Seventeen," the boy said in a steely tone.

From my seat, I could see his chest rise and fall rapidly against the fabric of his shirt. Like his parents, he wore nice clothes: a clean red

T-shirt, cargo shorts with a lot of pockets, and expensive-looking sneakers that had mud only on the soles. He scanned the congregation as if he wanted to fight each and every one of us with his bare fists. I hadn't seen that kind of intense anger in anyone in a long time.

"Wow," Aliyah whispered. "He looks so mean."

"Cute and mean," Juanita said, flicking a glance where the boys our age sat in the congregation. "Cuter than the other boys."

"Your brother is sitting over there," I whispered to her.

"And? I don't need to think my brother is cute." She peered at me through narrowed eyes. "Only you do."

"Your brother is cute," I said.

Octavio, her brother, was to court me after our first Prayer Circle. He was sweet and thoughtful, and we talked sometimes, when we could. It was rare to have time to talk to the boys in Edenton.

"I don't think the new boy is mean," I whispered, refocusing the topic on the boy onstage. "He doesn't want to be here."

"Who wouldn't want to be here?" Aliyah said, shaking her head.

Me.

"My children," the Reverend went on. "Tonight we welcome Daniel, his wife Evie, and their son Gabriel into the Eden family."

The congregation exploded into hallelujahs. Once everyone quieted, the Reverend continued with the welcoming ceremony. We spent over an hour in the pavilion, sitting, standing, kneeling, singing.

But all I could do was stare at Gabriel. I imagined what we looked like to him. Two hundred men, women, and children in stiff uniforms gazing up at the Reverend with tired eyes. It was already late, past our normal bedtime. I looked out beyond the pillars of the pavilion and watched one of the Edenton security guards saunter in and out of the shadows along the tree line. His gun, slung lazily over his shoulder, caught the light before he disappeared into the darkness between the trees.

After the ceremony, everyone dispersed. Gabriel fled the stage before his parents. Juanita and I watched as he shoved his way through the crowd, while Aliyah went on and on about Prayer Circle.

Once Gabriel had disappeared down the path leading to the boys' cottages, Aliyah, Juanita, and I walked toward the kitchen. It was my shift to prep for breakfast in the morning. The three of us sauntered along the dim walkway, in and out of the pools of light thrown by lamps, in silence. The night air was humid, heavy with the cloying scent of frangipani. I could feel the exhaustion weighing on my shoulders. The ceremony had gone on later than expected, and I longed to crawl into my bunk.

"I want to wear something pink, bright pink," Aliyah said.

I yawned. "We'll go see Sister tomorrow at the sewing cottage and see what she's got." I stopped below the flickering light at the back entrance to the kitchen. I took the hair tie from my wrist and pulled my hair into a knot. "Are you sure the Reverend is okay with you being out of uniform?"

"It's probably fine," Juanita said. "But check with Thaddeus first. You know how the Reverend feels about color."

Aliyah brought her hand up to touch the baubles cinching her ponytails. "But this is Prayer Circle! It's a celebration." She dropped her hand, eyes filled with anticipation. "There's singing and laughing—"

"How do you know?" I asked. "No one is allowed to talk about Circle."

"I'm guessing that's what happens." She leaned in, a conspiratorial tilt to her head. "You know I'll tell you guys, right? Everything there is to know about Prayer Circle. The second I come back."

"You shouldn't, Aliyah," Juanita said. "You'll be punished."

"You'll get your invite, too," she continued as if Juanita hadn't warned her. "Maybe it's just a mistake that I got the invite before you two. You're both older than me."

"We'll find you something pretty." I didn't care about an invitation to Prayer Circle, but I couldn't ruin her excitement.

With a giggle, she looped her arm in Juanita's. "Come on, Juanita," she said. "I need to get a good night's sleep."

"Don't we all," said Juanita, raising her eyebrows at me. "Don't stay too late prepping for breakfast, Mia."

"Yeah, well," was all I said as they turned away, Aliyah practically skipping toward our cottage behind the kitchen.

I peered down the dark and winding lane and tried to spot the warm glow of Mama's cottage, where she lived with my brother Max and another mother with a small child. Once the children of the Flock turned thirteen, we were separated from our parents and sent to live in different quarters with kids our age. I missed living with Mama, even though she infuriated me these days. But I missed someone kissing me good night before bed.

With a sigh, I opened the door to the kitchen. It smelled of disinfectant and dishwater. Inside the kitchen was cool, cooler than outside, the humidity swallowed up by the stainless steel of the appliances and counters. I remember being surprised when I first saw the professional kitchen, so different from the simple tables and benches in the dining hall. Cleanliness was taken very seriously in Edenton. Despite being close to Godliness, dirty was dangerous. In the jungle heat, germs multiplied. Scrapes festered into debilitating wounds and food poisoning could sicken entire rows of cottages. Which meant the Flock thinned; which meant the Reverend lost the workers that kept his utopia thriving.

My fingers ghosted along the back of my thigh, remembering the splinter. Once breakfast service was finished in the morning, I'd go to the infirmary.

I switched on my workstation lamp and began prepping the mangos, loving the feel of the chef's knife in my hand, the weight of it as it moved effortlessly over the cutting board; the thudding sound as it cut through.

A crash behind me made me whirl. A shadowy figure shot between the shelves lined with cooking utensils. Hanging ladles and spoons swung back and forth, the weak light from the window glinting off their handles. All I heard was my blood pulsing in my ears until my own voice broke through.

"Who's there?" I asked, hating the way my voice quavered.

I swallowed down the fear and stepped forward. The panic pulsing through me was so foreign, so different from the complaisant calm that had existed inside me since the day we came to Edenton. Part of me—and not a small part—thrilled.

"Who's there?" I said again, more forcefully.

From behind the shelves, someone moved in the shadows and took a deliberate step toward me. He moved forward until he was close enough that the small work light behind me revealed his features.

"Gabriel?" I asked.

Up close, his face wasn't as hard as it had appeared on the stage earlier. His cheekbones were sharp but his mouth had a softness to it, a plush quality that reminded me of the curving indentation on a cherry.

His tousled dark hair fell over his eyes. He seemed to realize I was staring at him because he stopped in front of me, eyes searching mine.

"That's not fair," he said. His voice was pleasant, subdued, the edge from earlier gone.

"What's not fair?" I asked.

"That you know my name, but I don't know yours." He smiled then, just a hint of a smile but enough to cause my breath to hitch.

"Mia," I whispered.

"Mia," he said as if testing my name on his lips. "Mia what?"

"Eden."

"Eden?" He sounded confused.

"The Flock's surname is Eden."

"So we're family?"

I shrugged. "If you put it that way, I guess so."

Gabriel's brows drew together as he regarded me. He leaned down, eyes shimmering with mischief, and whispered in my ear, "Good. Because I've always wanted a sister."

The heat of his breath lingered on my neck, his hair like feathers skimming over my cheek. A tingle I'd never felt before danced up my back and I let my eyes drift shut at the feeling. It wasn't until I heard the kitchen door slam that I realized he was gone.

And it wasn't until I looked down at my hand that I noticed he'd stolen my knife.

# Chapter Two

When I heard the knock on the door, I shoved my sketchbook to the bottom of the trunk at the foot of my bunk. My heart thumped faster than those three staccato taps. I thought I'd be alone for a few minutes while the girls from my cottage were on their way to physical training, and before I left to see Doc Gladstone. Sometimes, my moments alone with my sketchbook were all I had to look forward to in a day. I knew where I was going to draw, the upper-right corner of the twenty-second page. There were barely any blank pages left. All were packed with six years' worth of sketches, almost every inch of each page used, so I carefully planned out what was left of the open space, sacrificing some drawings to the kneaded eraser I'd kept balled at the end of my last pencil.

What I was going to draw, though, was a mystery until the lead slid across the paper.

I heard the pencil hit the tile floor and I scrambled around looking for it under my bed.

"One minute," I called.

I found the stubby thing and dropped it into my trunk. I couldn't get caught with the sketchbook—or the pencil. Personal items of any sort were strictly forbidden. But it was all that I had left of my other life—the life I still longed for outside of Edenton. A life of freedom and breathing space. A life where possibilities were my own to create. I was sure that outside of this regimented, scheduled place, there was something bigger than me, bigger than the God the Reverend wanted us to worship.

I shook the thought away as I shut the trunk and rushed over to open the door.

"Agatha needs you in the kitchen," Thaddeus said, looking down at me with his hands folded behind his back.

He was the Reverend's number two, whom the Reverend trusted above all others. He, like most of the men in Edenton, was tall and well built, imposing in an almost elegant way. His dark skin always had an unnatural luster, as if the surface were opalescent. Unlike the rest of the men, however, who wore plain gray collared shirts and black pants or shorts, he wore a simple white collarless shirt and gray trousers. His garb was the telltale marking of one of the Reverend's inner circle, with an embroidered Edenton crest on the left side of his chest. He waved his hand toward the path that led to the kitchen.

"Agatha?" I asked, and quickly realized my mistake. Thaddeus was never questioned.

"Yes." His pitch-black eyes bore down on me. "Agatha."

My hands began to tremble slightly. Thaddeus had spoken to me twice, as I could remember. Once when he welcomed our family to Edenton, and once when he'd thanked me for bringing him soup when he was ill. Otherwise, I was simply a member of the Flock. His presence alone made me nervous.

"I was on my way to see Doc Gladstone before training," I said, trying to keep the quaver from my voice.

He tsked. "Mia." My name sounded important in his deep-coal voice. "Agatha is the kitchen director and she needs you. Although I don't want to call her your boss, your contribution as a member of the Flock is to feed the congregation. And she's asked for you to assist in a task. I'm assuming it's not a dire situation for you to visit Doc Gladstone?"

"Splinter," was all I said.

"A splinter can wait."

I nodded and thanked him before I hurried toward the kitchen. I felt his eyes on me as I skittered away. A trickle of sweat slipped down my spine. It was unusual for Agatha to call me to the kitchen at that time of day, right after I'd left breakfast service, but it was more unusual for Thaddeus to come find me. Did she know about my knife? Our knives were our tools, expensive tools from what I understood. I'd have to work off losing the knife.

*You didn't lose it. Gabriel stole it.*

And like a fool—a tingly, girly fool—I let him.

When I opened the door to the kitchen, it was dark inside, the shades drawn over the windows. Agatha stood next to the opened door of the special provisions pantry, normally a locked closet at the back of the kitchen on the other side of the prep tables. A dim light from one of the workstations spilled over Agatha's lanky frame. The furrows along her forehead deepened. I couldn't see what she was unloading, but it made a tiny clinking noise, like glass.

"You requested to see me?"

Agatha jumped and pressed the palm of her hand to her chest. "Mia!" she said in a high-pitched voice. "You startled me."

"I'm sorry." I stepped into the kitchen and shut the door behind me. "Thaddeus said you needed me here?" I stressed his name, so she would understand how weird I thought it was.

She didn't notice. "I do." She stuffed something back into the pantry, the muscles beneath her sleeves flexing as she moved. "I'm baking today and need help," she said as she fished a key from her apron pocket and locked the pantry door. She slipped the keychain, a curly yellow cord, around her wrist.

"But we baked the bread this morning," I said.

"Not bread." Agatha grinned tightly, her hair pulled back in a severe bun. Her cheekbones were honed under her eternally sunburned skin. "We're making cookies."

"Cookies?" I asked.

She began removing the large canisters of flour and sugar from the shelves. "Yes, dear. Cookies."

We only made cookies—or any sweets for that matter—for holidays, like Christmas and Easter, when the Reverend allowed the Flock to celebrate. But other celebrations were rare in Edenton, about as rare as cold weather.

I didn't ask any more questions and got to work, as was expected of me. Agatha asked me to measure and mix the dry ingredients. She remained on the other side of the kitchen diligently weighing and measuring the wet ingredients, then incorporating mine. We worked in silence for a few hours, hundreds of cookies going in and coming out of the ovens. Agatha kept the other staff away from our work area, even as the smell of peanut butter cookies baking filled the entire cafeteria, prompting a few questions and many longing stares.

As I worked, though, my eyes kept going to where Gabriel had appeared the night before. He'd slipped out of the darkness and come toward me with such determination that my heart still stammered thinking about the look in his eyes. I'd never seen anyone look at me like that. Even Octavio didn't look at me like that.

But it was all a tactic, wasn't it? A ploy to get my knife.

My eyes flicked to the empty slot in my magnetic knife rack on the wall.

From where I stood in the back of the kitchen, I caught glimpses of the dining hall through the staff serving lunch. Because all the girls my age worked in the kitchen, my cottage mates were on the front lines of service. They stole glances back at me as I scooped cookie dough onto baking sheets. Agatha had lectured me earlier about not tasting the dough. It was disrespectful to the other members of the Flock. But I'd always tasted what I'd cooked, numerous times, throughout the process. It was how I understood flavors, and how they bloomed during the cooking time. Not tasting the dough as we baked went against everything Agatha had said during my kitchen duty training.

After I'd stored all the cookies in airtight containers, I headed down the path to the infirmary.

The back of my thigh stung. It grew more painful as the day went on.

"Mia!" I heard, and turned around. Aliyah ran toward me, grinning. "Sister agreed to make me a shirt for Prayer Circle. Come with me to the sewing cottage?" Her large eyes pleaded with me in that little girl way of hers, and I caved.

"Sure," I said and tried to keep up as she skipped down the path toward the sewing cottage.

Sister oversaw the sewing and laundry, although she preferred to call what she did textile arts. When we arrived, she was seated behind a large table inside, her graying hair escaping from a black-and-white floral headscarf. In her thin mouth she held a series of pins, the flat tops catching the light each time she bent her head. All around I saw gray, white, and black fabric, and boxes of Edenton emblems, the lids printed with the familiar tree.

Suzanne and Kori, girls a few years younger than we were, folded laundry in the back. We older girls were relegated to kitchen duty; the younger ones worked in the laundry. The Reverend believed in what he called "gender-appropriate chores." I loved cooking, but sometimes I longed to be with the boys catching fish on the beach or weeding and planting the gardens, bugs and all.

Sister's wrinkled fingers moved along a surprisingly pink stretch of fabric and they shook slightly with the effort. Beside Sister, Aliyah plunked down on a stool. Her eyes were alight as she stared at the spread of pink fabric like it was candy.

"Peony pink," Aliyah breathed.

"It's pretty," I said, leaning my elbows down on the table. It was, too. Her dark skin would look velvety next to the color.

"It's so beautiful." Aliyah's palm skated across it reverently.

"It's pink," Sister said, her voice rusty with age. "Pepto-Bismol pink. Calamine lotion pink." She flipped the fabric over and mumbled, "But this pink won't heal. Won't heal much at all."

"I just want to look pretty," Aliyah said.

"That you will, darlin'." Sister nodded, bobbing her head. "That you will."

But what Sister had said echoed in my head. "What do you mean won't heal?" I asked her.

Sister chewed the inside of her cheek like gum and shook her head at me. "Don't listen to me. I'm an old seamstress who talks nonsense."

Aliyah, as instructed, ignored her. "I'm also making banana rice pudding to take to Prayer Circle tonight. Do you think they'll like it?"

Before I could answer, Sister let out a long-suffering sigh. "You girls need to get on out of here. I need to work in peace. I've got these girls trained to keep quiet while I work." She thrust a knotted thumb back at Suzanne and Kori, both of whom glanced up. "I can't listen to all this talk. These ruffle sleeves ain't gonna ruffle themselves."

I grabbed Aliyah's arm and dragged her toward the door. By the look on her face, I knew she didn't want to leave.

"I'll be back after dinner service," Aliyah said to Sister.

She waved us off with a gnarled hand clutching a tiny needle, the pink thread swaying with the movement.

Outside, an occasional breeze eased the relentless humidity. Sister's sewing cottage sat on a small crest. Edenton, bordered by the jungle, stretched out in rows of wooden cottages and cobbled paths below. I could see the kitchen, behind it the herb garden, and behind that the path through the trees to the acres of vegetable gardens and fruit orchards.

Along the outside wall of the schoolhouse, painted a deep beet red, the younger kids lined up, Max among them, after recess in the play yard. Mama clapped her hands to get their attention before ushering them back into the schoolhouse through the large double doors. A strange echo caused the noise to sound a split second after her hands came together.

At the commune's gated entrance, men unloaded a truck of supplies, stacking boxes along the side of the road. The trucks were inspected and heavily guarded. Every box passed through a long building next to the Edenton front gates and came out on the other side, divided into piles.

As the wind shifted, I heard something strange. A beat. A deep, thudding beat.

"Do you hear that?" I asked Aliyah.

She cocked her head. "Hear what?"

"That," I paused, listening to it fade in and out. "That music."

"Music? Here?" Aliyah let out a small laugh. "You know the Reverend wouldn't allow it outside of congregation or . . . " her expression took on a dreamy quality, "Prayer Circle."

Ignoring her Circle worship, I stopped, trying to pick up what direction the sound was coming from. But the rumble of a truck leaving through the front entrance sounded, mingling with the kids' voices as they filtered into the schoolhouse.

"I heard it, Aliyah."

"It was probably coming from one of the delivery trucks. If the Reverend heard music around here, whoever played it would end up in Contrition for a week!"

Those who sinned—and were caught—were sent to confess their wrongdoings to the Reverend, then he doled out his punishment—anything from praying for hours on end to digging out the muck from the latrines in the work fields.

"But it wasn't coming from the trucks," I said, pointing to the entrance. Slowly, I spun around, finger still outstretched, trying to pinpoint where the music had come from. As I did, I caught a quick beat, and another before it was swallowed up by the wind. I froze. "It came from that direction."

"That's the jungle, Mia. There's nothing for ten miles."

I dropped my hand. "Can sound travel over that kind of distance?" I asked, mostly to myself.

"No," Aliyah said. "But it can travel from one of the trucks. The main road is pretty winding outside the gates from what I remember.

Maybe there's a truck out there." She grabbed my hand. "Come on, we have dinner to prep."

"Already?"

I looked up at the sun. It was lower in the sky, but as incessant as ever. Doc Gladstone, and the wound on my leg, would have to wait until after dinner.

I let Aliyah drag me down the hill, but I kept my eyes on the thick jungle encroaching on the border of Edenton. She was right. There was nothing out there but thick, wet foliage, brown recluse spiders, and poison dart frogs. Pit vipers that clung to branches, and birds, colorful and loud, almost mocking from their safe haven high in the trees. It was no place for people. Not ones who wanted to live, anyway.

# Chapter Three

After dinner service, the members of the Flock drained out through the dining hall doors as I collected the breadbaskets from the long tables. I spotted Mama slipping outside.

"Mama," I called. I placed the stack of breadbaskets on the gray cart and ran out through the door after her. "Mama, wait."

With a sigh, Mama turned. Her hair, a few shades darker brown than mine, hung in a braid that flipped over her shoulder. Ever since I was little, people told me I looked like her: the same wide green eyes, same rosebud mouth, same golden complexion. But the stiff gray of her uniform dress sallowed her skin in the evening sun. At her hip, Max held her hand and grinned at me.

"Yes, Mia?" she said.

Her cottage mate Jin Sang stopped as well. Bae John, her son, stood with his back up against her legs. Her arms were crossed over his chest protectively. She said nothing, but I saw the wariness in her almond-shaped eyes. She'd heard me argue with Mama the last few weeks, although I hoped she didn't hear what we argued about.

"Can we talk later?" I asked Mama. "I'll come by?"

She glanced at Jin Sang. "Will you take the boys back to our cottage?"

Jin Sang took Max's hand. "Of course," she said in her tiny accented voice.

Max waved goodbye to me with a curl of his fingers.

Mama glanced around before chucking her chin toward the outside corner of the dining hall. We walked behind a hibiscus bush studded with red blossoms. The perennial battalion of insects—mostly mosquitos—swirled in the evening air.

"You need to stop this, Mia," Mama said to me quietly.

"All I want is to talk about it. Calmly and rationally. We don't have to argue about it. Just discuss our options."

The lines in Mama's forehead deepened. "No. This conversation is over. And whatever you do, don't talk about it to anyone, understand?"

"But Mama—"

She thrust her finger in my face and dropped her voice to a harsh whisper. "Look, you're not the only one here who remembers life before Edenton."

"I'm the only one of my friends."

"It's a life we left behind," she said.

"A life you left behind! I was ten, what choice did I have?"

"What has come over you lately?"

What had come over me? I was finally doing what Papa had always told me to do before he left us all those years ago. Before he couldn't deal with her anymore. I was thinking. Questioning. Something no one did in Edenton. I placed my hands on my hips and stared her down.

"Good God, Mia," she said. "Stop it. Edenton is our home. This is where we belong. Bring this up one more time and I'll—"

"You'll what?" I said. "Turn me in to the Reverend because I want to leave?"

"Ssssh!" she said, and took a step back away from me. "Get back to work before Agatha starts looking for you."

I spun away from her, slammed through the dining hall doors, and wheeled the cart with the breadbaskets back to the kitchen. I spent the next two hours during dinner cleanup simmering about Mama and her closed-mindedness. I wasn't asking for the moon tied up in a perfect red ribbon. All I'd wanted to do was discuss options. Options that would lead me on the path out of Edenton. Maybe I'd have to find another way, without Mama's help. Without her knowledge.

"Mia," Octavio called, jogging around the corner of the building as I left the kitchen after dinner service. I'd been on my way to the infirmary to see Doc Gladstone about my leg, and looking forward to the short walk alone.

I smiled at him, as I always did, and he smiled back. A dimple in one cheek. His eyes were warm, like his sister's. But that rush of excitement, those stupid tingles I felt with Gabriel—someone I hardly knew—was missing when I looked into Octavio's eyes.

Octavio pushed the curls off his forehead. The sky above was flushed pink as the sun disappeared behind the tall trees. His dusky complexion, flawless and clear, practically shone in the light. Octavio was a beautiful boy. But he couldn't be my boy, even if he wanted to be.

"I wanted to see if you're going to be on the beach tomorrow," he said.

"Tomorrow?" I asked.

"Training is on the beach tomorrow instead of in the gym. You weren't in training today, so I was wondering—"

"Oh, yeah." I grinned at him. "I'll be there tomorrow."

His shoulders sagged in relief. "Good," he said. "Can I walk you back to your cottage?"

"I'm actually going to the infirmary," I said, and his expression turned to worry. "It's no big deal, just a splinter. And, yeah, walk with me over there."

"Okay." He shoved his hands in his pockets and tilted his head toward the path leading into the main walkway.

We walked together in companionable silence. Along the way, I wondered what there really was for us to discuss. How the fishing was this month? Were the papayas growing on schedule? Or maybe the Reverend's latest sermon on the importance of service in the eyes of God? What did any of us talk about, anyway? Nothing, if I thought about it. We talked about what the Reverend wanted us to talk about—benign and unworldly topics.

"Here we are," Octavio said as we approached the door to the infirmary.

I smiled at him again—it was easier than saying anything—and watched silently as he waved goodbye and walked back in the direction of the boys' cottages.

A hollow pain sat in my chest, and I let it linger there as I stood on the steps of the infirmary watching his liquid shadow dance along the cobblestones. He wasn't enough for me. Octavio was sweet, and caring. But I wanted so much more. I admitted to myself that I wanted what I'd felt when Gabriel was close to me, whispering in my ear. Why did the Reverend choose who our lifelong partners were anyway? What did he even know about me? About any of us, really?

Inside the infirmary, Doc Gladstone sat behind a small desk. Papers fanned out before him and he scratched a signature along the bottom of each. His fingers were long, holding the pen at a graceful, left-handed slant. I wanted that paper. That pen. Such a luxury to feel the ink slide across the surface. The small desk lamp illuminating the papers was the only light in the cool room and I caught movement in the shadows, closest to the back hallway. In a flash, the overhead fluorescent lights came on.

"We have a walk-in, Doctor," Nurse Ivy said in her rusted voice, the green cast of her scrubs reflecting her pallor.

She was skeletal, and creepy, and of indeterminate age. The glossy locks of her honey-colored hair seemed youthful and healthy, but the thinness of her skin, the tracing of bluish veins right below the surface, aged her.

"Hello there, Mia," Doc Gladstone said in his lilting Caribbean accent. He stood, gathering the papers into a pile. "What can I help you with this evening?"

I told him about the splinter, all the while watching Nurse Ivy cast a cold eye in my direction. Not until I was on the exam table did she leave the room, taking the papers into the darkened back hallway.

Doc Gladstone stretched on gloves. "On your stomach," he said. With gentle fingers, he examined the back of my thigh. "Mia, there's still a piece of splinter in your leg." Up close, he looked tired, the shadows under his eyes more pronounced. "Why didn't you come here right after this happened?"

I faltered for a moment. If I hadn't spent the day making those cookies and accompanying Aliyah to the sewing cottage, I would have been here taking care of myself. But Edenton was about community—thinking of others, not yourself. And that was so ingrained in me I was almost ashamed. I couldn't allow my health to be compromised. It was all I had.

"I had breakfast prep last night," I said, lifting my head from the pillow to turn back to Doc. I hadn't slept the night before. My neck was stiff from tossing and turning. "And then today I got busy."

A fan blew from the corner of the infirmary, oscillating evening air from the open window and I wondered idly why the infirmary's cots were more comfortable than my own bunk.

"Busy?" he asked. "Mia, without health life is not life, it is only a state of languor and suffering—an image of death." He grinned at me. "The Buddha."

"You're quoting the Buddha and referencing death because of a splinter?" I lifted an eyebrow. "I'm not sure about your bedside manner."

He laughed. "Infection, girl. It's rampant in this humid jungle and you know it." I felt a pinch and jumped. "This is going to hurt, it's in there deep."

As I tensed for the pain, I heard rioting voices coming from the infirmary's entrance. The shock of the sound, here in ever-so-peaceful Edenton, brought me up on my elbows.

"Stop squirming!" Grizz, one of Edenton's security guards, yelled.

His massive frame filled the doorway. Behind him, three other guards muscled forward, craning to see what Grizz held in his arms. He threw someone forward onto the polyurethaned floor. That someone landed with a thunk.

"Easy now, Grizz," Doc Gladstone said, going down on one knee. "This is one of God's creatures."

"This creature punched me!" Grizz said, his ham-sized hand motioning to the heap on the floor. "Twice! And it took three of my guys to wrestle him off me!"

Flickering fluorescent light washed over the dark figure crouched at his feet. The figure pushed himself up. Excitement electrified my skin as Gabriel lifted his head. Then I noticed a livid purpling bruise around his left eye and, beneath it, a cut trickling blood. Something tugged in my chest, and I realized I was worried about him. It had been so long since I worried about anyone.

Doc Gladstone gently lifted Gabriel's chin and examined his face.

Gabriel gazed blankly up at him through strands of unruly dark hair. "Who are you?" he asked with dazed fascination.

"Doc Gladstone."

"Don't you mean Dr. Eden? Isn't that our last name?"

"Gladstone is my first name."

"Sounds like a porn name."

Doc Gladstone shook his head and held up three fingers. "How many?"

Gabriel squinted, looked past Doc's fingers, and said, "Hey Doc, did you know your dreads are as thick as Snickers Bars?"

"Not blind, then," Doc Gladstone mumbled. "Are you hurt anywhere else?"

"Does my mangled soul count?"

Doc Gladstone fought a smile. "Up, come sit over here." He pulled Gabriel to his feet and led him to the cot next to mine.

Gabriel glanced at me as he sat on the cot. I flicked my eyes away.

"I'll be back in a moment. Grizz," Doc Gladstone said to the guard. "Let's talk outside."

Grizz lumbered back to the door, eyes never leaving Gabriel's. "Yeah, Doc. Let's talk."

"Nice meeting you, Grizz," Gabriel called, and then mumbled to himself, "I'm sure we'll meet again."

Once Doc escorted Grizz through the door, I silently studied Gabriel, from the top of his dark head to his mud-caked shoes. Neither of us said anything. He hadn't even looked in my direction, only kicked clumps of dried mud off his shoes onto the floor.

"You're making a mess," I said, still up on my elbows.

"And?"

"Someone has to clean that up. Nurse Ivy, probably."

Staring intently at me, he banged his boots together, raining more dried mud on the floor.

"Gabriel," I said in a flat tone.

"What?"

I glared at him for a moment, appalled. "Grow up."

I turned my head and put it down on the exam table. I remained there, listening to the fan purr and counting the seconds until Doc Gladstone returned. The white noise stretched out between us.

"Comfy?" Gabriel asked me in a silky voice.

"Huh?" I turned my head toward him and watched as his eyes traveled down the backs of my bare legs.

I realized, splayed out on my stomach like I was, my dress was rucked up high on my thigh, probably showing my underwear. My face felt hot. I scrambled into a seated position, ignoring the pain of the splinter.

"What did you do with my knife?" I asked.

"What knife?"

"My chef's knife. The one you stole from me last night. I had to prep fruit with a boning knife."

He mouthed "boning" with a look of mock horror.

I narrowed my eyes at him. "I don't know what kind of games you're playing, but this is my real life. This isn't some vacation. I have to work. I have a job to do every day and without that knife my job is ten times harder. So give it back."

He shrugged. "If I'd had the knife on me, Grizz would have used his irresistible charm to coax it from my hands."

"I need it, Gabe."

"Don't call me that."

"I'll just stop talking to you altogether, how's that?"

I stared straight ahead, trying to ignore him in the periphery of my vision. But I couldn't help peeking at him as he sat there. His arms were folded over his chest, biceps bunched up, straining the fabric of his shirt. I noticed the swirls of a dark tattoo peeking beneath his sleeve. The lines were beautiful and mysterious. Some of the older people in Edenton had tattoos, reminders of a life left behind, but the kids who'd grown up in Edenton didn't even have pierced ears, let alone something as exotic, and daring, as a tattoo.

"Do you like it?" Gabriel asked me.

My heart jumped. "Like—like what?"

"Edenton."

"Like it? I uh—"

At first, I had to tear my eyes away from his tattoo. Then, process his question. No one ever asked me a question like that. Of course I didn't like living in Edenton, but as far as I could tell, I was the only one.

I remembered life before Edenton. Suburban bliss: minivans, play dates, swimming pools, McDonald's. But it was also a sheltered life. I couldn't watch secular TV or movies. No secular music. I couldn't read a book unless Mama approved it. But Papa was different, sneaking songs for me to listen to and books for me to read. That's what made it a life of loud arguments in the middle of the night. My father disappearing for long periods of time. But it was emotional. When I was happy, it was the most electric feeling. When I was sad, it was the end of everything. High-highs tempered by low-lows. I missed that roller coaster of emotion.

But who was this boy to me? I hadn't known who he was twenty-four hours ago. I couldn't trust him. If Gabriel said anything to Thaddeus or the Reverend about how I felt about Edenton, about not liking it here anymore, I could be punished. Worse, every move I made would be watched by security.

Instead of answering his question honestly, if I liked Edenton, I answered like any other member of the Flock would answer.

"And the Lord God planted a garden eastward in Eden," I said, reciting the verse from memory, "and there he put the man whom he had formed. And out of the ground made the Lord God to grow every tree that is pleasant to the sight, and good for food; the tree of life also in the midst of the garden—"

"And the tree of knowledge of good and evil," he finished. "Don't quote the Bible to me."

"You know the quote?"

"I'm here in this hellhole, aren't I? So someone tainted my brain with religion."

"Gabriel," I said through gritted teeth, as I was about to say words I didn't believe to keep him at arm's length. "Edenton is a good place, where the world can't hurt us."

He shot me a look of disbelief. "This place is unbelievable. Even the goddamn teenagers are brainwashed here."

That hurt, because I wasn't. "I'm far from brainwashed—"

"You are. You all are. This place is not right." He waved his hand around the room. "Look at this place. Everything is so—so new. Modern. Expensive. We're stuck out here in the middle of the rainforest and looking around this room you wouldn't even know it. Edenton has everything. Where the hell do you get the money for all this stuff?"

I blinked at him. I'd never thought about it. "We sell produce and fish to the people in San Sebastian."

"You think peddling papayas is going to buy all those stainless steel appliances in the kitchen?" He shook his head in disgust, and shame unfurled in my chest. Did he think I was ignorant? "You really chose to come here? To stay here?"

"I—" I stared down at my work boots. I wanted to yell, No! I didn't. But I was too young and didn't know any better. I took in a breath and looked back at him. His eyes were slitted against black lashes. Blue, they were blue. Or maybe green? Regardless, they were livid. "Edenton is . . . um . . . a peaceful . . . "—and painfully boring—"commune."

"You're prisoners!" Trying to gain his composure, he squeezed his eyes shut and shook his head. "Mia," he whispered and my heart clenched. He remembered my name. When he opened his eyes to look at me, they were darker, serious. "I thought maybe you were different."

Different? In the last six years, had anyone thought I was different? Different from any other member of the Flock? My heart beat wildly. Because I knew what he suspected. I was different.

"What do you mean we're prisoners?" I asked, leaning closer to him.

Gabriel stared back at me, eyes scrutinizing me, and remained silent, as if weighing whether I was worthy of his words. "They're not keeping the world out," he finally said.

"Who?"

"The guards, Grizz and the rest," he said, glancing at the infirmary door. "Those guys who walk around with the guns. They're not keeping us safe. They're not keeping people from getting into Edenton. They're keeping the Flock—us—in."

The fan continued to whir, same white noise as before he spoke, but now it sounded distant, hollow, as if it were in another room.

"Keeping the Flock in?" I exhaled a breath. "How do you know?"

Gabriel dropped his voice. "Last night, I found—"

"Well, now," Doc Gladstone said as he came in the room. He smiled in that warm way of his that you knew wasn't a put-on bedside act. "I'm impressed, Gabriel. No one has landed a punch on Grizz in years. When he came here, at eighteen, he insisted we call him Grizz. Because of his size, you know. Big as a bear and loves to get scrappy and fight. I thought he was intimidating enough without the nickname." He shook his head with disbelief. "But you connected twice. Twice! Unbelievable." Doc Gladstone caught himself mid-laugh and sobered. "Now, whatever happened between you and Grizz is of no matter here in the infirmary. I do not judge that which the Reverend and the Lord must. The Reverend will decide your retribution. But I will tell you when you're being a bloody daft idiot. Don't cross Grizz. He prefers the Old Testament teachings on *lex talionis*. Eye for an eye and the like."

Gabriel nodded, shooting me a quick glance, as if to say *We'll talk about this later*. The idea that I'd see him later, that he might seek me out to talk to me, confide in me because I was different, sent a quivering thrill through my body.

"All right then," Doc Gladstone said, clapping his hands together. "Now, let's get to mending."

Before the curtain between the exam tables closed, Gabriel stared at me, gaze burning with determination. If I involved myself with Gabriel and told him about my yet-to-be-planned plan to escape from Edenton, I could make the mistake that could cost me my freedom.

# Chapter Four

The shrill cry of the Edenton loudspeaker alarm woke me with a jolt. I shot up, clutching my ears. My hair was still wet from the shower I'd taken before bed, so I couldn't have been asleep long. A sudden flash of light blinded me as the usually dormant floodlights nestled in the rafters of our cottage flared to life. I blinked, and saw the other girls in my cottage still in their bunks. Juanita lay back on her pillow, arm covering her eyes, rolling her head with its froth of black curls back and forth. Lily, above her, sat up with the sheet pulled to her chest, her wide gray eyes darting around with fear. Bridgette and Dina rose from their pillows with blind acceptance. Aliyah, above me, poked her head over the edge of the bed.

"Bright Night," she said over the noise.

"Dammit," I said.

"Mia!" Aliyah said, but she snuck a glance at Bridgette and Dina, the most devout of our little group.

Neither reacted, which meant neither had heard. They jumped from their bunks, gathering clothes folded neatly on their trunks.

"A what?" Lily yelled.

She'd arrived only six months ago with her adopted aunt and uncle. Her parents had died in a house fire, one she had, incredibly, survived. She'd told us her mother submerged her in the bathtub as her parents tried to find a way to escape. Lily called out in her sleep practically every night.

"Been a while since we've had one of these," Juanita said.

"Had one of what?" Lily asked.

Before any of us could explain to her about Bright Nights, the alarm stopped and Thaddeus's voice came over the speakers.

"Please join us in the pavilion in five minutes," he said in a low, rumbling tone. "By request of the Reverend."

Request was a kind word. It wasn't a request; it was an order. Those of us left in our cottages after five minutes were driven out and escorted to the pavilion by the guards.

Lily's fine blond hair fell into her eyes as she trembled. She looked so small compared to the rest of us. We'd been working for years in Edenton, building up muscle and endurance in our requisite physical training classes. Lily was still thin and somewhat frail, the tenacious sun constantly burning her fair skin.

"A Bright Night," I explained to Lily as I rose from my bed, "is when the Reverend calls for the congregation in the middle of the night to pray under the bright, white lights of the pavilion until dawn."

"Until dawn?" Lily asked in a disbelieving tone. "I have to bake bread at five A.M. I won't get any sleep at all."

"And you'll be better for it," Bridgette snapped. "Prayer at the Matins hours nourishes the soul so that sleep is unnecessary." She shoved her feet into her boots and flicked her bangs out of her eyes with a shake of her head. Snatching her worn Bible from below her pillow, she pointed it at us as she said, "You all act like this is a sacrifice—"

"But it is a sacrifice," said Dina, her breathy voice sounding childlike and serene. "Like the sacrifices the Lord made for us." She buttoned up her collar to the edge of her neck. "Girls, it's only a few hours. We don't need sleep—"

"I need sleep," I said as I stretched.

"Mia!" Bridgette said, flashing me an angry look as she brushed her perfectly straight hair. "Your attitude lately has been so irritating. What is wrong with you?"

"Calm down, Bridgette," said Juanita. "Bright Night is pretty intense, we all know that, so cut her a little slack."

"I wonder who it's going to be this time," Aliyah said.

Lily slid down from her bunk. "What do you mean?"

Juanita's gaze met mine from across the room. She tilted her head at me. So I needed to explain it. Great.

"Someone will be made an example of tonight," I said. "A member of the Flock will be brought up on that stage in the pavilion and chastised for sinning or going against the word of the Reverend."

I immediately thought of Gabriel. Although I wasn't altogether sure what he had done, other than stealing my knife and hitting Grizz. I hadn't told anyone about the knife.

Lily stepped into her dress beneath her nightgown. "The Reverend. He embarrasses the sinner?"

"Then we pray for whomever it is," Aliyah said.

"Not always," Bridgette said in a snappy tone. "A few times, he's punished the sinner onstage. A beating or whipping. It's a good reminder about avoiding sin for the rest of us."

"Beating a lesson into a person isn't teaching, Bridgette," I said.

She gaped at me, then looked to Juanita. "See, Juanita? Such a sassy attitude!"

Ignoring her, Juanita sat up and scratched her wild hair with curled fingers. "Let's hope it's not another sermon on chastity. The last one made my mother pray incessantly for days."

Carmen, Juanita's mother, came to Edenton almost two decades ago to cleanse herself of her sins. Her two most egregious sins were Juanita and Octavio, both conceived and born out of wedlock. The Reverend hadn't brought anyone onstage for that Bright Night's chastity lecture, but flashed warning glances at all the female members of the Flock, as if the sin of lust rested solely on our shoulders.

We all dressed silently. Bridgette and Dina darted out of the cottage door before the rest of us. I lingered over my trunk for a moment, weighing the chances of having two minutes alone with my sketchbook.

"Mia, come on," Aliyah said, standing at the door.

I dropped the lid of the trunk. It closed in a muted bang.

Outside, members of the Flock walked in eerie silence along the dimly lit paths to the pavilion, dutiful soldiers of the Reverend. On the hill in the distance, the pavilion's lights raged against the dark night. I glanced around for Mama and saw her carrying a sleeping Max draped over her shoulder. Kids five and younger didn't attend the Bright Nights. They stayed in the nursery with two elderly nurses. The Reverend, though, considered age six the age of comprehension. Seeing Max's sleepy little head, dark hair flopping over his eyes as Mama walked, made me wonder why. At six he understood and accepted many things, but being forced to stay awake and witness God-knows-what being done to one of the Flock was cruel.

As we took our places in the pavilion, the Reverend sat stone still on his throne, watching us. A self-assured half-smile almost disappeared under his thick, ginger-colored beard.

Aliyah settled next to me, Juanita on my other side. Next to her, Lily sat down, fiddling with the hem of her dress. I glanced behind me.

Bridgette and Dina, clutching their Bibles to their chests like life vests, stared with rapt attention at the stage.

Mama was seated next to Max, and surrounded by the rest of her students from the schoolhouse, all sleepy little satellites. Octavio and the rest of the teenage boys occupied their assigned benches, across the aisle from us. Gabriel was not among them. I spotted his parents sitting with the other married couples toward the front.

The Flock settled in with quiet reverence under the Reverend's stern gaze. I listened to the shuffle of feet, the occasional whispered question from the drowsy children.

"Let us pray," the Reverend said, his voice booming over the loud speaker.

Obediently, we bowed our heads. But I couldn't help peeking out from behind my hair, looking for Gabriel. I flicked my gaze to the shadowy wings of the stage. My stomach turned. Thaddeus stood by, as always, a looming menace.

But there was no sign of Gabriel. A small shudder went through me. It was going to be him tonight. It had to be.

"He who loves silver," the Reverend said, drawing our attention to the stage, "will not be satisfied with silver; nor he who loves abundance, with increase." He held his hands to his sides, palms up. "Ecclesiastes," he said, rising from his chair with some effort. The Reverend's bloated and sweaty appearance onstage disgusted me more than it usually did. A flush lit his cheeks as he lumbered back and forth. "Tonight I'll discuss the sin of greed . . . "

And he was off, on a Bright Night tangent. His intensity increased as he spoke, hands quaking, head shaking, sweat along his forehead. For two excruciating hours, I fidgeted on my bench, trying to look interested.

"Now," the Reverend said in a voice that shocked many awake. "Let's take a short intermission." He sat back down on his throne, ignoring the looks of shock on our faces. Intermission? Bright Nights didn't have intermissions. They were nonstop marathons of preaching and praying. "Agatha?" he called to the back of the pavilion. "Are you all set up?"

I saw Agatha placing plates on a long table, piled with what looked like the cookies we'd baked yesterday. She looked pale and drawn under the fluorescent lights.

Aliyah placed her hand on mine. "Are those the cookies you made?" she whispered with an edge of excitement.

"They are," I said, dread settling over me.

Was I to be the example tonight? Should I have questioned more, resisted the idea of baking a treat for the Flock? Was I greedy to think that I, an ordinary member of this congregation, could bring such happiness to everyone with a simple gesture?

"Please," the Reverend said. "Help yourselves to some refreshments and we'll continue in fifteen minutes."

People made their way to the back of the pavilion, lined up in an orderly fashion. Lily filed out and we followed her, Juanita mumbling something about milk. Aliyah squeezed my shoulders with eagerness.

As the line inched along, my eyes kept snapping to the Reverend and Thaddeus, now huddled together, talking quietly. As if they'd felt my stare, they both looked up, eyes meeting mine. I instantly grew light-headed and turned away.

Ahead of us, children jumped up and down, tugging at each other's hands. I noticed Max and Mama at the start of the line, very close to the buffet table. Max's expression darkened like a stormy sky as he examined the table's contents. He began to cry.

"Excuse me," I said as I moved past people in line.

I followed Mama, who had picked him up and was making her way back to their seats. Max was allergic to peanuts. I knew it, too. But when I was making the cookies, I didn't realize they were for the Flock. I sat down beside them.

"Cookies have peanuts," Max sobbed.

I stroked the hair out of his eyes. "You know what?" I said. "I don't even want any cookies."

Mama smiled at me, her anger from earlier melting away, and patted Max's arm.

"Why not?" Max asked.

"Will they make me healthy? Will they give me strength? Could I work harder, longer, after I ate one?" I shook my head, making a show for Max. "No, Maxie. No, they couldn't help me. Those cookies would taste good, then what? They'd just give me cavities and probably make my stomach hurt if I ate too many."

35

"You have a point, child." I turned to see the Reverend had over-heard me. "You do indeed have a point."

His expression was unreadable, his eyes two flat black circles. But I did hear the slightest bit of admiration in his voice.

Mama, Max, and I watched the Flock as they ate, savoring each bite. The girls from my cottage huddled around our seats, eating their cookies and grinning. In the six months I'd known her, I hadn't seen Lily smile so generously. There was a sweetness to her that reminded me of Aliyah.

Octavio caught my eye and held up a cookie. He pointed to it, then to me.

I smiled and nodded. I made them, I mouthed.

He grinned, his wide mouth spreading across his face. I'd never known someone to smile with his entire being, but Octavio did. He shot me a thumbs-up and pointed to his other hand. He had a pile of cookies wrapped in a napkin. Placing his palm over his heart, he bowed his head in a regal, and sincere, thank you.

The Reverend allowed the Flock to eat and sip on little cups of milk. Everyone chatted about how delicious the cookies were, and I couldn't help a small feeling of pride bloom in my chest.

From what I could tell we went a full fifteen minutes without inter-ruption. Then, in a flat, almost disgusted tone, the Reverend called us back to our seats. I kissed Max on the forehead and my mother on the cheek, and joined the girls. I felt the buzz of excitement around them, like sparks in the air. A few months after I began cooking in Edenton, I understood the power of food. Food nourished, it made people feel safe, cared for; but food bringing joy to Edenton was so rare.

Once the Flock settled down, the Reverend said, "Delicious, weren't they? Agatha has such a talent for baking."

Agatha, standing on the side of the stage with her hands clenched in front of her, smiled politely, glancing over the Flock as people let out a series of "Amens." Out of the corner of my eye, I saw my mother bring Max to her chest in a protective hug. He wasn't crying any longer, but his eyes were rimmed in red.

"Now," said the Reverend. He stood then, folding his hands behind him. He began to pace. "Tonight, I've orchestrated the ultimate lesson on greed."

All movement ceased. Only wide-eyed gazes shifted to follow the Rev-erend walk back and forth along the edge of the stage. Silence reigned.

He smiled out over us. "Those of you who ate one cookie will be fine."

I shot a confused look at Juanita. She shrugged.

"Those who ate two cookies will experience a little stomach trouble, nothing more."

Around the pavilion hands went involuntarily to abdomens. My own stomach, even though I hadn't eaten any cookies, roiled. My palms began to sweat. I rubbed them against my skirt.

"Those who ate three will spend the rest of the night vomiting."

Panic stabbed me. A round of gasps swept across the Flock.

"And those who ate four or more?" He paused, scrutinizing us as we sat staring up at him, dumbfounded. "Will be dead before sunrise."

# Chapter Five

The last words Lily said to us before she died were, "My mom used to make peanut butter cookies." Unshed tears glistened on her lashes.

Then, before we could say goodbye, she and ten others were escorted from the pavilion.

Octavio was among them.

I called out his name, the shriek of my voice echoing through the pavilion, and ran out from under the roof onto the shorn grass leading to one of the pathways through the jungle.

Octavio pivoted around, wrestled his arm free from the guard, and sprinted toward me. Light from the pavilion washed out his features. In the sickly glow of the pavilion's too-bright lights, his lips looked parched. He swallowed and his Adam's apple bobbed.

"I'm sorry," he said in a dry voice.

"Sorry for what?" I asked.

"For being greedy." He slowly lifted one shoulder, confusion darkening his eyes. "For wanting to eat something you made."

My gut heaved. Something I made. A warm tear tracked down my check and I swiped it away. "You shouldn't be sorry," I whispered.

"Of course I should," he said. He hooked his finger under my chin and lifted my face to meet his. "I sinned, and I'm being punished for it. I deserve this. And you—"a small curve of his dry lips—"take care of Juanita for me." He nodded to his sister, waved to his mother, and joined the guard who waited patiently behind him.

"No," I whispered, watching helplessly as they were led off, away from the pavilion. "Freddie!" I said to the guard. "Where are you taking them?"

Freddie allowed Octavio to join the ill-fated group on his own and turned to me. "To the cove beach."

"Why?"

"That's where we're taking them to die."

Something in me twisted and I leaned over, placing my hands on my knees as a wave of nausea overtook me. I had done this to them.

Guilt pressed down on me, darkening the edges of my sight. I swallowed down bile and straightened, looking up to watch the group wend their way along the path, the bordering lights blurring in the humidity, as if they were walking through clouds.

From where I stood outside the pavilion, I could see Juanita sitting in her seat, hands intertwined in her lap, her eyes fixed on me. I silently pleaded for her forgiveness, for her understanding, but she slowly turned to face the stage, unblinking, along with the rest of the Flock. All focused on the Reverend. As if simply looking at the sinners would taint their souls.

"Child," the Reverend called to me. "Your concern is commendable, but poorly directed."

"Poorly directed?"

The words didn't even make sense to me. My head was cloudy, confused. All I could think was that I'd killed eleven people. Killed.

Someone caught me by the shoulder and my heart jumped. Doc Gladstone stood next to me, a dark leather bag in his hand. "Go back into the pavilion, Mia."

"They're dying, Doc Gladstone," I whispered.

He dipped to my ear. "Mia, go sit down."

"Doctor?" the Reverend called. "Shouldn't you tend to the sinners? Ensure that the rest of their time here in Edenton is as painless as it possibly can be. Now, God wanted these folks to suffer, let me be clear about that. And I, the Reverend Elias Eden, am going against God to provide them comfort in their final hours." He bowed his head. "Let us pray God absolves me for my sin."

Doc Gladstone patted my shoulder. "Go on," he said and then ran off to follow the path to the beach. He looked so strong and powerful, dreadlocks flying behind him like a cape.

But I couldn't move. My feet seemed rooted to the ground. No one would look at me, not Juanita, Aliyah, nor Mama. Like I was as expendable as any tree in the jungle behind me. Like what I was feeling—the shock and horror of it—didn't matter.

Like those eleven people didn't matter, either.

"Why pray for your absolution?" I asked aloud, my throat tight.

The Reverend raised his head and deliberately, slowly, turned to glare at me. "Excuse me, child?"

I licked my lips, swallowed, and spoke. "Why does the Flock pray for your absolution? Shouldn't those eleven people be absolved?"

A round of horrified gasps echoed in the pavilion.

"They were punished for their greed," the Reverend said through his teeth.

"They ate a few cookies," I answered.

The Reverend's eyes narrowed on me, a wicked twist on his mouth. "Maria, come take your child back to her seat."

Mama stood, straightened out her skirt, and wove her way through the little kids seated on the benches. She didn't look at me until she drew closer. Her eyes were emotionless, but her grip was tight on my upper arm.

"Don't do this, Mia," she said under her breath. "It's not your place to question what happens here."

I jerked away from her, disgusted by her complacency, and pointed to the Reverend. "You killed eleven people!" I said.

"No, you did," he snapped. "You assisted Agatha in baking, correct?"

"I—" I stopped.

Mama's expectant stare bore into me. "Answer him, Mia."

"I did bake them," I admitted, but the rest of the words—I didn't know about the poison—were stolen from my lips by her softening, warm expression.

"It's as if the hand of God reached down through you to teach our Flock a lesson on greed." Mama brushed my hair back from my forehead. "I'm proud of you, Mia."

"P-proud of me?" I said, searching her eyes, looking for something to make sense of her reaction. "Those people are dying, Mama!"

"Thaddeus!" the Reverend yelled. "Take Mia away. Find something for her to do until she comes to her senses about this."

Mama stepped away from me, hands dropping to her sides.

The Reverend stood, pushing himself up from his throne. "Have someone watch her."

Thaddeus, who had been charging toward me, paused. "May I suggest she stay with Grizz, sir?"

"Yes." The Reverend grinned. A wide, callous grin. "With Grizz."

* * *

40

I heard the rhythmic thumping sound before the jungle opened up into the clearing. Thaddeus walked behind me. He hadn't spoken since snagging my arm and dragging me through Edenton to an unlit path I'd never been down before. I'd never needed to in the six years I'd been in Edenton. Because it led to the cemetery.

Thaddeus's flashlight cut a swath of light across the dark path. My shadow, walking stiffly, stretched out and made its way over the knotted roots and fallen leaves, then into the clearing. There was no breeze. Heat radiated from the surrounding jungle. Thaddeus reached down and opened a rusting iron gate set into a concrete threshold. Headstones poked out of the ground like crooked teeth. In the flickering torchlight, two figures stood, one shoveling, the other standing, arms folded, watching the other with disinterest.

"Grizz!" Thaddeus called.

Grizz's hulking silhouette lumbered over. He hitched his gun strap over his shoulder and jerked his chin at us.

"You said eleven, right?" Grizz asked Thaddeus. "The kid's digging the fifth one now."

In the distance, Gabriel sunk the shovel into the earth and threw the dirt into a pile. Clots of soil tumbled down the mound, scattering on the ground.

"Only five so far?" Thaddeus said, shining the flashlight in Grizz's eyes.

He held up his hand to shield his face. "Yeah, but the ground's soft. He'll have them done soon enough."

"Here's another to help." Thaddeus blinded me with the flashlight. "Mia needs to reflect on her actions during Bright Night. Give her a shovel and put her to work."

Grizz shrugged. "Okay. Come on, Mia."

"Wait," I said, looking at Thaddeus. "You're going to make me dig their graves?"

"Yes." He handed me to Grizz and turned back to the path. "Oh, and Grizz," Thaddeus called over his shoulder, "why don't you help dig, too? We'll need to bury the bodies soon. We can't leave them on the beach in this heat."

Grizz cursed under his breath, but not loud enough for Thaddeus to hear. "No problem," he said.

Gabriel looked up as we approached, wiping his brow with the shoulder of his shirt. "Grizz, you didn't tell me we'd have visitors. I would have made tea."

"Shut up." Grizz handed me a shovel. "All the graves are outlined with spray paint. Start digging here." He pointed to an orange rectangle painted on the patchy ground.

I glanced at the shallow, open graves lined up next to the one Gabriel was digging; beyond them I saw the gravestones of Edenton residents long since gone. I didn't recognize most of the names, except for Eduardo, Enrique and Angél's father, Edenton's original fisherman. It had been a while since anyone had died in Edenton. The milky-white marble of the headstones remembered who and when, but not how. I was glad for it. I didn't want anyone to remember how these eleven people died.

"Mia," Grizz said, snapping his fingers.

I blinked. The weight of the shovel in my hands made everything that was happening so real. "I don't know if I can do this, Grizz."

"I've seen you train," he said. "You can lift weights, you can dig a damn hole in the ground."

"That's not what I—"

Grizz cut me off, thrusting a pair of work gloves in my face. "Dig. I'm going to get another shovel. If either of you moves from this spot, I will hunt you down myself, got that?"

"Promise?" Gabriel asked.

Grizz slumped visibly and sighed. "You are exhausting, Gabriel." He pulled up one of the torch lights wedged in the dirt and walked away, leaving us to dig.

"Why can't you do this?" Gabriel asked once Grizz was out of earshot.

I stared down at the shovel, the dull metal blade against the rich dirt beneath my feet, and wondered whose body would be buried in this grave.

"Doesn't matter," I said, stabbing the shovel into the ground. It sunk into the dirt easily enough, but with each thwack of the blade, I counted in my head to eleven, then began again.

Gabriel watched me for a few moments. "You knew them? The ones that died?"

"Of course."

"Grizz told me about it. He sounded like, I don't know, almost proud about how clever the Reverend was. The Flock learning a lesson in greed and all that shit." He paused, regarding me with a thoughtful expression. "You know what the Reverend did was screwed up, right? Stuff like that doesn't happen in the outside world. Well, it may, but there are investigations and people get caught and go on trial for murder."

Shame and anger rose up in my throat. The Reverend had made me an accessory to murder. "I know what the Reverend did was wrong."

Gabriel looked surprised. "Really?"

"I know wrong from right." I stopped shoveling and met Gabriel's gaze. "And do you know how they died?"

"Something about poison in food?"

"Cookies. Poisoned cookies." I poked the shovel into the ground. "That I baked."

"Oh. Okay," he said, nodded once, and went back to shoveling.

I leaned against the handle of the shovel. "You don't seem too surprised that I murdered eleven people."

"You didn't do it," he said.

"How do you know?"

"You just told me you knew wrong from right." He threw a shovelful of dirt on the pile. "You wouldn't have knowingly put poison in any cookies."

"You're right," I said.

"Of course I am." He shot me a sly smile. "Like I said, I thought you were different from the rest of the Flock. Any one of them would have done it without blinking an eye. And wouldn't feel bad about it afterward. Like you do."

We dug without speaking for a while, the thwacking sounds from the shovels ringing through the trees.

"You want to hear another reason how I know you're not a murderer?" Gabriel whispered.

The gate squeaked, heralding Grizz's entrance. He trudged forward dragging a shovel behind him.

I nodded, stealing a quick glance at Grizz.

Gabriel leaned toward me. "Because, Mia, I'm a murderer."

# Chapter Six

When I entered the dining hall through the swinging kitchen doors the next morning the talking stopped. I heard the tinny sound of silverware clanking against plates. The squeaking ceiling fans hanging from the rafters. Birds shrieking outside the open windows. But no one spoke. I grabbed a large gray bin from the cart and scanned the long tables for dirty plates. Backs stiffened as I passed. I reached between Enrique and Angél, both reeking of fish, and they gave me a wide berth, as if I were the one who stank.

Across the table from me, Juanita collected the breadbaskets. She grinned in thanks as Enrique stacked baskets and handed them to her. I tried to catch her gaze but she turned away the moment our eyes met. And she wasn't the only one. A stack of dirty plates was shoved in my direction. When I looked down to thank Suzanne, she twisted in her seat and I kindly thanked the back of her head. I threw the plates in the bin and took bitter satisfaction at her startled wince.

Speaking out against the Reverend was like speaking out against God Himself. The Flock would outcast me for my heresy until the Reverend told them I was to be forgiven. I wasn't expecting that commandment to be handed down any time soon.

Mama sat with Max at the end of the next table. Jin Sang was seated next to Bae John. His dark eyes were like hers, but his caramel-colored hair sometimes caused me to wonder about his father. I collected the plates at the edge of the table and Max glanced up, stealing a smile at me while Mama whispered to Jin Sang. Jin Sang's small arms reached out and hugged Mama, giving her a consoling pat on the back. Hiding her face from me until I walked away.

I took a deep, calming breath and trudged to the corner of the dining hall with the bin full of dishes and slid it on the cart. My eyes stung, lids heavy with exhaustion. I was beginning to feel every movement of my muscles in my arms and back, the hours of shoveling until dawn taking their toll.

"Agatha needs you in the kitchen," Juanita said from behind me, her words cold and flat.

I nodded over my shoulder at her but didn't try to meet her eyes again. I rolled the cart through the dining hall. In that minefield of disregard, I felt the weight of a solitary gaze on me. Gabriel tracked my progress to the kitchen. He sat with the rest of the boys from his cottage, next to the empty space once occupied by Octavio. The end of his hair was wet and curled around his face and neck, like he'd showered. He didn't smile. Didn't nod. Simply watched me, as if flipping a decision over in his head.

What had he meant—he was a murderer? Once Grizz had returned to the graveyard, we couldn't talk anymore. I'd spent the rest of the time wondering and stealing glances at Gabriel as he worked. If what he'd said was true though, and he was a murderer, wouldn't he be in prison? That's how they punished people in the outside world, wasn't it?

I backed through the swinging doors to the kitchen, towing the cart along. Aliyah and Bridgette mechanically scraped out large frying pans over the trash cans. Dina pulled the buffet servers from the service line. Without even turning their heads, they seemed to sense my presence and immediately tensed.

"Mia," Agatha snapped. She stood in the center of the kitchen wearing a spotless white apron. She pointed to the magnetic strip over my workstation. "Where is your chef's knife?"

My pulse quickened. I looked over at my station. I'd arranged my knives so the empty space would be less noticeable. But they'd been reorganized, sizes descending in perfect order, a yawning gap where the chef's knife should be.

"It's got to be around here somewhere," I said, keeping my voice steady on the lie. It wasn't exactly a lie. Gabriel still had it, so it was around here. Somewhere.

Bridgette turned back to her frying pan, her mouth half-twisted with satisfaction.

A flush of anger heated my cheeks. I shoved down the rage and faced Agatha.

"Find it," she said. "Those are expensive knives. We can't just be leaving them about!" She threw an open palm at the cart. "Load the dishwasher and then I have a new assignment for you."

I sighed inwardly. I placed the dishes I'd collected in the washer and set it for a two-minute cycle. When I turned back around, I caught Aliyah, expression wrought with pity, flicking a glance in my direction. I ignored her. I didn't want her pity. I didn't want Bridgette's vengeance. I didn't want Agatha's wrath. But it all swarmed around me like flies.

"Now," Agatha said, hitching her hands on her waist. "The traps need to be cleaned."

"Traps?" I asked, and heard a snicker from Bridgette. "The grease traps?"

Agatha shot Bridgette a warning look. "No, Mia. The rodent traps. Once we're finished in here, you're to empty the traps from around the kitchen and the trash bins in the back. After lunch service, you need to take the carcasses and burn them."

"I . . . what?" I glanced around the room, at those dark and shadowy places under the counters and behind the refrigerators. "Isn't there someone else who does that?"

Agatha's eyebrows lowered, three creases appearing between them. "Excuse me? Are you implying that you're too good to clean the traps?"

"Uh, no, I didn't say that—"

"See here, young lady," she said, pointing a bony finger at me. "I'm not sure who you think you are, or what you think you have been put on God's Green Earth to do, but it is to serve the Reverend and the good people of Edenton. You are going to clean out those traps. You are going to burn those carcasses, and you may end up doing it again if you don't watch what comes out of that smart mouth of yours, understand?"

I nodded, fighting back the score of angry words I wanted to scream in her bitter, haggard face.

"Girls," Agatha said. "Get this kitchen cleaned up quickly. It's going to take Mia a couple hours to collect and empty the traps. And I want them cleaned out of here before we begin lunch service." She curled her lip. "I don't want those disgusting things anywhere near my food. We don't want to serve any contaminated food," she eyed me, "do we, Mia?"

\* \* \*

The acrid, smoky smell clung to me as I pushed open the door to my cottage. Inside, the bunks were made, blankets pulled tight over the mattresses, and the other girls' aprons missing from the pegs on the wall. Except for two. Mine and Lily's.

Fading sunlight edged through the blinds, enough that I didn't bother turning on the light. The fan circled overhead, wafting down the stink of my hair and cooling the layers of sweat and smoke coating my skin. My gray dress was streaked with black, and, I noticed then, dried blood. I checked myself for cuts or scrapes, but found none, and ripped open the dress from the neck, peeling it off of me. I wasn't going to pull that thing over my head. I emptied the deep pockets, throwing my ID tag and a burned stick wrapped in plastic onto my bed.

In the bathroom, the sink still had pooling water around the edges of the drain. So I hadn't missed the girls by that much time. I was relieved to not have to face them—even if it was just until dinner service was over. Agatha hadn't wanted me anywhere near the kitchen in my current condition, and I was thankful for it. I'd been granted an hour to shower and dress and I planned on using all of it, if not a little more.

I twisted the shower on and stuck my hand into the stream of water, knowing I'd have to wait for it to get hot. I went back in the bedroom, and eyed Lily's bunk. Someone had made it. I touched the blanket, and wondered who would fill that bunk next. Would she come and go as quickly as Lily had? I shook the thought away. Lily had died, not escaped. And death wasn't preferable to living in Edenton, was it?

I snatched the stick off my bed, unwrapped the plastic I'd snuck from the kitchen, and grabbed my sketchbook from the trunk. After I erased a patch from an old drawing, I scratched the end of the stick onto the paper, and watched the charcoal scrape across the surface. The color was rich, no reflection in it like the lead of the pencil.

It wasn't until I noticed the steam pouring from the bathroom that I really looked at the image I'd drawn. Gabriel stared back at me, the way he'd looked last night. Face half-draped in shadow, the light of the torch outlining the strength of his jaw, the straight line of his nose, that cherry-skin indentation on his bottom lip. I liked looking at him, I realized. The way he spoke, the way he moved. Was that normal in the outside world? Because it didn't seem normal in Edenton.

After hiding my sketchbook and charcoal, I headed to the bathroom, stripped off my bra and underwear, and tossed them into the hamper in the corner of the room. I heard the front door of the cottage squeak open.

"I'll be out in a bit," I called, stepping into the bathroom and kicking the door closed behind me.

I didn't even bother to wait for an answer. If whoever-it-was needed to use the bathroom, she'd just come in with me in the shower. It's not as if we had locks on the doors. Or privacy.

I slid the shower curtain closed. I watched the dark water fade to clear at my feet, then scrubbed myself until my skin was raw red. By the time I got out, the bathroom was filled with opaque steam. I wrapped myself in a towel, went out to my trunk, and snatched up a clean uniform from the pile.

When I returned to the bathroom, most of the steam had cleared. A dark shape next to the mirror caught the light. I drew closer. Stuck into the wall next to the mirror was my chef's knife. Then I saw the writing on the steamy mirror.

*Meet me on the fishing beach after curfew. Come alone.*

# Chapter Seven

The ocean was black and still in the moonlight, waves folding quietly in on themselves. It would have been beautiful if it hadn't been for the jangling of my nerves. I stayed close to the tree line, inched my way off the cove path, and onto the sand. I scanned the cove, but knew no guards were here. They always patrolled the jungle, not the water.

*They're not keeping people from getting into Edenton. They're keeping the Flock—us—in.*

If what Gabriel had said in the infirmary was right, then I understood why they didn't patrol the waterfront. We didn't have boats, no small inflatable dinghies, or even life preservers. There was no way the Flock could escape out onto the water, so why waste the manpower? With our limited number of guards, it made sense to patrol where we could get away on foot.

Still, I remained close to the trees and hoped to make it to the jetty of rocks that separated the cove from the wide fishing beach without being seen. I'd changed into the dark T-shirt and jeans I'd been given for heavy-duty work—for most of the Flock that would have been their Contrition punishment—and my work boots. No breeze came off the water in the cove and my shirt stuck to my skin. My thick-soled boots shifted around unsteadily in the deep sand.

I saw deteriorating indentations stretching along the beach. Eleven. A curtain of dread dropped over me and I glanced up at the star-drenched sky. That was the last thing Octavio and Lily probably saw, all that beauty coaxing them into the everlasting night.

The jetty reached far out into the ocean, separating the cove where we were occasionally allowed to swim for training, and the fishing beach. Instead of taking the path to the beach, I decided to climb over the jetty. Enrique and Angél's cottage was at the mouth of the fishing beach path. I couldn't risk being seen by the fishermen. The rocks were slippery, though. Water from the breaking waves sprayed my face, feeling cool against my heated skin. A sharp rock scraped my palm and I hoped the salt water would clean it because I didn't want to have to lie to Doc Gladstone.

My boots hit the sand on the other side. It was wet and easier to walk in than the deep sand on the cove side. I walked slowly, scanning the wide expanse of beach. On this side of the jetty, the small waves broke far out, low tide expanding the beach into a wide stretch of sand. In the half moon's milky light, the humidity hung in the air like steam, blurring everything. I squinted and off in the distance saw what looked like a large rock at the edge of the water, as if it had come loose from the jetty. Slowly I approached, the wet sand sinking below my heavy soles. A figure unfurled from the rock-like shape and began walking toward me.

"You came," Gabriel said as he moved closer, no surprise in his tone.

He'd expected me to show, and, in a way, I didn't really care what he'd expected. I was out on the beach, late at night, with a boy. That tingle came back; excitement mingled with fear. This time I welcomed it. Because, why not? I glanced up at him. Same as me, he wore dark clothes. Wind sweeping off the water blew wisps of hair from his forehead and I could see a spark of satisfaction in his eyes.

"If the Reverend finds out we're here, we could get in a lot of trouble," I said.

"But you don't care about getting in trouble, do you?"

He was right. I didn't care. Not anymore.

"Why did you ask me here? I have to be at breakfast service at six A.M."

"Don't plan on sleeping," he said as he grabbed my hand.

The warmth of his palm electrified my skin. It ran all the way up my arm as he led me down the beach.

"Where are we going?" I asked, peering back over my shoulder.

He didn't answer, only darted forward, dragging me toward the high rocky bluff towering over the far side of the beach. My breathing rang in my ears as we moved farther from the shoreline, the ocean breeze disappearing as we headed inland.

We stopped at the edge of the bluff. Above us, the rocky ridge peaked high into the night sky.

"It's not as steep as it looks," Gabriel said, following my gaze.

"It's not as—huh?"

"Have you ever climbed a rock wall?"

"A what?" I dropped his hand. "I can't climb that."

His eyes skated over me. "Something tells me you can."

"Why would I want to?" I asked.

"Because I want you to see what's on the other side."

I glanced up the steep hill. It was high. A fall could kill me.

*Because, Mia, I'm a murderer.*

Or a shove.

I felt instantly stupid for coming out here to meet him.

"Having second thoughts?" Gabriel asked.

"No," I said and glanced at him. His hair fell into his eyes, a curling bruise dark around the eye where Grizz had punched him. Is this what a murderer looked like? "Maybe."

Gabriel kicked the toe of his shoe against the craggy wall then bent down and fiddled with the heel of his shoe. He drew something from it. It glinted as he held it up and flipped it open with a tinny sound.

"You have a lighter?" I asked, shocked. "How did you get that into Edenton?"

"They took all my fun stuff. I hid it in crazy places, too. Like in the linings of our luggage." He examined the façade of the cliff with the little flame. "Except this. Guess they didn't think to search my mom's ladytime supplies. Now, if I can just find where I climbed last night . . ."

"Ladytime?"

He turned to me, the lighter's flame flickering between us. "You ready to climb?"

My hands began to tremble. A flutter built in my chest.

"Why do you want me to go up there?" I asked.

"Come on, Eden. Man up."

"Eden?"

"That's our last name, right?"

I paused, thinking about my name. Mia Eden. It was like an actress's name. A made-up name.

"Ricci," I said, my last name—Papa's last name—feeling strange on my tongue. It had been so long since I'd said it. "Mia Antonia Ricci."

"Gabriel Herbert Tallon," he said, taking my hand and shaking it once.

I sent him a questioning look. "Herbert." He nodded. "Yeah, I know. But it's really my only flaw."

I laughed, and felt an unexpected burst of lightness in my chest, so strange and wonderful that it almost made me forget everything for a split second. The sound of my own laugh shocked me, too. It was warm and smoky, not much different from my voice, but in laughter it became saturated. It had been a long time since I laughed.

Gabriel said nothing. He only stood, eyes fixed on my mouth.

I swallowed back my laugh.

"Follow me," Gabriel said and placed his foot on a jutting rock. "Try to put your hands and feet where I put mine."

I watched as he scaled the wall almost effortlessly. Determined, I followed him. Occasionally, I lost my footing and my boot slipped out from under me. My anxiety skyrocketed, bursting in my chest and spreading out into my limbs until they prickled with rushing blood. I loved the feeling of it. Like I'd been wading in a lukewarm kiddie pool for years, then plunged down a water slide, careening almost uncontrollably.

When I reached the top, Gabriel grabbed my hand and lifted me to my feet. We were both breathless and sweating. He stood so close I could feel the heat coming off his body before it was whisked away by the wind.

"Thanks," I mumbled.

"No problem." He glanced down the side of the bluff we'd just climbed. "That was pretty hardcore. I wasn't sure you'd do it."

I looked down, too. Once I saw the height we'd scaled, the shock and elation made my head swirl. The wind caught the fabric of my clothes, and for a moment, the idea of flying didn't seem that crazy. Maybe it was the sudden sense of freedom rushing through me.

I tried to sound indifferent. "So, now I'm up here, what do you want to show me?"

Gabriel let the question hang, the corners of his mouth quirking. "This way," he said finally, leading me toward the other side of the bluff.

Once there, we mounted a smaller hill with a gradual slope and climbed it side by side. As the next beach came into view, my jaw dropped.

"That's not Edenton," I said.

"Nope."

Down on the beach, lights winked around what looked like a small town square plopped in the middle of the jungle. Modern buildings, much more sophisticated than in Edenton, bordered a perfect plot of well-manicured land. One paved road led to it from the surrounding jungle, a few blue-hued headlights driving toward the outcrop of buildings.

The beach itself boasted rows of little sun huts and a large deck out over the sand, lined with lights.

"That can't be San Sebastian," I said. "It's too small—and it's supposed to be farther away. The Reverend says the government granted us a ten-mile border radius."

Gabriel's tone was flat. "Either the Reverend is easily confused by the science of cartography, or he's lying."

I turned and saw the low, muted lights of Edenton just over the trees that lined the beach. The sparkling little beach encampment was just about two miles away.

"Why lie?" I asked Gabriel.

"The Reverend killed eleven people. I'd imagine he's prone to lying—especially to himself."

"Is it a resort?"

"No idea. Could be? If it was, why would the Reverend allow the corruption of the outside world so close to his paradise?"

"I want to see what's down there."

"I tried that last night," he said. "I couldn't get very close because of the guards and when I tried to make it back through the jungle to Edenton, Grizz caught me."

I thought for a moment. "But you already got caught," I said. "Would they think you'd be dumb enough to try again?"

"Grizz would. He doesn't think as highly of me as you do," he said.

"I don't think that highly of you," I said and hid the smile tugging at the corners of my lips. "We'll come back up the way we came."

He gestured to the rocky slope below. "This side's steeper than the one we climbed up. I was able to slide down this, but couldn't gain enough footing to climb back up."

I peeked over the edge. "We'll find our way back though the jungle, then."

Gabriel stared silently at the lights on the beach for a few moments. Finally he said, "How long have you been in Edenton?" He turned to me, moon behind him, eyes cloaked in shadows.

"Six years."

He inclined his head, almost imperceptibly. "I wasn't here six minutes when I knew I wanted out." His voice became a sharp whisper. "I'm escaping from Edenton, but I'm not making the same mistake I made last night. They're going to be looking for me out there tonight, no matter what you may think about their security procedures. And if you—"

"What if I want out, too?" I asked in a rush.

His mouth snapped shut.

I faced the little beach resort's lights. "I want to see what's down there. I want to know why the Reverend lied about the ten-mile radius." I paused, letting my voice drop to a whisper. "And when you escape, you aren't going alone. I want to go with you."

# Chapter Eight

I didn't remember changing into my pajamas and slipping into bed after sneaking back from the beach. I hadn't slept since before the Bright Night and must have passed out when my head hit the pillow. While asleep, I was dragged down by guilt and worry. The faces of the eleven stared at me, cradling the cookies I'd made in their hands as if they were precious and rare, all looking at me with trusting gazes. I saw Octavio. Laughing, smiling, eating . . . dying. Choking and gaging, blood pouring from his mouth and down his chin, staining his flawless skin.

I woke with a start. The light from the windows was gray and murky, barely dawn. A shadow passed between the bunks. The bathroom door closed with a soft click. I glanced at the other bunks. All were occupied, the girls curled under their thin blankets. Except for Aliyah's. And, of course, Lily's.

I peeled back my sheet and got out of bed, quietly making my way to the bathroom door. Listening silently, I heard the water running, and, beneath the hiss, what sounded like sniffling. After a few moments the water continued to run, so I softly knocked.

"One minute," came Aliyah's voice, nothing more than a weak sound on the other side of the door.

"Are you okay?" I whispered.

The door cracked open. "Sure." Her smile was bright, but it didn't match her eyes. "I'm changing for breakfast service." She motioned to her serviceable uniform dress and bib apron.

I glanced at the clock on the wall. Only two minutes until the cottage morning alarm would go off. Although I'd been haunted by chilling dreams, I wanted more sleep. I really did love sleep. Probably because I always felt deprived of it. I couldn't recall ever sleeping past five-thirty since coming to Edenton.

"How was it?" I asked Aliyah. "Prayer Circle."

She cocked her head, one braided ponytail falling over her forehead. "Fine."

I waited for more information, the tell-all she'd promised me about what happened in Prayer Circle, but her smile only grew wider.

"What is it, silly?" Her deep brown eyes looked hollow, lost. Vacant.

"Nothing," I said, backing away one step. "Just making sure you're okay."

"I'm fine." Before she shut the door, I saw a flash of pink in the trash can. Peony pink. The special shirt Sister had made Aliyah to attend Circle was stuffed in the garbage.

"You're not going to get any information," Juanita said from her bunk. Her tone was flat, eyes focused just beyond my head at the wall, unable—or unwilling—to meet my eyes.

Bridgette shot up, the sheet whipping back away from her. "She won't talk about it," she said. "We don't talk about it."

She motioned to Dina, who was silently crawling from her bed, less sanctimonious than her bunk mate in the morning. Both Bridgette and Dina had attended their first Prayer Circle a few months ago, but had only been back twice since. Prayer Circle for many of the Flock was a two or three times a week event.

Bridgette thrust her chin forward as she swung her feet over the edge of her top bunk. "Prayer Circle is a sacred rite in the Reverend's church. We offer our silence as a sacrifice to the sanctity of the event."

I glared at Bridgette. Her tone, her attitude, along with how Aliyah was acting, gnawed at me. "Is it hot up there?" I asked Bridgette.

"On my bunk?" she asked.

"On your cross."

Bridgette gasped. "Mia! You are so nasty these days. You're lucky I don't report your attitude to Thaddeus."

I shot a worried look at the bathroom door. Maybe I wanted to face Thaddeus again and ask some real questions—about the cookies, about the little town just over the ridge, about the mysterious Prayer Circle.

"Go ahead, Bridgette. Tell him whatever you want," I said, and turned to my bunk.

Bridgette slipped down off her bed, her feet hitting the floor with a thud. I heard the rustle of sheets being flipped aside. "You didn't do him justice, you know," she said.

I turned back. She held out my sketchbook like an offering, open to the page where I'd drawn Gabriel. The breath slowly left my lungs.

"You went through my things?" I breathed.

"Your things?" Bridgette's eyes sharpened on mine. "There is no yours or mine in Edenton." She swung the book to face her and held it up to eye level. She cocked her head to the side. "Your drawing of the new boy isn't as pretty as he is," she said. "God blessed him physically, but the Lord sure didn't give you the talent to translate his beauty to the page." She began flipping through the sketchbook.

"Give it back," I said, moving toward her.

Bridgette tsked. "Mia, you better not be seen with the new boy. You know you'll get punished for seeking out his company. This drawing is pretty damning evidence that you're coveting him."

"Give it to me, now!" I yelled.

"Let's see." She twisted away, putting the corner of her bunk between us. "Oh, there's writing in this, too. It's like a little diary. Looks like you're a little bit of a daddy's girl." She read in a sing-song voice. "'Things Papa used to say: Doubt everything, find your own light . . . Knowledge is freedom . . . Faith is not wanting to know what's true.'" She gasped, placing her hand theatrically over her heart. "Mia, these quotes are sacrilegious!"

"They're not." The heaviness of everyone's gaze was on me. I glanced around. "They're just things I remember him saying when I was little," I said to the girls.

"They are sacrilegious!" Bridgette said to everyone, waving a hand around the room. "Faith is not hiding from the truth. Faith is confidence and trust in Our Maker. Doubt is the temptation of the devil." She slammed the book closed and pointed it at me. "This whole book is awful! You shouldn't even have it!"

"It's all I have left!" I yelled.

Bridgette dropped her arm to her side, my sketchbook in her hand tapping against her leg. "Left of what?"

"My life before Edenton," I snapped.

Aliyah, who had been standing in the bathroom doorway with her hand on the knob, slipped inside the bathroom and I saw her reflection cowering behind the door. Dina stood strong at Bridgette's side. Juanita, though, still sat on her bunk, eyes on me, looking like I'd punched her in the gut. I'd said something terribly wrong.

"There is nothing before Edenton," Bridgette said. "Edenton is our one true home. It's where we are meant to be." She looked down at the book in her hand. "I'm going right to Thaddeus about this. This book should be burned."

I envisioned my sketchbook, along with my fading memories of Papa, being tossed into the fire like those rigid rat carcasses. My sight went angry red. I lunged forward, trying to swipe the book away from Bridgette, but Dina darted in front of her. Dina was small, strong enough, but smaller than me and I easily batted her aside. All I could see was my sketchbook clasped in Bridgette's hand, as if I were looking down a long tunnel at it.

My sketchbook.

The one thing I had that kept me sane. The one thing that I could confide in without judgment. The one thing that was truly mine.

In someone else's hands.

In Bridgette's hands.

And she was going to hand it over to Thaddeus. To the Reverend.

I wasn't going to lose it without a fight. I curled my hand into a fist and swung. It connected with Bridgette's cheek. She tumbled back, hand clasping for the bedpost as she fell. She cried out in pain. The sketchbook toppled to the floor, pages fluttering open. She grabbed the side of her face, eyes wide with shock.

"How dare you!" she yelled at me.

I scrambled down on my knees and gathered up the sketchbook, clutching it to my chest. Glancing up, I saw Juanita's confused expression. She looked at me as if she wasn't sure who I was. A stranger. She reached down a hand to help me to my feet.

"Thanks," I mumbled.

Dina sat next to Bridgette on the bed, stroking Bridgette's hair back away from her face and inspecting her cheek. A red mark flamed on Bridgette's skin.

I should have regretted hitting her, but the solid feel of my sketchbook in my hands again erased the regret.

"I'm going to Thaddeus," Bridgette said, struggling to her feet.

"No," said Juanita.

We swung our surprised gazes at her. She stood in the center of the room, her eyes narrowed on me. A sense of calm emanated from her, her breathing steady and deep.

"What do you mean, no?" Bridgette said. "She broke a rule. Obviously she's had that diary here since she came to Edenton. Snuck it in somehow. Mia can't be allowed to keep it."

Juanita didn't look at Bridgette as she spoke, she kept her focus on me with a look of curiosity mingled with disappointment. "She's not going to keep it," Juanita said. "She's going to burn it herself."

A slow smile crept over Bridgette's face. "That will make up for you hitting me, too."

"What?" I asked, clutching the book closer. "No, I can't do that—"

"You will, Mia," Juanita said. "You have to. You keep that and she's going right to Thaddeus."

Bridgette stood, brushing Dina away like a pesky bug. "We'd all go to Thaddeus about this. Not only me."

"I wouldn't." The meek voice came from behind the bathroom door. Aliyah peeked her head around the corner and met my eyes. "I would never say anything, Mia."

"You're a fool, Aliyah," Bridgette said. "Willing to put your friendship before the Reverend's rules."

"I'm not a fool!" Aliyah exploded. "Don't ever call me that!"

Bridgette's jaw dropped. "We'll chalk up your attitude to exhaustion. Prayer Circle takes a lot out of you, doesn't it Aliyah?"

Aliyah cringed back into the bathroom and nodded.

I looked up at Juanita. "I can't burn this, Juanita. Please."

"I'll help you do it," she said. "Get dressed and we'll take care of it before breakfast service."

"But Thaddeus should know," Bridgette whined.

Juanita placed her hand out toward me, asking for the sketchbook. "He doesn't need to know about this, Bridgette," she said as I handed her the sketchbook. "We're getting rid of it, no harm done." She snagged her apron off the hook on the wall and wrapped the book in it. "And besides, Mia isn't the only one hiding something around here, is she?"

Bridgette scowled, clutching at her neck, where beneath her nightshirt she wore a silver dog-tag style necklace engraved with Romans 13:13. "This necklace was sanctioned by the Reverend," she said.

"I wasn't talking about that, Bridgette." And Juanita left it at that.

By the time we got to the heap, the sky was lightening in the east, a pale dusty gray. Juanita, her mass of curls pulled away from her face in a tie, held my sketchbook inside her apron under one arm. Her hands were shoved into her uniform dress's pockets.

We stood at the edge of a smoldering mound of trash, tiny wisps of smoke curling up and away, as if trying to escape the rotting stink of the heap. Lights were still on, even as the morning brightened, casting stark shadows in the piles around us.

Juanita pulled my sketchbook from under her arm and stared at the black cover. "How long have you had this?" she asked.

"I've always had it, Juanita," I said. "I smuggled it into Edenton when I came."

"I don't understand what you need it for."

"It's where I draw, write. It's where I put my thoughts and memories. It reminds me of who I am."

"Who you were," she corrected.

My gut clenched. I didn't like to think of the younger me as the better, freer, happier me. Weren't things supposed to improve as you got older? You grow into yourself, understand who you are?

She turned away and walked toward the recycling bins. Grabbing a cardboard cereal box, she tossed it onto the smoldering pile. Flames began to lick up the sides, black smoke swirling into the air. She handed me the sketchbook.

I glanced again at the flames. They ate away at the box. The thought of my sketchbook eaten by fire made me weak with disgust.

"Hide it," Juanita said, watching the flames.

"What?"

"Hide your book. Hide it someplace Bridgette and Dina won't find it." Her brown eyes met mine. Sadness edged her gaze. "I know you wonder about your father. I wonder about mine, too. The only difference is that I never knew my dad. But if I did, I would never forget him and I would do everything I could to hold on to those memories. Octavio—" Her voice hitched. "Octavio and I used to talk about what our fathers were like. He never met his either. His father died right after he was born." She looked up into the pinking sky. "Anyway, they're together now."

After a moment of watching the golden clouds move across the sky, she turned away and walked toward the entrance to the heap. Then she stopped and turned around. "Bridgette is right about Gabriel. If the Reverend knew you were interested in him, you'd get in a lot of trouble."

"I know."

"You're not betrothed to anyone anymore, true." She said the words without pause. "But Gabriel may already have been chosen for someone else."

I nodded. "I understand, Juanita."

"Good. I'll cover for you at breakfast prep. Go hide your book now."

"Thank you," I called to her.

The relief lasted until I arrived at the kitchen twenty minutes later. Bridgette glared at me as I pushed my way through the door and hustled over to my station. When no one was looking, I slipped my chef's knife from my apron pocket and placed it quietly on the magnetic strip.

Bridgette narrowed her eyes at me but didn't say a word.

"Mia," Agatha snapped. "You're on dining hall duty. Go set up."

"But what about the fruit?" I asked, nodding my head toward the box of mangos on the counter.

"Mia," she spoke through clenched teeth.

Pushing the box aside, I left, shoving my way through the kitchen doors with too much force. They swung back, one banging against the wall. I heard Agatha's frustrated sigh and saw her peeking through the service counter window at me. She slammed the window's sliding door closed with a sneer. The sound resonated through the vast dining hall.

With an answering sigh, I lifted a stack of clean plates and placed them on the end of the service line. The muscles in my arms ached from climbing the ridge. I rubbed my bicep and leaned over to grab another stack when I heard his voice.

"Hey, Ricci," Gabriel whispered.

He stood on the other side of the open window, hair mussed and falling into his eyes, as if he'd just gotten out of bed. The dawning sunlight picked out the gold in his hair. It wasn't nearly as dark as I'd thought.

I rushed over to the window. "What are you doing here?" I asked, glancing over my shoulder for signs of Agatha.

"Tonight," he said.

I met his gaze. In the morning light, his eyes were startling, the color deep and . . . different in each. One was slightly greener, the other slightly bluer. The difference was subtle, but it was there. It was almost a perfect gradient of color from the green left eye to the blue right one.

"Why are you looking at me like that?" His voice broke my thoughts.

I blinked at him. "Huh?"

"Why are you—never mind. It's tonight."

"What is, exactly?"

"Tonight, Ricci, you and I are going to a little place I know on the beach."

# Chapter Nine

My legs were spattered in mud. With every step, the clammy denim chafed my skin. I followed Gabriel through the crunching fallen leaves and limbs on the jungle floor. Surprisingly, the brush was thinner than I'd expected, as if it had once been cleared and recently reclaimed by the jungle. There was only enough dappled moonlight to make out shapes as we trudged toward the sparkling lights of the strange little beach town.

"Stop," he whispered, clamping his hand on my shoulder and pulling me to his side. His arm curled around my waist and he positioned us behind a tree. "Don't move," he said in my ear. It was barely a whisper.

Fear coursed through me. The softness of his breath sent shivers down my spine. I scanned the darkness, but then I realized his body was pressed against mine, the firmness of his arm coiled around my lower back holding me close. I had to remind myself to breathe.

A figure appeared in the distance, moving between the trees. A man. He walked idly, as if bored. My heart pounded heavily and, with our chests pressed together, I knew Gabriel could feel it. My teeth began chattering. Gabriel brought his index finger up against my mouth. A spear of light illuminated his face and he mouthed, "Ssssh," lips pursing.

The cracking of fallen leaves grew louder. I curled myself into Gabriel as he pulled me closer. We held our breath. Between us sweat gathered, our shirts growing wet and slick.

I heard a crackle of static on the other side of the tree—it sounded like a radio—and a man's voice I didn't recognize said, "I'm heading back to base. My shift was done ten minutes ago. Over."

A thready voice on the other end said, "Grizz can't make it out for another twenty. He's on assignment for the Reverend. Over."

The man let out a guttural sigh. "Screw Grizz. I'm heading back to H.Q." I heard a high-pitched noise and a click. He'd turned off his radio.

Gabriel and I clutched each other, listening intently to the heavy footsteps thudding away. Even when we couldn't hear him any longer, we didn't move. Eventually, we breathed evenly, and Gabriel detached my arms from his waist. He took one step back, out of the shaft of light that had lit his face. I couldn't see his expression.

"You want to keep going?" he asked in a low voice.

"Yes," I said, trying not to sound like I was wavering.

But the guard spooked me. Scaling a wall of rock, sliding down a muddy embankment, picking my way through the jungle at night—challenging but not impossible. Getting caught with so many strikes against me? Nightmare.

"All right," Gabriel said. "Let's move."

He took off through the jungle and I tried to keep up. My wet jeans didn't make it easy. I kept my eyes on my feet, avoiding fallen branches and slithering things. I'd worn my heavy boots, hoping to avoid a little thing like a venomous snakebite.

I crashed into Gabriel's back. He'd stopped a few feet before the edge of the trees. Pain shot through my nose and I landed hard on my tailbone.

"Jesus," he said, kneeling down next to me. "You trying to tackle me? I know I'm irresistible, but really, control yourself, Ricci."

He pulled up the hem of his T-shirt and brought it to my face. In the low light, I saw the taut skin on his stomach, the waistband of his jeans pulling lower to reveal more swirling lines. Another tattoo—right above his—

"Eyes up," he said.

I looked up and saw that he was smirking.

"Bloody nose," he said and put his shirt to rights. "You okay?"

"Okay enough," I mumbled, trying to ignore my throbbing face, and the feverish embarrassment.

"Okay enough to keep going? Or do you want to head back?"

"Keep going."

"I could carry you the rest of the way."

I stood. "I don't need you to carry me."

"Piggyback?"

"No."

He followed me, standing up, and grinned. "You sure?"

"Yeah, Gabriel. I just fell. I'm not feeble."

He eyes raked over me, that curl still on his lips. I wanted to shrink beneath his scrutiny. "Nope, you're not that," he finally said. "Let's go."

We trudged closer and closer to the twinkling lights. When we reached the edge of the little town, the jungle ended and we were met with a carpet of fine grass. We stood at the tree line, crouched low in the shadows. We'd approached from the side of the town and now that I was closer, I could see I'd been right before. It was less like a town and more like a very exclusive beach resort. A long road stretched out into the distance, cutting through the jungle. It was lined with tall streetlights and, in the grass beside it, spikes that would pierce tires instantly. What was the point of the spikes? To keep animals out? To keep the cars from driving into the jungle? As I'd seen from the bluff, the road led to the buildings, which faced the beach some fifty yards away.

"We need to get closer," I whispered.

"Between the buildings," he said. "There isn't much light. Less likely we'll be seen. Stay low and follow me."

He scooted out from under the trees, hunched down, and took off toward the closest building. I followed. The grass was slippery and wet. My feet slid from under me as I ran and I landed on my hands and knees in a circle of light thrown by a floodlight at the corner of the building. I glanced up to see Gabriel make it safely between the two closest buildings. He waved me over and I scrambled to my feet, dashing to join him in the shadows. Gabriel's hand found mine and we inched our way down the dark alley, ducking under windows, toward the front of the buildings where they faced the beach.

We peered around the corner of the building. From where we stood, we could see a large gazebo in the center of a cul-de-sac, a tinkling fountain in the middle. Flowers bloomed everywhere. Even in Edenton, where flowers bordered houses and pathways, I'd hadn't seen—or smelled—these kinds of flowers. In the flickering light thrown by burning torches at the columns of the gazebo, the colors of the flowers were as vibrant as if they were in daylight. The same torches lit a path leading from the gazebo out to the beach. Points of dancing light dotted the sand, torches standing like soldiers next to the beach huts we'd seen from the ridge. It was then I noticed it wasn't a full circle, but a half-circle driveway in front of the buildings.

Light flooded my vision. Gabriel's hands on my shoulders pushed me to the ground. When I looked back up, I realized the light came from car headlights on the road from the jungle.

The car stopped in front of one of the buildings. A man got out of the car. It was shiny and rounded, like a U.F.O. in one of the rare cartoons I'd seen when I was little. Not like any car I'd ever seen personally. I only saw Jeeps and delivery trucks in Edenton. The man opened the passenger's side door and a woman stepped out, dressed in a sleek, close-fitting dress. Her hair tumbled down her shoulders, falling over her face in flirty waves. A sparkly clip cinched part of her hair at the nape of her neck. I couldn't see the detail at this distance, but I knew it must be beautiful because of the way it caught the light. That hair clip mesmerized me with how it glittered. The man led her into the building through a frosted glass door with a shiny chrome handle. The door shut behind them silently.

"Let's go over there," I whispered to Gabriel, "and check out the building they went into."

Gabriel glanced over his shoulder. "This way."

Instead of heading toward the driveway, Gabriel turned and dashed down the alley between the buildings. I tried to keep up. He was fast. We clambered along the perimeter of the buildings' backyards, all fenced in with tall stone walls, at least seven or eight feet high. Plants and flowers fringed above the fence line. All the backyards glowed with a beautiful, liquid aqua-blue light, the humid air amplifying the effect.

"I think it's this one," Gabriel said, pointing to the building at the far corner lot.

We ran over to it, dodging the beams glaring from the floodlights, and backed against the building's stone fence under the shelter of a wide-leafed tree. Even with my heart pounding in my ears, I heard a low, rhythmic pulsing—music playing—coming from the other side of the fence. This must have been what I'd heard that day with Aliyah as we'd come out of Sister's sewing cottage.

"Stay here," Gabriel whispered and he disappeared around the corner. Nervously, I waited for what seemed like forever, focusing on the soft beat of the music, so strange and foreign after years of only hearing songs during service over the jangle of the acoustic guitars.

Gabriel thunked something down next to me. It was a cinderblock. He was breathing heavily, biceps bulging below his shirtsleeves. "I saw it when we passed one of the buildings," he whispered. He flipped it on its end, placed his foot on it, and lifted himself up, so he could see over the top of the fence. He waved me up.

I glanced down at the cinderblock, at the small square where his foot perched. I placed my foot next to his but stopped. There wasn't a lot of room. I shrugged.

With a look of impatience, he grabbed my forearm and pulled me onto the cinderblock. It wobbled and I grabbed the top of the fence to steady myself. Again, I was crushed up against him, but this time my back was to his chest, his arms bracketing mine.

Behind the fence it looked like a little paradise. From between the leaves of the tree above us, I saw a kaleidoscope of blossoming tropical flowers bordering a manicured yard. A large, kidney-shaped pool graced the center of a stone patio, glowing that aqua color I'd noticed earlier. Two lounge chairs with thick, white cushions sat at the far end of the pool. A sliding glass door opened and a man, dressed all in black, stepped out with a tray holding one short glass and another tall, triangular one.

"We're living like prisoners," Gabriel whispered, "and there's a freaking Club Med less than two miles away."

The man in black put the glasses down on a small table between the chairs. He looked over at the sliding glass door as someone walked out onto the patio. A man and woman emerged, both dressed in white robes. Their faces were hidden, but I could tell it was the couple from the car. The woman had that same fall of hair over the side of her face, the sparkling clip at the nape of her neck. The man in black excused himself with a bow and disappeared through the sliding glass door. With a slow, mechanical movement, dark curtains closed on the inside, obscuring the patio from the interior of the building.

The man lay back on a lounge chair, one arm behind his head. With the other he made a sweeping gesture to the woman, motioning for her to stand before him. He was big, this man, barrel-chested and muscular, yet there was an air of cultivation to him, as if he'd been raised with the manners of a prince—and the demands of one, too. The woman took her cue and stood before him, her back to us. He gave her an impatient wave and picked up the short glass. He kicked back the liquid inside, drinking it fast.

The woman untied the robe. When it slipped to the ground, I heard Gabriel mutter a curse. She was naked. Completely, unquestionably naked. I felt my eyes grow wide. Her body was athletic and healthy.

Gabriel shifted behind me on the cinder block, his breath warm on my neck.

The woman leaned down, picked up the triangular-shaped glass, and took a sip. Then another. There was a confidence in her stance. I couldn't see her face, only her very nude body, but she seemed to be keeping eye contact with the man as she placed the glass back on the table. She reached out and cradled the man's face, fingers lingering on his cheek. She bent her head and kissed him passionately, while removing the clip from her hair with her other hand. Then she turned, the soft waves of her hair falling over her face as she watched her own feet step toward the pool. After stopping briefly at the edge, she dove in with a fierce determination.

The man stood and walked to the edge of the pool with a swagger. The light hit his face. It was square, jaw pronounced, with a beard that looked more like long stubble. His skin was tanned and his eyes glinted with hunger beneath heavy dark brows as he tracked the woman swimming across the pool. She streaked beneath the surface, hair fanning behind her like a mermaid.

"I don't think we should keep watching," I whispered to Gabriel.

"We shouldn't," he whispered back. "But I can't seem to stop."

I couldn't stop, either. The scene was so foreign, so riveting—unlike anything I'd ever seen. Something about it caused my stomach to tense. Watching this was forbidden, and I had been raised with such inflexible morals, that the word rang through my head.

Wrong.

If Mama knew what I was doing, what I was watching, her disgust and fury would alienate me for hours, possibly days. And she'd never forget. Mama never forgot anything.

Wrong.

The woman swam toward the edge of the pool that was closest to us. Gabriel and I both ducked, our eyes just above the ledge of the fence. She shot to the surface with a splash, face bursting through the water. She pushed herself up on the pool's edge. Water sluiced down her curves.

Wrong.

As she flipped her hair back, light from below the water danced over her in a broken pattern of waves. When I saw her face, it hit me like a punch to the stomach. My voice sounded small.

"Mama?"

# Chapter Ten

A hand clamped down hard over my mouth from behind and I was dragged under the cover of the tree line. Floodlights blinded me and in the whiteness all I saw was Mama, naked, kissing that man with the hungry eyes, taunting him with her body as she walked toward the pool. The shock of that moment was so intense that blood drained from my limbs, a sudden cold enveloped me, and the image—that image—seared into my memory. I wished I could erase it as easily as I erased drawings in my sketchbook.

"Hey," I heard Gabriel whisper and I blinked the blinding light away. "You're shaking."

"That was my mother." The words sounded foreign. "That was my mother."

"The naked woman?"

I winced and nodded. She was naked. So very naked. And Gabriel saw her, all of her. My cheeks flared with heat.

"You didn't recognize her?" I asked.

Gabriel winced. "I wasn't exactly looking at her face." He looked as if he wanted to say something else. I saw concern in his eyes, but instead he stole a glance over his shoulder. "We need to get out of here. I hear voices coming this way."

I listened for a moment and heard nothing. Nothing but the splash of a sleek dive, the explosion of water as Mama shot out of the pool. Sounds that reminded me of being young, carefree. Summer days spent at the neighborhood pool; waddling through the women's locker room, floaties squeezing my upper arms; the biting sting of sunburn and clean smell of sunscreen; hot dogs and Popsicles from the snack bar. Those memories now tainted by what I'd just seen.

Gabriel clutched my arm and dragged me to my feet. "The only way back is through the jungle," he said as he wrapped an arm around me and steered me into the copse of trees. "Can you keep it together until we get back to Edenton? Then you can lose it, okay?"

Back to Edenton. How could I even go back? I didn't want to see Mama in the morning, serve her breakfast, watch as she avoided eye contact with me. How did she get to that fancy resort, and how could she be with that entitled and haughty man? Had she been seeing him all along, since we left our home to come to Edenton? And why would the Reverend allow her do that? No wonder she didn't want to leave.

Gabriel waved his hand over my deadened gaze. "Ricci, you with me?" he whispered.

"Yeah," I replied. I realized we were now walking through the jungle, his arm circling my waist, guiding me along.

"Good, because we need to move a little faster." His arm tightened and he corralled me forward, moving quickly. "Don't think about what you saw," he said in a surprisingly soothing tone. "Just don't think about it right now."

"How can I not think about it?" My voice shook. "I'm never going to be able to stop thinking about it."

"Years of therapy should help with that."

"Years of what?"

"Nothing. Keep walking."

After twenty minutes of picking our way over the jungle floor in silence, Gabriel came to a sudden stop. I heard a snapping crack. Then saw a light sweep across the tree trunks and leaves in front of us.

I stiffened. Gabriel pulled me into the shadows of wide leaves. Neither of us moved.

The beam of light arced closer.

Through the trees, I could see the dim glimmering lights of Edenton. We were so close, and I would have preferred the oppressive safety of Edenton to where we were now.

Gabriel peeked around a tree and I felt his heart pound harder.

"Shit," he mumbled.

My pulse throbbed in my throat. I looked up at him. Before I could see his expression, he pressed his lips to mine with a blinding pressure. One hand tangled in my hair, the other cinched my waist. My body felt feverish. Through the sweaty material of my shirt, I could feel the muscles of his chest, hard and smooth. The effect made me dizzy and I would have fallen back against a tree if he weren't holding me. All I heard were our hearts, the noises of the jungle around us, the footsteps of the person approaching with the flashlight. Everything else faded away. There was only sensation. The softness of Gabriel's lips pressed hotly on mine, the hard planes of his body pressed against my curves. I didn't even want to wonder why he was kissing me, he just was. My stomach fluttered. It was as if my body began to blossom, awaken, after seasons of cold. I snaked my arms over his shoulders and pulled him closer. I opened my mouth tentatively. He went rigid.

"Hey!" I heard and Gabriel tore himself away from me. Light shone in our eyes, and we shielded our faces with our hands. But as Gabriel looked at the man with the flashlight, I looked at him. What just happened?

"Goddammit," Grizz said, swinging the flashlight beam to Gabriel's face. "I told them you'd be trouble." His eyes focused on me and he actually growled. "Mia! Is that—it's you?"

I nodded, my body hot all over, slightly terrified and very, very confused.

Grizz took a step toward Gabriel. "If you did anything to hurt her—"

"We were only kissing!" Gabriel held up his hands. "That's all that happened."

Realization dawned. Gabriel had kissed me so Grizz would think that's why we were out here on the edge of Edenton alone. To kiss. Or do other things. Disappointment lodged in my chest, my heart seeming to miss a few beats.

"Come on." Grizz grabbed Gabriel by the arm. "We're going to see Thaddeus. Mia, let's go."

"But I didn't do anything!" I lied, trying to hide my disappointment.

"Let's hope that's the case," Grizz said. "Both of you, move."

We trudged the short distance to Edenton. I stole glances at Gabriel the entire way. His cheeks were flushed and he licked his lips. Those lips just gave me my first kiss. The thought sent excitement then dismay through me. It had been my first kiss, yes. But it wasn't sincere, or real. It was only a ploy. So maybe it didn't count. I watched Gabriel stalk quietly beside Grizz, that air of confidence still surrounding him like an impenetrable cloud. As much as I didn't want to admit it, I wanted that kiss to count.

Grizz grumbled into his walkie-talkie, telling Thaddeus to expect us. We approached a wide, wooden gate located at a mouth of trees. The gate was ajar, with a slumping guard leaning against one of the posts, arms folded over his chest. His face, lolling forward, was hidden.

"Freddie, wake up," Grizz snapped and Freddie popped to attention.

"Yes, here!" Freddie said.

"We're going in." Grizz kicked the gate open and shoved Gabriel forward through it.

I lagged behind, wary. This section of the commune housed not only the Reverend's cottage, but the offices and cottages of Edenton's administrators. People like Thaddeus. I'd only been to this part of Edenton once, when I'd delivered soup to a sick Thaddeus in his office. Or outside his office. He'd cracked the door and asked that I leave it on the front step.

"You too, Mia?" Freddie asked when he saw me.

"Her, too," Grizz grumbled. "But not a word of this to anyone, understand, Freddie? Not. A. Word."

Freddie agreed with a mumbled, "Not a word," and we continued past him.

I kept my eyes on my feet as we passed a number of cottages. I didn't want to make eye contact with Gabriel, or Grizz. By the time we reached Thaddeus's office, the lights were burning bright in the windows.

The door opened and I was hit with a blast of cold air, almost like opening the large refrigerator in the kitchen. I immediately shivered and tried to cover my arms with my hands. Thaddeus's office was air-conditioned. I didn't know any place in Edenton was air-conditioned. I felt betrayed. First, because how could Thaddeus be so selfish? He extolled the importance of sacrifice for the good of the community. I was positive an AC unit was siphoning more than its fair share of electricity. And second, why didn't anyone in Edenton talk about it? People must have known. What other things didn't people in Edenton talk about?

Like Mama.

Naked.

Kissing a strange man.

There were bigger secrets than air-conditioned cottages.

Grizz threw Gabriel in a chair in front of the desk, then nodded his head at the other chair. "Sit, Mia. Thaddeus will be here in a minute."

I sat, and felt the coldness of the leather seep through the fabric of my damp jeans.

In the silence that hung around us, the hum of the air conditioner sounded unnatural and strange. His office seemed that way, too. It was very clean, and very luxurious—at least, in comparison to the interiors of the other cottages. The walls were painted the color of raw liver. On the floor, a richly detailed rug stretched below a large mahogany desk. The surface of the desk itself was empty except for a phone with a lot of buttons and a manila envelope. Behind the desk, shelves lined the wall. On each shelf were skeletons. Animal skeletons. Cats, birds, what looked like a small monkey. Some I couldn't identify at all.

A door opened in the back of the cottage and Thaddeus walked in. He was tall and imposing in his monk-like intensity. His eyes never left Gabriel's as he sat down behind the desk. He said nothing as he picked up the envelope and slipped on a pair of dark-framed glasses. On the front I could see my name typed on a label. What was it? My health records? Information about me? A list of everything I'd ever done wrong since I arrived in Edenton? I couldn't see through the packet of papers he removed. Intentionally or not, he flipped through the papers without bending the sheets far enough for me to see what was written on them.

"Grizz, you may leave," Thaddeus said in his chestnut voice.

"He says all they did was kiss." Grizz gave Gabriel a hard look. "Let's hope that's all he did to her."

"Yes," Thaddeus said. "Thank you. You may go."

Grizz seemed put off by Thaddeus's dismissal, but tromped to the door mumbling under his breath. It shut behind him with a bang. That noise rang in my ears until the hum of the air conditioner took over.

Thaddeus slid the papers back in the envelope and folded his hands neatly on the desk.

Yesterday, before I'd attacked Bridgette, I'd wanted to face Thaddeus, ask him why Agatha chose me to bake those damn cookies, ask about Prayer Circle, and so much more. But the way his placid face betrayed none of his emotion, the solemn line of his mouth, set my nerves on edge. I could never confront Thaddeus, and was foolish to think so.

"Gabriel," he said quietly. "I cannot say I'm surprised to see you back here again."

"You're a sparkling conversationalist," Gabriel said, folding his arms over his chest. "I missed our discourse."

A muscle in Thaddeus's jaw jumped. "Gabriel, you'll see soon enough that God has given me the gift of endless patience." He turned to me. "Mia, did this boy take advantage of you?"

"Advantage?" I was sure my face lit bright red. "Um, no. No he didn't."

"So you went with him willingly?"

I glanced at Gabriel. He stared straight ahead with the side of his mouth kicked up in a smirk.

"Yes. I went willingly," I said.

"Mia," said Thaddeus slowly. "You know you are not supposed to . . ." he cleared his throat ". . . be with a boy until after you've attended your first Prayer Circle."

"Be with a boy?" Oh, God. He thought I had sex with Gabriel! "Oh, no. We didn't . . ." I couldn't bring myself to say it, especially after seeing Mama.

Gabriel spoke up. "We only kissed. And it's my fault. I asked her to come with me and I got a little carried away."

"A little carried away?" There was a hint of outrage in Thaddeus's voice. "Are you saying if Grizz hadn't found you—"

"Hell, no!" Gabriel looked genuinely offended. "I don't make a habit of taking advantage of young girls."

"Young?" I said. "I'm barely a year younger than you!"

"Mia."

Thaddeus dropped my name like an anvil. I felt the force of it in the pit of my stomach. He picked up the phone and pressed a button. I heard a voice answer on the other end.

"Gladstone," Thaddeus said. "I need you to perform an examination immediately." I heard mumbling. "It's not an emergency." He paused. "Yes, I realize it's one in the morning, but this is important." More mumbling on the other end, and by the pitch of Doc Gladstone's voice, it sounded like a question. Thaddeus's eyes locked on mine. "Pelvic."

At the edge of my sight, I saw Gabriel sink in his chair. I kept my gaze on Thaddeus, confused. Pelvic? Why would . . . ? A cold wave of disgust slithered down my spine. He wanted to know if I was still a virgin. I should have been mortified, but I was too furious.

The phone hit the receiver with a clank. "Report to the infirmary immediately, Mia."

"We're telling the truth," I said with steel in my voice. "We only kissed. And that's if you really want to call what happened out there a kiss. It was more like being licked in the face by a dog. Except a dog would have had better breath."

Gabriel had the audacity to glare at me, insulted.

"Mia." Thaddeus stood, towering over us. "You are to go to the infirmary immediately. I'm sparing you Contrition, because this clearly wasn't your fault. However, you are not to speak to each other. Don't even look at each other. If you're caught together before Mia attends her first Prayer Circle, you'll both be seriously punished."

"I haven't attended my first Prayer Circle," Gabriel said, still slouched in the chair. "I'm getting the feeling I'll never be popular. Throw me a bone, Thad."

"Why until after I attend Prayer Circle? What about him?" I asked, then saw that was a mistake.

Thaddeus's famous patience was beginning to disintegrate. He clenched his fists on the surface of the desk. "The canon of the Flock of the Promised Land is not to be questioned. Now, Mia, go. And you," he turned to Gabriel, who lazily raised his eyebrows as if to say, yes? "You are going to learn that physical labor can cleanse the soul."

"I thought I was already learning that lesson."

"We are doubling your studies," said Thaddeus.

"See, Thaddeus?" Gabriel said. "We have such engrossing repartee."

Thaddeus banged the desk, once, and said, "Mia, go."

I backed out of the cottage under Thaddeus's fierce gaze. Pulling the door closed behind me, the darkness of the Edenton night drew the shadows close. I felt the full weight of what had happened on my shoulders: the poisoned cookies, the secret town, Mama's other life, Thaddeus's cooled cottage, the mystery of Prayer Circle, Gabriel. And his searing—his faked—kiss.

Determination rose in me like a tide. I was going to find a way to escape, with Max, and we'd leave Edenton behind to drown in its secrets.

# Chapter Eleven

The envelope was cradled in Mama's hands. It was crushed in on one side, as if it had been snatched away in haste. On the front, my name was written with flowing cursive in deep indigo ink.

"You got the call," Mama said.

She sat in the chair in the corner of her room, across from me. Inside her cottage it was stuffy and hot. A slow drip of sweat slid down my back. In her starched dress, she looked stern, like the schoolteacher she was—so unlike the naked, carefree woman from six nights ago.

She leaned forward and handed me the envelope.

I didn't meet her eyes, and avoided touching her hand. On the back of the envelope was a waxy seal, that familiar symbolic tree of Edenton, pressed into the shiny gold, metallic wax. I cracked open the seal. Handwritten in small letters, I saw my name—Mia Eden—along with a date and time. Below that, The Cottage of the Reverend Elias Eden was scrawled larger than the rest. The paper itself was beautiful, thick and pulpy. But I wouldn't save that paper, even as my own supply disappeared under layers of pencil lead or disintegrated by an eraser.

"When?" she asked.

"Tomorrow night." I folded the envelope, threw it on the dresser, and focused my eyes on my feet.

Tears of anger and frustration welled in my eyes and I blinked them back. She was a liar, more deceitful and manipulating that I ever imagined. I studied my boots with more focus. My brown utilitarian boots, dusted with flour from this morning's baking. I'd been given the early shifts for food service this past week. Punishment, I guessed, for my transgression with Gabriel.

"So soon." I heard her get up from her chair. "You're still so young."

"I'm sixteen," I said, willing my tears away. I needed strength to face her. "Almost all the girls in my cottage have been to Prayer Circle. Only Juanita and I haven't gone." And Lily, I couldn't help but think.

Over the past week, I'd thought a lot about Prayer Circle. Wondered why Thaddeus had emphasized the importance of it, why it was significant as a sacrament in the Reverend's church. I needed to know why Prayer Circle mattered. The more I knew about Edenton, the easier it would be to plan an escape. I'd tried to talk to Aliyah about Circle but she avoided the topic with glazed smiles and inane questions about cooking. It infuriated me. Not because she wouldn't tell me anything, but because she wasn't altogether there anymore. In mid-conversation her focus would drift, or I would find her in the corner of the kitchen staring off into space.

"Why are you suddenly so eager to go?" Mama asked, suspicion sharpening her voice. "Is it because of that boy?"

My head shot up. "Gabriel?"

She stood before the small mirror above a chest of drawers scraping her hair back away from her face with a small gray comb. She narrowed her eyes at my reflection. "Did anything happen with him, Mia? Other than a kiss?"

"I told you, nothing happened. And if you don't believe me, ask Doc Gladstone for the examination results."

"Things can happen that don't show up on an exam." With seething accuracy, she flipped her brown hair through an elastic and pulled it into a bun. "I can't believe you even put yourself in a position to have to be given an examination like that!"

"Me?" Rage clawed at my gut. I'd spent most of the week successfully avoiding her, and now she stood before me, my judge and jury, as if my morality was on trial. "What about you, Mama?"

She spun around, anger flaring. "What about me?"

I stepped back but my temper blazed, too, and I lifted my head. "Go for any midnight swims lately?"

She blinked, wariness clouding her gaze. "What are you talking about?" She slowly sunk onto the edge of the bed.

I didn't answer. As much as I wanted to confront her, if I did, she'd figure out that I was somewhere I wasn't supposed to be that night—other than in the jungle kissing Gabriel.

She rubbed her temples, and closed her eyes.

"What's wrong with your head?" I asked.

"All the stress you've caused this week," she said. "I've had headaches."

"Oh, so it's my fault?"

"Yes. It is." She sighed and looked up at me. "Mia, please. If this is about leaving Edenton—"

I glanced at the clock on the wall. "I have to go. I'm late for dinner service," I said.

I left Mama alone in her cottage, staring after me. She was a hypocrite. Warning me to stay away from Gabriel when she was with that man in that place.

Stepping outside was a relief. The air was cool. It was early evening—later than I'd thought—and long, indigo shadows stretched across the paths lined with cottages and flowers. I hurried toward the kitchen to report for dinner prep.

The kitchen was already buzzing with activity. Aliyah sliced bread and placed it into baskets. Juanita alternated stirring two large pots on the stove. Dina added chopped cucumbers to large salad bins on the buffet. Bridgette stood by the rice cookers, spoon in hand, glaring at me as I walked in.

"Mia," I heard and turned to see Agatha standing behind me with a clipboard. "You're late."

"I'm sorry, Agatha. I was with my mother. She needed me for something." I decided then not to tell anyone I'd gotten the call to Prayer Circle.

"Well, we're almost ready for dinner service, anyway. Why don't you take the compost and recycling to the heap?"

Out of the corner of my eye, I saw Bridgette grin.

Back to the heap, where I'd burned the rats and pretended to burn my sketchbook. The heap was a miserable place. Even the most devout of God's creatures didn't like the stench at the heap.

I gathered up the waste bins beneath the work areas. None of my cottage mates spoke to me, which meant Agatha was probably complaining about my lateness before I'd arrived. Once again I resigned myself to being the pariah for the evening. I said nothing and carried the bins, one after the other, through the back door of the kitchen and dumped each type of waste into the proper containers. The waste containers sat on a dolly, which made them easier to transport to the heap.

I dragged the dolly down the path, passing the dining hall, where members of the Flock sat at tables, waiting for dinner service. I threw a smile to Max when I saw him sitting next to Mama, but it faded as soon as Mama met my gaze.

Darkness encroached along the edges of the road leading to the heap, the fading day slowly illuminating the lights on either side. My eyes had trouble adjusting. Everything looked flat. The heap was located in a wide circle of trees, bordered by a fence topped with razor wire.

*They're keeping us in.*

I rolled the dolly to the large compost receptacle and began dumping the kitchen scraps when I heard a dull thumping sound. I turned. In the dim light Gabriel stood, hunched over, shovel in hand, sorting the trash pile.

My stomach lurched. I hadn't seen him all week, but I still felt a stab of rejection, fresh as it had been after that kiss. Where had he been this whole time? Working here? And was this his punishment for kissing me in the jungle? A flush warmed my cheeks at the memory. I could still feel how he tugged me to him, the softness of his lips.

"Hey," I said, tossing aside the compost container and marching toward him.

He didn't turn around. "Hey to you," he said, still shoveling.

The uniform shirt he wore stretched over his back, damp down the center with sweat. I could see his muscles roll and tense beneath the fabric.

"Where have you been?" I asked, my tone surprisingly demanding.

He stopped then, shovel frozen in the air, and glanced over his shoulder at me. "Where have I been? Oh, you know. Here and there." He drove the shovel into the pile of trash at his feet where it remained speared in the ground. He faced me. "But mostly here."

"Mostly here," I repeated.

He stepped closer. "I've been wanting to talk to you."

"Really."

"First, I need to apologize for what happened. I didn't know you'd have to go through . . . " He paused as if searching for the words.

"An examination?"

"Yeah, that."

"I'm assuming you didn't have one?"

He shook his head. "No."

"How very nice for you." I turned to walk away.

"Hey," he called. "Aw, Ricci, come on." He grabbed my shoulder and flipped me around to face him. "I'm sorry."

I wasn't sure what he was apologizing for—the kiss or me having to get an exam. I hoped it wasn't the kiss. He looked sincere, though, and I felt a tug in my chest.

"I got the call to Circle," I blurted.

He stared at me blankly for a moment, then recognition hit his eyes. "Prayer Circle?"

I nodded. "Yeah. My mom got the invitation this morning."

"I see." He folded his arms and studied me. "Are you hitting on me, Ricci?"

"Excuse me?"

"You know, what Thaddeus said." One eyebrow lifted in a perfect arc. "That you can't be with any boys until after Prayer Circle—"

"No!" I stepped back. "Of course not!"

He smiled a little. "Oh, well."

I rubbed my forehead. Grizz was right. Gabriel was exhausting.

"What else did you want to talk to me about?" I asked.

"I've been pretty isolated the last week, since we saw what we saw." He shifted his feet in the dirt. "I mean, that resort or whatever it was. I've asked a couple people about it but they don't have a clue. Did you, um . . . " he glanced away for a second " . . . ask your mom what she was doing there?"

"No," I said. "I didn't want her to know I was out near that place. She might say something to Thaddeus. But maybe having some insight into Circle could help me figure out how to escape."

"Wait a minute," Gabriel said, holding up his hands. "You? I thought *we* were escaping. As I recall, you demanded I take you with me. Now you're going to leave on your own?"

"Well, I, uh, changed my mind." I tried for confidence in my voice, but I sounded more confused.

"Obviously." He turned away from me abruptly, and snagged the shovel speared in the ground. "Maybe I'll see you in the outside world sometime."

My head spun with confusion. He'd kissed me so we wouldn't get caught sneaking back into Edenton. It wasn't his fault I wanted that kiss to be more than simply a ruse to fool the security guards. I'd overreacted, and escaping on my own wasn't only dangerous, but stupid.

"Look, Gabriel—"

"What the—?" I heard and spun around. Grizz stalked toward us, hands curled into fists. His gun was slung over his shoulder and it bounced as he walked. "I can't even take a piss! What's going on?"

Gabriel whispered a curse.

"Nothing's going on," I said, my voice pitching higher than I intended.

Grizz stopped, boots clomping in the trash-ridden dirt, and loomed over us. The light behind him limned his shaved head in a yellow glow. "You two aren't supposed to be around each other. And here you are." He swirled his finger in the air between us. "Around each other."

I glanced at Gabriel. He stood, one hand on the handle of the shovel, the other on his hip. Lazily, he gave me an expectant look. I guessed I had to come up with the excuse because it didn't look like he was going to even bother trying.

Fine.

"I was breaking it off with Gabriel," I said. "He needs to know it's over." I gave him a pitying expression. "He just won't give up hope."

Gabriel inclined his head, the corners of his mouth curled up in a tiny smile, as if to say touché.

"Good!" Grizz said, too exasperated to notice our exchange. "Hold up. I mean, not good. There shouldn't have been anything to break off to begin with! Stay away from each other, you hear me? No more antics." He swung a bandaged hand at Gabriel. "I have to keep beating him up because of his antics."

"Honestly, Grizz, you hit like a girl," Gabriel said, rubbing his jaw. He glanced at me. "No offense."

"Maybe," I said, "you need to be hit by a real girl."

"Is that a promise, Ricci?"

"Stop the flirting!" Grizz yelled.

"We are not flirting," I said and wondered with a flush of embarrassment if that was, indeed, flirting.

Grizz took in a labored breath and exhaled with a growl. "You," he said to me, "leave. Back to the kitchen."

"But I have trash duty," I said motioning to the abandoned dolly.

"I'll take care of it," said Grizz. "I'll tell Agatha you did it all. Get the hell out of here before someone sees and Thaddeus is on my ass again."

"Okay, okay," I said backing away. "But the bins need to be scrubbed out." That was a tiny lie.

"I got it!" Grizz said, waving impatiently. "Just go."

Because I was supposed to be at the heap for another twenty minutes or so, I snuck back to my cottage and hid out with my sketchbook until it was time to return to the kitchen for cleanup and breakfast prep.

When I returned, the kitchen was practically empty. Only Juanita and Dina were on duty, cleaning up pots and dishes and placing them in the dishwasher. I found the dolly Grizz had returned parked outside the back of the kitchen, the bins scrubbed out and still damp. Silently, I returned the bins to the workstations and began taking fruit from the cartons to prep.

"How was the heap?" Juanita asked me.

"Stinky," I replied.

"Maybe next time," Dina said airily, "you won't be late for dinner duty."

"Maybe," I said through a tense smile.

I continued concentrating on cutting mangoes to keep from saying something to Dina. She was only Bridgette's minion, but she was a pupil to the master of pious scolding.

"Here." Juanita placed a bowl of beans and rice next to my cutting board. She held another bowl in her other hand. "I saved you some dinner."

"Thank you," I replied, genuinely touched by her thoughtfulness. If she hadn't made me a plate, I would have had to sneak bites of fruit as I prepped and wait until breakfast to eat. "Who's that one for?" I asked, eyeing the other bowl.

She tilted her head toward the open service line window with a clear view of the dining room. "Him."

Alone at the center of a long table, was Gabriel. He sat, elbows on the edge of the table, hands clutched together in front of him. Between his hunched shoulders he hung his head, dark hair hiding his face.

"Grizz brings him here for every meal after everyone leaves," Juanita said. "But usually it's later than this. Grizz said he needed a shower. He smelled pretty rank."

"Ah," was all I said.

I hadn't been scheduled for any late shifts in the kitchen, probably because they didn't want me running into Gabriel as he was served meals.

I returned to prepping the fruit, but peeked at Juanita as she placed the plate down in front of Gabriel and sat across from him. He thanked her politely, smiling. They began talking, about what I couldn't hear, but they spoke to each other like they'd been friends for a while. Jealousy bubbled inside me. I had no right to be jealous, though. I wasn't courting him, and had no plans to do so.

I furiously cut up mangoes and scraped them into a bowl.

"You're making a mess," Dina said, now standing beside me.

"I'll clean it up," I snapped.

"Okay," she said, but remained next to me.

"Can I help you with something?" I asked her, not in the mood to listen to her breathy, childlike voice.

"No," she sighed, staring off at Gabriel and Juanita seated at the table. "They make a cute couple."

I tensed, fingers strangling the handle of my knife. "Yes."

"I think he's going to ask the Reverend to court her."

The knife slipped, almost slicing my finger. Dina threw me a questioning look.

"Working too fast," I said, trying to cover up my shock. "So, why would Gabriel ask to court Juanita?"

"They talk every meal. He comes here after the kitchen is closed to eat. Guess he got into some trouble or something. Anyway, she's been serving him his meals and she stays to chat with him." Dina's voice dipped to breathy awe. "I like watching him smile."

I looked over to see Gabriel laughing at something Juanita said. My stomach pitched, either out of jealousy, or from the effect of his smile. Either way, I would have rather shoved the knife through my hand than feel that way.

"She got the call, you know," Dina said.

I blinked at her. "Huh?"

"Juanita got the call. You know, to Prayer Circle."

"When?" I asked, throat tight with an emotion I didn't understand.

"Her mother received the envelope this morning. She goes to Circle tomorrow night." Dina's wide eyes gazed dreamily at Juanita and Gabriel. "After that, they'll be free to start courting."

# Chapter Twelve

Juanita sat across from me on her bunk, combing out her curls. Her hair was still wet and tiny droplets of water dribbled onto the beige blanket folded neatly at the end of the bed.

"Are you nervous?" she asked me.

I tore my gaze from her hair. I was sitting on my bunk, dressed and ready, waiting for her to walk to the Reverend's cottage with me for Prayer Circle.

"Yeah." I nodded. "What about you?"

She patted the ends of her hair with an eggshell-white towel. "Not as much as I thought I'd be." The corners of her mouth hitched up. "Especially since you're going with me. And, if you think about it, it's really a rite of passage. Once we attend Prayer Circle, we're no longer considered kids."

"And we'll be free to court," I said in a tone weighty with accusation.

Immediately I wanted to take it back. Whatever was going to happen between her and Gabriel tomorrow was none of my business. But I couldn't ignore the pang of disappointment.

Juanita sent me a confused look as she braided her hair into one large plait. "You okay?"

Before I could answer, the door to our cottage opened and Aliyah came in, her apron and dress splattered with what looked like tomato sauce. Her hair sparkled with tiny water droplets.

"Sorry," she said, gingerly lifting the apron over her head. "I didn't mean to interrupt. I spilled stuff all over me during dinner cleanup."

"You're not interrupting," I said, standing. "We're just on our way to Prayer Circle."

Aliyah's eyes widened. "I didn't know you're going, too, Mia."

I still hadn't told anyone about the invitation, except for Juanita. I'd wondered if Gabriel would have told her during one of their mealtime conversations, but she seemed both surprised and pleased at the news.

"Mama got the call yesterday—"

"And you didn't tell me?" Aliyah sounded hurt.

I fought the urge to yell at her, to remind her that she'd been the one who hadn't told me anything over the past week. All she'd done was throw me emotionless smiles when I'd asked about Circle. Instead, I apologized lamely and stood.

"Come on, Juanita. We're going to be late."

As I passed Aliyah, I thought I heard her whisper, "Good luck." Although anxiety caused my limbs to tremble, I kept walking. Why do I need luck? Luck didn't exist in Edenton. God's will determined the outcome of the events in our lives; nothing was a matter of mere chance. If a person rolled the dice to play a game, God caused the dice to land in a particular way to fulfill His divine plan for our lives. Did Aliyah not believe that anymore? Was she questioning things, like me?

Juanita got to her feet and followed me to the door.

"Wait!" Aliyah called.

We turned back to look at her. Conflicting emotions chased over her expression: confusion, sympathy, and finally resignation.

"Take umbrellas," she said quietly. "It's raining."

* * *

Outside, steel-gray clouds hung low over Edenton and a steady, light drizzle misted the heavy air. Behind the clouds, the sun was setting, and the light was slipping quickly away. The patter of raindrops sounded against my umbrella, cocooning me with my thoughts as Juanita and I walked to the other side of Edenton, to the Reverend's cottage. My pulse throbbed wildly in nervous anticipation.

As I passed Mama's cottage, I saw her at the window, curtain parted in her hand. A dim light shone on her face, deepening the furrows pinching her forehead. I resisted the deep-rooted urge to wave and turned away from her, as if I'd never seen her there.

"It's getting worse," Juanita said through the rain. "I hope Circle is inside."

I liked the gloomy rain. It reflected my mood. Although I was sharp with curiosity, a persistent feeling of doom hung around me. Death and secrets clung to Edenton like a fog and I needed to get out before I slowly evaporated. Tonight I would find information to escape. I had to.

We approached the gate to the part of Edenton where the Reverend lived. Grizz stood at the gate, his bulky figure blurred by the rain. Juanita took the lead and I walked cautiously behind her. Grizz's hood was pulled up over his head and water dripped down from the brim over his face. Above him, a beam of light from the lamppost captured the falling raindrops in crystal perfection.

"Right on time," Grizz said. "The Reverend will be pleased."

"Are we the only ones attending Prayer Circle tonight?" Juanita asked.

"No," he said and led us inside the gate. He tugged a walkie-talkie from beneath his raincoat and requested Freddie to take over his post.

We passed a few cottages and I recognized one as Thaddeus's office. Inside each building, shades were drawn. But through the slats in the blinds, I could see a flickering sterile-white light.

"What's in those buildings?" I asked Grizz, trying to glean as much information as possible, hoping it seemed more like natural curiosity.

"Offices."

"Offices for what?"

"To keep Edenton going."

"I thought that's what we do every day."

Grizz stopped and whirled, the force of it throwing rainwater off his hood. He hunched down under the rim of my umbrella and pinned me with a hard gaze. "Look, Mia. No attitude tonight. It won't help, got it?"

Juanita shifted her umbrella to shield her face from mine.

"Got it," I said to Grizz, keeping the anger from my voice. I resisted the urge to ask, *help what?*

He turned away and trudged forward along the path again, expecting us to follow, which we did. I'd learned my lesson, though. I needed to keep my questions to a minimum and observe what I could. The path led up an incline. At the top of a hill a cottage perched, pretty and perfect. Unlike the offices we'd passed, soft warm light glowed from the windows. This cottage had a porch, dotted with rocking chairs, and a chimney from which a curling stream of smoke lifted into heavy slanting rain.

Grizz led us up the wooden steps. Moths orbited an ornate porch light by the door, a few of them dead and crusted on the exposed clear bulb. Grizz pressed a lighted button beside the door and a buzzer sounded.

The front door swung open smoothly. On the other side of the screen door, Thaddeus stood, expression hidden by the reflection on the mesh.

"Thank you for escorting them here, Grizz," he said. "You may go to your next assignment."

Grizz didn't look pleased at all with Thaddeus's dismissal, probably because Thaddeus dismissed Grizz a lot, like a servant, or a pet.

The screen door opened silently with Thaddeus's touch and he looked us over with mild apathy. "Please come in, the Reverend will be joining us shortly."

Inside, the lights were low and peppered throughout the room. The room we entered was large, wider than it was long, furnished with a plush blue velvet sofa and four chairs upholstered in a tiny swirling pattern, surrounding a low table. Behind the couch, a lamp with a stained-glass shade illuminated another table. Row upon row of bookshelves lined the walls, each filled with books. The books were meticulously organized, with labels attached to each of their colorful spines. All those books here, in the Reverend's cottage, so close but not accessible. The Edenton children had been taught to read, but not encouraged to do so for any leisure activity. We had our Bibles, but no novels or encyclopedias. Even in the kitchen we only had two cookbooks, and they just listed recipes. No opinions on the outcome of the final dishes.

"Please sit," Thaddeus said.

Juanita chose the chair closest to the couch, and I sat next to her. The chair was so comfortable, so soft, reminding me of the furniture we had at our house before coming to Edenton.

Thaddeus took a book from a table next to the couch and sat down, his long legs crossed before him. He opened the book, placed it on his lap, and began reading. To himself.

Juanita and I exchanged confused looks.

"Thaddeus," I said.

"Yes, Mia." His eyes did not leave the book as he turned a page.

"I thought we were attending Prayer Circle."

"You are."

Juanita shook her head. "Then shouldn't we be, uh, praying?"

"If you wish to pray before we begin, that is approved by the Reverend."

"So we haven't begun yet," I said, trying to keep the impatience from my voice.

Thaddeus turned another page. "We have not."

We sat in silence, the wind outside picking up. Rain clinked against the windows. Lightning flashed and burst into the darkness huddled in the corners of the room. I tried to see what book Thaddeus was reading, but couldn't read the hidden title. It appeared to be new, though. The paperback cover was red and shiny, the binding solid. If I'd thought about it, I'd have guessed Thaddeus would consider it frivolous to read a novel.

Juanita fidgeted in her seat, fingers twining around themselves. Above the sound of the howling wind, an unseen clock ticked nearby and counted each odd tock almost unintentionally.

"Good evening, children," a familiar voice said.

Even though I'd heard it before, it was strange to hear his voice without amplification. The Reverend's voice still resonated, though, as if he could throw his own echo.

Juanita and I stood, obediently.

Thaddeus dog-eared a corner of a page, folded the book closed in his large hands, and set it aside. He nodded at the Reverend, but did not stand.

If the Reverend felt disrespected by the gesture, he didn't let on. He stood in a wide doorway, nothing but darkness behind him. His eyes were their usual, wide-set and round, but his lids blinked lazily. Thoughtfully. Like he was seeing us differently. The sight unnerved me.

The Reverend cocked his head. "Thaddeus," he said. "We're missing some of Flock for the Circle tonight, aren't we?"

"Yes," Thaddeus said. "But that will be remedied shortly."

"Excellent." The Reverend smiled at us then, his teeth flashing against his red beard. He stepped forward. "Girls, please sit."

As we did, a man appeared from the shadows with a tray of three tall, thin glasses, each filled with a bubbly pink liquid and two bright-red cherries at the bottom. He leaned down and offered one to me. I plucked one from the tray; the glass felt cold and wet in my hand, beads of condensation on its surface. I thanked him and he nodded stiffly. I'd never seen him before—and it was so rare to see an unfamiliar face in Edenton. After Juanita took a glass, he placed the third one carefully on a coaster on the coffee table between us and Thaddeus on the sofa.

"Who are you?" I asked the man serving the drinks.

"My name is—"

"You may go," Thaddeus said.

As he faded away in the shadows, Thaddeus said, "We employ a few people from San Sebastian to assist the local economy."

"That's very gracious of you," I said in a low voice.

Juanita threw me a warning glance. Thankfully, Thaddeus didn't hear me.

"So, are you girls excited about your first Prayer Circle?" the Reverend asked. He hadn't moved from his position in the doorway.

Juanita took a sip of the drink and grinned. "Yes, sir," she said and took a bigger gulp. She placed the half-empty glass on a coaster.

I took a small sip of the drink. It tasted of vanilla, orange, and cherry, and sweetness bubbled over my tongue. It had been so long since I'd tasted anything so vibrant, I took another sip.

The screen door banged behind us and Juanita and I turned. Gabriel stood just inside the room, Grizz on the other side of the screen. My heart leapt to my throat.

"Gabriel!" Juanita said and I grew inexplicably angry, as if she didn't have the right to say his name.

But it was only a name, and I didn't have any hold over Gabriel. I shouldn't have cared.

"How did I get an invite behind the velvet rope?" Gabriel asked.

"Excuse me, child?" the Reverend said.

Thaddeus stood then. "Gabriel, it was decided that you should experience Prayer Circle as well."

"Experience, huh?" Gabriel said. "Sounds intriguing. But why didn't I get one of those special little envelopes delivered to my parents? Or did you think Grizz leading me here at gunpoint was more memorable for my first time?"

Thaddeus shot Grizz a dark look.

"This kid is impossible!" Grizz said. "Sometimes he needs persuading."

"I think you need to look up what persuading means, Grizz," Gabriel said.

"Dammit, Gabriel—" Grizz started.

"Grizz, you're dismissed," Thaddeus said, impatience lacing his tone. "Gabriel, sit."

Surprisingly, Gabriel sat in the chair next to mine without question. As he did, we all heard Grizz mumbling to himself in the pattering rain as he pounded down the wooden porch steps.

Thaddeus sat back down. "Have a drink, Gabriel." He pointed to the glass in front of Gabriel, small bubbles floating to the surface of the liquid.

Gabriel glanced at the glass, then leaned back in the chair, folding his arms. "Thanks, Thad. But pink isn't my favorite flavor." He turned to us. "Hey, girls," he said to both of us, but he was only looking at me, directly in the eyes. As quick as a flutter of a moth's wing, he flicked his gaze to the glass in front of me and met my eyes again. Almost imperceptibly, he shook his head. "Having fun so far?"

The drink. Like the cookies, was it poisoned? Why would the Reverend invite us to Prayer Circle then poison us? I clenched my teeth to keep from gagging up the small sips I'd already taken.

"We haven't really done anything yet," Juanita replied. Her glass was almost empty.

Before I could react, the Reverend chuckled. "You are spirited, Gabriel. Quite spirited." He stepped back, into the darkness behind him, and said, "Children, please join me and we'll get started."

A nervous flutter went through my stomach. This was it. The mystery would be solved in a matter of moments. I stood, along with Gabriel and Juanita. Gabriel led the way, seemingly unafraid. Juanita followed. But I hesitated, as if my feet were stuck to the wood floor.

"Mia?" Thaddeus said, noticing my uncertainty. "It's time."

"Yes," I whispered. I watched Gabriel and Juanita disappear into the dark room.

"Come along." Thaddeus started toward me, reaching to take my arm.

I flinched away. The backs of my calves hit the chair.

"I'm coming," I said, although my legs were beginning to shake almost uncontrollably.

The storm outside swirled around the cottage as violently as my thoughts. I was about to find answers, possibly clues to how I could escape from Edenton. I had no reason to feel nervous. I should have been excited, curious. But something about this didn't feel right. Who was that man who served us the drinks? Why hadn't I ever seen him before? Why would Gabriel assume the drinks were poisoned?

"Mia," Thaddeus said my name with a hint of a threat. "Is something wrong?"

"No, nothing." I forced a smile. My lips, suddenly parched, stretched painfully. "Just anxious about my first Circle. I'm trying to savor the moment, I guess."

"Ah, yes. Of course. But the hour grows late." His long arm swung toward the door. "Please," he said.

I walked to the door and glanced at the couch. The book Thaddeus had been reading sat face up, its red cover shiny.

*The Art of War.*

War? The Church of the Promised Land didn't believe in war. We were taught that violence can't lead to peace.

But I couldn't let myself be distracted by that now, so I stepped over the threshold as quickly as I could, then stopped. Light from behind me illuminated only a few feet into the room.

"Down the hall, Mia," Thaddeus said from behind me.

"Hall?" I asked.

My eyes adjusted to the dark. What I thought was a room was actually a small antechamber with another door on the other side. I stepped toward it, quickly, because if I didn't move fast, I'd turn and run the other way. My feet moved quietly over the floor, my hands grazing the walls in the narrow hall. A low light winked at what looked like the other end. I moved faster. The light disappeared, a shadow moving before it.

"Hello," I called out.

"Mia," I heard Thaddeus say from behind me and I darted forward.

I tripped, hands going down to brace myself. I fell, pain shooting up my arms, a sharp ache in my knees as I hit the floor. In the blackness, I heard a groan. A familiar voice. Gabriel? I reached back and felt skin, an arm. A shadow moved ahead of me and light stretched out from the other end of the hall, shining on Gabriel's prone body, sprawled on the floor. I'd tripped over Gabriel. And next to him was another body.

"Juanita?" I whispered.

My arm stung as if pricked by a needle. I tried to scramble to my feet but they slipped out from under me. I needed to scream, call for help. I opened my mouth to yell. I tasted blood on my tongue. A fog descended over my eyes. I succumbed to the shadows, and they swallowed me whole.

# Chapter Thirteen

I heard music. Real music. Pounding, beat-driven, pulsing. So loud the bass traveled down my spine, though my limbs, and over my skin in throbbing waves. I jumped and danced and howled like an animal. Wind whipped my hair and cool water droplets hit my face. I wasn't sure if it was the rain sheeting outside the gazebo or the water flowing from the fountain in the center, but I didn't care. I was alive. The music was alive. The crowd dancing around me was alive.

I twirled in a circle, looking down at my dress swirling out around me. Green, or was it blue? I blinked to focus my eyes and moved a little closer to one of the flickering lanterns hanging from the underside of the roof. Green. A soft, bay leaf green.

"Mia!" Juanita danced toward me, her hair a free-flowing, curling mass over her bare shoulders. She wore bright red, the neckline top low and bouncing loosely over her chest. She grabbed my cheeks in her palms. "This is amazing!" she yelled over the music.

Juanita was right. It was amazing.

"And you look so pretty," she said taking strands of my hair in her fingers. It curled at the ends, the light-brown color shining in the low lights.

"So do you!" I smiled.

I pulled away from her and let the music, the crowd, envelop me. Lights blurred at the edges of my vision. Faces shimmered in and out of focus. People writhed around me, bumping my shoulders, making me laugh. It was as if I could feel the music on my tongue—deep, dark, sensual flavors like cherry, chocolate, and coconut. I sensed every part of my body—my hair brushing my back, my calves tensing and aching, air cooling the skin under my arms. All I wanted to do was feel.

"I never want this to end!" Juanita said close to my ear, causing me to jump. I'd forgotten she was there.

"Me neither!" I yelled back to her.

We danced. I twirled my arms around me, throwing off the heat from the people around us that clung to my skin. I lifted my hands above the heads of the crowd to feel the cool night.

Through the bodies moving to the music, I saw Gabriel leaning against one of the gazebo's pillars. He wore a black dress shirt, unbuttoned at the collar, with the sleeves rolled up to his forearms. A woman I didn't recognize pawed at his arm with a predatory gaze, but his eyes were fixed on me. Shoving off the pillar, he dismissed the woman with a shrug of his shoulder and negotiated the crowd. My entire body flushed as he approached and I stopped dancing, even as the other people jostled me.

"Hi," I said to him.

"Hi," he said back. His eyes were dark, pupils swallowing up the gradient color of his irises. "You're a good dancer."

"You're nice to say that," I said, words slurring as I said them. I bit the inside of my cheek to keep from grinning foolishly, but I couldn't keep my mouth from slowly curling upward.

"No, Mia. I'm not nice." He took my hand and tugged me against his chest. "I'm not nice at all." My grin faded as we began to move, slowly, dancing as he looked down at me with glittering dark eyes.

I should have felt nerves coursing through me. I'd never danced with a boy before, let alone someone like Gabriel, but a hum of excitement lit my insides. My body was loose, my mind unencumbered by doubt or worry. I was light and free and alive and—to my surprise—happy.

Over Gabriel's shoulder, a few feet away, a large man stood stiffly among the dancers, scanning the crowd. His face was familiar, but I couldn't place it, as if I'd dreamed about him long ago. The man called someone over, someone I couldn't see. Then Gabriel spun me around and backed me up against a column. Rain splattered my shoulders, my back. The thin material of the dress offered no protection.

The dress. A thought bubbled up to the surface of my euphoria. Where did I get this dress?

The way Gabriel gazed down at me, fierce with craving, washed the question from my mind.

"You know what else you're good at?" he asked me.

I leaned toward him. "I hear I'm a killer baker."

We laughed, although inside I knew it wasn't funny. It was cruel, and I would never joke about the eleven who'd died. Gabriel wouldn't either. But we couldn't seem to help ourselves.

His laugh died down first. He held me with an unreadable look.

I went still and said, "What else am I good at?"

"Kissing," he said as he leaned down. His mouth crushed mine. The memory of his kiss in the jungle rushed back like water storming the shore. This kiss was different. It was fervent instead of fake, passionate instead of pretend. I was hot, and cold, and shivering, and sweating. I curled my fingers into his shirt, tugging him against me with such strength I was sure the material would tear. I wanted him closer.

Abruptly, he jerked away and tried to catch his breath. "Let's go someplace else."

"Someplace else?" I repeated.

I glanced around. I didn't think I knew where I was to begin with. Before I could ask, say anything really, Gabriel grabbed my hand and towed me through the crowd. We dashed down the gazebo's steps and into the rain. The droplets were cool as they dripped onto my heated skin. I tilted my head back and let the water moisten my face. I'd never had this sensation of buoyancy before, like I'd been weighted down by guilt and shame my whole life, then all that was cut away and I was finally free.

Gabriel yanked me into a tiny hut on the beach. Diamond-like droplets of rain beaded our skin, our clothes, our hair. Sand spilled over the tops of my shoes. It was cool and damp. We collapsed onto a tufted lounge, buttons digging into my back. It was dark in there, but light still hit his glassy eyes as he brought his face close to mine.

"What the hell am I doing?" he asked himself, eyebrows knitting together.

"Kissing me, again," I answered.

"Yeah. Again," he said with an intense, swift heat.

All I saw was his face, in perfect focus. Everything else fell away into a blur of nothingness. One tiny rivulet of rain traveled down his cheek from his damp hair, and over his lips. I reached a finger up and caught a droplet before it fell from his bottom lip. And, with an erotic boldness I didn't recognize, I drew the wetness over my own lips.

Gabriel grumbled a curse, and kissed me. Colors and sparks burst behind my eyes and I swayed, almost falling back, but he caught me. I knotted my fists in his shirt, to keep myself from toppling off the lounge, but also from sheer, absolute need. His fingers lingered on my waist, playing with the curve of my hip, then the tied sash at my waist.

We kissed for either minutes, or hours, I wasn't sure. I had no sense of time, only sensation.

Things began to change. The passion inside me gave way to a droning pain gnawing in my head. I drew back and leaned my head against a wall behind me. Gabriel saw it as an invitation to trail kisses down my neck, and I let him, unwilling to give up the warmth of his mouth.

For a moment, everything was almost unrecognizable. The stripes on the ceiling above me vibrated in the dim, winking light. Or was it the breeze snapping the fabric back and forth? Lines shifted and jumped, shaking with a nauseating vibration. Waves pounded the shore and in the noise of it all I heard Gabriel whisper my name, over and over.

"Stop!"

The word crashed down from above. I squinted up to see Thaddeus towering over us, eyes fixed on where my body touched Gabriel's. His nostrils flared with an uncharacteristic anger, and the pain in my head grew worse.

Gabriel laughed, an infectious laugh. And I would have joined him if Thaddeus's ominous expression didn't frighten me so much.

When Thaddeus grabbed us by our arms, lifting us both with inhuman strength, and tore us apart with a violent jolt, Gabriel sobered. He tried to rip his arm from Thaddeus's grip, but failed.

"You two are coming with me," Thaddeus growled.

"We're not going anywhere," Gabriel said in a slow, low voice. "We're staying right here."

"Where is here?" I asked and watched as confusion washed over Gabriel's features.

In that moment, shock rattled me and the blurred beauty of everything melted away, as if condensation had been swiped from a mirror. How did we get here from Edenton? I reached back in my memory and couldn't remember anything after dinner service.

Thaddeus dragged us from the hut, and I saw where we were: in that strange little town Gabriel and I had seen from the cliff, not two miles from Edenton. We'd approached it from the beach, dotted with identical red-and-white striped beach huts. The gazebo sat in the cul-de-sac, and through the crowd I could see the fountain bubbling in the center. Bordering the street were new and sleek buildings, so different from the homey cottages in Edenton. Parked around the cul-de-sac were futuristic cars.

The little resort brimmed with people, dancing, swaying, hanging onto one another, even in the rain. Unidentifiable faces filled the crowd and I remembered Juanita. Somewhere out there. Who was she with? Was she now as scared as I was?

Thaddeus shifted Gabriel in front of him, and me behind, to wedge our way through the crowd and past a few cars. Heat still rose off the hood of one, vaporizing the rain into swirling steam. I marveled at the beauty of it, then caught the choking scent of smoke and coughed.

"Why are you doing this?" Gabriel asked Thaddeus. "What did we do?"

"You were to stay away from her," Thaddeus barked.

"You expect me to stay away from her? How, Thaddeus, when we're partying together, and both of us look this damn good?"

I looked down at myself. Where did I get this dress? The front wrapped over my chest in a V. A belt, the same color and fabric as the dress, was tied at my waist. The sleeves were short, capped over my shoulders in ruffles. It was green, pretty, and simple.

"You're right," I said, almost dreamily, "We do look damn good."

Gabriel threw a covetous look over his shoulder. "Damn right," he said.

"Shut up, both of you."

Thaddeus shoved him forward onto a footpath leading to one of the buildings on the other side of the street and dragged me along behind. My limbs were losing their lightness, the echo of the music pulsing in my muscles fading away. But even as I tried to recall the exhilaration of the dancing and the kiss, nausea quivered in my stomach.

"Thaddeus?" I called. "I'm feeling a little sick."

He didn't answer, only swung open a door and pushed Gabriel through it. He tugged me along behind him and deposited me on a seat. I shielded my eyes from the brightness of the room. My stomach churned and I slumped back with a moan.

"Get her a glass of water or something," Gabriel said to Thaddeus.

I heard heavy footsteps rush over tile, and a thud.

"Do not order me about, boy, understand me?" Thaddeus boomed, sending a dull ache through my head.

I kept my hand over my eyes and leaned my elbow against my knee. Beneath my feet, the floor began to spin.

I heard the creaking sound of a door opening, and Thaddeus's voice. "Do not leave this room. Do not go near Mia. You two have caused enough problems tonight with your disappearing act." And the door closed with a click.

I swallowed down another nauseous wave. "Gabriel?"

"Yeah?" I heard him rasp from the other side of the room.

"I feel like I'm going to throw up," I said softly.

"Am I that bad a kisser?"

He stood by the window, peering out through the curtains with a steely gaze.

I ignored his joke and asked, "Do you feel like you're going to vomit?"

"No." He let the curtain drop and rubbed a spot on his upper arm. "But I don't feel right." Gabriel took a few steps toward me, studying me, eyes heavy-lidded and thoughtful.

"What is it?" I asked.

He knelt before me and grazed his fingertips over the skin on my bicep. I tried not to jump at his touch. A lump had formed there.

"Is your arm sore?" he asked, lightly pressing the spot.

"Yes." I dropped my head again, squeezing my eyes shut.

"An injection," he said. "I wonder what they gave us."

"Gave us?" I asked, but the words caused my abdomen to tighten.

I lifted my head then and squinted around the room. It was all white, bright. Sleek low furnishings crouched on the floor. Black-and-white photographs hung on the walls—images of the jungle and the beasts that inhabited it.

"Are we where I think we are?" I whispered as softly as I could.

"In the resort we saw from the cliff."

"Why?"

He stood up. "I'm not sure."

We remained silent, Gabriel pacing the floor, me staring blankly at it. My head swirled with confusion and bewilderment. Memories were cloaked by the fog in my mind. It felt as if I could reach out and touch them, like sparkling fish swimming just beneath the surface of the water. But when I tried, my head ached more.

"You're dressed up," I said.

His black dress shirt was damp, but it still looked pressed. His dark jeans were new, too, but he still wore his same Edenton-issued boots. He paused in the middle of a thick white rug and glanced down at himself.

"Huh," he said. He picked up his foot and examined his boot. The edges of the sole were dark with mud. With a dismissive stomp, he wiped the mud on the rug. "Guess you're not the only one."

"The only one?" I looked at my lap. Oh, right. The green dress. It was pretty, flaring at the waist and draping at my knees like it did. My shoes were flat, delicate, a small leather flower curling at the top of each.

"Where did we get these clothes?" I asked.

"I don't know, Mia. All I remember is being in the gazebo, watching you dance then . . . " he trailed off, further explanation unnecessary. "Dammit," he said, rattling the door handle. He seemed to sway on his feet, squeezing his eyes shut. He grasped the handle harder.

"Are you okay?" I asked.

"This door is locked." He paused. "Locked from the outside."

Another wave of nausea overtook me. I hung forward again, and it helped, but only a little. "Have we been drugged?"

He stabbed his fingers through his wet hair. "Yeah, Mia. We've been drugged."

"Why? Why are we here?"

Gabriel shrugged.

"And what did Thaddeus mean when he said our disappearing act caused problems? Problems for whom?"

"I suppose problems for him. Or the Reverend."

I fought a gag. Thaddeus must have been the reason we were here and why we were like this, whatever this was. We needed to hide and gain control again. We had nothing if we didn't have control. I lifted myself to my feet.

"We need to get out of here before Thaddeus comes back," I said.

"Lead the way."

"Try that door," I said, swaying slightly as I pointed to a door at the end of the room.

Gabriel made his way to it, hanging onto furniture along the way.

"Locked," he said.

"Window." I pointed to the back of the room.

With a sigh, Gabriel judged the distance between himself and the window. He slumped down on the closest chair. "Probably locked."

Next to me, on a small table, sat a heavy-based lamp. Gathering the strength I had left, I ripped its cord from the outlet and hurled the lamp across the room at the window. The lamp shattered the window into tinkling glass.

"Shit, Ricci," Gabriel said, "I can't take you anywhere."

"I'd rather be anywhere but here." I started forward on unstable legs.

"You're in luck then," came the voice from behind. I turned to see the Reverend in the doorway Thaddeus had dragged us through. He was flanked by guards, neither of whom I recognized. "Because you're about to go someplace else," he said with an eerie certainty.

Gabriel forced himself to his feet. "Where?"

"Knowledge of God's word is the bulwark of temptation." The Reverend stepped into the room, the guards following and fanning out on either side. "But that didn't seem to deter the two of you. Your foray into the forbidden has cost us time."

"We aren't going anywhere," I said, trying to strengthen my voice.

But my put-on bravado melted away when I saw the small woman step out from behind one of the guards. It was Nurse Ivy, from the infirmary in Edenton. Her skin was thin and translucent, veins creeping blue over her arms. Her usual green scrubs were replaced by black. In her hand she held a small case. I heard the ripping sound of a zipper and she folded it open. Inside were two syringes.

The Reverend's mouth stretched into a wide and terrible smile, teeth peeking out from behind his thick beard. "You're going to go anywhere—and do anything—we want, child."

# Chapter Fourteen

Blackness. No dreams, no thoughts, only a sense of floating peace. Through the dark, a thickly accented voice hissed, "I wanted her awake, not comatose." The razorlike anger of his tone cut through my serenity.

"She will awaken soon enough, and you can continue your evening." I recognized Thaddeus speaking.

"There is not much evening left. You must do something about this situation."

"We had a bit of a hiccup earlier, and we apologize," said Thaddeus. "Time got away from us. Perhaps we should schedule another time, then?"

"No." The word was a violent sound. "No. Remedy this now."

I felt submerged in dark, lukewarm water. My arms tried to push against the pressure around me but they couldn't fight it. My legs were pinned together and any attempt to move them was met with more resistance. I couldn't fight it. Almost didn't want to fight. I tried to pry my eyes open, but the darkness grew more comfortable, so soft, embracing me in warmth. I wanted to remain there longer. Just a little longer.

A sharp sting on my thigh jolted me out of the embracing twilight. I fought it as much as I could. A new strength bubbled up in me and chased away the tranquility, like noon-day sun bleaching out shadows. Light stabbed my eyes as I blinked awake and all I wanted to do was close them again. But I felt as if I were being watched, the force of that gaze like a lead blanket over me.

A blurry silhouette of a man sat in a chair in the corner of the room. He was big and broad-shouldered, arms hitched on the armrests as if he couldn't pull them closer into his sides. His cruel laugh sounded around me, shaking me from the shadows.

"Finally, she wakes," he said in a rumbling sound. He stood, and with a slow sureness, came toward me.

I wanted to scurry away, to a corner, to protect myself with my arms, but my body wouldn't move. "Who are you?" I dragged the back of my hand over my eyes and wiped away the clouding tears. "Where am I?"

"I am only able to answer one of your questions, Mia," he said. "Thaddeus forbids I say too much."

"How do you know my name?" I asked.

"I know many things about you." He knelt by me, his face still a blur.

I blinked to try to clear my eyes again, but it seemed to only make things worse. Bright anger cut through the listlessness of my body.

"What do you know about me?" My voice was weak, yet demanding.

"You're beautiful, you're young." His finger slid up my arm. "You're devout, a member of the Flock."

"I'm not devout," I ground out. "And don't touch me."

I managed to rise up on my elbows, the room spinning around me, following the circuit of the ceiling fan. Slowly the haze over my eyes began to lift and I saw I was in an unrecognizable place. The room was dark. One light in the corner threw the room into stark relief. Heavy drapes covered the single window. They shifted occasionally as if the window behind them were open. I focused on listening and heard the telltale sounds of the jungle outside the window.

"You don't believe you are devout? Is that so?" The man peered at me. His eyes were indistinct, not blue, not green, not hazel, not gray, but a mix of all.

"Where am I?"

"Where you're supposed to be," he said, standing.

"I have a feeling I'm not supposed to be here at all."

He laughed at that, not as cruel as before, but with a hint of amusement. With his back to me all I could see was his size, the expanse of his shoulders. He half-turned to me. The side of his face was leathery, a laugh line like a parenthesis slashing down the corner of his mouth. A thick, dark eyebrow arched in question.

"Are you thirsty?" After choosing a bottle from many lined up on a long table by the door, he opened one as he spoke, hands working with agility as if he'd done that a thousand times. I heard a pop and tiny swirls of mist came from the top of the bottle.

"No," I said. "I want to know where I am."

He turned then, glass in one hand, bottle in the other. "You're very demanding for someone who is here at my request." He placed the bottle down on the long table.

"Your request? I don't even know you."

"Oh, but I know you, Mia. You look so much like her. But untainted by time and regret, as she is."

"Who?" I asked, finally able to sit upright. I grabbed the edge of the seat—no the bed—to gain balance.

"Maria."

I saw the man clearly. He stood at the end of the bed, swirling liquid in the glass, around and around in a small circular motion, a gesture I'd seen before. He was the man I'd seen in a dream when I was with Gabriel. And we were dancing. Gabriel and I were dancing—maybe doing more than dancing. A familiarity about the man had struck me in the dream, as it did now. The way he swirled his drink, his barrel chest, the hungry gleam in his eyes. Awareness slammed into me like a slap across my cheek. It was the man who watched Mama swim naked across that pool, who looked at her with a propriety in his eyes below those dark brows, as if he owned her.

"My mother's name is Maria," I managed to say, ignoring the tremble in my voice.

"Yes. I know Maria well. She's been a friend for a while."

"A friend," I said, forcing my limbs to move, but I could only manage to remain sitting up on the bed. I glanced around the room. It had only one door, one window with a small round table next to it, no alcoves or hallways. "Is my mother here?"

He chuckled then, as if I'd said something impossibly adorable. "No."

"What is wrong with me?" I swayed to the side, shifting so I wouldn't tumble off the edge of the bed.

The man tipped his head back, pouring the drink into his mouth, all the while keeping eye contact with me. He swallowed loudly. Nausea bubbled in my stomach at that sound.

"That damn daft nurse. Why is she administering the medications instead of the doctor from San Sebastian is what I would like to know? They have not been very professional this evening."

"Who are they?"

"It doesn't matter," he said, placing the glass on the table next to the door. He gazed at me, eyes lidded with a yearning, a yearning that reminded me of how he looked at Mama.

"Why am I here?"

He prowled toward me and growled, "You're here for me."

I shrieked, numbly grasping the bed to cower away from him. A fingernail caught on the bed and ripped, the sharp little pain lancing through my finger.

"You see?" he said, waving an arm to me on the bed. "You see!" His face was growing red with anger as he looked up into the rafters of the room. I followed his gaze and saw a tiny flashing green light. "You fools did not medicate her properly!"

"Medicate me?" I asked, feeling my stomach churn.

I had been drugged . . . oh, God. The vague images blinked in my head and I remembered being with Gabriel—it wasn't a dream. I was really dancing with him, doing things with him. Flashes of him kissing me, of me kissing him back with no restraint or questions. I fought the flush overtaking me to focus on what I needed to remember. What happened in between? My mind held only snatches of memories.

"I want to go now," I said, trying to get up again, but failing. My limbs quivered, trying to support my weight. They were weak and as useless as my own mind.

"You are not going anywhere until I get what I paid for. But I will not take it by force." The man looked up again. "Thaddeus! Send that damned nurse here and get this girl under control! She was supposed to be compliant."

A crackling noise sounded. "Right away, Monsieur Lambert. We apologize for the inconvenience." It was a voice I didn't recognize.

Monsieur Lambert laughed at that. A thick hearty laugh, a laugh that caused the bed beneath me to tremble. "They apologize," he said, then mumbled words in what I assumed was French.

"I was supposed to be compliant?" I asked, confused. "Why?"

Monsieur Lambert sat in a chair by the window and crossed his ankle over his knee. "They truly keep all of you in the dark. It's quite miraculous." He barked a laugh. "Leave it to the Reverend to perform miracles while delivering the innocent unto sin."

"Enough, Lambert." Thaddeus stood in the doorway. "You've already said too much to her."

"What does it matter?" said Lambert, crossing his arms over his bulky chest.

The short sleeves of his shirt strained over his arms, his fleshy skin swelling in bulges beneath the fabric. A breeze fluttered the curtains, and stringy strands of black hair flipped forward over his forehead. He raked them back with mild disgust.

"Isn't erasing the memory what you do best?" Lambert continued. "She will remember nothing of this, so I can tell her anything I please. I've done the same with her mother, told her secrets and stories, yet each time we meet is like the first time." He stood. "Speaking of the first time, I'd like to move this along. I've waited long enough and I grow anxious."

I felt an icy-cold hand take my arm.

"Thaddeus," Lambert said. "That woman does not know what she's doing with those drugs! This is not like the times with Maria!"

"It will have to do for now," said Thaddeus.

Nurse Ivy stood next to the bed, syringe in hand.

"No," I said, batting it away.

"It's for the best," she said in a creaky voice.

"The best for whom?" I asked, glancing at Lambert.

She wiped my skin with a small white square of cotton. I jerked away, almost toppling over off the bed.

"Get away from me, Ivy."

"Mia," she said in a warning tone as she snatched my arm.

The room spun again and I was too weak to fight her off. She held onto me with bruising force, nails digging into my skin.

"Please speed this along," Lambert said. "It's quite late and I have a plane to catch in the early afternoon."

"Yes," Nurse Ivy said with a touch of impatience and wrestled me down, the tips of her nails digging into the tender flesh beneath my arms. Her bloodshot eyes were fierce and angry.

My arm stung, a tiny pinch. Before she could push the plunger down, the room began filling with thick, black smoke.

I looked up and saw the flames, the curtains being eaten by long licks of fire.

Lambert shouted in French and lunged away. Both Lambert and Ivy ran to the door; he shoved her down to the floor before escaping. She clambered to her feet and didn't glance back as she let the door slam shut behind her.

I pushed myself unsteadily to my feet. My knees buckled and I fell to the floor, the needle slipping out of my arm. Smoke choked me, burning my eyes and mouth. I clutched the bed and hauled myself up again. I managed a few unsteady steps toward the door before dropping to my knees. I heard a whooshing sound beneath the crackle of the flames and glanced back over my shoulder to see a wall of fire sweep across the room.

# Chapter Fifteen

"Mia!" The shout came from the window. "Follow my voice!"

Adrenaline pulsed through me, shoving aside the murkiness in my head, and I clawed my way toward the sound. I crouched low as billowing smoke rose to the ceiling.

The curtains fell away, a fiery drape of fabric drifting back into the room. I felt hands on my upper arms, lifting me to my feet, and I tumbled out the window onto something hard, my knees and palms taking the brunt of the blow. Coughing, I tried to stand.

"Come on, let's move away from the fire," she said softly in my ear.

I blinked up at her. Juanita?

"How did you—?"

"I'll tell you later." A piece of burning lumber crashed next to us. "We have to move away!"

She hiked my arm over her shoulder and half-carried me past a burning fence, toward a planting of trees at the edge of the yard. Depositing me on the ground, she turned and looked back at the burning building.

Burning buildings.

My eyes, stinging and watery, blinked several times before I could see what was happening. Fire. Not just the building I was in, but at least four others were burning. Around us was chaos. People in various states of dress sprinted around, screaming, wrapped in blankets. One woman, wearing only a robe, its hem singed at the bottom, yelled to no one in particular about her purse being inside. Black tears trailed down her cheeks. She clutched her lapels together. I'd seen her before, but couldn't place where. Certainly not Edenton. People didn't look like her in Edenton. Security guards screamed into their walkie-talkies, some tugging long garden hoses and spraying the fire to no avail.

"I have to find Gabriel," Juanita said. "Stay here and I'll be back."

"No!" I yelled. "Don't leave me here. I'm coming with you."

She glanced around, worry furrowing her brow. Her dress, glowing bright red in the orange light from the fire, was ripped on one shoulder and knotted. Black smudges dotted her cheeks, her forehead, all along her arms. I looked at mine. They were marked up, too. I touched my face and my finger came back stained with black ash.

"Okay, but stay close."

Juanita hung my arm over her shoulder again and brought me to my feet. My legs didn't seem as shaky as before, the adrenaline pulsing through me, giving me strength. We lumbered together, through the throng of onlookers and panicked people, scanning the crowd for Gabriel.

"Do you know where we are?" I asked her.

"Not sure," she answered. "I remember leaving one of these buildings with some man, I didn't know who he was. But he was dressed like the security guards in Edenton." Almost absently, she touched the torn shoulder of her dress. "When we got outside, there was smoke everywhere and Gabriel was running toward us."

"Gabriel?" My heart picked up.

"After he knocked out the man with one punch," she said with admiration, "he told me what building you were in and to get you out through the window."

We made our way around the front of the circle of buildings, where the gazebo in the center of the little town burned with the same intensity as the buildings. I realized we were in the little resort Gabriel and I had seen from the ridge—and I felt as if I'd had that same realization before, recently. With Gabriel.

"He told me he'd be around here," Juanita said.

Out front, people were piling into cars. A line of red taillights formed around the cul-de-sac as they filed onto the long road toward the jungle. Away from the smoke, the night air was cool on my sweaty face.

Juanita craned her neck, looking for Gabriel over the heads of the people dashing around us. I peered through the crowd as best I could, my eyes still tearing from the smoke. Between the bodies I saw him, crouched on the ground. He was rifling through a bag, tossing things aside and putting others in a pile.

"There!" I said to Juanita, pointing.

I felt her shoulders sag in relief. And, I guessed, mine did, too. Gabriel stood, folding the bag beneath his arm. He was sorting through a large keychain when we approached.

"Who carries this many keys?" he asked us casually, as if we'd approached him in the dining hall rather than limping toward him, clothes disheveled and faces streaked with ashes, while the population of a weird resort screamed around us. He easily picked out a black fob, a symbol resembling a peace sign on it. "Are you girls okay?"

Juanita nodded. "I am. You, Mia?"

When Gabriel's questioning gaze met mine, I instantly remembered the soft pressure of his lips, and I hoped the flush didn't show through the soot on my face. His eyes, though, showed only concern for me, not glowing with the heat from earlier. That look of his was seared into my memory, one of the few things I could remember clearly from the last few hours.

"I'm good," I said.

"Good." Gabriel smiled faintly, his expression warm with relief.

I couldn't help but think how beautiful he looked just then. Even with the soot streaked down his left cheek and his hair looking as if it were trying to escape his head. Maybe it wasn't how he looked that was beautiful, but how he looked at me.

He blinked and turned his focus on the cars parked around the cul-de-sac. "Come on." He waved us forward as he held the fob out, pressing buttons.

"Where are we going?" Juanita asked.

"Away from here," Gabriel said.

"Why?" she said.

"You want to hang out here in the middle of Armageddon?"

I glanced around at the fires burning, the people, confused. "But where will we go?"

"Back to Edenton," said Juanita.

*Beep.*

One of the cars lit up. We rushed toward it, Gabriel leading the way. The car was low and curvy. In the dim light I could see it was a dark shade of red.

"C-class," Gabriel said, mouth curving up. "It's no Maybach, but it will do."

As he opened one of the back doors, we heard Thaddeus's booming voice.

"Where are the children?" he asked loudly.

We could see him frantically looking between the bodies panicking around him, an envelope of guards searching alongside. He yelled the question again into a walkie-talkie in his hand and more guards appeared at the far end of the cul-de-sac.

"Get in," Gabriel hissed. "Now!"

"No, wait," Juanita said. "It's Thaddeus! Look!"

"I see them!" I knew that voice. It was Grizz. "Over there!"

Gabriel cursed vividly, shoving Juanita into the back seat.

"Wait!" she protested. "They can take us back to Edenton!"

He shoved me into the passenger's seat. "Sorry, Ricci," he said as he slammed the door. He scrambled around the car to the driver's side and slid in. He fumbled with the keychain. It dropped in his lap with a distressing jangle.

"Why are we leaving?" Juanita asked. She stole a look over her shoulder and I followed her gaze. Thaddeus and the security guards pushed their way through the crowd.

"Thaddeus is coming," I said to Gabriel. "Hurry! What's wrong with you? Start the car!"

"I'm not shaking on purpose!" Gabriel said, sliding the key into the ignition. It roared to life. I heard his foot slam into the pedal and we idled, not moving forward or back. From the backseat, I saw Gabriel's gaze dart around the dashboard. "Shit!" he yelled. "It's a stick?"

"You can't drive manual transmission?" I asked.

"Not since I was eleven!" said Gabriel.

"Eleven?" I said, mouth agape.

"I was an adventurous youth."

Gabriel began hitting pedals with his feet and shoved the gearshift into place. The engine made ugly grinding noises. We jolted forward, the sound of crunching metal filling the car.

"Shit, shit!" he exclaimed.

A bang at the window next to me caused me to jump. A building beside us, lapped by flames, illuminated Thaddeus's face as he stared through the glass into the car. His skin, damp with sweat, shimmered under the orange-yellow light.

"Open this door," he yelled, his fists pounding the window.

A screeching sound. The car shot forward.

"Wait!" Juanita tried to open the back door, but it was locked. She darted forward, squeezing her arm between the driver's door and Gabriel's seat, and pecked at buttons on the inside of the car door.

"What are you doing?" Gabriel yelled, trying to swat her away.

"Trying to unlock the doors!"

"No!" I yelled, frantically searching the buttons on my door, but the symbols didn't make any sense to me.

Movement at my window. I glanced up and saw Thaddeus running alongside the car. Distantly, I heard a thunking noise.

I fell sideways when the car door next to me opened. Thaddeus clutched my arm, his grip tight and burning against my skin. I heard Juanita call his name.

In a panic, I twisted around. With a vicious grunt, I kicked him in the chest. Pain shot up my leg.

"Faster!" I yelled to Gabriel and the car shot forward. Juanita and I fell against the seats. I pulled the door closed, breathing hard. "How do I lock this?"

Gabriel elbowed Juanita back. "Sorry," he said and searched the door next to him and jabbed a button.

"Mia!" cried Juanita. "How could you do that to Thaddeus?"

"Juanita," I said, my voice strong despite how brittle I felt. "I can't explain why we're here, how we got here, but Thaddeus had something to do with it."

Thaddeus had shoved himself to his feet and ran along the side of the car. He rushed the door again. This time, when he pounded the window, it spiderwebbed into tiny cracks.

Gabriel twisted the car around the cul-de-sac. We hit something, hard. The window next to me shattered, showering me with glass. The underside of the car scraped a curb. We bounced onto the median surrounding the gazebo—and stalled. From below the horizon of the car's hood, I saw people dashing around, diving into cars.

"You okay?" Gabriel asked.

"Yeah!" I said. "Just go!"

Juanita was strangely silent. She gazed out the window at the panic-stricken crowd.

"I'm trying!" Gabriel shifted the car and it rolled, back and forth, until we pitched forward.

"They're coming!" I said, looking over my shoulder. They were so close I could hear the static from their walkie-talkies.

"Come on, baby," Gabriel growled at the car. "Come on."

I heard another scraping sound deep in the engine. Then we shot forward, the car bumping down off the median and onto the road. Gabriel steered the car around the other vehicles waiting to exit the resort, unafraid to knock into their pristine, metal surfaces to force them out of the way. A few people stared at us in horror, probably wondering if they needed to leave with the same sense of urgency. Others glared at us with unadulterated anger in their eyes.

Finally, we made it onto the stretch of road leading away from the resort and drove, bookended by cars in front and in back.

"How fast are we going?" I asked staring back out the window.

"Not fast enough," Gabriel said.

"Go faster!"

"Don't you think I would if I could? The midlife-crisis-mobile up ahead isn't being driven to its full potential."

A white car with long red taillights, like a pair of demon eyes, drove ahead of us at a leisurely pace.

I glanced back at Juanita. "You okay?" I asked her.

"I think so." She peered at the road in front of us. "This road will take us back to Edenton?"

Gabriel and I exchanged a look. This was it, our chance to escape. Neither of us could fathom going back now.

"I'm not sure," I answered honestly.

"Screw this guy." Gabriel swerved the wheel to the right. "He drives like a grampa."

I saw metal glint along the border of the road. And remembered the spikes I'd seen the other night. "No! Don't!"

But it was too late. The tires burst and the flapping sound echoed inside the car. We began to wobble, the back of the car spinning around to the front. Somehow, Gabriel steered the car back onto the road where we spun out.

"I can't control it," Gabriel said, punching his foot on the brake.

We came to a stop, a sickening metallic screech sounding as we did. The car landed perpendicular, front and back straddling the road, blocking the cars behind us. Gabriel slammed the flat of his hand into the steering wheel and cursed.

"What do we do now?" Juanita asked. "Walk back to Thaddeus?"

I looked back at the cars, all at a standstill. People were exiting the cars; a few came toward us. We couldn't go back there. I peered through the driver's side window and saw the white car ahead of us had stopped. The door opened.

After finding the right button to unlock the car, I shoved open the passenger's door. Glass spilled out onto the black asphalt, sparkling like sugar under the blue-white glow of the headlights.

"What are you doing?" Juanita asked.

"Get out," I said. "We're going to get help."

"From whom?" She waved her hand around the car. "Thaddeus?"

"No."

Cars began honking. The road back to the resort was long and lined with headlights, backed up because our car blocked them from moving ahead.

"Move that car!" someone yelled. "We can't get out!"

Maybe that was what we needed to make our escape. If they couldn't drive down the only road leading away from the beach resort, then Thaddeus couldn't follow us.

I marched toward the white car ahead. In the distance, I could see the silhouette of someone getting out of it.

Gabriel caught up with me first.

"Hey, just so you know," he said, "that dude may not be inclined to help us."

"Probably not." I glanced at him. "When was the last time you punched someone?"

"About ten minutes ago."

"Entirely too long."

Gabriel grinned, the shadows lining his face giving him a roguish appearance—not much different from his normal appearance, actually.

As we approached, the darkness gave way to the ambient light from the car and I saw a large, barrel-chested man standing in the middle of the road, hand shielding his eyes from the headlights behind us. I recognized him immediately. My stomach dropped.

"What is going on here?" Lambert asked with the indignant voice of an aristocrat.

"Hello, Monsieur Lambert."

"Mia!" he said, voice bright with surprise.

"You know this douche?" Gabriel asked as he stepped in front of me, shielding me from Lambert.

"Douche?" Lambert asked, drawing out the word so long I could practically see a trail of letter Os rushing out of his mouth. With little subtlety, he sniffed under one of his arms.

I threw Gabriel a questioning look.

"Aw." Gabriel reached back and stroked my arm. "I keep forgetting you've been so sheltered all these years. How about asshat? Know that one?"

But when Gabriel touched me, Lambert puffed up, scowl descending over his face.

"Do not put your hands on her," Lambert said with a sharp edge to his voice.

"Why not?" Gabriel said, taking one step closer to him. "So you can?"

"Mia, get in the car," said Lambert, motioning to the passenger's side door.

"No," I said.

Gabriel squinted at Lambert. "Oh, wait—I know who you are." Obviously, he remembered seeing Lambert that night with Mama.

"You know who I am, do you? Listen to me, young man. Mia is—"

But before he could get the rest of his sentence out, Gabriel slugged him in the nose and Lambert went down like a thick-trunked tree. He fell against the open driver's side door then onto the hard surface of the road, groaning.

"That was so brutal," I said to Gabriel.

Gabriel bent over and shoved Lambert out of the way of the door, rolling him away a couple of feet. "Don't forget I have a sweet side."

"Hey!" Juanita ran up to us. She looked at Lambert, groaning on the ground. "Who's he?"

Gabriel eyes bore into mine. "Did he touch you?" He jerked his hand toward the lights in the distance. "Back there. In that place?"

I shook my head, trying to fight through the fog in my brain. "I—I don't think so."

Down the road, more and more cars attempted to drive off the road and into the surrounding grass. Flapping sounds filled the air, along with curses and angry yelling.

Juanita stared off into the distance. "Do you think Thaddeus is back there looking for us?"

"Yep." Gabriel smiled. "And probably frustrated as hell."

"He's going to punish us when we get back to Edenton," she said to me.

I couldn't meet her eyes. We weren't going back.

Gabriel placed a hand on Juanita's shoulder. She instantly brightened.

"Get in the car," he said to her, opening the back door of Lambert's car. "We'll see where this road leads."

She smiled at him and folded herself into the backseat, behind the driver's seat. He shut Juanita's door. "You're riding shotgun, Ricci."

That little flair of jealousy rose up in my chest. I pushed it back down and quickly made my way to the other side of the car.

"Lucky me," I said, grabbing the handle.

He caught my eye over the roof of the car. "Hey, Ricci."

"What, Gabriel?"

"I thought you wanted to escape without me." His eyes shone in the night between us.

Lambert groaned again. Gabriel turned and kicked him.

"Well?" he said, turning back to me. "Are we going to do this? Together?"

We were going to escape. Together. And at least for a little while, I wouldn't be alone in the outside world.

"Yes," I answered. "We're going to do this."

# Chapter Sixteen

The constellation of instruments in the car's dashboard danced with every adjustment Gabriel made while driving. I'd never seen anything like it, the colors, the intensity of the lights. Each was like a compass, mapping our way to freedom—or a clock, ticking away the time until we were caught.

I was still processing all that had happened, at least what I could remember. Bits and pieces of what transpired before I woke up in that room with Monsieur Lambert were coming back to me, little flashes of light and sensation. Prayer Circle and the cloying taste of vanilla and cherry. Dancing with Gabriel, and kissing him. Getting caught by Thaddeus and seeing the anger in his eyes. Crashing a lamp into a window in an attempt to escape.

Trees and plants blurred by outside the car's window, disappearing into the darkness as the headlights passed by, like a black curtain closing over the jungle, keeping its secrets. Only a small shard of the waning moon shone in the sky. Inside the car, it was cool and soft, the seat cradling me. I allowed myself to love the luxurious feeling of it. It kept my mind from wandering into dangerous territory. Namely, the future.

Gabriel pressed a few buttons. A small TV screen unfolded from the top of the dashboard and glowed. Juanita leaned forward, awe in her eyes. I'm sure I looked no different.

"What is that?" she asked.

"GPS."

"What does it do?"

"What does it do—oh, right." Gabriel smiled a little as he fiddled with the controls. "It can tell us where to go."

A disembodied voice sounded from somewhere in the cabin of the car, speaking French.

"This car talks?" I asked.

"Lots of cars talk," Gabriel said, scrolling through jumbling words on the screen.

"And you understand this car?" Juanita said. "What language is it speaking?"

"French. It was a requirement at my prep school. And now, I'm thoroughly prepped to drive through the Amazon and translate the prompts of a snotty navigation system." He glanced in the rear view mirror at Juanita. "I keep forgetting how long you guys have been in Edenton."

"Since I was three," she said in a faraway voice. "Thirteen years." She leaned forward, hand resting on the back of my seat.

"That's a long time," Gabriel whispered.

She heard him. "I don't remember my life before. Is this GPS thing going to tell us how to get back to Edenton?"

I turned in my seat. "Back to Edenton?"

"Yes, Mia," Juanita said with impatience. "Back to Edenton. Our family is there, it's our home."

"We aren't going back to Edenton," Gabriel said definitively. "It's not safe."

"Driving through the dark jungle in the middle of the night is safe?" Juanita asked. "Edenton is where we belong."

"But what happened back there, Juanita?" I asked. "Explain how we ended up in that place with those people if we were so safe in Edenton."

She thought for a moment. "I can't."

"Well, I can't go back," I said. "I won't go back."

"What about your mom?" she asked.

"What about her?'

"Mia!" Juanita gasped. "I can't believe you would say that! We can't abandon our families. I can't leave my mom. She's already lost one child."

Guilt descended over me in the silence that followed. With Octavio gone, Juanita was now the only child her mom had. Because of me. Was it, though? I stared at the long road before us, the dark, mangled jungle on either side. I didn't belong out here. I didn't think I belonged in Edenton either, but whatever had happened to land me where I was, it wasn't my fault. It was the Reverend's. He was a liar, a manipulator. He got us out of Edenton somehow, endangering us. And he was responsible for the deaths of those eleven people. Those people didn't die because of me. It was because the Reverend used me. I couldn't take responsibility for Octavio's death.

Gabriel sensed the tension, his brow furrowing as he glanced at me. "Let's get to the nearest city," he said. "What's it called again?"

"San Sebastian," I mumbled, staring at my reflection in the dark window next to me.

I looked different, older. I swiped my finger over my eyelid and it came away darker. Not the same gray-black as the soot. More like a mossy green color.

"Once we get to San Sebastian," he said, scrolling through words on the GPS screen, "we'll figure out something. Juanita, if you want to go back to Edenton once we're there, we'll find a way."

"But Gabriel," Juanita said. "Your parents are in Edenton, too."

He didn't say anything, only shifted his focus from the GPS to the road.

"What are they going to say when they realize you're gone?" she asked.

"They won't do anything. I turn eighteen next year and I told them I was leaving Edenton anyway."

"But they love you."

"If they loved me, they wouldn't have brought me to Edenton," he said bitterly.

Juanita turned to me, realizing it was impossible to rationalize with an angry Gabriel. "Running away isn't the right thing to do, Mia. You know that. Edenton is our family. I don't know anything else. And what about little Max? He needs you."

A small pain lodged in my heart. I couldn't leave Max in Edenton without me. "You're right. Max—" I started.

"Ssssh!" Gabriel said suddenly and cocked his head to the side. "Do you hear that?"

We all froze, listening. Softly, in the distance, I heard a buzzing. It was faint, but it was there.

"What is that?" Juanita asked.

Gabriel shot a look over his shoulder, then through the sunroof. He flipped off the headlights and the road ahead of us disappeared. The car slowed with a soft rumble and he brought it to a stop in the middle of the road. Before he turned the car off, he slid open his window.

"What are you doing?" Juanita asked.

Darkness swallowed up everything around us; only the sliver of moon cast a dim glow through the sunroof. The sounds of the jungle slowly faded away as the noise grew louder, closer, a rhythmic thwomping, a thick, heart-like pounding approaching.

Gabriel cursed and twisted in his seat, looking up.

Overhead, a helicopter passed us, shining lights like tentacles over the road. A flash of blue-hued light came through the sunroof, almost blinding us.

We watched with numb disbelief as the helicopter plowed ahead of us, a red light on one side and a green light on the other. Before I could blink, it climbed higher into the sky and the red light on its left side disappeared in the dark.

"It's turning around," I said.

"How desperate are they?" he asked, not expecting an answer. "Why don't they just let us go?"

"Who?" Juanita asked.

It couldn't be. I looked at Gabriel in disbelief. "Is that—?"

"Yes!" Gabriel blindly grasped for the key in the ignition and started the car. He revved the engine and pealed forward, tires screeching, toward the helicopter.

"Don't drive toward them!" I yelled.

"If we drive toward them, they'll have to turn around again. It could buy us some time."

"Oh," I said lamely.

"Stop the car, Gabriel!" Juanita said. "Maybe they can help us get back to Edenton."

"They're the reason you're not in Edenton!" Gabriel said. "Whoever is up there drugged us and took us out of Edenton to that weird resort."

"How do you know who's up there?" Juanita asked.

"Jesus, Juanita." Gabriel looked at her in the rearview mirror. "It's not the local police nabbing us for a speeding ticket. Who the hell else do you think it is?"

The helicopter barreled toward us, sinking lower, following the road. A spotlight from its underbelly hit us like a weight and I felt cold fear slide down my spine.

"Mia," Juanita said, trying to reason with me. "This is insane. How are we going to get away from a helicopter? Let's pull over and let them—"

"Let them what, Juanita?" I asked. "Drug us again?"

"But—"

"No!" I said, immediately feeling guilty for snapping at her. But she was being unreasonable. We couldn't trust anyone.

The helicopter stopped mid-air and drifted down to the asphalt in front of us, blocking the road. Gabriel hit the brakes and we spun out. I was thrown against the side of the car, knocking my head and shoulder on the window. I opened my eyes and we all stared, rapt, at the helicopter perched in the middle of the road. The doors flew open and four brawny figures ran out, each cradling something in his hands. Then we heard Thaddeus's voice resonating through a loudspeaker, calling our names.

"Out of the car," he said. "Now. We don't have time for this."

"What do they have in their hands?" I asked.

"Guns," Gabriel whispered.

"Go," I said, the men coming closer. "Go, go, go!"

"No!" Juanita yelled, trying to open the back door, but Gabriel hit the gas, turning the car away from the helicopter and we surged forward. Thaddeus yelled behind us, his voice ringing through the car. The helicopter blades picked up speed again, beating like wings.

Juanita yelled something at Gabriel from the backseat, but my pulse pounded in my ears, drowning her out. Why did they have guns? I leaned forward, squinting through the windshield.

"What's that?" I asked, pointing. "There, on the right, a break in the trees." As we whizzed by, I saw the beginning of a rutted dirt road. "Turn around! There's a road leading into the jungle!"

Gabriel slammed on the brakes and twisted the steering wheel. The tires squealed, the acrid scent of burning rubber wafting into the car. I clutched the dashboard as I bashed into the door again. My shoulder ached. The car bounced violently as he drove onto the dirt road. I clutched the door handle and heard the helicopter whizzing off behind us. Leaves slammed across the windshield and branches scraped along the sides of the car causing ominous high-pitched screeches. I looked up to see only a small break in the trees above us.

"They're going to follow us," Juanita said matter-of-factly and sat back in her seat, crossing her arms over her chest.

"But we'll be harder to see from the air," Gabriel said. "The trees will shield us." Even in the dim light, I could see the approving expression on his face as he glanced at me. I couldn't fight the little thrill that ran through me. "Let's make it even harder," he said and flipped off the headlights.

The jungle around us plunged into darkness. Only small lights near the ground at the front of the car illuminated our way. We bounced along the dirt road, mud kicking up and splattering the windows. Parts of the car rattled under the onslaught of the bumps and jolts. My stomach and head ached.

"Does that GPS thing know where we're going?" I asked.

Gabriel glanced at the screen. "No. This road isn't on the map."

"Great," I said.

"Don't worry," Gabriel said, maneuvering the car through a particularly rough patch of road. "Yet."

"I want to go back," Juanita said. "Let me out, I'll walk back to the road."

"No," Gabriel said sharply and shook his head. "Look, Juanita, I'm sorry about this but I can't let you out here in the middle of the jungle." His voice softened. "Please trust me." The car slowed as Gabriel held her gaze in the rearview mirror. There was an intimacy to it that embarrassed me, like I was intruding. I turned away and stared ahead.

"Okay," Juanita said, and I heard the shy smile in her voice.

"Okay," Gabriel agreed.

My eyes found the battered road ahead and I focused on every rut and bump I could see. The deeper we drove into the jungle, the more deteriorated the road became. Gaping furrows ran along either side; the car's tires dipped into puddles and thick mud.

Above us, the trees opened up into a wide circle, light from the slivered moon peeking through the night. Gabriel flipped on the bright lights and brought the car to a stop.

"Is that supposed to be a bridge?" he asked.

"I hope not," I said.

We both opened our doors and got out to have a closer look.

Slabs of battered wood stretched across a gaping hollow in the road, some pieces splintered with wear and age. Twisted roots shot up through the mud like arms reaching skyward. I couldn't see the bottom of the ditch; it was either too dark, or too deep.

Gabriel bent down to adjust a few slabs of wood.

"We're not driving over that, are we?" I asked.

"You want to go back that way?" he said, hitching a thumb over his shoulder.

"Not really," I said. "No."

Juanita got out of the car and came toward us. She stared at the ditch. "This is a sign from God, you know."

Gabriel slowly turned to her. "Really?"

"That we should turn back," she continued. "We aren't meant to go forward."

I shook my head. "What if it's a sign that we are meant to go forward? It's a bridge."

"You know, Gabriel," Juanita said, "the word bridge isn't used in the Bible."

"It's not?" Gabriel asked and I couldn't help feeling he was humoring us. "And why is that?"

Juanita's face fell as she remembered one of the Reverend's sermons.

"Because," I said, reciting what I could recall, "God's people must pass through the dangerous currents of suffering and death, not simply ride over them."

"Suffering and death for God's people, huh?" Gabriel peered down into the ditch. "I guess if I was going to fly my atheist flag, now would be the time."

I laughed, and Juanita couldn't fight a smile.

That's when I saw the flicker of light through the trees and my stomach plummeted. It was a car, following us.

"Someone's coming," I said.

We scrambled back into the car, nervously watching the lights bob in and out of view between the trees.

Gabriel flung the car into reverse and draped his arm over the seat back. "Running start," he said.

He backed up a good distance from the ditch, then shifted into drive and jammed the accelerator to the floor. The force threw us back against the seats. Ahead, the rickety, makeshift bridge appeared even more fragile, as if it could barely hold a person, let alone a sports car. I snapped my seatbelt on as quickly as I could.

Juanita and I gasped as the car hit the boards of the bridge with bouncing force. The car listed forward. I grabbed the door and watched helplessly as the boards flipped backward, shooting into the sky above us.

I heard the crunch of metal as the car dove into the ditch.

# Chapter Seventeen

"I'm guessing that string of words that just came out of your mouth were all bad," I said to Gabriel as we hung in the ditch, the front bumper of the car wedged deep in the mud.

"Your guess is right," Gabriel said.

"I'd never heard some of those before. 'Dammit' is about as adventurous as I get."

"It's the miracle of the modern English language, all the different ways to curse. I know other, more colorful combinations if you want to hear them."

"That's okay," I said, adjusting the seatbelt as it dug into my shoulder. "Something tells me I'll be hearing plenty in the near future."

"Are we going to wait here for that car to show up?" Juanita asked hopefully. She was pressed forward against the back of my seat, strands of her hair ticking my cheek.

Gabriel slung open the driver's side door. It hit the end of its hinge with a metallic creak. "No." He peered over the edge of the door. "Now we hide." Before either of us could protest, he climbed out onto the door and pushed himself up on the edge of the ditch with the grace of a big cat. He reached out his hand. "Come on," he said.

"You go first," I said to Juanita.

She shimmied over the seat and managed to fold her tall body behind the steering wheel. With the shift in weight, the car jerked and slid downward in the mud.

"Faster, Juanita," Gabriel said as she made her way onto the door. "You too, Mia, move!"

I scrambled to the driver's side after Juanita, feeling the car slip further into the ditch.

"Hurry up," Gabriel hissed to Juanita. "Those headlights are getting closer."

She clambered out of the ditch and Gabriel pulled her to safety.

I crawled to the door. As soon as I put my weight on it, it groaned under the pressure and began to bend back. Jerking away from the door, I twisted around and planted my foot on the back of the driver's seat. With confidence I didn't think I had, I scrabbled onto the roof, shoes slipping on the metal. I began sliding down the roof of the car and clawed my way up, trying to gain my footing. Blindly, I reached up toward the edge of the ditch and Juanita, then Gabriel, grabbed my hands. They hauled me up, my knees dragging through warm mud and twigs.

Breathing heavily, I asked, "Now what?"

"We go up." Gabriel said.

"Up where?" Juanita asked.

He hustled us to our feet and motioned to the edge of the jungle where tall trees framed the edges of the road. "Pick a tree and climb it. Go!"

I stole a glance over my shoulder at the approaching headlights and dashed toward one of the trees. I caught a low branch and heaved myself onto the trunk, as I'd done hundreds of times before, trying not to think about the snakes that might be lurking in the branches. Except, it was dark. The ambient light thrown by the car's interior light and headlights wasn't enough to help me see beneath the thick leaves of the tree. When I reached for a higher branch, I misjudged the distance and fell back down, clutching the lower branch.

I felt a hand on my lower back pushing me.

"Get back up," Gabriel said. "And pull me up behind you!"

For a second, I couldn't move. No one had ever touched me there, on my lower back. To be honest, it was probably lower than my lower back.

"Mia!" Gabriel said.

I flung myself over the branch and reached down to pull him up. He was so heavy he almost dragged me off the branch. But I tightened my legs to gain balance and he hauled himself up behind me.

"Where's Juanita?" I asked.

"In that tree over there," he said, pointing to another tree a few yards away. "I don't know how she climbed up so fast, but she was too far up to help me."

"You can't climb a tree, Gabriel?" I whispered.

He leaned over my shoulder, his breath hot on my neck. "Nope. Grew up in Manhattan. But I can do a lot of other things, Mia."

I tried to hide the hitch in my breath, sneering back at him. "We're hiding in a tree with people chasing us. Do you really think this is an appropriate time to make suggestive comments?"

He grinned at me, shadows trying to mask the wicked light in his eyes, but it was impossible.

We heard the car approach, then saw the headlights illuminate the trees ahead of us. I saw a quick flash of Juanita's red dress between the leaves.

Car doors slammed shut and I got a glimpse of people below the branches. Heavy boots, dark pants, gun barrels swinging near their hips. Edenton security guards. They stopped at the edge of the ditch.

"They trashed a really nice car," one said.

"Any sign of them?" said another.

"No, car's empty."

"Sweep the area." Thaddeus's voice. He must have gotten out of the helicopter to chase us by car. "Grizz, stay here and watch the car."

"Why?" Grizz asked. "It's not going anywhere. It's stuck in a ditch."

"Grizz," Thaddeus said in a warning tone. "Keep an eye on *our* car."

"It's not going anywhere either. You have the keys."

"Grizz!"

"Staying here, *boss*." Grizz emphasized the last word with a tone of contempt.

Along with the retreating footfalls of the guards, I heard the helicopter approaching. I looked up to see how much coverage we had above us from the leaves and could barely see the sky. I wondered if Juanita was as lucky to have picked a tree with thick foliage.

The helicopter swept overhead. Leaves flapped above us frantically, opening a hole in the canopy. Gabriel folded me beneath him as it passed us. My heart kicked up. I told myself it was only the intensity of our situation. We were being hunted. But I knew that was only a part of it. I was caged beneath Gabriel, and I felt safeguarded, and carnal.

I lifted my eyes and looked over at Juanita's tree. I caught sight of a flash of red rippling beneath a large swathe of leaves. My heart rushed to my throat as the helicopter paused above. Through the fluttering leaves, a circle of light surrounded the car we'd left in the ditch. A walkie-talkie crackled, then the light swept off into another direction, deeper into the jungle.

The wind and noise died down as the helicopter flew off. Gabriel sat up, bringing me with him. Slowly, he ran his palm down my arm, as if he were watching the goose bumps form on my skin, but it was too dark to see. With the helicopter somewhere off in the distance, the sounds of the jungle flared to life around us. I wondered if snakes were slithering along the branches around us. But the way Gabriel was touching me, that simple skimming of his skin along mine, made me think he was more dangerous than any other creature in the tree.

As if I'd singed him, he pulled his hand away and tensed. I heard a single pair of footsteps crunching leaves somewhere under the tree branches. I saw Gabriel glaring down at Grizz as the guard wandered into view below us. Gingerly, Gabriel inched away from me and brought his leg back over the limb so both legs swung out beneath him. He moved to the edge of the branch, dislodging a few leaves. I watched with nervous fascination as one landed on the ground in front of Grizz. He didn't look up.

Gabriel turned to me, a wide smile on his face, and I knew what he was planning to do. I shook my head in panicky agitation and reached for him. But he slipped from my grasp and dropped to the ground, landing on Grizz. Both tumbled to the ground in a heap of limbs. Fabric tangled around my thighs, and I cursed the dress I was wearing as I scrambled out of the tree. I landed on the ground in time to see Gabriel standing over an unconscious Grizz, punching his face.

"Hey!" I hissed, glancing around to make sure we were alone. "He's already knocked out."

Gabriel shook out his hand. "Yeah, but do you know how long I've wanted to do that?"

I raked my fingers though my hair. "You're completely reckless."

"Not completely." He lifted the gun from Grizz's shoulder and, with a brief moment of hesitation, hauled it over his own.

"Do you know how to use that thing?" I asked.

"Not really," he said, but there was a peculiar darkness to his words.

He skated his fingers over the barrel and for a moment I wondered if the gun held a certain fascination. He dropped his hand, shaking his head slightly, and walked over to Juanita's tree. He helped her down.

I bent down to see if Grizz was still breathing, if he had a steady pulse. He seemed okay, passed out cold with blood tricking from his nose, but okay. I untied the bandanna wrapped around his head and held it to his nose.

"Oh, Grizz." Juanita knelt next to me. Seeing Grizz like that, laid out before us, unconscious and bloody, was unnerving—he'd always been around, protecting us with the fierce determination of a bulldog. Or so we'd thought. "Is he okay?"

"I think so," I said.

"Grizz was chasing us," she said, as if trying to convince herself. I nodded.

"And he's not alone," Gabriel said, looking into the driver's side of the car. He tested the door handle. It was locked. "Come on. We need to get out of here before they come back."

"And go where?" Juanita asked.

"Back to the main road."

I checked to see if Grizz's nose was still bleeding, but it looked like it had stopped. I stood up, next to Juanita, and watched Gabriel glance around. Not nervously, though. It was almost as if—

"You're enjoying this," I said to him.

"Enjoying?" he said. He took our arms and shepherded us away from Grizz. "You make me sound like a sick bastard who likes violence and near-death experiences."

I raised an eyebrow at him.

Gabriel pulled me along. "Do you think you can walk and dissect my psyche at the same time? I'd prefer not to die today."

"Die?" Juanita said, following alongside. "They aren't going to hurt us, they just want us back in Edenton."

"Then why did they have guns?" I asked.

Juanita didn't answer my question, she stared at her feet. I saw the struggle within her, the hesitancy in her limbs as she walked.

Gabriel led us into the mangled trees and brush at the edge of the dirt road. "If we can make it to the road, maybe a car will pick us up. But on the GPS, it looked like San Sebastian wasn't too far away."

"How far?" I asked.

"Seventeen or eighteen miles."

"I thought San Sebastian was ten miles away from Edenton!" I looked down at my dainty shoes. My feet throbbed.

"Ten miles as the crow flies, probably," Gabriel said. He led us to the edge of the dirt road wending between the trees. His voice dropped to a whisper. "One of them may have doubled back to the main road, so stay alert."

We walked in silence, moving as quickly and quietly as we could along the edge of the muddy road. If we heard a noise, we slipped behind a tree and tried to melt into the darkness. Gabriel, in his black clothes, faded into the shadows with a deft swiftness. I followed his movements, surprised at how ungraceful I felt slinking along behind him. Juanita, her mass of hair shielding her face, took tense step after tense step, watching her feet, occasionally looking back down the road as if waiting to be saved.

We reached the mouth of the dirt road, where the mud met the asphalt. The heat of the road's surface bled through the soles of my flat shoes. Unlike the damp air, it hadn't cooled off yet.

"We were driving that way," I whispered, pointing up the road.

Gabriel and I started in that direction, but Juanita didn't move. We turned back to her in unison. Although the moonlight was faint, it was enough to let me see her features. I couldn't see her eyes, but I could see the furrow between her eyebrows.

"I'm sure if we talked to Thaddeus," she said quietly, "let him know we're scared, he'll help us."

"He won't," I whispered fiercely to her, losing my patience. "He did this to us, Juanita. We're here because of him. I saw him back there in that, that place where they took us. He knew we were being drugged. He knew what was happening to us. Get it through your head, Juanita. They don't care about you."

Gabriel shot me an angry expression then took her hand. "Come with us to San Sebastian. I know you're scared, but he won't help us. Not in the way you think."

She glanced back over her shoulder. "How can you be so sure? I know you told me to trust you, Gabriel, and I do. But the more I think about this, the more I'm convinced that Thaddeus, or anyone in Edenton for that matter, wouldn't hurt us. I can't explain what happened to us back there, but—"

A beam of light suddenly arced out from the dirt road behind Juanita, her red dress shining like a beacon in the night. I lunged back, into the shadows, and watched, paralyzed, as she released Gabriel's hand and turned, waving her arms over her head.

"Thaddeus!" she called into the light. She held a hand up to shield her eyes. "I'm here and we're fine. We want to come home—"

A sharp noise—like a crack of thunder—split the air.

Juanita reeled back, falling onto the asphalt. Her head hit the hard surface and bounced, once, before it fell sideways, away from me.

The beam of light remained trained on her, and an oval of darker red expanded on the fabric of her red dress.

I clapped my hands over my mouth and stifled a scream.

# Chapter Eighteen

For a long, awful moment I stood staring at Juanita on the ground, the watery fringe of the blood darkening the red of her dress. A tug at my waist caused me to blink out of my haze. Small things surrounding her came into focus: the frayed hem of her dress, a smudged black mark on the road next to her knee, tiny pebbles glittering like gemstones in the light.

The light.

From the shadows, the light shining on Juanita shifted and bounced. A person holding a flashlight walked toward her. Toward us.

Gabriel dropped something that clattered to the ground and the noise snapped me awake. I glanced down to see the gun he'd been holding now lying at our feet. He yanked my dress.

"Run," he whispered fiercely in my ear. "Run!"

All impulse and nerves, I spun and darted up the road, legs pushing and pushing, blindly leading me away from Juanita. I didn't feel I was moving fast enough, like running in deep sand. I drove harder and kept going until my knees gave out from sheer shock.

They shot her.

Shot.

If it weren't for Gabriel, I would have fallen on my knees on the black asphalt. He held my arm and swept me to the edge of the road, so we could flee beneath the cover of the trees.

"Don't look back," he said in my ear.

"I shouldn't leave her," I said, a tremor of fear in my voice. Hearing my broken tone made everything real. Horribly real.

"They have her now." He glanced over his shoulder. "Keep moving."

A riot of arguing voices rose up behind us, but I couldn't make out any words over my own rushing breath. We sped up, cresting a small hill on the road.

Running footfalls slapped the pavement somewhere behind us.

"Faster," Gabriel said.

I ran, full speed, my feet protesting with every step. Minutes swept by and I focused on the pain from my dainty shoes, the burning ache of my muscles, to keep from thinking about Juanita, about the men stalking us. I thought about the clamminess of my dress, sticking to me like my bathing suit did after a swim in the cove beach; the moisture collecting at the roots of my hair; the dry sandiness of my mouth. I was so thirsty. Still I kept running. A quick glance over my shoulder proved we were still being followed. The men's flashlights swept through the heavy air in intersecting beams. From above, I heard the deep whomp of helicopter blades. Wide leaves flapped overhead, peeling away to reveal us dashing along the edge of the road. No searchlight circled us, though. Instead, it shone on some point behind us. The helicopter swept past. With the onslaught of cutting air, the skin on my back and neck became chilled and oversensitive. I expected a bullet to hit me any second. The wind slowly faded as we sprinted away. It sounded like the helicopter landed in the road.

We followed a wide curving bend.

"This way," Gabriel said and tugged me off the road, through the trees.

The brush was thick, thistles and branches slicing into the skin of my calves, but I followed, concentrating on the brightness of the pain. It was dark under the canopy of leaves. I only saw tall columns of dull black surrounding us, like endless corridors. Each tree we passed was thicker than the last. The hem of my skirt caught on a branch. I pulled it free and plowed forward, trying to gain as much ground as I could. Gabriel ran as fast as before. I'd been able to keep up with him so far, but now the pain searing the skin of my legs, my breath sawing in and out of my lungs, made it more difficult.

Keep going for Juanita. Get to the police in San Sebastian and save her.

"Stop!" someone yelled from the road into the jungle that surrounded us.

But I didn't hear the telltale crunch of underbrush behind us. They weren't following us into the trees. I listened hard and heard one of them complaining of snakes.

Gabriel came up short, throwing his arm out to the side to keep me from moving forward. I saw a sudden break in the jungle. Light from a distance revealed another road. This one was gravel.

I turned and peered through the darkness behind us. The men's voices collided as they argued. One didn't want to proceed. The other shouted, "That's an order," over and over again until I heard the sound of flesh hitting flesh. One beam of light flickered between the dead-still leaves. Underbrush snapped as the man broke the boundary of the jungle. The footsteps were slow as he picked his way carefully through the gnarled, thick growth covering the ground. He was coming toward us.

"What do we do now?" Gabriel asked, breathing hard.

I glanced up and down the road. "There!"

Headlights approached. I darted to the center of the road and waved my hands over my head. The truck skidded to a sudden stop a few feet ahead of me, kicking up gravel as it did. I rushed to the driver's side window, which was already open, revealing a man and a woman dressed in identical white shirts. Some kind of uniform.

"Will you take us to San Sebastian?" I asked in Spanish.

The man's eyes took me in and I looked down to see what he saw. My dress, tattered and sweaty, hung around my scratched and bleeding legs. I swiped the hair out of my face in hopes of appearing a little less psychotic.

The man glanced at Gabriel standing in the illumination of the headlights, and looked momentarily worried. Gabriel looked strung out and tense, hands balled into fists. His shirt hung open at the neck and his skin was slick and glistening. But his blazing eyes probably frightened the man the most.

"Hey," I hissed to Gabriel in English, "try to look less lethal!"

Gabriel swung his hand in the direction of the jungle. "We need to get out of here, now."

"Señor," I said to the man. "We need help. Please."

"Get in the back." He jerked his thumb toward the bed of the truck. "We'll take you."

We clambered in as quickly as we could. The bed of the truck was empty except for a large box crisscrossed with bungie cords strapping it in. We sat between the box and the rear window of the cab. I heard the man and woman mumbling to each other.

The truck sputtered out on the gravel. The man drove like someone had yelled *Go!* I clutched the side of the pitching truck to keep from toppling out. I looked wide-eyed at Gabriel. He shot me a grin.

Even over the rumble of the truck, I heard the man who'd been chasing us break out of the trees. With the box as a shield, we ducked down and peeked over the edge. He glanced around in confusion, then saw the lights of the truck. He started running. But we were already too far for him to catch up and he stopped abruptly, sliding through the gravel.

The empty road stretched before us. Above, billowing clouds moved over the slivered moon. I curled my legs to my chest, wrapping my arms around my knees, trying to catch my breath. In the semidarkness, all I could see was Juanita, her head bouncing on the hard asphalt of the road. Bouncing. That jerk of her head, how it ricocheted off that unforgiving surface, seemed unnatural. Unsurvivable.

We heard the thwack-thwack of the helicopter circling again. The man in the driver's seat ducked his head out the window and peered into the sky, still speeding along the gravel road. He met my gaze in the rearview mirror and examined me with suspicious dark eyes. He leaned over and mumbled to the woman in the passenger's seat. She half-looked over her shoulder at us, but said nothing.

"They're coming after us," I said to Gabriel as quietly as I could. I wasn't sure if the couple spoke English.

Gabriel glanced up at the helicopter. "I don't think so," he said, pointing. "No searchlights. Looks like they're following the other road. I wonder why they aren't pursuing us."

"It sounded like they were arguing. Maybe they didn't mean to . . ." I sucked in a breath but it sounded like a sob. I refused to cry. Juanita was not dead, she didn't need my tears. "Maybe shooting her was a mistake and they took her to the hospital in San Sebastian." I could only hope that was the truth.

The helicopter buzzed off on its determined route, leaving us barreling down the gravel road, rocks spitting from the tires in our wake.

I stared at the lights disappearing in the distance. "Do you think she's still alive?" I asked Gabriel in a small whisper.

He placed his hand on my shoulder. "Yes."

I felt the heat of his skin through the fabric of my dress. I hadn't realized how cold I'd become with the wind whipping around us in the back of the truck. It felt good, safe. The simplicity of that touch grounded me for a moment. I smiled at him.

A look of confusion washed over his features. He jerked his hand from my shoulder. I fought down a stab of disappointment. Touching me wasn't so terrible before, at that strange and ethereal party.

"What are you doing out here?" The truck driver called back to me through the window. He sounded concerned and almost fatherly.

I hesitated. Did I tell him the truth? Make up a lie? If so, what? After a few moments of indecision, I said, "We're from a place called Edenton. We—"

"Edenton?" the man exclaimed and the truck lurched sideways.

For a moment I went weightless, as if lifted into the air. A bruising force cinched my arm, and before I'd realized it, Gabriel pulled me back into the truck, fingers digging into my arm as he tucked me tight against his side.

"Jesus," he breathed, lips parted, eyes wide and dark. "Mia, you almost—" he searched my face.

"Why aren't you in Edenton?" The man yelled back to us, oblivious that I'd nearly been thrown from his truck like an untethered box. Worse, his tone was now devoid of any friendliness.

Gabriel released me with surprise and scrambled to the other side of the flatbed. Breathing hard, I stared at him, unsure what to say. I rubbed my arm and mouthed, "Thank you." He nodded, once.

Through the cab, the woman's shrill and frightened voice rang out. Complaining. She was complaining to the man. They never should have picked us up.

The truck began to slow.

I tore my gaze away from Gabriel's and began pleading with the couple not to dump us here, on the side of the road, words tripping off my tongue in frantic, sharp syllables.

Once the truck stopped, the man turned and threw his elbow over the seat. "Why aren't you in Edenton," he repeated to me through the open window, but peered at Gabriel, as if he'd dragged me from Edenton like some kind of chest-thumping caveman. "The Reverend does not allow his Flock to wander."

"How do you know?" I asked.

"Edenton is not the kind of place that goes unnoticed here," he said. "Many people know of it. But you're in my truck, so answer my question, or we won't take you to San Sebastian. Tell me why you are not in Edenton."

"We—" I shot a look at Gabriel, hoping for help, but realized he didn't understand what we were saying. I guessed his fancy prep school didn't teach Spanish.

The man shook his head in disgust, slapping a hand on the seat with a shot of fury. "Why," he asked in thick English, "are you not in Edenton?"

"We escaped," Gabriel said with a shrug.

The woman gasped. The man's expression changed from virtuous anger to wondrous fear.

"Escaped?" he said with surprise.

"Edenton is not what it seems, sir," I said, grabbing the rear window's frame and ducking my head so I could see the other side of his face in the rearview mirror. "It's a dangerous place. The Reverend is cruel and, well, dangerous. We're going to San Sebastian to talk to the police."

"We are?" Gabriel asked.

Shushing Gabriel, I switched back to Spanish, and said to the man, "There are people there who need help. The Reverend is doing horrible, twisted things to his Flock."

The man slid a glance at the woman, who looked away, blinking back tears. He faced the steering wheel. In the mirror I could see exasperation flicker in his eyes.

Did they need more convincing? "I can cite examples, sir," I said. "The other night in Edenton, the Rev—"

"Do not say another word to us about Edenton," he snapped and shifted the truck into drive.

# Chapter Nineteen

The drive to San Sebastian rattled my teeth and bones and mind. By the time we reached the city, exhaustion and worry dragged me further down into the bed of the pickup. The lights lining the streets and outside the shops shone so brightly I had to squint to see the details along the sidewalks.

The storefronts were painted vibrant colors, tropical fruit colors: just-picked shades of green, sun-ripened yellows and oranges. Wires were strung above the street and hung between the buildings, delivering electricity in an intricate web. Small motorcycles buzzed by the pickup truck, leaving trails of choking smoke. Stray dogs, and the occasional scrawny chicken, wove through the legs of pedestrians along the busy street.

The truck came to an abrupt halt. My head hit the cab behind me on the ricochet. Pain lanced my skull and I reached back to rub it away.

"Get out," the man said in English and without ceremony. "You tell no one who drove you into the city."

"We don't even know your name," Gabriel said as he hopped from the truck bed. He stretched out a hand for me. I accepted it and followed him down onto the sidewalk.

"The police station is one block away." The man pointed out the truck window down the street. "Around the corner to the right."

The woman in the passenger's seat kept her face turned away, but I saw her reflection in the truck's side mirror. She worried her lower lip between her thumb and forefinger, her eyes darting from person to person on the street. She whispered something in Spanish I couldn't make out over the street noise.

With a curt nod, the man steered the truck into traffic and it rumbled away from us, tearing down the street, almost sideswiping a couple on a teetering motorcycle. Pedestrians jumped back onto the curb as the pickup swung around a corner.

"He's charming," Gabriel said.

"Well, he did bring us here," I said, and started up the sidewalk.

The city smelled like grilled meat and hot tar, open-air cooking fires billowing out storefronts. I tried to ignore the gnawing pain in my stomach. I'd guessed it was an aftereffect of the drugs, or the stress, or the impeding sense of doom hanging over me.

"Wonder why he didn't want the police to know who brought us."

Gabriel walked beside me with a self-confidence that belied his bedraggled appearance. I couldn't tell which of us was drawing more stares from passersby.

He said, "Maybe he's in trouble with the cops or maybe he's paranoid. Who knows. Everyone has crazy in them. Earth is the mental institution of the universe."

I stopped and swung him a confused look.

"It's a quote . . . I heard. Somewhere." He fidgeted with his shirt-sleeves, trying to shove them further up his arms. "Hey, look, we don't have to go to the cops, you know. Cops aren't always," he paused, "on my side of things."

"Your side of things? What do you mean?" I dropped my voice. "Are you talking about when you told me you were a murder—"

"Ricci," he snapped. "Look, forget I said anything about cops." He snagged my arm and dodged people as we hustled up the street. "We'll go. We'll get it over with. They'll help us and everything will be cool, right?" He answered his own question. "Right. It will." His voice tightened when he addressed me. "But don't bring that up while we're in the station, got it?"

"Of course I won't—ouch!" I twisted my arm out of his grip. "What is the matter with you?"

"You want an alphabetical list?"

A few moments later, we pushed our way through the police station's glass doors, the large star-shaped shield painted on the glass obscuring our view of the lobby until we stepped inside. A man in a black button-down shirt with a stern, hard face stood at a counter and looked up as a beep sounded, broadcasting our entrance. His eyes widened as he took in our torn clothes and soot-smeared faces.

I approached the counter and quietly, carefully, tried explaining our situation. As I spoke, my gaze swept over the people behind him. A sleepy-eyed man sat next to a wide, paper-filled desk with his wrist handcuffed to the arm of the chair. A few others huddled around a bright, glowing screen, pointing to it while stealing glances my way. A younger-looking man, with a few days' growth of beard and a loose navy-colored tie dangling from his collar, watched us with an interest that sharpened my nerves.

When I said the name Edenton to the police officer at the counter, he took a step back. His expression grew guarded.

"One moment," he said, picking up a phone and mumbling into it.

"What's going on?" Gabriel whispered.

"I'm not sure," I replied, unable to hear what the man was saying.

After a minute or so, the police officer hung up and eyed us warily. I knew how we appeared—two kids who looked like they'd hiked the length of the Amazon in their Sunday Best. But, to my growing disappointment, I didn't see sympathy in anyone's eyes.

A woman walked out from a steel door connected to the lobby. She was dressed in a stark white shirt and gray pants with a gun slung at her hip. At the sight of the gun so close to me, I had to snap my thoughts away from Juanita. The woman's hair was forced back from her face in a severe braid, but even pulled back so tightly it didn't straighten the kink from her scalp. She approached us with a cruel determination that caused my stomach to sink.

"You must leave," she said in accented English. She spoke just softly enough for no one else to hear. "We cannot help you."

"Why not?" I asked.

"Edenton is not our jurisdiction. Now, leave. Please."

"But—" I started.

"You can't do this," Gabriel snapped. "We're teenagers. Underage. We have no place to go. Don't you have some legal obligation to help us? You swore to uphold the law. If we were back in the States—"

"You are not in the States," the woman said, pointing a long finger in Gabriel's face. Her nails were chewed and ragged. "And, as I said, we cannot help you. Leave. Now." She dropped her hand and with the tips of her fingers, she grazed the gun at her hip before letting her hand rest at her side.

I tugged on Gabriel's arm. "Let's go."

But he stood there, eyes locked on hers, silently challenging her threat.

"Gabriel, let's go," I repeated and managed to drag him though the doors under the suspicious gazes of all the people in the station.

We walked a block on the hectic sidewalk without speaking. My mind ran with panicky thoughts, one leading to the next like a runaway train. We had nothing. No money, no help, no way to get back to Edenton even if we wanted to. And there was no way in hell I was going back there if I couldn't walk back out with Max. The chances of that seemed slim—or more likely impossible. My shoulder slammed into someone rushing by and I muttered an apology in Spanish.

"We should find the hospital," I said to Gabriel, snagging his wrist. "Get to Juanita."

He slouched, looking tired beyond his years, and gently guided me to a niche in one of the buildings. "Why are we so sure Thaddeus brought her here? She could be anywhere."

Or nowhere. I shoved the thought away.

Gabriel continued, "What happens if we see Thaddeus at the hospital? Do you think he's just going to let us walk out the door with her?"

"I know, but we have to do some—"

"A guy is following us," Gabriel said, eyes trained just beyond my shoulder.

He shoved me into the crowd again. I navigated around an older woman carrying overstuffed plastic bags and tried to throw a casual glance over my shoulder. The sidewalk behind us was filled with too much chaos, too much for me to even process. It melted away into a blurred mass.

"I don't see anyone," I said.

"I recognize him. He was in the police station, sitting at a desk."

"Why would he be following us? The police won't help us. No one will help us." My feet ached; the skin on my legs was shredded from the underbrush in the jungle and stung. My head pounded and my stomach stirred. I wasn't sure how much more my body, and soul, could take tonight.

"Enough," I said, stopping in the middle of the sidewalk. I was done with all this. Sick of running. If someone was following us I was going to find out why.

"Ricci, are you crazy?" Gabriel said.

"No, Gabriel. I'm tired."

Someone approached. He looked like a rough sketch of a man, all harried and darting lines, his face slowly coming into view. The man with the scruffy beard, the navy tie flapping over his shoulder, came toward us with a purposeful gait. When he stopped in front of us, his eyes scanned the people on the street before speaking.

"Is it true you're from Edenton?" His voice was a harsh whisper.

"Why would I lie about that?" I said, trying unsuccessfully to keep the flatness from my tone.

"People lie for many reasons." He searched the street, as if someone were following him. "Come, this way. We must talk."

"We're not going anywhere with you," Gabriel said.

"But I am a police officer—"

"Yes, sir. I know," Gabriel said with put-on politeness. "But I happen to be scared shitless of the police."

"You have no reason to be afraid of me," he said.

I resisted the urge to scream my frustration in the man's face. Instead, I said, "That woman in there said the police won't help us."

"I can help you. I will help."

"You will?" I said, not wanting that spark of hope igniting in my chest, not wanting the expectation that someone—a stranger at that— would help us.

The man waved for us to follow him down the sidewalk. "I can take you to others who will help you, too." When he saw the doubt in our expressions, he urged us on. "Come, please. I won't harm you. I only want to get you to a place away from here. The Reverend has too many eyes in this town."

A jolt of alarm trembled through me at the thought. "Okay," I said.

Gabriel snagged my wrist. "No, definitely not okay," he said. "Will you give us a minute?" he asked the man. Not waiting for an answer, he pulled me away. "You don't actually think we're going with this guy, do you?"

"Why not? Without help what do we have? You heard him. The Reverend has people in town watching—which doesn't surprise me now, based on how the police reacted. And you know Thaddeus is looking for us. Do you want to stay here and let them find us? We don't exactly blend in." I flipped the ragged edge of my dress. "Gabriel, if they catch us . . . " I let the conclusion rattle around silently between us. Over Gabriel's shoulder I saw the man bobbing from one foot to the other impatiently. "I'm going with him, with or without you. I have nothing to lose."

"I have plenty to lose. I'm young and in my prime." I could tell Gabriel wasn't entirely serious from the half-defeated tone. He sighed. "But I won't let you go alone."

I placed my hand over his, which still held my other wrist, and gave it a squeeze. The gesture was just as unexpected to me as it was to him. Our eyes locked and something passed between us. A truer connection than we'd felt before. Something less like the lust from earlier at the party and more like trust.

Gabriel and I faced the man, who now looked at us with hope. I nodded consent, and we followed him to a small green car. In nervous silence, Gabriel and I ducked into the backseat, dread settling over me as if I were in a funeral procession. The car started up and we drove out of the city and into the night.

# Chapter Twenty

The air blowing in through the open car window grew cooler as we chugged up the mountain. Gabriel sat, long legs folded in front of him, cramped into the tight space and unfazed by the cold.

"He's taking us pretty far into the country," he whispered over the groaning of the small car's struggling engine.

"Looks that way," I said.

I glanced at the officer—Officer Santiago, as he'd introduced himself earlier. He was talking into a very small, flat phone asking the person on the other end for directions up the mountain.

"And how do you know he isn't taking us someplace for, I don't know, a ritualistic killing?"

"Oh, you mean a traditional Amazonian Pit Viper bloodletting? That's strictly a rainy-season ritual."

In the soft glow coming from the dash, I saw Gabriel force down a grin. I smiled back. It felt good, that moment of levity. But the nagging returned, that clawing at the back of my mind reminding me that feeling good was wrong, improper. Before I'd known what was happening, everything had changed. For the first time in as long as I could remember, I was outside of Edenton. I had been running from Thaddeus and Edenton security guards with guns. Juanita had been shot. A sensation of numbness settled over me. It was too much to feel, too much to think about. As much as I hated my life in Edenton, I wasn't sure how I could ever go back for Max. I'd never see Mama or Max again. I swallowed the lump in my throat.

"Should we have stayed there with Juanita?" I asked Gabriel. "Was going to San Sebastian a mistake?"

"No." His voice sounded hoarse. "There was nothing we could do to help Juanita."

"Why are you so sure?"

"What were we going to do, Mia? Fight them then take her to a hospital?" He sounded tired, a bone-deep and raw kind of tired. "They had guns."

"You had a gun. Grizz's gun. You could have used it."

"I'd dropped it. But even if I hadn't, I wouldn't—couldn't have used it."

"But—"

"It doesn't matter now, does it?" His eyes drifted away from me and he watched the trees that lined the road.

We were quiet for a few minutes, each lost in our own reverie.

Finally he spoke. "Listen, about earlier." He glanced at the officer who was paying more attention to his phone than to us. "At that weird party. Whatever drugs they gave us were intense. I haven't been on anything like that in a long time." He paused. "I did some things I wouldn't normally do."

"What do you mean?" I asked, even though I knew what he meant.

"I don't want you to get the wrong idea. We aren't together or anything. The kiss in the jungle that night, the one earlier at the party, they were only incidents of circumstance, understand?"

"Perfectly," I said, though his words stung. My heart twisted in my hollow chest. I wasn't sure what I expected from him, but the words sounded so cold, clinical. Incidents of circumstance. "I'm actually glad you said something. I didn't want you to get the wrong idea."

His mouth twisted and he looked away. "Good."

I shifted farther from him.

Moments later, we pulled up outside a small house nestled among trees. It was a low-slung building with a sloped tile roof. Security lights blinked on, shining wide cones of illumination into the darkness. The windows' glass was slatted, like the cottages in Edenton, and I was surprised to feel a pang of homesickness. White chairs were stacked on the covered porch by the front door, which swung open the moment Officer Santiago turned off the car.

Light spilled onto the porch as a large woman lumbered out, leaning heavily on a cane. From what I could see beyond the glare of the security lights, her face was round and pretty, dominated by enormous eyes, framed with a halo of curling blond hair. She wore a red robe tied around her thick middle with a mismatching length of fabric. She paused at the bottom of the steps as she squinted at us in the back of the car.

Officer Santiago got out, leaving Gabriel to shoot me a suspicious glance.

"What?" I asked him. "Do you think she's going to brain you with her cane? She looks pretty harmless."

Wordlessly, he jumped from the car and, to my surprise, held out a hand to help me. I tentatively placed my hand in his. His skin was hot, and my heart thudded. I took in a deep breath, trying to get my pulse under control.

*An incident of circumstance.*

"These are the people from Edenton?" the woman with the cane asked in Spanish. She spoke the words with a lazy tongue, obviously not a native speaker. "Dear God, Santiago. They're children."

"They came to the police station," Santiago said.

"In San Sebastian?" the woman asked with surprise. She took us in, her eyes raking over us with worry. "How did they end up there?"

"They told me there was a fire," said Santiago.

"Where?" she asked.

"I believe she described Las Casitas." He said the words like a proper name. "They did not escape from the Edenton compound."

I'd explained to Officer Santiago about waking up in the little resort, but he hadn't said anything about it on the ride out of town.

The woman gasped, horrified. "Truly? These children were at Las Casitas tonight?"

He glanced at me and took the woman's arm, speaking with her in low, urgent tones.

"What is Las Casitas?" I called to them in Spanish, and suspecting I already knew the answer.

"Excuse me," Gabriel said in English, raising his hand. "The Ugly American here. Do you plan on subtitling this conversation or should I go ahead and make up a story in my head? Because my version includes a hot shower, about fourteen hours of sleep, and fried chicken."

"Oh, my apologies," the woman with the cane said in a crisp British accent. I was surprised that her native tongue could be so sharp yet her Spanish so edgeless. She came forward with an outstretched hand. "Veronica Rosendale," she said, shaking Gabriel's hand vigorously.

After he introduced himself, Gabriel rubbed his palm with his other hand. "And this is Mia," he said. The introduction was unexpected and considerate.

I didn't extend my hand. "Hi," I said.

"Are you truly from Edenton?" Veronica leaned on her cane and asked with an edgy interest.

"Yes," was all I offered.

Her eyes lit with a flash of excitement. "Excellent. Please come in." She waved us toward the house with her cane. "Santiago, are you coming?"

"No," he said in English. "I don't want to arouse too much suspicion with my absence from the station." He inclined his head to us in goodbye.

I watched helplessly as he pulled away in the car, realizing we had no way back down the mountain. I didn't see a car parked near the house. My nerves began to sing with apprehension.

Gabriel and I followed Veronica to the house. The porch floor was tiled in large squares, the shiny surface dulled with dust. At the far end, a colorful hammock was strung between the concrete wall of the house and a porch rail, a stack of newspapers scattered about below it, as if someone had spent a lazy afternoon reading. We ducked through the front door and entered a large room, painted the same ocher as the outside of the house.

"Tea?" Veronica asked, limping over to a tea service sitting on a small dining table under a tarnished brass chandelier. A few of the bulbs were dark at the tips and burned out.

"Yes, thank you," I said absently, watching Gabriel as he examined the room. His eyes anchored on every crevice, every shadow, and every space behind the furniture. "What were you expecting?" I whispered to him.

Gabriel sat down on one of four matching green lounge chairs that circled a cluttered coffee table. He relaxed a fraction and whispered back to me. "Before? Maybe an ambush, Thaddeus jumping out of the shadows to take us back." He watched as Veronica busied herself with a teakettle, her cane propped against the ornate table. She hummed tunelessly. "Now? An *Antiques Roadshow* marathon and about thirty cats."

"So," Veronica said, glancing over her shoulder at us. "I'm not even sure where to start. What a boon this is!"

Gabriel mouthed the word "boon" to me.

Ignoring him, I asked, "What's the place you and Officer Santiago mentioned outside, Las Casitas?"

The teacup rattled in her hand, and her expression darkened. "Las Casitas del Jardin," she said.

Before she could say anything else, a shadow appeared in a doorway off the living room. Another woman entered, followed by a man. Both appeared to be deadly serious, in contrast to Veronica's cheeriness.

The woman was smaller than Veronica, almost petite by comparison, with a spill of black hair gathered in a tie over one shoulder. Her olive skin was clear and slicked with a sheen of sweat. She and the man wore the same type of clothing: khaki shorts, tough hiking boots, and dusty shirts, hers a button-up white blouse with a tank top underneath, his a white T-shirt.

"Veronica," the woman said, a slight Spanish accent honing her words. She stared down at us with disgust. "You're offering them tea? Have you seen the wounds on the girl's legs?"

I looked down at myself. Dirt and blood streaked my legs, the cuts clotting in patches along my skin. "It doesn't feel as bad as it looks," I said.

"Right now, but if those wounds get infected you'll be in a lot of pain. And trouble." The woman stomped across the room into what looked like a kitchen.

"That's Ibbie," the man said. "I'm Edgar."

He sat heavily on a green chair across from us. The springs of the seat protested with a series of squeaks. He was bulky, and tall, taller than Gabriel, and slightly familiar, though I couldn't place exactly what about him was familiar.

"Now, how do we know you're really from Edenton?" he said.

"And the point of lying would be?" Gabriel asked. "So we could have a complete stranger chauffeur us to another complete stranger's house for proper English tea at," he looked at a clock on a bookshelf, "two in the morning? Mia, he's discovered our nefarious plan."

Edgar rubbed his palm over his black shorn hair and squinted at Gabriel. "Smartass teenagers. My favorite."

Ibbie hurried back into the room and knelt at my feet, depositing a first aid kit on the floor. She flung it open and began scrabbling around its contents. "You're both so young," she said, and it sounded as if she were about to cry. "So, so young."

"Excuse me," I said. "Can one of you tell us why we are here?"

146

Veronica laughed. It was high-pitched and trilling. "We are so thrilled you are here. You have absolutely no idea what we've been through."

Edgar cleared his throat. "Veronica," he said in a dry, warning tone, then turned to me, leaning forward with his elbows on his knees. "Mia, is it?"

I nodded.

His heavy eyebrows lowered over his eyes. "We have a vested interest in Edenton because all of us have relatives who live there."

"Live," Ibbie scoffed. "Imprisoned is more like it."

"Who?" I asked, shocked. With the exception of my own father, I rarely thought about the Flock's relatives outside of Edenton.

"My daughter-in-law," said Veronica, handing me a teacup, clinking on a saucer. "Chamomile. Nice and relaxing."

"Thanks." I smiled a little. "Who is your daughter-in-law?"

Veronica took in a heavy breath, as if saying the name would cause her physical pain. "Jin Sang Rosendale."

Mama's cottage mate. Her last name in the outside world was Rosendale?

Veronica continued, "She was married to my son, John. When he passed away five years ago, she began following the Reverend Eden's teachings. Three years ago, she moved to Edenton with my only grand-child." Her large, round eyes glistened with unshed tears. She paused to gather herself. "That sweet boy is the only part of my son I have left."

Edgar reached over and took Veronica's hand. She patted it with her manicured hand and forced a smile on her lips.

"Is my Bae John okay?" Veronica asked me hopefully. "My grandson?"

I nodded. "Yes, he and Jin Sang live with my mother and my brother. The boys are about the same age." I tried to smile, but it may have looked more like a wince.

"My brother is there, too," said Edgar. "He's been there for so long. I worry about how that place has changed him."

Gabriel peered at Edgar with a fierce intensity. "No."

Edgar quirked his brow. "Pardon me?"

"Oh, now I can see it," Gabriel said, pointing at Edgar. "You have the same Neanderthal forehead."

Edgar's fingers touched the skin above his bushy brows and I stared in fascination as the familiarity of his features clicked. "Grizz is your brother," I said.

Edgar crossed his bulky arms over his chest. "Is Eugene still going by that ridiculous nickname?"

Gabriel burst into laughter. "Eugene?" He grabbed his stomach and dipped back in the chair.

When I noticed Edgar's annoyed sneer, I slapped Gabriel on the leg. "I wouldn't laugh so hard there, Herbert." I said his middle name quietly, but not too quietly. We couldn't afford to anger the only people willing to help us. Especially not someone the size of Edgar.

A piercing sting shot up my leg. "Ow!" I cried. I spilled tea on my hand, the pain nothing compared to the slashed skin on my calves.

"Sorry," said Ibbie.

She cleaned away some of the mud and blood from my legs. I shifted, uncomfortable and fidgety. I didn't know this person, yet she was motherly and caring—like a member of the Flock. Except she wasn't.

I held my hand out. "I can do that."

"Oh," Ibbie said. "Of course." She surrendered the washcloth with a discouraged tilt to her mouth.

I bent down and wiped my legs, trying to keep from wincing with every brush of the rough material against the tender scrapes.

"Can you tell us why the police wouldn't help us?" Gabriel asked.

Even though he spoke to Veronica and Edgar, he watched me intently as the washcloth grazed up and down my legs. I felt his eyes on me, and my face warmed.

"The Reverend gives the government in San Sebastian hefty allowances to let his Flock be," Veronica said. "He reigns free in this area with no fear of interference from the authorities."

"He also employs locals," Ibbie added. "Infusing funds into the local economy."

"Many work for one of the Reverend's more successful ventures," Edgar said.

"Ventures?" I asked, handing Ibbie the washcloth.

My legs were as clean as I could get them. Blood oozed from the newly cleaned scrapes. Ibbie lowered her head and concentrated on coating my cuts with ointment. I glanced up in time to see Edgar and Veronica exchange a look.

"Las Casitas del Jardin," Veronica said, "is a resort, of sorts, that the Reverend operates to entertain very wealthy patrons."

"A resort," I said. A sick suspicion twisted in my chest. I felt like I knew what they were going to say. But I couldn't help asking, "Entertain? How?"

Edgar scrubbed his hand over his forehead, then dropped it onto the arm of his chair. I jumped at the noise. "The people of Edenton, Mia, are for sale to the highest bidder."

# Chapter Twenty-One

I stood stiffly, leaning over the back of a chair, my eyes fixed on a knife-edge thin computer screen as Edgar traced his fingers over a silver square beneath the keyboard.

"This isn't the actual website," he said, inclining his head toward the brightly colored display. "The live site is under airtight security. It's password protected and an IP address must be given permission to access it. These are only screen captures that were sent to us last week."

"Screen captures?" I asked, feeling as if Edenton had locked me away in a box while the world evolved around me, everything speeding by while I remained still as a dead tree.

"Like movie stills," Gabriel said with a hint of patience. He sat at the edge of one of the two beds, the light from the screen illuminating the green in his left eye. "They're pictures of a website."

As he went on to explain, I saw the pity etched in Veronica's expression. She stood on the other side of the small bedroom as if the two single beds bisecting the space were protection from the desk and computer.

I shifted my focus back to the screen. Faces of the Flock scrolled by. The pictures I recognized: each of us, wearing our simple uniforms, against an indigo background. A few faces smiled, but more wore serious expressions that seemed to dare the camera to take their photos. The pictures were the same as the ones laminated on our ID cards.

"It's essentially a catalog," Veronica said, voice pitched high with a nervous tremble. "A human catalog."

"What do you mean, a human catalog?" Gabriel asked.

"The members of the Flock are for sale, man," Edgar said, running a hand over his hair. "There are people in this world who are willing to pay for their—for your—companionship."

"Companionship." Gabriel paled.

Edgar continued, glancing at the screen with distaste as he spoke. "Very exclusive people, very wealthy people, gain access to this website by donating to corrupt politicians in this country and in other countries in the Western hemisphere. Including the United States."

He waited for a reaction from us, Gabriel and me, but I could barely follow what was happening, my head foggy and confused. Gabriel only stared, his lips curled in disgust.

"This is a catalog of the members of the Flock, the ones who have been made available for sale to the highest bidder."

"Have been made available?" Gabriel asked. "What makes a member of the Flock available?"

"It used to be age," Edgar said. "When members of Edenton reached the age of eighteen, they were put up for sale—"

"Rent," Veronica whispered. "They're rented."

"—in the catalog," Edgar continued. "But over the years, that's changed."

Veronica let out a long breath. "Drastically."

"How drastically?" I asked.

Veronica folded a blanket, patting down the edges as she placed it on the end of one of the beds. "This is rather much for tonight, don't you think? Maybe some rest—"

"Where am I in this?" I asked Edgar. My pulse pounded through my limbs and head. A vein pulsed at my temple. I touched it, as if I could calm my heart. "On these screen captures? Where am I listed in the catalog?"

Edgar pointed to the screen. "It's organized in such a way that you are all categorized. By gender, age, physical characteristics, and . . . " He cleared his throat. "Sexual experience."

"Edgar," Veronica hissed. "They're children!"

"We aren't anymore," Gabriel said, a haunted, distant sound to his tone. "If the Reverend is doing this to us, we aren't children anymore, are we?"

I met his eyes over Edgar's head.

"Here you are, Mia." Edgar scrolled the image on the screen and my face came into view.

Burning acid gurgled in my stomach at the sight. I pressed my palm to my diaphragm to try to push it down. I read the words listed below my photograph.

Mia; Female; Age: 16; Hair: light brown; Eyes: green; Date of Last Encounter: —/—/—

"Date of last encounter?" I asked.

"We're whores, Mia," Gabriel said. "That's the date of your last sexual encounter."

The words stung, and my skin prickled hot under his glare. "Whores?" I asked, disbelief clawing at my throat.

Edgar threw Gabriel a disapproving look, but didn't correct him. "That's why you were in that resort—Las Casitas del Jardin—because people paid to be with you there."

"To have sex with us," Gabriel said with a certainty that unnerved me. "Just say it, Edgar. Don't be gentle about it."

"Sex?" I asked. Their eyes were on me. They knew I was inexperienced. Lambert paid for me because I was inexperienced. I flushed with embarrassment. "I . . . uh."

"This is too much," Veronica said to Edgar. "Too much information for these children tonight." She called Ibbie's name.

Ibbie appeared at the door, having changed into a loose-fitting shirt and baggy plaid pajama pants. She reached her hand toward us. "Come with me. We have a change of clothes for you, you can shower and clean up. Afterward, you can have a little something to eat, and hopefully get some sleep."

"We can certainly chat about our proposal with you in the morning," Veronica called as we headed out the door, and I didn't miss Ibbie's reproachful glance over her shoulder at Veronica.

"Proposal?" I asked.

I was light-headed, cloudy, trying to feel the floor beneath my feet. Maybe Veronica was right, this was too much information for tonight, and I wasn't sure I wanted to hear any more. I could still feel the adrenaline coursing through me. The horrific image of Juanita on the ground still burned into my sight.

Gabriel silently stalked past us out of the room. Behind me, I heard a dull thumping sound and turned to see Edgar had folded the computer closed. He leaned his elbows on the desk and clasped his head in his hands, weary and shut down like the computer.

Ibbie led me to a bedroom with a double bed. The walls were covered in a dull, peeling beige wallpaper. Over the single window hung crooked blinds, sheer curtains barely concealing the missing slats.

"I've changed the bed and put fresh towels in the bathroom." She motioned to a door to the right of the bed.

"Thank you," I said as I stood staring into the room, unsure what to do next.

Ibbie placed a hand on my shoulder. I flinched away.

"I'm sorry," she said, clasping one hand with the other in front of her. "Is there anything you need?"

I glanced at her and she looked at me with concern. Who were these strangers and why did they want to help us?

"Who do you know in Edenton?" I asked her.

She moved to the bed, grazing her hand along the blanket folded across the end of the mattress. "My father left our family when I was young," she said as she sat down on the bed. "He had to leave our country for his own safety." Her lips twisted and she stared off into the corner of the room as if reliving a memory. She didn't elaborate further.

"Your father is in Edenton?" I asked.

"Yes, and my two brothers. He took them with him when he left. Eduardo is my father's name." Her eyes snapped up to meet mine with an expectancy that caught me off guard.

Eduardo. The name was familiar, but there wasn't anyone in Edenton with that name. "Who are your brothers?" I asked, trying to cover up my confusion.

"Angél and Enrique."

Of course. Eduardo was their father. But—

"Eduardo," I said, not wanting her leaden stare on me. It was unfair that I had to deliver this news to her. Did news never travel outside of Edenton, just as we never heard anything about the outside world? "I mean, your father passed away a few years before I came to Edenton."

A moment passed, and then another, and I looked down to see my hands tightly balled into fists, the knuckles as white as the bones beneath my skin.

"So," Ibbie finally said, "the boys have been without a father since they were very young."

I nodded once, and wanted to say I hadn't had a father since I was very young, either. But I didn't. It probably wouldn't bring her any comfort. She didn't look much older than her brothers, or me for that matter, maybe in her early twenties.

She shot to her feet, rubbing her eyes with the heels of her hands. "Thank you," she said. "I've tried for years to find out if he had died. He wasn't well when he fled." She dropped her hands. "And my brothers? How are they?"

"They're doing well," I said. "They're in charge of fishing in Edenton. They help feed the Flock." I tried to smile at her, but I was so tired I was sure it looked more like a grimace. "Angél and Enrique are very good at what they do. They followed in your father's footsteps."

"Thank you for that," Ibbie said and placed her hand on my arm. I couldn't help but jerk away from her touch again. It had been a long, horrific night. Ibbie sensed my discomfort and brushed past me to the door. "I'll let you rest," she said with a maternal gentleness.

I drifted down on the bed. It was overly soft and I sunk low into the mattress. Or was this the way beds outside Edenton were supposed to feel? Thinking back, I couldn't remember what the bed felt like when I woke up in that room with Monsieur Lambert. That acid gurgled up in my stomach again. Lambert. He'd paid to be with me—to have sex with me. Even if I'd had no experience? I swallowed down the rising acid in my throat.

Lambert's voice in my head caused my lips to tremble and sweat to bead on my brow. *Speaking of the first time, I'd like to move this along. I've waited long enough and I grow anxious.*

Just as I suspected, he'd paid money to take my virginity.

"Mia?" I heard Ibbie say from outside the bedroom door, but I was already running for the bathroom.

*  *  *

When I woke, it was still dark. Faint moonlight streaked through the bedraggled blinds, throwing dim stripes of light on the windowsill.

Even thick with grogginess, my mind went to Juanita. Was she okay? Where was she? What was the last thing I said to her? I thought back.

*Get it through your head, Juanita. They don't care about you.*

Guilt and tears clawed at my chest. I rolled over in the bed. The dampness of my hair made the pillow clammy and warm. I rose, about to flip the pillow, and froze.

Gabriel leaned against the doorjamb, dressed in loose-fitting clothes, his hands shoved in his pockets. His hair was beginning to dry, curling lightly at the ends near the collar of his shirt. Because of the light seeping in from the room behind him, his face was deep in shadow.

"Hey," he said.

"Hey," I said. "Were you watching me sleep?"

He didn't reply.

"Because if you were, that would be pretty damn creepy."

"Some people would find it romantic."

*Romantic? What about us is romantic? Especially after your little speech in the car earlier.*

I didn't say it, but with his eyes shielded in silhouette, I couldn't tell if he was joking. I sat up fully, tugging the covers up to my throat, although I suspected the borrowed shirt from Ibbie more than covered me.

Gabriel glanced down at his feet. "Can I ask you a favor?"

"I guess so."

He spoke tentatively. "They have me in that room with Edgar. And he snores like a son of a bitch." He paused. "I was wondering if I could sleep in here with you."

"With me?"

He held up his hands, palms facing me. "Just sleep, I don't want to make you uncomfortable, really. But I'm exhausted and still confused about what happened tonight. And . . . " He shoved a hand through his hair. "And the only person I trust, the only one who understands how I'm supposed to feel right now, the only one who experienced what I went through tonight . . ." he said softly, ". . . is you."

I couldn't breathe. A small tug in my chest and a tingle in my belly made me shift uncomfortably, and I realized I didn't have pants on, only the borrowed shirt and my underwear. But he wouldn't try anything, especially not after blaming his kisses on circumstance. I willed myself to drag in a breath. "Okay."

Gabriel took a step into the room, closing the door quietly behind him. The room grew pitch black quickly and I felt for the light next to the bed. But before I could turn it on, he darted into the room.

I heard a thump when he tumbled to the floor.

"Ow."

"Let me turn on a light for you." I switched on the light.

"Thanks."

"No problem."

He pushed himself to his feet and sat on the side of the bed. "I can sleep on top of the covers."

The mountain air had grown cool as the night passed, and if the house had heat, it didn't seem to be on. I glanced at Gabriel's borrowed clothes. He wore a thin button-down shirt, the sleeves rolled up, and gym shorts that went to his knees. I wished I'd thought he looked ridiculous, but to me he didn't.

"No, it's okay," I said and scooted over to the edge of the bed. He pulled back the covers and caught sight of my bare thighs. His lips parted.

"Are you sure?" he asked.

I knew I shouldn't have, but I enjoyed his little drug-free reaction to catching a peek of my legs under the covers, even with the bandages. "Yeah, I'm sure."

I reached over and turned off the light, throwing the room into darkness again. I heard him pat his way into the bed and the mattress dipped as he slipped in.

We lay side by side, still as planks, each staring blindly at the ceiling. Slowly, the dim moonlight faded in, chasing some of the darkness away, and I watched the ceiling fan wobble with every rotation. Even through the blanket that dipped between us, I felt the heat radiate off his body and sensed the solidness of it. It was so strange, foreign, being with him like this, but part of it felt right and natural, too. Not so long ago, he was a total stranger.

After a few minutes of tortured silence, I turned my head and asked, "How did you end up in Edenton?"

Gabriel draped his arm over his forehead. He inhaled deeply, keeping his gaze fixed on the ceiling. I studied his profile while waiting for an answer, or a refusal to answer. The fine lines of his nose, the thick smudge of his eyelashes, supple contours of his lips . . .

"My parents thought coming to Edenton would be good for our family," he said. "Because I killed my brother."

# Chapter Twenty-Two

*You want to hear another reason how I know you're not a murderer? Because, Mia, I'm a murderer.*

I shot up in bed and twisted to look at Gabriel. He hadn't moved. He was still staring at the ceiling.

"Are you serious?" I asked.

"Deadly." Bleak amusement deepened his voice.

"That's not funny."

He sat up and leaned back on his elbows. He watched me closely. Dark hair fell across his forehead, shadows shielding his eyes. "It wasn't meant to be. My brother died because of me."

"But you didn't kill him, did you?"

"I did," he said simply. "My actions were responsible for his death, what's the difference?"

"There's a difference." I traced the quilted pattern on the blanket with my index finger. "Do I still feel responsible for the deaths of those eleven people during the Bright Night? Yeah, I do."

"You were the Reverend's pawn."

"I know that. And he would have gotten someone else to help Agatha with the baking if it wasn't me. I still have a vague sense of responsibility for what I was a part of, but I understand that I didn't kill them." I glanced back at him. "Can I ask what happened to your brother?"

He shook his head with a doubtful cast. "It's a twisted bedtime story, Mia. Not something that will usher you into a peaceful night's sleep."

"I'm far away from having a peaceful night's sleep. It'll be dawn in a couple hours." I lay back down, curling sideways on the pillow. "You don't have to tell me, it's okay. I thought maybe, I don't know, it would help."

"I've had lots of help," he said, then muttered, "psychiatrists are as crazy as everyone else." Gabriel let out a long exhale and dropped back onto his pillow. He folded his arms over his chest, tucking his hands under his arms, as if shielding his heart.

He'd lost a sibling, like Juanita. Maybe they spoke about it, maybe it was what had brought them close together so quickly.

"My brother was almost ten years older," Gabriel said. "I worshipped him. Worshipped. When he was fourteen he went to parties and clubs—"

"Wasn't he a little young to get into nightclubs?"

"First, I think my grandmother called them nightclubs back in the eighties."

"How old is your grandmother?"

"And second," he said, ignoring me, "we were rich and lived in Manhattan."

"Is that some kind of explanation?"

He shrugged. "Pretty much."

"Fine." I waved a tired hand at him. "Go on."

"My mom worked all the time. She was a lawyer for a five-name law firm in Midtown. Corporate law. The most soul-crushing. My dad is—was—a writer."

"Was," I whispered.

"Yeah. He tried to bring his computer into Edenton but they confiscated it." When he shifted in the bed, the mattress beneath us wobbled. "Before, though, he'd be holed up in his office all the time trying to write a follow-up to his *New York Times* best-selling novel, which, by the way, was a sappy, self-serving piece of crap I could barely get through."

"What was it about?"

"Oh, undying love, terminal cancer, and time travel. You know, the usual."

"Of course."

Gabriel continued, "I had a nanny I was with all the time. She was supposed to watch Griffin, too—"

"Your brother's name was Griffin?"

"My mom found the letter G endearing."

"Why?"

"Gaia, Ganesha, Guanyin, Gandhi, God. It was a different religion, different beliefs for her practically every few months." I couldn't see his face clearly, but the dim light in the room reflected in the sheen of his eyes as he stared off into the distance. "We had a room in our house dedicated to her spiritual evolution. It was filled with statues and altars, incense and bells, beads and books. When she wasn't working, she locked herself up in there. We hardly saw her. I guess her job may have been soulless, but she was determined to keep hers intact, no matter what the sacrifice."

"What was her sacrifice?"

"Her sons. She set us aside to go on a spiritual journey that didn't include her family."

"What about your dad?"

"He worshipped at the altar of the Amazon Sales Rank."

"The Amazon is for sale?"

He let out a sigh that sounded a bit like a laugh. "Never mind." He shifted his arm behind his head. "Griffin would ignore Miss Beverly. He didn't give a crap about where he was supposed to be and what he was supposed to be doing. It was awesome."

"How is that awesome?"

"When you're a kid and your older brother is a badass, off running around Manhattan, acting like he owns the island, it's awesome." He went quiet then, staring off into the darkness, head tilted away from me. "Until it's not."

I remained silent, waiting.

"Griffin began to change," Gabriel continued in a rasping voice. "He didn't go out with his friends as often, didn't talk to many people. He'd ditch his phone on the kitchen counter and leave it 'til the battery died.

"It started to get worse," he said. "For hours he would stay in his room. Hours. Sometimes days. It got to a point where he didn't even go to school. Griffin wasn't dumb. He may have skipped school, but he was smart enough never to get in trouble for it." A faint smile graced his lips. "He could talk his way out of anything." He dragged out the last word and stopped talking, staring, maybe sifting through memories.

I studied his profile again, the grace of his straight nose, his full lower bottom lip with that cherry indentation that kept drawing my eye. I wondered about Griffin. Did he look like Gabriel? Dark hair and gradient blue-green eyes?

"How old were you when your brother was born?" he asked suddenly.

"I was—" I started, refocusing. "I was nine."

"And how did you feel when he was born?"

"How did I feel?" I asked.

"Yeah. You were old enough to remember when he was born. What did you feel when he and your mom came home from the hospital?"

"He didn't come home from the hospital."

"Was he born in Edenton?"

"No. He was born right before we came to Edenton. My mom wanted to give birth at our house, not in a 'cold, unfeeling' hospital."

"That can't be sanitary," he said flatly.

I smiled. "She had a midwife. If my Dad had been there, he would have been furious."

"Your dad? You have a father?"

"Yes, I have a father. He just . . . " I trailed off, grief cinching my throat. "He didn't come with us to Edenton."

Gabriel didn't say anything, only waited for me to continue.

"It's not that he didn't want to come with us," I said, repositioning myself onto my back so I wasn't facing him. I focused on the crooked wobble of the ceiling fan and wondered how much I should tell Gabriel. There was so much I didn't want to remember, so many emotions I didn't want to bubble up. Especially now, after what we'd been through earlier. "He left us before Max was born."

"Oh," he muttered. "Sorry."

"It's okay."

I wasn't sure what I was saying was okay, Gabriel bringing it up or Papa leaving us. I hadn't talked about what had happened between my parents to anyone, really. The girls in my cottage never asked. As far as the Flock was concerned, your life before Edenton was insignificant.

"But when Max was born," I said, shifting the conversation back to his question, "I was excited. I was an only child and always wanted a brother or sister. I wanted to hold him all the time. And as he got older, and we could have little conversations, he became more precious to me—"

I stopped, a small choking sound escaping my throat. Max was still in Edenton. Would I ever see him again? I placed my hand on my stomach, at the pain beginning to bloom there, and inhaled.

"You okay?" Gabriel asked.

"Yes," I said in a hoarse whisper. "Why did you ask about how I felt when my brother was born?"

"Sibling rivalry," he said. "Seems like it happens when kids are closer in age, you know what I mean? A two-year-old not understanding why he isn't the center of attention anymore. Sure—that makes sense. Why would you be jealous of your baby brother if you're a lot older?"

"I wasn't jealous of him."

"But my brother was of me. He hated me. I worshipped him like a dumb little kid and he absolutely hated me."

"Hate is a very strong word."

"Extreme dislike doesn't exactly cover it," he muttered. "Like I said, Griffin changed and my parents barely noticed. I overheard Miss Beverly telling my mom that she was worried about Griffin. My mom said something idiotic, like his spirit will light the way to a happier path. Or whatever." He sat up, punched the pillow, and repositioned it against the headboard. He leaned back against the pillow. "And my dad couldn't have cared less. He was so caught up in his own world it was like we didn't even exist to him. Until it came to taking a family photo for some book-marketing crap. I remember in one picture we all wore matching khakis and white shirts on the beach. And my dad rented a golden retriever for the photo."

"How do you rent a golden retriever?"

"The Amazing Animals casting agency," he said, rubbing his eyes with his fingertips. "It's not important. Anyway, one afternoon when I was eight, my mom was at work and my dad was who-knows-where. Griffin came into my room and asked Miss Beverly if I could play a game with him. Miss Beverly glanced at me, then at him, and I thought *me*? Why me?" He seemed as taken aback now as he must have been when he was eight. "Miss Beverly said it was okay. I remember what he said when he saw the shocked look on my face. 'Come on, Gabe. Come play a game with me.' So I followed Griffin down the stairs to our family room." Gabriel let out a long breath but stayed silent for a while; the only sound was the early morning birds chirping outside the window.

"I thought people in New York lived in apartments," I said, trying to sway the subject temporarily away from his brother because the tone of his voice sounded like he didn't want to continue. But my curiosity was piqued. Where was his story going? "Did you live in a house? Was it big?"

"Pretty big place, I guess. Upper East Side brownstone. The family room was in the basement. I was the only one who really hung out down there, so my toys were everywhere, Legos and stuff. When I got down there, I saw a box on the coffee table. Griffin told me to open it." He hesitated. "Inside was a gun."

"A gun?" I asked.

"Yeah. It wasn't unusual, really. I played with toy guns, giant water pistols that looked like machine guns. But this didn't look like a toy. It was black, and looked heavy and real. Griffin asked me if I wanted to play a game called Deer Hunter. He said the rules were simple, it was like Marco Polo." He turned to me. "You know that game?"

I thought back to when I was little, playing with the kids in the neighborhood pool. If I remembered correctly, it was tag, but in a swimming pool. I was "it" a few times, yelling "Marco" with my eyes closed, swimming to the closest "Polo" I heard from someone in response, trying to tag that person. Then my memory clouded with visions of Mama swimming, naked with Lambert. My stomach roiled.

"Yeah," I said softly. "I know the game."

"Anyway, he said we'd play it just like that, except he was the deer and I was the hunter. He put a blindfold over my eyes. And at first I was freaked out and asked what kind of gun it was. He told me it was a paintball gun. I'd never seen one before, so I was pretty excited. I thought about how pissed Mom would be if we got paint on her rugs.

"Griffin placed the gun in my hand. It was so heavy. I asked him what I was supposed to do next. He told me to say 'deer' when I was ready, and he would answer 'hunter.' And I had to find him and shoot. But then he said, 'Remember, Gabe. Even the deer doesn't want to die alone. That's why he has the hunter.' I nodded at him, not sure what he was talking about until . . . "

Anxiety prickled its way over my limbs. As much as I didn't want to hear what happened, I couldn't stop listening to his story.

"I held the gun out." He mimicked the movement with his hands. "And I said, 'deer.' I actually was excited to pull the trigger. I heard him reply, 'hunter.' " Gabriel drew out the word. "I remember how he said it. He spoke very slowly and sounded far away. I turned to where I heard him and squeezed the trigger. And suddenly my face was on fire. The gun kicked back and clocked me in the nose, and I was in so much pain I started crying. I didn't even take off the blindfold." He touched his head between his brows. "There was a scream, and it sounded like I heard it through water—it was muffled. And then someone whipped the blindfold off my face and it hurt like hell. I remember bringing my hands up to my nose and they came back covered in blood.

"I looked down to see Miss Beverly crouched over Griffin. When she moved away, I saw him. He wasn't far away from me at all. He had been right in front of me when I pulled the trigger."

The air rushed from my lungs in horror. "It was a real gun?"

"Yeah," he said quietly. "A real gun." Bringing his hand up to his forehead, he pressed his index fingers to his temples. "I stood there for what felt like hours, looking at his face—it was completely unrecognizable. All I could think was that it looked like raw bloody meat."

"Oh, God." I swallowed a gag at the thought. "Why did he do it? Did he leave a note?"

"He . . . he didn't leave a real suicide note or anything. The cops had no clues why he did it. But I guess he hated me just that much."

"No," I said and wondered if a person like that could hate his own brother.

"I told you, he'd always hated the fact I was born."

"But that doesn't mean he hated you."

"What the hell is the difference, Mia?" he retorted. He brought his fingers to his eyes and rubbed them. "I'm sorry."

"Gabriel, don't be sorry. I'm the one who asked you to tell me this story. And I think what he did to you was like child abuse."

"I know that now. But when you're an eight-year-old kid, all you can think is that you killed your goddamn brother."

I slid my hand across the bed sheet and placed it on his wrist. My fingers prickled at the touch. "I'm so sorry you went through that."

He tensed beside me, then relaxed when I didn't pull my hand away. "Thanks," he said. "After all that, you know, we went through a lot. Investigations, a trial. I ended up in therapy for years. My parents— God, my parents. Some days, they would clutch onto me like I was all they had left. Other days—" he broke off and shrugged.

I tightened my grip on his wrist.

"Finally," he said, "when I was thirteen, I stopped going to therapy, stopped dealing with my parents' insanity."

"Why?" I asked.

He hesitated, and said tightly, "Because I had a good reason to." He didn't elaborate on that reason. "All I wanted was to hang out with friends, party, wanted to forget everything that happened. I did whatever I wanted, whenever I wanted. Drugs, tattoos, girls—" he stopped.

"Sounds like fun," I said, but didn't mean it. I didn't want to hear about him with other girls, and he knew I didn't.

"Yeah. It was a hell of a lot of fun." He didn't sound convincing. "You know, I was never punished for it."

"For the accident?"

"It wasn't an accident, Mia. I should have been punished for it." Before I could tell him he was wrong, he said, "Or maybe my mom persuading my dad that we needed to come together as a family in Edenton was my punishment."

"Well, we're not in Edenton now," I said.

"We're not." In the dark, I saw the silhouette of his eyelashes drift closed. Silence stretched out, so long that I imagined he'd fallen asleep.

I let go of his wrist. Before I could pull my arm away, he reached for my hand and snagged it, intertwining our fingers. I couldn't hide my gasp of surprise.

"Sorry," he whispered, eyes still closed. "Like I said before, you're the only one who gets what happened to us earlier. I—" he broke off and tugged me closer to him. "When I saw Juanita like that—the sound of the gun, the blood . . . "

"I understand," I whispered.

"I know." His voice sounded pained, as if the words hurt. "You see, that's exactly it. You're the only one who understands everything—my brother, Edenton, what happened at that place by the beach."

He turned his head, and his eyes opened slowly. Even in the low light, I saw they were unguarded and earnest. Gone was the boy who covered up his emotions with sardonic quips; all that put-on strength and bravery faded away and I was left with Gabriel.

Slowly, I reached up and placed my hand on his cheek. To my surprise, he leaned his head into my palm, keeping his eyes locked with mine. I guided his face down to my own, placing a soft kiss on his forehead. He didn't pull away. I kissed him tenderly on his temple, on his cheek, on his jaw, then brought his mouth to mine. And hesitated before I kissed him. It was a light press of lips on lips. We stayed like that for a bit, tenderly brushing our lips together with our breaths mingling.

He pushed me backward onto the mattress and his tongue slipped inside my mouth, both gentle and demanding. The weight of his body on mine was astonishing and phenomenal and terrifying, and I snaked my arms around his neck and pulled him closer. I felt him—all of him—against me. It was as if a fire ignited in the pit of my stomach. All I wanted to do was melt into him. I tangled my fingers in his hair as the kiss grew more desperate. I heard myself make small whimpering sounds, and him groan in response. The light stubble on his face rasped my cheek but it didn't matter. It only made it more exciting, more real. His hand flattened on the small of my back, pressing me tightly against him. His mouth left mine and he trailed kisses down my neck as he whispered my name against my skin.

I unbuttoned his borrowed shirt with trembling fingers and peeled it off his arms. His skin was brilliant, smooth and taut. Once his hands were free, they traced their way down my body, leaving heat in their wake. We rolled on our sides, legs tangled together, our bodies pressing closer and closer. I couldn't breathe but I couldn't stop. We rolled back and I placed my palms on his shoulders, skating down his sinewy, flexed arms as he lifted himself up over me. The tattoo on his arm swirled in the darkness. His shorts slung low on his hips and I saw his other tattoo peeking out on his lower abdomen.

I reached up and pulled his mouth back on mine.

"Gabriel," I whispered against his lips. I wanted him closer so badly. An ache in my chest burned with the need, spreading to my stomach and limbs and skin.

Gabriel dragged his mouth softly over my cheek and down my neck. He rasped my name and my skin shivered under his breath. Cool air hit my shoulder as he pushed down the collar of my shirt with one hand, the other sliding up my back, fingertips tracing my spine. He kneeled between my legs and bowed me up with the force of his hand. Our chests collided along with our mouths. Our kisses grew deeper and deeper until his fingers toyed with the waistband of my underwear and I wriggled my hips closer to his.

I pulled away from our kiss.

"Gabriel?" I whispered again, loving how perfectly our bodies fit together. I reached his shorts, slipping my fingers between the rough elastic of his waistband and his feverish skin.

"Yeah, Mia?" he breathed and I felt the words on his breath as it traveled over the hollow of my neck, right before he kissed me there.

"I—I—" I stuttered, knowing I needed to say something about how I felt about him, but unsure how. "I think I'm falling—"

"No." The word was sharp and Gabriel froze when he said it. Slowly, deliberately, he lifted his head and our eyes met. He looked dazed for a moment. But quickly it was as if someone shut a door behind his eyes. They turned to ice.

"Don't," he said.

I shrank back onto the mattress. My heart, beating so quickly, stopped cold.

"Don't?" I asked.

"Just don't, okay?" His body tensed and rolled off me. He stood at his side of the bed dragging his hands through his hair. Snapping up his shirt from the bed, he turned and started toward the bathroom.

"What's wrong?" I asked, sitting up and pulling the bed sheet up to my chest.

He paused at the bathroom door and placed his hand on the jamb. He hung his head and shook it.

"Once we leave here," Gabriel said, not facing me. "Once we get off this mountain, I think it's best if we go our separate ways. I'm going back to New York. It's where I belong."

"Okay," I managed, so confused and lost my voice rasped in my throat.

"Okay," he echoed and stepped into the bathroom, closing the door behind him.

# Chapter Twenty-Three

When I woke, a deep-orange sunset glow striped the room. Glancing at the clock, I saw the time and realized I'd slept sixteen hours. The day was surrendering to night again, and I stretched, my muscles coming to life before the aches, and the memories, set in.

I wondered what was happening in Edenton. Our absence would be noticed by now, but probably not felt, at least as far as chores were concerned. It was about the time for dinner service to begin, and Agatha would have recruited two of the younger girls from Sister's sewing cottage to help. Sister would make do. Our absence in the kitchen, Juanita's and mine, would simply be patched over, like adding more dough to a hole when it's stretched too thin.

I glanced to my left to see Gabriel in bed, his back turned to me. I remembered the heat that had built up between us, and how, just as suddenly, he'd cooled. He breathed softly, ribs rising and falling in a languid rhythm. I wondered if my fingers would slide perfectly in the indentations between each rib, how warm he would be to the touch. A quiver went through my stomach. Turning my thoughts away, I slowly swung off the bed and wove my way around it to the bathroom.

"You moan in your sleep."

I whirled. Gabriel's eyes were open, but he still lay on his side, head on the pillow.

"I do not," I answered.

"Oh yes, you do." His gaze was heavy, but not accusing. The air of the room was cool on my legs and I forced myself to keep from pulling down the T-shirt.

"I think the girls in my cottage would have told me," I said.

"Maybe you only moan when you're in bed with me." He sat up, grinning at his innuendo.

"You're ridiculous."

"But you like my brand of ridiculousness, don't you?"

Yes. "No."

"Okay, maybe you weren't moaning exactly. Mewling. More like a—" He made a little whimpering sound.

"Why do you feel the need to tell me this?"

He stood and shrugged. "Just thought it was cute. That's all." Snagging his—Edgar's—shirt off the floor, he tugged it over his head, a couple of the buttons down the front still clasped.

"Next time you think something about me is cute, keep it to yourself."

"No problem." He gave me a quick once-over, then said, "I'm hungry," and made his way out of the room so fast I didn't feel my cheeks warm until after he was gone.

I forced myself to remember Gabriel was broken. Messed up. But I couldn't help feeling he was playing with me. But why? What would be the point of hurting me?

The kitchen was crowded by the time I'd washed up and dressed in more clothes lent by Ibbie: a pair of too-long jeans, rolled up to my ankles, and another simple T-shirt, this one the color of oatmeal. She'd even lent me a bra, which was surprisingly too small, but I wedged myself into it anyway. My feet were bare, cold on the tile floor.

"Good evening, dear," Veronica said as I walked in.

She sat at the round kitchen table, a small glass in her hand filled with a garnet-colored liquid. Ibbie sat to her right, smiling at me and picking at a piece of bread. Gabriel, to her left, hovered over a plate of food. He didn't acknowledge me.

"Good evening," I replied to Veronica. "Sorry I slept so long."

"Oh, don't apologize," she said. "Edgar has made some dinner. He can fix you a plate and we can talk."

"About your proposal?" I asked Veronica.

"Ah, yes." Veronica gestured to an empty chair. "Join us, please."

I sat in a plastic chair. The seat was cold, seeping through the fabric of my borrowed jeans. It was strange. I hadn't felt this kind of cold in a long time. No, I'd felt it recently: in Thaddeus's office. But this wasn't air conditioning, artificial and piercing, it was the clear, pure, cool air of the mountains.

Edgar placed a steaming plate of food in front of me. It was simple fare: grilled chicken, rice, and a side of colorful, chopped-up fruit. My stomach gnawed at the sight. I scooped up the fork as soon as he put it down and dug in.

The room was silent while we ate. I should have been embarrassed, scarfing down the rice in great scoops, but I couldn't help it. I'd been too upset last night to eat. I couldn't believe something as simple as rice could taste like that, with a depth of flavor I'd never created in Edenton. Or maybe I never needed food like this, appreciated food as much as I did now. I never knew real hunger in Edenton. I gulped down ice water and slumped back in my chair, inhaling deeply.

"Good?" Edgar asked.

I nodded, smiling.

Gabriel got up and went to place his dish in the sink. "Thank you for taking us in last night," he said.

"Don't thank us yet," Edgar said.

"We have a favor to ask," Veronica said without preamble.

I snapped my attention to Edgar's face. His thick eyebrows knit over his wide, crooked nose. I wondered if it had been broken.

"All right," Gabriel said. "What's your favor?"

Veronica spoke. "What we showed you last night, the human catalog—"

"Can we not call it that?" I asked.

"Why?" Gabriel asked. "That's what it is, isn't it?"

"Yes, Gabriel," I said slowly, "that's exactly what it is. You're right. Forgive me for not wanting to think of the people I've lived with for six years as something you can order at the click of a button."

"But that's what they are, Mia." He sat back down at the table. "That's what we are."

"Not anymore."

Veronica volleyed glances between us. "Well, then."

Edgar flipped a chair around and straddled it, hanging his heavy arms over the seat back. "It's not just the three of us trying to free our relatives from Edenton. We have a network of people, all with loved ones inside the compound, working with us. We got here and rented this place to be as close as we could without breaking the perimeter boundary and causing suspicion."

"Why all the way up on this mountain, though?"

Edgar glanced at Veronica and Ibbie. Veronica nodded in consent. Then he said, "Why don't we go outside?"

We made our way through a strange little room. A rundown sunroom with a dirty translucent roof and cushioned garden furniture. Along the walls, painted the same color yellow as the rest of the house, hung rustic-looking instruments: dull, rusted machetes, worn leather whips, and horseshoes of different sizes, their opened ends facing up. The sky outside had taken on a burnt-orange sheen that began to darken to twilight. It was such a strange sensation, to wake up so near evening and imagine the whole day passing while I slept.

The air outside was cold, colder than last night when we'd arrived. I wrapped my arms around myself. Behind the house, the patchy yard stretched on until it disappeared over an edge; a sudden drop-off where below a valley carpeted the land to the ocean, lines of trees like fences dividing off sections of land. It was a majestic view.

"Whoa," I whispered.

Gabriel, standing near me, heard and inched closer. "Not afraid of heights, are you Ricci?"

I shook my head. "It's just . . . I haven't seen anything like this in a long time."

"Since we saw Las Casitas from the ridge?"

"That wasn't this high." I turned to him. "It reminds me of the view from the airplane. Before we landed at the airport in San Sebastian when I was ten."

Gabriel's profile was black against the fiery sky. "That's a long time to not see a view."

"There." Veronica pointed into the distance, to a dim jumble of lights. "That's Edenton. And there . . . " she slid her finger through the air " . . . is Las Casitas on the shore."

I watched the lights of Edenton glint beneath the leaves, wondering again what was happening there. Dinner service would be finished, the girls would be cleaning up the kitchen. Mama would be getting Max ready for bed.

"We get it," Gabriel said. "It's a nice view. But I'm not sure how this helps you."

Edgar released a long breath and walked over to a small shed. He dragged out what looked like a telescope on a tripod, but it wasn't long, it was wide and round. He placed it on a wooden platform, three dots painted on its surface to position each of the tripod's legs. Then, from his back pocket, he pulled out a small rectangular device that lit up when he touched a button.

"What is that?" I asked, awed by the brightness of such a small, compact thing.

"A very small computer," Edgar said. "It controls this scope." His fingers skated over the surface of the screen and suddenly the head of the scope twitched and honed in on a target. "It's programmed to focus on specific areas of the compound. We just got this working a week ago." He held out his hand. "Come here, Mia, take a look."

I walked over to the scope, trying to find a viewfinder, but Edgar stopped me.

"No, look here." He swiped his finger across the small screen. An image came into view, blurring in and out before becoming clear.

"That's the pavilion!" I said. The image on the screen wasn't perfect, but I could see the stage of the pavilion, the Reverend's empty throne located in the center, and a few boys straightening the benches, preparing for evening prayer. "That's amazing," I breathed. "What else can you see?"

"Not as much as we would like," Veronica said, taking the tiny computer from me. "The pavilion seems to be on higher ground, as well as what we believe is the laundry, and a few other buildings. But our information is sparse."

"We have someone on the inside," Edgar said. "In Edenton, giving us information."

"Someone on the inside?" I asked, stunned. "You mean someone who lives in Edenton is working with you guys?"

"It's not your brother," said Gabriel.

"Not Eugene, no."

I saw Gabriel swallow a laugh. So childish. It was only a name. A kind of hilarious-sounding name for someone as gruff as Grizz. I fought a smile.

"Who is it then?" I asked.

Edgar's gaze shot to Veronica, then Ibbie. "We can't say," Edgar said. "Concern for that person's safety. But we do have a network of people working with us on the outside. We received the screenshots of the human cata—the website from a politician in this country who's dedicated to our cause. One of his staff has been assisting us, as well as Officer Santiago from the San Sebastian police. Unfortunately, because the Reverend's money-making ventures outside of Edenton contribute so much to the local economy here, the politician is having difficulty convincing the government and law enforcement that the Reverend's activities are illegal."

"It's astonishing, really," Veronica said. "So much corruption at such a high level."

"How lucrative are his businesses?" Gabriel asked.

Ibbie, who'd been quiet until now, finally spoke up. "We believe he has close to $15 million on site, and another forty-five in accounts all over the world."

"Sixty million dollars?" I asked. "Sixty?"

"And that's only what we know about," Ibbie said.

Gabriel gazed at the image on the hand-held computer. He tapped his finger on the surface of the screen and the telescope buzzed.

"Give me that," Edgar said.

Gabriel handed it over reluctantly. "So you have all this stuff, people helping you, what do you need from us? More information?"

Veronica and Edgar exchanged a look. Ibbie sunk into a white plastic chair a few feet away.

"The Reverend has made some very real threats," Edgar said. "When he purchased the land from the government, both parties signed a contract that Edenton would be a municipality under totalitarian rule. Any invasion or show of force against the municipality could be met with equal force—"

"Self-defense," Veronica said. "But the Reverend has his own definition of self-defense."

"The guards are armed," I said. I flashed a glance at Edgar, thinking of Grizz. "They're the only ones who are armed in Edenton."

"Yes, we know," Veronica said. "And that's one way he's said he'd defend Edenton."

I stepped toward her. "What are the other ways?"

"There's only one other way," Ibbie said. She slumped forward, elbows on her knees, hands folded in front of her. She cast a squinty glare out toward the lights of Edenton. In the long shadows of the fading sunset, her face was dusky colored. One dark eye caught the light as she looked back at us. "Before his Flock could be captured or released, he vowed to kill them all."

# Chapter Twenty-Four

"What do you mean, kill everyone in Edenton?" I asked with disbelief. Immediately, my thoughts went to the Bright Night and the poisoned cookies. Was that how he planned to do it? Poison everyone?

Veronica balanced on her cane and hung her head. "Ibbie," she breathed. "There were loads of other ways to tell them about the Reverend's plans."

"They need to know the truth," Ibbie said, standing, "without breaking it to them gently or tiptoeing around it. You keep saying they're children, but you certainly don't plan to treat them that way, do you?"

"Ibbie," Veronica said in a warning tone.

"What does she mean?" Gabriel asked, addressing Veronica with a steely glare. "How exactly do you plan to treat us?"

"Now, now," she said. "Why don't we go back inside and discuss this?"

"What's the difference, Veronica?" Edgar said, his tone sounding low and defeated. "Inside, out. The request is the same."

"Just tell us," I said.

Veronica let out a labored breath. "We need your help. As we said, we have someone on the inside, an informant who has been working with us to leak information, but reports are sporadic. This person can leave the compound occasionally, but not long enough for us to meet up."

"We have new technology," Edgar said. "Although we're able to see into the compound, we can't listen to conversations or understand what exactly is happening."

"I don't like the sound of this," Gabriel said.

"The Reverend is getting sloppy, arrogant." Edgar pocketed the small computer. "He's beginning to change his offerings in the human catalog."

Ice crackled over my bones. "What do you mean, change?"

"For years, he'd offered to sell teenagers and the state of their purity," Veronica said.

"Virginity, you mean," said Gabriel in a dull tone.

"Yes, right." Veronica nodded quickly. "The subjects were always fifteen or older. But he's finding there are people who will pay exorbitant amounts for encounters with much younger members of the Flock."

I felt my jaw slacken. "How much younger?"

"We don't know right now," she said. "Our belief is if the customer can pay the asking price, the subject is given willingly, possibly regardless of age."

"But it hasn't happened yet," I said.

"No, we believe they are still gauging interest," she said. "The subject is taboo, and although selling the virginity of teenagers is—believe it or not—a more accepted practice, the selling of younger children may not be something they are willing to advertise yet."

I thought of Max, only six. And the rest of the children in the schoolhouse—innocent and wondrous with a lifetime ahead of them to discover cruelty and depravity.

"What does this have to do with us?" Gabriel asked.

Edgar pulled a couple of chairs from a stack by the shed. "Why don't you sit down?"

"No one ever asks you to sit down before delivering good news," Gabriel mumbled, sliding into the chair.

I followed, sitting in the seat next to his.

The sun had finally slipped below the horizon. Evening descended upon us, the damp air carrying the cold from the recesses between the trees. Edgar folded up the telescope, placing it back into the shed. Ibbie threaded her fingers through each other nervously, over and over, as if finding the right position for her hands to deliver a prayer.

Veronica, however, still stood with the handle of her cane clutched in her fist, knuckles paling.

"We need to know what is happening inside the compound," she said. "When the Reverend plans to begin offering the younger children for sale, and how he's decided to kill the Flock in the event of an attack on the compound."

Edgar leaned back against the shed, shoving his hands into the pockets of his shorts. "We had planned to attack Edenton and rescue the Flock a year and a half ago," he said. "But we lost the support of the U.S. government because of lack of evidence."

"Lack of evidence?" Gabriel said, disgusted. "Isn't it obvious that what's going on there is illegal?"

"Up until recently, no," said Edgar. "With the leak of the website we now have undisputed evidence of sex trafficking. But we suspect that there's so much more. Forms of bonded labor, child labor."

"What do you want from us?" Gabriel asked with a hint of impatience. "We have information, but it sounds like you know a lot already. If you need maps of Edenton, or schedules, Mia has been there for over six years, she can provide that kind of information."

"Yes, well, that information would be helpful, but we need to know what the Reverend will do if we invade Edenton. How will he react to an invasion, what fail-safes does he have in place to follow through on his threat to destroy the Flock?"

"I don't understand," I said. "Why kill everyone?"

"If there's no one left alive in Edenton, there's no one left to testify against him."

"But he'd be guilty of murder!"

"He would," Veronica said. "So he must have a means to absolve himself from any responsibility. Perhaps he's planning on finding a scapegoat for his actions." She took in a breath and let it out slowly. "We need to have more information in order to formulate a strategy."

An awful, oily blackness sank into my chest. "You want us to go back. You want us to find out the Reverend's plans so you can storm Edenton—"

"And save the Flock."

Gabriel barked a disbelieving laugh. "You're out of your minds. We just got out of that hellhole."

Ignoring Gabriel, Veronica took a step toward me, her cane sinking in the soft turf. "Think of your relatives, Mia. Your friends. The people you've spent the last six years living with, taking meals with, praying with—"

"Stop!" I said, jumping to my feet. "Just stop."

Everyone sank into silence. Edgar busied himself with his pockets. Ibbie, still hunched over in the chair, dropped her forehead in her hands. Veronica traced patterns on the top of her cane with her index finger. Gabriel, however, looked up at me, searing emotion in his blue-green eyes. I couldn't tell if it was disgust, disbelief, or determination.

My head swirled with words and phrases, blinding me with shocked horror.

Human trafficking.

Slave labor.

Prostitution.

Murder.

No, not simply murder. Mass murder.

"All of this can't be true," I said.

"It is, dear," Veronica said.

"No. You don't understand. Edenton may not be perfect, but it is a society of people who love and care for each other—"

"They're not talking about the Flock," Gabriel snapped. "They're talking about the Reverend. He's doing this to his own people."

"But—"

"Mia," said Edgar, "don't let how you've spent the last few years keep you blind to what is going on in Edenton. We aren't lying to you about this."

"All those people," I said. "How could this happen and no one knows it?"

I gazed at the lights of Edenton again—lights that could be extinguished in an instant, at the Reverend's whim. I took off toward the house, bare feet slapping against the cold grass. I wanted to crawl back into that soft bed, curl up in the quilted blanket. Slip back into that long, dreamless sleep.

*Back to Edenton.* I'd only barely escaped. And only by luck. It wasn't part of a plan I'd cleverly put together. It wasn't as if I'd snuck away in a delivery truck or broken my own arm so I could be air-lifted to San Sebastian. It was just dumb luck.

Now I was free but where would I go? How could I settle into a new life? Find a place to live and get a job cooking in a restaurant? But how could I move on with my life, be a citizen of a world I didn't know, leaving behind a world I wished I didn't, and all the while wonder about the people I'd left behind? I'd assumed if I left, Edenton would go on as usual: routines and rituals, prayers and provisioning.

But now I knew the truth. And any threat against the Reverend was a threat against the Flock.

Out of the corner of my vision, I saw Gabriel in the doorway. I hadn't realized it, but I had come directly to the bathroom and slumped on the tiled floor, my back against the tub.

"They're afraid to come in here," Gabriel said. "They think they pushed you too far."

I only nodded.

He squatted down across from me. "But they didn't push you too far, did they? Because the only way you'd feel pushed is if you were actually considering going back to Edenton. Which you're not."

I examined a broken tile near my bare foot.

"Mia?"

"My brother Max is six years old."

"I know."

"What if they drug him up, like they did us, and send him to Las Casitas? What if someone like Lambert gets his hands on Max and . . ." The rest was too horrifying to comprehend, let alone say.

Gabriel sunk down to the floor. "How do we even know what Veronica and Edgar are telling us is the truth? They may have their own reasons for wanting to send you back in there." He paused. "What if they work for the Reverend?"

The idea caused my breath to catch. I shot to my feet and paced the floor, heart beating too fast. I thought of Officer Santiago chasing after us in the streets of San Sebastian. I thought of Ibbie's instantaneous need to clean and bandage my legs, the concern and worry dragging through her features. Of Veronica's excitement upon our arrival, of Edgar's rough manner, so much like his brother's.

"They don't work for the Reverend, Gabriel. All they want to do is save the people they love. They don't want them to die."

"Of course not."

"But I know how to stop him from killing them all. The cookies, from the Bright Night—I know where Agatha keeps the poison. In a locked provisions pantry in the kitchen."

I stopped and placed my hands on the edge of the sink. I looked at my reflection in the cracked mirror, a sliver of silver bifurcating my drawn face. Who was that girl staring back at me? Green eyes dulled, skin sallow and scratched, brown hair lank and straggling? She appeared beaten and exhausted. But more than that, what happened to her spirit?

Had it fizzled out, like a snuffed blaze that had once burned so brightly it lit the way forward, lit the way out?

I twisted around, my back against the sink.

Gabriel, still on the floor, gazed up at me, and shook his head. "You're not going back in."

\* \* \*

I needed sleep. If I was going to return to Edenton, I needed a clear mind. But the more anxious I was to sleep, the more awake I became. I turned onto my back, tightening the covers around me. Tonight, I was alone in the bed. Gabriel decided to sleep in Edgar's room, bear-like snores and all.

Sick of tossing and turning, I flipped off the covers, dragged on Ibbie's jeans, and shoved my feet into borrowed sneakers. Stripping the blanket off the bed, I wrapped it around me and made my way outside.

Stepping out of the sunroom's back door, the grass beneath my shoes crunched, and I looked down. In the light thrown from the eaves of the house, the grass glistened. Frost. I didn't remember ever seeing frost except in the freezer in the Edenton kitchen. I plucked a blade of grass and placed it in my mouth, the little crystals of ice melting immediately.

The night air was different up on the mountain. No heaviness, no oppressive humidity leached the energy from my skin. I took in a deep breath and dipped my head back. Above me, the stars glinted in the pitch-black sky with unwavering persistence. Without that darkness, the stars couldn't shine.

In the valley below, the lights of Edenton blinked through the trees and those of Las Casitas, overly bright, as if spotlights shown on the buildings. I stepped a little closer to the edge to see if I could make out what was happening.

"They're rebuilding," came a voice from behind me and I jumped.

Gabriel came up next to me. He wore a large hooded sweatshirt, his hands fisted in the kanga-pocket in the front. "From the fire," he said. "They're rebuilding what I burned down."

"What you burned down?"

"That night at Las Casitas, I started the fires. They didn't put different shoes on me when they changed our clothes while we were drugged. I had my lighter hidden in the heel of my boot."

"Why are they rebuilding at night, though?" I asked.

"I would imagine they're doing it 'round the clock. They have a business to run, money to make, people to sell."

We stood in silence overlooking the valley below, watching the lights dance in the distance.

"Don't go," Gabriel said in a low voice.

I turned to him, but said nothing.

He blinked, and looked down at his shoes. He toed the frost. "We're free, Mia. This is what you've wanted for years. To be out of Edenton. To live your life, not the Reverend's idea of what your life should be. Now you're going back with some twisted idea that you can save two hundred people from certain death?"

When he put it that way, the whole idea suddenly seemed absurd. Any confidence I'd bolstered began to deflate.

Gabriel glanced up at the sky. "Our parents put us in that place. It wasn't our choice. But this is. You get to choose, Mia, how you want your life to be. The power of choice is a basic human right."

"Not for everyone," I said.

"No, not for everyone. But make the right choice for the people who don't have the ability to make their own choices. Choose for them."

"What about your parents?" I asked.

"What about them?"

"You want to leave them there, in Edenton, wondering where you are? What happened to you?"

He shrugged. "Maybe. And maybe they deserve whatever happens to them."

"You can't be serious. Knowing what we know now—you'd really let them die at the hands of the Reverend?"

"They dragged me to Edenton against my will," he spit out.

"I'll let them know you're okay when I see them," I said.

Gabriel grabbed my arms. "You can't do this. It's suicide. Thaddeus saw us running from him. He'll know something is going on with you. What if he shoots you on sight? And what about Juanita? If she survives, don't you think she'll tell everyone that you and I were running away that night?"

"I can only hope she's still alive," I said quietly.

"Quit being a goddamn martyr, Mia." His grip grew tighter. His eyes were fierce. "You go back in there, you're not coming out. At least not alive."

"Why do you even care?" I asked him. "You don't care what happens to your parents. Why would you care about what happens to me?"

He remained silent.

"You're free too, Gabriel." I wrenched myself from his grip. "Free to make your own choices, so go and make them."

He stepped back, his expression cooling, and walked back to the house, leaving me standing in the frost.

# Chapter Twenty-Five

The tattered green dress hung on me like seaweed, damp and musty, straggled over the scabs on my knees. Ibbie sat at my feet, legs curled under her, gently peeling the bandages from my legs. We were gathered in the room I'd been sleeping in, standing next to the bed neatly made by Veronica moments before.

"This is going to hurt a little bit," Ibbie said as she used alcohol to wipe away the remnants of adhesive.

It stung, but the nerves jumbling in my stomach chased away the piercing pain.

"These are microphones," Edgar said, placing a handful of tiny plastic boxes on the bed. Inside each was a small circular device. "Each has adhesive on one side, a magnet on the other. Make sure you put them in places they cannot be spotted."

"Right, of course," I said. "How am I going to smuggle them in?"

"We'll put them in your bra," Veronica said. "Turn around, Edgar."

He faced the wall, hands folded in front of him. I stood like a statue, afraid to move, as Veronica unwrapped the front of my dress and placed the microphones inside the cups of my bra.

"When you get into Edenton, our informant will contact you," Edgar said.

Ibbie finished with my legs and gingerly placed the flat, tight shoes I'd worn back on my feet. If possible, they seemed even tighter. The leather dug into my heels like the edges of glass.

"Officer Santiago will drop you off on the service road to Las Casitas," Edgar said. "Wait a little bit before you start down the road and either you'll make it to Casitas or a worker will pick you up and bring you in."

"You remember the service road?" Veronica asked. "You said that couple picked you and Gabriel up there."

"Of course." The sound of his name was like a punch to my stomach.

After we'd argued outside last night, he left the house for the rest of the night. I suspected he'd snuck back in, sleeping in one of the green lounge chairs in the living room, but left again before dawn.

"Returning to Las Casitas makes the most sense. You've never been outside Edenton, correct?" Veronica asked.

"No, I haven't." I squirmed as the microphones folded uncomfortably beneath my breasts.

"Good," she said. "Then you wouldn't know how to get there if you were lost in the jungle. Close to where they were tracking you makes the most sense."

With the microphones in place, Veronica patted my breasts. My face felt instantly hot. It was a maternal kind of pat, but my breasts didn't get a lot of touching, let alone patting. By a woman. A proper English woman. Wearing a rose-print blouse.

"Turn," she said to Edgar.

"Mia," Edgar said. "I know this is additional pressure on you, but it's imperative you tell them you don't remember anything, understand? You woke up in the jungle, alone, unsure how you got there. No matter what, you must never let them know you remember."

I nodded. "Understood."

Veronica enveloped my hands in hers and dragged her watery gaze to mine. "You can't imagine," she said, "how much this means. How we've struggled for years for this kind of opportunity. We've tried to send people into Edenton to become members of the Flock so they could help us, but all were turned away because the Reverend or members of his ministry became suspicious."

Ibbie, Edgar, and Veronica all stared at me standing there in that dress I'd once imagined as beautiful. My tongue felt thick in my mouth. I wasn't sure what they wanted me to say.

"You're their Obi-Wan," a familiar voice said from the doorway.

We all turned. It was Gabriel, looking like he'd been trudging through the wilderness. Mud splattered his legs. His—Edgar's—shorts were torn at the hem. His hair was mussed and his green-blue eyes were half-opened and lined in red. He raked them over me in a way that sent shivers over my skin.

"What do you mean Obi-Wan?" I asked.

"You, Mia Ricci, are their only hope."

* * *

Gravel crunched under my feet. The midday sun seemed to pierce my exposed skin, like it never had before in Edenton. This sunlight was different, harsher. It stirred the fear and nerves, and my skin burned with anxiety. I didn't care about the Reverend and his lackeys, but the people of Edenton were the ones who'd be sacrificed if I failed. If the Reverend was to mete out revenge for this betrayal, I hoped it wouldn't be on them. But neither did I want to be a martyr as Gabriel had said.

I'd been walking for about an hour before I heard the rumble of a truck behind me. I turned. A large truck carrying lumber approached, and I flagged it down. The truck rolled to a stop. An older man in a worn straw hat sat behind the wheel. He gazed down at me with a confused expression on his face, lines sketched deeply in his sun-browned skin.

"Can you help me?" I asked in Spanish. "I'm lost."

"Lost?" the man asked. "All the way out here? Where are you from?"

"Edenton," I said.

He removed his hat. Sweat trickled down his brow and he mopped it with a folded red kerchief. "You live in Edenton?"

"Yes," I said and went on to explain how I'd awakened in the jungle, in strange clothes, unsure of where I was. I kept talking, adding in details I might or might not remember later. I finally told myself to shut up.

"I can take you to Edenton," he said, not without trepidation. "But I don't want to be involved. I'll take you as far as the gates."

The last time I'd seen the gates of Edenton from the outside, I was awed by the intricacies of the grillwork. It swirled and curlicued like leaves of the Tree of Knowledge, bearing perfectly formed fruit. Then, it had been beautiful and glimmering in the golden afternoon sun. Now, I wondered why they needed to have such an ostentatious gate, a magnificent corral to confine us? Was it to seduce us into thinking we were safe and loved?

I climbed out of the truck and thanked the man. Just outside the gates, a guard stood in the small surveillance house. It was Freddie.

"Mia!" he said, coming toward me. "What happened to you?"

"I—I don't know. Can you please open the gates and let me back in?"

I wished the tears that formed in my eyes weren't genuine. I wished they were part of the act I'd been asked to play. But fear, and misplaced relief, caused a tear to track down my cheek.

"One minute."

Instead of opening the gates, he went back to the surveillance house and called in on his radio. I couldn't hear what he was saying, his words were muffled by the harsh caws of the birds sweeping above.

I wrapped my arms around my waist, trying to calm the churning in my stomach. Freddie kept glancing back at me as he spoke into the radio. There was no one else in sight. The Edenton entry gate was at the end of a driveway that wound through the trees, away from the encampment itself, so there was no one passing by who could see me standing there ragged and misplaced. No witnesses to see that I'd made it back alive.

Freddie walked back to me, hitching up the gun holster over his shoulder. "You need to wait here, Mia. I can't let you back in."

For a moment I froze in fear, eyes locked on his. Finally, I said, "Freddie, this is my home. I need to be inside. I . . . I want to see my mom."

"Thaddeus said to wait here. I'm sorry, Mia. I really am." He glanced at my shredded clothes, the healing cuts on my legs. "Come inside and sit."

Slowly, I walked on unstable legs over to the little guardhouse by the gate. I tripped, and Freddie took me by the arm.

"You okay?"

"Just need to eat," I lied, fear coursing through me in such a rush I could barely stand. Why wouldn't he let me into Edenton?

Inside the guardhouse he motioned to a stool and I sat, eyeing the intricate radio on the desk before me.

"Lots of buttons," I said to fill the silence.

Freddie nodded. "Took a while to figure out how to use it. Just a glorified phone."

Outside, I heard the sound of tires skidding to a stop. We left the booth to see Thaddeus hopping from the driver's seat of a Jeep, moving with the predatory grace of a wolf.

"That was fast," Freddie said.

Thaddeus stormed to me. "Not a word about her being here to anyone," he said to Freddie, pointing his long finger. "Understand me?"

"Yes sir," Freddie said.

"You," he said to me. "Keep your mouth shut and get in the car."

I did as he said. Anxiety and terror blurred my vision as we took a dirt road I'd never seen before, one that led around to the back of Edenton.

I wanted to hang my head outside the car and vomit. What was he going to do, shoot me?

We stopped at a much humbler gate made of wood and wire. He pressed a button on the dashboard and the gate swung open like a great pair of wings. Thaddeus, angrily brooding during the entire ride, parked the Jeep in a spot next to a small, concrete building. We both got out. A winding path through the trees led to the back entrance of another building, but it wasn't until I was inside that I realized it was his cottage.

The second I walked in, my skin burned with the cold; the air inside felt weighty and thick.

"Sit down," he said, gesturing to the chairs in front of his desk.

The chill of the chair seeped through the thin material of my dress, causing me to shiver. I'd thought about how I was going to handle this moment, but my mind went blank with fear. I blindly watched as he lowered himself into the chair behind his desk and clasped his hands in front of him, spindly fingers twining. For long moments, we said nothing, my heart pounding so furiously I was sure he could hear it.

"Well?" he said, the planes of his face stark with anger.

I inhaled, trying to focus. What was I supposed to say?

*Act like you don't remember anything.*

"How did I get out there?" I asked him, hearing the words as if from a distance.

The tension in his face visibly drained. "What do you mean, Mia?"

I was so afraid he would see through me, know I was lying, that I began to shake. Slowly, the story I'd rehearsed in my head after Santiago dropped me off came back to me. "How did I get out there?" I said. "In the middle of the jungle, wearing clothes I'd never seen before? What happened after Prayer Circle? You know, don't you? I was there, in the Reverend's cottage, then—" I threw up my hands. "I woke up on the side of some road, wearing this—" I tugged at the collar of the dress. "I was so scared, Thaddeus. So scared!" I dropped my face into my hands, so nervous that he'd see through my story, I couldn't look at him any longer.

"Really?" he said. "You simply woke up in the jungle, lost and confused?"

I nodded, hands still over my face. He didn't believe me. Tears began welling in my eyes. I wiped them away with my fingertips and looked down at my shoes, then eyed the door.

"Mia, you have caused many issues over the last few weeks."

"I know." I met his stern glare. "I'm sorry."

"Are you? I'm surprised. You never showed any real remorse before."

"I've never been alone on the outside before. Never been so afraid and alone. Edenton is my home, Thaddeus."

He stared at me for long moments through squinted lids. I stared back. Strands of hair dangled over my eyes, and with every beat of my heart I saw them tremble.

His hand reached for the phone, arm stretching across the desk, not losing eye contact with me. "Gladstone," he said. "I have an emergency."

By the time Doc Gladstone came to collect me from Thaddeus's office, I'd been thoroughly frozen through, both by the air conditioning and by Thaddeus's icy demeanor. He hadn't said a word to me after my bawling confession and I was too afraid to elaborate on my story. He handed me off to Doc Gladstone as if I were nothing more than a dirty bag of laundry to be cleaned and pressed.

"Take care of this," Thaddeus said to Doc Gladstone. "Use whatever meds you need to put her mind at ease." He pinned me with a hard stare.

A pit of dread settled in my stomach. I didn't like how that sounded.

Doc Gladstone gave me a warm smile after Thaddeus shut the door. "We can talk once we get to the infirmary, but first we need to get you there without anyone seeing you like this."

"But how?" I asked. We were still inside the gates of the Reverend's protected village, but the infirmary was located close to the center of Edenton.

"We'll take the tunnels," Doc Gladstone said.

"Tunnels?"

Doc Gladstone led me back down the path I'd followed to Thaddeus's cottage, to where the Jeep was still parked inside the wood-and-wire gate.

"Here," he said.

We stood before the little concrete building I'd seen before. He pressed the numbers 123456. After he punched the numbers into a keypad above the door handle, it beeped and swung open. A light blinked on. Inside a set of stairs led down two levels. The concrete was clean, untouched by the quick decay of the jungle surrounding the building.

"Where are we?" I asked.

Doc Gladstone sighed, as if he didn't approve of where we were. "Beneath Edenton is a series of tunnels, built when the water and sewer systems were put in place."

"What are they used for?"

"Getting around the encampment undetected," he said as he descended the stairs. "This is something the Flock knows nothing about, Mia. And I trust you can keep quiet about this."

"You have my word," I said, showing Doc Gladstone the respect he'd earned from me over the years.

The tunnel snaked along, lit intermittently by caged lightbulbs along the ceiling. It smelled dank, like the basement of the house where I lived when I was young. Every thirty feet or so the tunnel forked, with no sign or indication where the other branch led that I could see.

"How do you know where you're going?" I asked Doc Gladstone. My voice echoed off the concrete walls.

He pointed to a series of small circles on the wall, spaced the same distance away from each other as the lights shining above. Each circle was divided into four sections, the upper left section filled with blue, the other three left blank. "This tunnel is leading northwest, toward the northwest section of Edenton, where the infirmary is located. If the tunnel were leading directly north, then the line at the top of the circle, pointing north, would be colored blue. If it were leading southeast, then the lower right section would be colored in, and so forth." He pointed to the wall on the other side of the tunnel. "The symbols are reversed there, so if you were coming the opposite way, you'd be traveling southeast. Keep to the right to know which direction you're traveling."

"Why not simply have signs saying where each tunnel is going?"

"If necessity is the mother of invention, paranoia is the father."

Finally, we made it to another set of stairs. The metal handrail chilled the skin of my palm. When Doc Gladstone opened the door at the top, we emerged through a closet in the infirmary, the smell of alcohol and adhesive permeating the air.

"Take one of the exam tables," he said as he gathered some supplies from a cabinet.

The weight of my nervousness made it difficult to walk without wobbling a little. Trying to get my breathing under control, I sat at the edge of one of the tables, feet dangling. To my right, within arm's reach, a series of instruments lay neatly on a tray. One with a long handle and a short blade looked very sharp.

"So," he said, approaching me. "Let's take a look at the cuts on your legs before we address the state of your mind, shall we?"

My legs. I'd forgotten. Ibbie had removed the bandages, but surely he'd noticed the cuts and scrapes were cleaned, most healing properly. If I'd awakened in the jungle, like I'd claimed, infection would have set in by now.

"You know, they're fine," I said, tucking one leg under myself. "I washed them off with some river water."

Doc Gladstone's eyes rounded in surprise. "River water?" Before I could pull the other away, he knelt down and grabbed my calf, examining the scabbing skin. "River water could not clean the cuts so neatly, Mia." His eyes flicked up to mine. "But it is good to see that Ibbie hasn't lost her touch."

# Chapter Twenty-Six

"I've been working with the outside network for months now," Doc Gladstone said quietly. He stood then, glancing about the infirmary. The silence in the room cocooned us in an eerie but explicit kind of privacy.

"You know what happened with us?" I asked. "At Las Casitas? On the mountain?"

He nodded. "I was sent to Las Casitas that night to help anyone wounded in the fire." He cocked a little grin. "But there were none. Only hysterical wealthy folks worried about their possessions. Thaddeus told me you, Gabriel, and Juanita had run. Veronica sent me a message yesterday. I knew to expect you back."

"But how could she send you a message?"

Doc Gladstone walked to a large bookshelf tucked into the corner of the room. He drew his finger over one row of slender books with white spines.

"Because I'm not allowed access to medical journals online, they're delivered in print weekly. All items that come into Edenton are scanned by an X-ray machine, so the network sends messages inside the journals as footnotes." He smiled faintly. "No one reads footnotes."

My mouth hung open in shock. "I'm having trouble comprehending this," I said. "I mean, I get it. You're helping the network—"

"I'm part of the network."

"But—why are you doing this? You're here in Edenton, aren't you? You came here for a reason."

"When I came here I believed in what the Reverend had to offer. A self-governing, utopian society, bound by respect and love. The Reverend was idealistic and hopeful, but began to change as the idea of Edenton as a self-sufficient community began to falter. Funds dwindled and the jungle began to conspire against us in its inherent ways. The Reverend brought in Thaddeus to help manage and grow Edenton.

"The encampment itself began to transform—buildings were renovated, expensive equipment was added to the kitchen, to the infirmary, to the security of the grounds. The guards began to patrol. I'd never seen a gun until the Edenton sentinel was assembled. The Reverend shut himself off from the Flock within his own secured zone. What was once a transparent council of leadership became a cloistered ministry of secrets. During that time, Thaddeus never left the Reverend's side. He counseled him on everything, from what he ate to the content of his sermons. The Reverend grew more obsessed with power, taking Edenton to the next level. And, as this happened, I was contacted by the network."

"Aren't you afraid of getting caught?"

"I'm afraid every day." Doc Gladstone rolled a stool over to sit beside me. "I took an oath, and part of that oath states that I remain a member of society with special obligations to all my fellow human beings. Edenton is a society, Mia, regardless of how it's changed. And what is happening here, how the Reverend is exploiting these people, must be stopped. Until now I've been at this alone on the inside."

With a surprising feeling of dread, I realized he now had me to help, to figure out how to save the Flock. Just me.

"Do you know about the Reverend's threat against the Flock?" I asked. "How he's planning to kill everyone if there is an attack on Edenton?"

"I do." He rubbed his palm on his forehead, then down the back of his dreadlocks. "But the Reverend, Thaddeus, and the rest of the ministry know my passion for healing. Anytime I get close to finding out the Reverend's plan to thwart rescue attempts by the outside, I'm shut out."

Passion for healing.

"So, Juanita? Is Juanita alive?" I asked.

"They haven't told me where she is. All they told me is to expect her return soon."

"Will she live?"

"They didn't tell me." He looked at me with sorrow in his eyes.

I rubbed my temple with my index finger, trying to focus and not worry about Juanita. "What was the rest of Edenton told?" I asked. "About what happened to us?"

"At morning prayer yesterday, the Reverend told the congregation that you were on a special undertaking for the Flock with the poorer communities outside of San Sebastian. He asked for prayers for your success, and left it at that."

I thought of Mama, of Max, of Juanita's mother. No one left Edenton, except for Doc Gladstone to go to the hospital in San Sebastian and a few others to go into the city for supplies. They must have suspected something was wrong. Or were they too far under the Reverend's spell to question our whereabouts?

I needed to find a way to let Gabriel's parents know he was all right. Stubborn as hell, determined to move on from Edenton, but all right. Or was it my place to do so? If Gabriel didn't care whether his parents died by the hands of the Reverend, would he care if they knew about how he was doing? That, somehow, he would be okay?

Doc Gladstone sat hunched over on the stool, eyes half-closed with a haggard kind of tiredness.

"What do we do now?" I asked him.

He exhaled and glanced at a cabinet. "Once you get changed into your uniform, I'll need to give you a shot." He gave me an apologetic look.

"What is the shot for?" I asked.

"Thaddeus is going to debrief you. The drug I should give you would make you very open to suggestion, make insinuations memories, so you can return into Edenton with a clear mind and an open heart."

"Should give me?" I asked, feeling anger rise in me. "You've been giving these drugs to the Flock all along? How could you do that to these people you claim to love?"

"Either I give them the drugs, or they die for what they remember." He shook his head sadly. "Death or the drugs. The choice was simple for me, Mia. Now, we must take care of you."

"I can't let you do that," I said, eyeing the scalpel on the tray next to me.

"I know." The corner of his mouth kicked up. "And I wouldn't do it to you. Not now that you're going to help the network."

"The network. Sounds so official."

"In a way, it is. We have very significant people trying to help the cause. And you, Mia, are our linchpin."

"I'm not sure I like the sound of that."

"Well, first things first. We need to prep you for a debriefing by Thaddeus."

A tremble started in my limbs. "Do you mean he's going to interview me?"

"In a way. He'll suggest to you how you ended up back in Edenton, what happened the night of the Prayer Circle, where you were during that time, understand?"

I nodded. "Does the real drug work?"

"Does it work? No one has ever told us it hasn't because if they did, if they remembered what happened at Las Casitas and discussed it—questioned it— they would be punished. And everyone fears punishment."

"Punishment? Like Contrition? Heavy labor?" I asked, recalling Gabriel's penance in the heap.

Doc Gladstone filled a syringe with a clear liquid, flicked it once, and gingerly placed it on the tray next to me. "The Reverend is not a forgiving man, regardless of the teachings of the Lord's scripture." He sat back down and folded his arms. "In Ecclesiastes, it is claimed that lack of punishment leads people into evil. The Reverend uses the Bible's lessons in penance as models for torture. Days of hard labor, like on the heap, is one thing. Slicing a man's legs and arms, then packing him in salt to suffer stinging pain is quite another." At my look of horror he added, "A twisted translation of Lot's wife's punishment. Now go clean yourself up. You'll find a uniform dress in the bathroom. And hurry, Thaddeus will be here any moment."

I undressed and swiftly removed the tiny microphones from my bra. Then I quickly showered and changed into the uniform laid out on the counter by the sink. I took a tiny microphone, removed it from its small plastic case, and slipped it into the pocket of my dress. The other microphones went back into the clean sports bra I usually wore. By the time I'd returned to the exam room, Thaddeus stood by Doc Gladstone's bookshelf, skimming the titles on the spines as Doc Gladstone looked on nervously.

"So much to study up on, eh Gladstone?" Thaddeus said.

"Yes, must keep current. Perhaps if I could use a computer to access the medical journals there would be no need to kill so many trees."

Thaddeus tsked. "Have you looked around? There's an abundance of trees. We drown in them every day. We spend so much on manpower to keep them from encroaching upon Edenton—" His eyes snapped up and saw me standing in the doorway, neatly dressed in my Edenton uniform. "Mia."

"Thaddeus," I said, nodding once. I took my place on an exam table.

"Much calmer now, are you?" he asked me but looked at Doc Gladstone.

Doc Gladstone shook his head, indicating he hadn't given me the drug. The syringe alone lay on the tray; the sharp instruments that had been lined up alongside it were gone. Perhaps Doc Gladstone worried I'd do something rash to Thaddeus. He wasn't wrong to worry.

"Let's move on with this," Thaddeus said. "The Reverend has decided to join us once the procedure has begun."

"The Reverend?" Doc Gladstone asked with an unsteady pitch to his voice. He inclined his head toward Thaddeus, who still eyed the medical journals with a certain curiosity. "He rarely attends these sessions."

"This is a special circumstance." His slipped a book from the shelf and traced his fingers over the spine as if it were the handle of a knife. "Mia, I take it the doctor has explained what will be happening?"

I nodded. I wasn't sure what I was supposed to say. Was I to admit that I knew he would be suggesting new memories through the medication?

"Very well. Doctor, please administer the medication."

Doc Gladstone approached the exam table with a stunted gait, perhaps realizing he hadn't told me what to say when Thaddeus arrived. With his back to Thaddeus, he said, "Now, Mia, as we discussed, this medication will relax you and help you remember what happened to you. Why you ended up in the jungle." His dark brown eyes widened a fraction.

So that was it. I was supposed to think the medication would help me regain my memories, when really, through Thaddeus's suggestions, it would wash them away like a wave eroding footsteps in the sand.

Again, I nodded, deciding that remaining mute was my best defense. The needle went into my arm with a sharp stab. I looked away as the clear liquid shot into my arm, deep under the skin. Almost immediately, I felt a wave of dizziness and swayed on the table.

"Easy there," Doc Gladstone said, grabbing my shoulder. "Just lie here for a moment."

As if I could do much else. The edges of the room became unfocused, prism-like colors moving in a twisting rainbow. I felt as if my body melted into the examination table beneath me, shoulders slouching, head listing to the side. Frantic thoughts raced through my brain: Is this the real drug?

"Can you hear me, Mia?" Doc Gladstone asked.

Of course I could. I could hear everything. In fact, despite how my body sagged, I could think clearly as well. I gave Doc Gladstone a weak dip of my chin to acknowledge I heard what he was saying.

Thaddeus slid the book he'd been holding back between the other white spines with a push of his index finger. He came over and sat on the stool next to the exam table. I tried to keep my eyes focused on the ceiling.

His voice was soothing, quiet. "The other night, you went to Prayer Circle. You devoted yourself to prayer, to readings from the Bible, to the Reverend's own teachings. You remember this, yes Mia?"

"Yes."

"Then, you stayed late, not wanting the evening to end. It was a joyful occasion. The Reverend complied, allowing you, Gabriel, and Juanita to continue on in silent meditation all night long."

At the mention of Juanita's name, I forced myself to remain still, face placid.

"The next morning," Thaddeus said, "the three of you, so enlightened by the experience, dedicated your time at the Reverend's cottage to packing boxes of food and necessities for the needy in the nearby villages."

"That was nice of us," I said, unable to keep from mocking the ridiculous scenario.

There was a pause. Suspicion perhaps? Dread swept over me.

Then he said, "Yes, it was. So nice, in fact, that you delivered the boxes of supplies yourselves and stayed to help the families. Understand?"

"Yes," I replied automatically.

"Very well."

There was another long pause. I listened for movement, for whispering, but the only sound was the sharp cawing of the birds outside.

"Juanita and Gabriel," Thaddeus said with volume that jolted me from my concentration, "remained behind in one of the villages outside San Sebastian."

Even under the influence of the drug, my lips twitched with anger, but I said, "Yes. Stayed behind."

The door creaked, breaking the intensity of my rage, as the Reverend entered the room.

"Good afternoon, Mia," he said pleasantly. He wore a long blue shirt, crisp and dry, over long khaki-colored pants. His red beard had recently been trimmed, close to his face, making him appear younger, friendlier.

"Good afternoon," I slurred.

"Ah, regaining your memories, I see," he said.

I tried to nod, but my body felt so sluggish.

"Thaddeus," the Reverend said, slightly turning his large torso toward Thaddeus. "We've had another development." He smiled at me. "A joyous development."

Immediately, my thoughts went to Juanita. Was she out of danger, returning from the hospital here to Edenton? I wanted to jump off the exam table and find her, let her know I didn't mean to abandon her, didn't want to, but I didn't have much choice.

"Grizz," the Reverend called.

Grizz shouldered his way through the door, dragging someone behind him. When he deposited Gabriel on the floor, my heart beat furiously, despite the calming drug pulsing through my system. With shocked awe, I whispered his name.

The Reverend smiled down at him. "We're so pleased to have you back here, son."

Gabriel, dressed in the same torn and dirtied clothes he wore the night we'd escaped Las Casitas, tilted his head up to glare at the Reverend. He looked very tired; the exhaustion, though, exaggerated the fierceness of his features. I couldn't rip my gaze away from his face, both surprised by his presence here and fascinated by his beauty, like the time he'd approached me in the kitchen, his first night in Edenton. But I knew my fascination was like being fascinated by a sharp piece of glittering, broken glass.

Finally, Gabriel spoke. When he did so, he looked directly at me as I lay still on the exam table. "I'd say I'm pleased to be back, Reverend, but the reality is I'm only here because I make terrible choices."

# Chapter Twenty-Seven

With the help of Nurse Ivy, whom I could barely look at without confronting her for what she'd done to me at Las Casitas, I was taken to Doc Gladstone's office to recover—but not before planting the microphone from my pocket in a lip below the exam table as the others turned their attention to Gabriel.

Two hours later, I'd made it back to my cottage on my own. A few members of the Flock nodded at me as I walked by, staring at me with curiosity lighting their eyes, but no one said anything to me, no one asked any questions.

Because it was early evening, the girls in my cottage were at dinner prep. I splayed out on my bunk, noting the hardness of the mattress, and hoped I could keep up my acting and lies. The network was going to invade to save their loved ones. That was certain. How many people would die in the process, though, was what tugged at my soul.

I slid off the bed and made my way to the bathroom. With the tips of my fingers, I lifted the edge of the mirror over the sink. It came away easily. I slipped my hand in to find my sketchbook wedged between the mirror and the wall. I carefully took it out and wiped my fingerprints from the corner of the glass.

I sat back on my bunk. My nubby pencil was still shoved between the pages. I looked at my drawing of Gabriel—mocked by Bridgette—and quickly flipped to the next page. One of the last pages left. An image remained on the flip side, one I'd drawn when I first got to Edenton: a crude, ten-year-old's drawing of Papa.

I began sketching out a map of Edenton, from memory. Although I understood the system of tunnels Doc Gladstone had explained, I couldn't figure out where everything was off the top of my head. When I finished, I ripped the map out and stuck it in my pocket, then lay back on the bed, my body still aching from the chase the other night.

"Hi there," I heard and looked up to see Aliyah coming through the cottage's front door. Around her head she wore a sweat-soaked black handkerchief, a streak of powdery flour over her forehead. "You're back," she said with no enthusiasm or disappointment.

"I am," I said, placing my head back on the pillow.

Aliyah walked toward her trunk, located on the other side of my headboard, and opened it. "So," she said. "How was your first Prayer Circle? Sounds like you guys really . . ." she paused, ". . . helped out some needy folks."

"Yeah," I said, throwing my arm over my eyes. "We helped."

She riffled through some things in her trunk. "You must be exhausted," she said. "I know how draining Prayer Circle can be, with all the chanting and . . . touching."

I lifted my arm from my eyes. "Touching?"

"You know," she said quickly. "Hugging and stuff."

I sat up and looked at her. "Hugging?"

She closed the lid to her trunk without looking at me. In her hand she twisted another handkerchief, this one red. When her eyes finally met mine, they glistened. "Your Prayer Circle didn't have any . . . hugging?"

I shot out of bed and faced her. It took everything in me to keep from grasping her arms and shaking her. "You know."

She remained silent. She wrapped the handkerchief tighter around her hand, the tips of her fingers paling.

"You remember, don't you? You remember what happened during your first Prayer Circle."

Aliyah turned away from me, flipping the red handkerchief over her shoulder and untying the black one from around her head. She snapped it out on the trashcan and a poof of powder burst into the air. Then she dropped the black kerchief on her trunk. As close as we were in that quiet room, I could barely hear her voice. "I remember."

"So do I," I said.

Relief washed over her features, her dark eyes flooding. "Oh good!" She shook her head. "I'm sorry. It's not good—that you remember like I do—but good that you told me. I've been so lonely keeping this secret."

I hugged her. "You're not alone," I whispered.

The fabric on my shoulder grew wet with her tears. I willed myself to cry, so she wasn't crying alone. Crying alone amplified the loneliness. But tears wouldn't come. Her chest heaved in another sob. I wrapped my arms tighter around her. And we stood there, holding each other until outside the windows twilight fell and the sounds of the nocturnal jungle droned through the slatted glass.

\* \* \*

Avoiding Mama, who'd been informed that I'd returned from my "mission with the poor," I went to the kitchen with Aliyah for after-dinner cleanup. I wasn't ready to face Mama. Lambert had said that each time he'd spent with my mother was like the first time for her, because the drugs she'd been given kept her from remembering any of their former encounters. But how she acted when I received my invitation to Prayer Circle, saying over and over again that I was so young, made me think she must have remembered what had happened at Las Casitas. So young. But I was too young, I suppose, to be told the truth.

The kitchen smelled of bleach, and a lingering scent of roasted meat. Piles of compost remained in the bins, stacked by the back door, ready to be taken to the heap. Aliyah went right to work disinfecting the wooden cutting boards.

"Look who's back!" Bridgette's voice screeched in the metallic space. "So enlightened at Prayer Circle that the light of the Lord speared your heart and drove you to help the needy, huh?"

I grabbed a rag from the pile on the counter. "Go away."

"Oh, not feeling Christ's love this evening?" Bridgette asked. She stood by the special provisions pantry, apron spotless, her hair pulled back from her face so tightly her eyebrows appeared raised in surprise.

Dina stood behind her, piling plates into the dishwasher. Her apron, by contrast, was covered with muck and stained with dark, bile-colored splotches.

"What did you guys make for dinner?" I asked trying to sound casual. My attention kept snapping to the special provisions pantry.

Dina smiled cautiously. "I made greens with bacon and pepper."

"Too much pepper," Bridgette said under her breath. "You missed dinner, Mia, because you had your other plans to help the poor. Unfortunately, we don't have anything left over for you."

She hung her hand on her hip and tilted her head, waiting for a response. I didn't give her one.

"You're too good now to address me, Mia?" Bridgette sneered. "Your mission with the poor must have robbed you of your humility."

Instead of downplaying my fake mission with the poor, I decided on a different tactic. I was feeling just that shallow, and exhausted.

"To be honest, Bridgette, it was an enlightening experience. The Reverend was so proud of our selfless actions, he's asked me to oversee a program to help the poorer villages. I'm sure you'll be more than happy to dedicate your time?" I took a spray bottle and misted disinfectant onto a dirtied counter. "That means, of course, you'd have to work for me. Because, you know, I'd be in charge."

Her mouth stretched in a fixed grimace, as if she were a monkey baring its teeth in threat. "Of course."

She twisted away quickly, and something glinted on her wrist. A yellow spiraled plastic bracelet circled her wrist, and from a silver chain dangled the key to the special provisions pantry. My heart sped up. Why did she have it? Why would Agatha entrust her with it?

"Oh," she said in an offhand tone. Her back was turned to me. "You'll be interested to know that, while you were away on your special assignment for the Reverend, Agatha gave me the position of kitchen manager."

Hence, the key.

"Congratulations." I squirted another spray of cleaner and wiped down another section of the counter with a sweeping arm movement.

"So, you can stop doing what you're doing, Mia, and take the compost to the heap."

I swung around, spray nozzle aimed at her like a gun. "Excuse me?"

"You heard me. Now move along before it starts to stink in here." She batted her eyelashes. "I'm in charge, remember? Agatha wouldn't want to hear you're not cooperating."

I glanced at Aliyah. She looked back at me and nodded once. I heaved a sigh and dropped the bottle and paper towel on the counter. I didn't need to cause trouble, although I wanted to smack Bridgette in the head.

Outside, there was a sinister silence. The birds, usually cawing and calling, had quieted. Their sounds were still there, but it seemed as if they'd been dampened, as if I were listening to them through a wall. I looked into the sky and saw the clouds hanging swollen and dark, iron gray. Yellow flashes of lightning, followed by more silence, meant a storm somewhere in the distance was rolling toward Edenton.

No one was on the path to the heap. I wheeled the buckets of compost through the corridor of trees. A light shone on the tall lump of trash, a shovel bobbing from behind it every few seconds.

Gabriel.

I abandoned the compost and rushed over to him, glancing around for a sign of Grizz.

"Hey," I whispered.

Gabriel jumped, trash flying into the air from his shovel. "Jesus Christ, Mia!" he said, spearing the shovel into the soft ground. He was back in uniform. His damp shirt stuck to his wide shoulders. "Why the hell are you sneaking up on me?"

"I wasn't."

He placed both his hands around the handle of the shovel and leaned on it, back bowing forward with exhaustion. "I'm back on pile duty."

"Obviously. But why are you here in the first place?" I crossed my arms over my chest. "Why did you come back? Aren't you supposed to be living your life somewhere? Somewhere other than here?"

"Did you think I was going to let you do this on your own?"

"Yes."

"Well then, Ricci, you must think little of me."

"I—" I started.

Did I think that little of him? Didn't something inside me know he would show up? He may have been furious with his parents for bringing him to Edenton, but he wouldn't let them die at the hands of the Reverend. I shifted uncomfortably.

"So," he said, glancing around. "You still have those microphones?" His gaze darted to my chest.

I dropped my arms and crossed them again. "Yes," I whispered. "I've already planted one in the infirmary and one in the kitchen."

"The kitchen? Why there?"

"Agatha keeps the poison in a pantry in the kitchen. The poison we—" I cleared my throat, "she used for the Bright Night cookies."

"Ah."

He leaned a little closer, palms, one over the other, planted on the shovel's handle. He smelled of soap and clean sweat. The incorrigible glint in his eye didn't seem to break the surface of his expression. I could see that below his boyish charisma worry and anger threatened to surge forward.

"What we need to do is get one of those microphones into the Reverend's or Thaddeus's office." He cocked a grin. "I can get in trouble again and have Thaddeus give me a good talking to. I could plant one in there then."

"And how exactly would you get in trouble this time?"

A deeper, broader smile rose from somewhere elemental in him, causing my eyes to widen. A flush of heat rose to my cheeks.

"You said you weren't interested," I said.

"We'd be doing it for the network." He leaned in a fraction closer. "For the greater good."

"You're an ass."

"Well, I've heard that before."

"I'm sure you have." I glanced around again, worried Grizz was somewhere close and could hear us talking. I spoke quietly and quickly. "I think we can plant more microphones without sacrificing ourselves for the greater good."

His smile dropped like an anvil. "I'd be a sacrifice? Damn, Ricci, your words can be razor sharp."

"You wouldn't be a sacrifice—" I caught myself when he grinned again. I inhaled audibly. "Meet me later, two hours after curfew, in the infirmary. There's something I need to show you."

"The rest of the microphones?" he asked, looking pointedly at my chest.

"Really?"

"You're too much fun to tease, you know that? Of course I'll meet you later."

*Of course.* At those words my pulse jumped.

I stepped away. "Just be careful and don't get caught."

Gabriel thrust the shovel into the pile of trash. "No promises, Ricci. No promises."

# Chapter Twenty-Eight

Through the sheets of rain, I picked my way around the puddles toward the infirmary. The winding path through Edenton seemed to disappear ahead of me, the lights lining either side reflecting off the water and creating an almost opaque white curtain of water. Rain slanted as sharp wind blew cool spattering drops on my face, and I pulled my hood tighter.

"Mia? What are you doing out here this late?"

I saw a figure come toward me. It was Agatha, poncho pulled tight around her body. Her face was taut with tension. Cheekbones protruded out from her narrow face, streaming with water. She squinted at me through the rain.

I'd thought of excuses before I'd snuck out of the cottage while the other girls slept. "I was just going to ask Doc Gladstone for some aspirin. Headache." I pointed to my forehead. "What about you?"

She shifted from one foot to the other. "A few things to take care of in the kitchen." At my questioning look she said, "Your new kitchen manager didn't finish her duties this evening." She didn't elaborate further. "Hurry along or you'll catch your death out here."

I watched as she rushed past me and veered off down the path toward the kitchen.

A curl of malicious joy unfurled in my chest. Good. Bridgette wasn't so perfect after all. I had planned on sneaking the key from her wrist while she slept, but it had been so dark in our cottage when I snuck out, I didn't want to risk waking her and listening to a righteous lecture on the Eighth Commandment. I couldn't miss meeting Gabriel, after all. I'd find a way to get the key. I only needed to be patient.

I didn't want to run into anyone else, so I stepped off the path and trudged through the mud, darting between buildings to the infirmary. The rain kept most of the patrolling security guards at the places most needed: the entrances and out in the jungle. But when I realized what I'd done, I almost launched into one of Gabriel's string of vivid curses. I had to pass one of the guard buildings to get to the infirmary, or double back. I was losing time. I crouched down. The one window was open, so I started to slowly pass under it when I heard noises from inside. Not just noises, but giggles and—moaning?

I stopped below the sill. Gradually, I lifted my head until I could see inside. The light was low; only a desk lamp had been turned on and the illumination reflected against the stark-white wall above the desk. Deep shadows clung to the corners of the room. Once I could make out what was happening inside, I had to stifle a gasp. Freddie was stripped to the waist. The muscles of his back rolled and tensed, and he held someone in his arms. He half-turned toward the window and I quickly ducked down. I listened for a moment and heard a giggle. With extreme care, I peeked up over the windowsill again—and saw a very giddy, very naked, very carefree Bridgette.

It took me a few moments to process the scene. This was Bridgette. Holier-than-thou, sanctimonious, preachy, smug Bridgette. Now she was lustful and needy, pulling at Freddie's waistband. And he seemed pleased to be the target of her greediness. How long had this been going on? I'd never noticed anything between them. They certainly weren't courting. Since her first Prayer Circle, she hadn't been matched with a boy by the Reverend, and never really seemed to care. I knew Edenton was filled with secrets, but I never realized some would shock me so much more than others.

Her uniform dress was strewn across the desk and her bra was dangling off the arm of the desk chair. Her hair, normally so neat and pulled into a ponytail, flew freely about her head, wildly, as if the wind from outside were lifting it into the air. Her face was flushed, relaxed. And she looked so happy—not viciously happy, or self-righteously happy, but simply happy. The malicious joy I'd felt earlier was replaced by an inexplicable envy. I wanted that kind of happy. Lustful and exciting, the kind of happy that would make my cheeks glow pink and my body awaken. I remembered the last time I'd felt that, and with whom.

Then, I saw it. Lying on the windowsill next to her silver dog-tag necklace with the Romans 13:13 scripture quote, was the yellow bracelet with the pantry key.

I inspected a small rip in the screen. While their attention was on each other, I stuck my finger into the small slit and ripped it, tiny wire by tiny wire, until it was wide enough to slip the key through. By the time I had the bracelet halfway out of the opening, Freddie's pants were off, and he was naked.

I froze and stared. I'd never seen a boy naked. I immediately thought of Gabriel, the tattoo on his stomach, and what was below that tattoo. I squeezed my eyes shut and heard words exchanged, sweet, low, whispered words I couldn't understand over the rain. Blindly, I pulled the bracelet out the rest of the way, ducked below the window, and sighed with relief. Then I dashed away, feet slipping on the muddy turf.

By the time I made it to the infirmary, a strange mix of emotions churned inside me. I didn't understand the yearning I felt, why my thoughts pinged right to Gabriel. He'd made it clear he wasn't interested in me. Fine. Maybe I wasn't interested either. Maybe it was just my first experience with anything sexual, and that was making me obsess a little more on the subject than I should.

But he came back to Edenton. Did he come back for me?

*Did you think I was going to let you do this on your own?*

A few soft lights burned in the infirmary. The door wasn't locked, so I slipped inside and shook off my raincoat, the patters of water hitting the floor in little tinkling sounds.

"Doc Gladstone?" I called in a loud whisper.

"He's not here." Gabriel's eyes gleamed in the shadows. "No one is."

I threw my raincoat on an exam table. "Maybe he's with a patient in one of the cottages."

"What took you so long to get here?" he asked, stepping closer. Instead of the usual gray collared uniform shirt, he wore a black T-shirt and black cargo pants.

"I ran into Agatha," I said. "And Bridgette."

"What were they doing out in this weather?"

"Agatha was headed to the kitchen. And Bridgette was in the security guard shack with Freddie the security guard, having sex."

Gabriel's eyes widened. "Wow. No metaphor for you, huh? And how, may I ask, did you run into them having sex?" He drew out the last word with a particular kind of interest.

I tried to remain dispassionate, clinical, but Gabriel's eyes on me felt almost like a touch. "I was passing by the security building on my way here and I heard something. So I looked in the window and there they were."

Moving slowly, deliberately, Gabriel stepped forward. He was very close now. I drew in a breath, feeling a little dizzy.

"Did you watch them, Mia?" he asked in a low, rumbling voice.

I answered without looking him in the eye. "No."

"I think you did."

"It doesn't matter if I did or not." I held up my wrist, the key dangling from it. "She left the key to the special provisions pantry on the windowsill and I snagged it."

"Impressive. And one hell of a sacrifice you made to get it."

"Shut up. Come on, you need to see something."

He didn't make a smart comment back to me, which meant he was either taking me seriously, or had his mind on something else. I could only imagine what that something else was.

The back hall of the infirmary was enveloped in shadow. I'd only been back there a couple times, so I wasn't familiar with the space. I felt around on the wall for a light switch, and found it, flipping it on. Everything went sterile white for a split second, and the hallway came into view.

I twisted the handle to the closet door, where Doc Gladstone and I had emerged earlier from the tunnel, and motioned for Gabriel to walk in first.

"What's in there?" he asked.

"You'll see."

"Look, Mia, do you have to be so creepy about this? Edenton is weird enough as it is. Just tell me."

"There are stairs that lead to a series of underground tunnels beneath Edenton."

"And it just got weirder." Gabriel shook his head. "Underground tunnels? For what?"

"For people to get around unseen. For the Reverend's inner circle to travel around as they please. Doc Gladstone said they were constructed when the plumbing and stuff was put in."

"Where do they lead?"

"All over Edenton. I think every security building has access to them, as well as some of the more important buildings and cottages. I bet we could get to Thaddeus's cottage as well as the Reverend's and plant the microphones."

"How do you know how to get around?"

"Doc Gladstone showed me how to tell which tunnel is going in which direction."

"And this idea doesn't scare you shitless?"

I tugged at the pocket of my dress. "We have to get these microphones planted."

Gabriel's face lit in a glorious smile. "Yeah, we do, don't we?"

Realization dawned. "You really like all this, don't you?"

"What do you mean?"

"The danger, the adrenaline. You enjoy it."

He shrugged. "I do."

"So that's why you came back," I said. "The outside world didn't have the immediate adrenaline rush that freeing the Flock from certain death would have?"

"I have my own reason for coming back."

"And what is it?"

Ignoring my question, Gabriel walked into the closet, found the light, and turned it on. "Shut out the light in the hallway," he said.

He stopped when he saw the keypad by the door inside the closet. From behind, I reached around him and punched in the numbers I remembered seeing Doc Gladstone use earlier: 123456. The door made a clinking sound.

"You're kidding," he said. "That's their passcode and the network can't hack into their systems? I bet all their passwords are 'password.'"

Slowly, he opened the door. The staircase led down two flights. Without any hesitancy, Gabriel bounded down the steps and I followed as quickly as I could.

He froze at the bottom of the steps. "Holy shit. This is unbelievable."

The tunnel looked the same as I remembered it, walls of concrete, but now dingy, dripping stains crept down the sides, water seeping in from the rain above. It smelled of mold and dampness. The cage lights above burned at a low wattage, just enough to see from one circle of light to the next.

The stairway was in the middle of a long stretch of tunnel. To our right the tunnel curved away from us, to the left it snaked along a few feet then banked suddenly behind us.

"Which way?" he asked.

I fished out the map I'd drawn from my pocket. The edges of it were damp.

"Did you draw that?" Gabriel asked, looking at the image on the other side.

"When I was ten," I said, studying the map.

"It's good. Who is it?"

"My father."

"You miss him?"

I looked up, and felt my brow pinch. "I don't know."

Gabriel nodded. "It's okay, you know. Not to miss them. You need to live for the living, not the dead. I mean, I don't always miss my brother. And it's okay."

I tilted my head at him.

"At least, that's what my ex-therapist told me." He didn't wait for a reaction from me. "So where to?"

We needed to get to the Reverend's cottage—the first, and most terrifying, place to plant a microphone.

"Follow me," I said, shoving the map in my pocket.

The tunnel was silent, except for the echoing drips of water. Gabriel followed closely behind, so close I could feel his warm breath fight through the chilly damp air on my neck.

I stopped at a three-way split in the tunnel, and tugged the map from my pocket again. I studied it, still confused as to where we were. Putting the map away, I shut my eyes and imagined the layout of Edenton. Gabriel, to his benefit, said nothing, but I could feel his adrenaline-fueled bouncing behind me.

"This way," I said, pointing to the right.

"You sure?"

"Yes."

I wasn't, but I plowed ahead anyway. We'd figure out where we were eventually. There were only so many places the tunnels could go.

We came across a stairway, the third we'd seen. It was the first, though, that seemed familiar. It wasn't that it was clearly different from the other stairways, but the way the tunnel turned to the right next to it, the way the caged light above was slightly crooked, part of the clear bulb cracked but not broken. There was a stain at the bottom of the last step—dark with sweeping crisscrossing scrubbed marks.

Gabriel pointed to the stain. "Have we been here—"

A murmur of muffled voices.

A clicking metallic noise from the top of the staircase.

Fear ripped through me. People were coming down the stairs.

Gabriel snatched my arm and shoved me into the tiny space below the staircase's landing. Beneath the landing, the damp walls loomed over me, encroaching on the cramped, but secluded space. Gabriel tucked himself into the small gap in front of me. We were facing each other, knees tangled together, panicked breaths mingling.

Footsteps came down the steps. They were heavy. Thudding, the sound resonating off the walls around us. My heart beat so frantically that I saw everything vibrate around me in time to my pulse. I'd known there was a chance of this happening, but stupidly, I didn't think about what we would do. What was our excuse? I kept my body from trembling, but the terror was too hard to control. My lip began to quiver and I bit down on it. Cold leached from the concrete wall against my back, my shoulder. My wet hair clung to the back of my neck. The chill and the tension drained any warmth from my body, and I cocooned myself into Gabriel. To keep from trembling. To hide.

Light slanted across Gabriel's face. His gaze was fixed on mine, his green-blue eyes twinkled beneath their thick lashes, stripped of his usual humor. Then my heart beat frantically for a different reason. His eyes were clear as glass and focused on me—and full of desire.

# Chapter Twenty-Nine

"The progress at Las Casitas is going well," Thaddeus said, stomping down the steps, causing the metal treads screwed into each to rattle.

I tore my gaze from Gabriel's. I couldn't look into the depths of his eyes and concentrate on what the two men were saying.

"Okay," the Reverend responded. His step was also heavy, but his shoes made a soft sound each time they hit a stair.

"We've paid the workers twice as much per hour to speed up productivity," Thaddeus said. "So, be sure to mention how impressed you are with their work."

There was a pause. "Yes, I'll do that," the Reverend said. His tone was flat.

I felt Gabriel's arm around me, pulling me closer. His breathing had grown heavier, deeper, heating the chilled, wet skin on my neck. His breath made me shudder.

"The clients that were in the fire," Thaddeus said, "have been refunded their money with guarantees it won't happen again."

"That was prudent," the Reverend said. "And what will I say when I see them again?"

"I'll take care of it. You don't say anything. Once we're back in business, offer them a handshake and nothing more."

I shivered as Gabriel shifted his hand and circled his fingertips over the skin of my calf, between each healing scratch. It burned where he touched me. My mind, first clouded with fear, now clouded with lust. I didn't understand why he was doing this, how we could ignite so quickly, like dry leaves catching from an errant spark. I watched his fingers trail down my leg but sat still, too afraid to move. I tilted my head up slowly and met his eyes again.

"It better not happen again," Thaddeus said.

"I'm sorry," the Reverend said. "I thought Ivy knew what she was doing."

"We both did. She claimed to know how to administer the drugs." Thaddeus sounded angry. "A few of our clients reported seeing a teenage boy setting the cottages on fire. It must have been Gabriel. He should be severely punished for what he's done."

Gabriel's gaze went blank. I blinked. What did they just say?

"Then punish him," the Reverend said. "You've done it before. How difficult would it be?"

"I have him on the heap."

"Maybe a harsher punishment?"

My mind went back to what Doc Gladstone had said: The Reverend uses the Bible's lessons in penance as models for torture. But it didn't sound like the Reverend was making the decisions about Gabriel's punishment.

"If he remembered his indiscretion," Thaddeus said, "then a harsher punishment would be the answer. I don't think we should injure him in any physical way, as he promises to make us a lot of money at Las Casitas. We have a long list of bids for his time, and we've just raised his asking price significantly. No one has withdrawn their bids."

Gabriel's eyes swam with confusion.

"And Mia," Thaddeus continued. "Lambert has doubled his offer. He could certainly go higher if we asked."

I watched Gabriel's expression drop into cold fury. I turned my face away from his, disgusted and embarrassed that they so casually spoke of our bodies as playthings for others.

"That other girl still in a coma?" the Reverend asked.

"Yes." Thaddeus paused. "And there is another problem we're dealing with tonight with another member of the Flock, but you don't need to know about that now. It should be solved before dawn regardless."

I heard the shuffle of feet, and saw the Reverend's bloated belly lead him a few steps down the tunnel.

"Reverend, stay here," Thaddeus said and I watched the Reverend freeze in place. "Freddie should have been here ten minutes ago to drive us over."

A crackling noise.

"Grizz, where is Freddie? The Reverend wants to inspect the progress at Las Casitas now."

A garbled reply echoed in the tunnel.

"Freddie will be here any moment," Thaddeus said.

The Reverend blinked a few times and hung his head. He looked broken standing there, alone and hunched over. He inhaled a great breath and puffed up. In the small sliver of space, I could see his expression darken, as if he were putting on a mask of anger.

Seconds later, the sound of a motor, a small motor, barreled toward the staircase.

"I'm so sorry I'm late," was Freddie's rushed announcement as he pulled up. I saw a glimpse of a golf cart as it passed the far edge of the staircase.

"What the hell happened?" the Reverend snapped. Now he sounded more like the Reverend I knew.

"Rain," Freddie said, "caused some problems. Couldn't get this thing started."

"It's not raining in the tunnels, boy," the Reverend said. "Shouldn't have affected it."

"The dampness," Freddie said quickly. "Things are very . . . damp."

From the bouncing squeaks, I could tell they were getting into the cart. A few moments later, they drove off down the tunnel, the buzz of the motor fading away.

We stayed in that cramped space a few moments, not looking at each other, either making sure they were gone, or too embarrassed for our gazes to meet. Finally, Gabriel crawled out of the space and reached his hand down to me. I took it. I glanced down either side of the tunnel before stepping out from behind the staircase. It was empty.

"This is where they took us," Gabriel said, voice subdued and haunted with memory. He stepped into the center of the tunnel and gestured in the direction the cart had driven. "After they drugged us at Prayer Circle, in the Reverend's cottage. This is how they got us to Las Casitas. I remember a little."

Images flashed. My feet stumbling down the steps. The strange dark stain on the floor that was only half scrubbed away. The bent cage light, casting twisted tree-branch shadows over the concrete floor. Juanita, next to me in the golf cart, dark ringlets of hair covering her face as she hung forward.

"Then," I said, turning to the stairs, "we plant the microphone right up there. Behind that door. It must be the Reverend's cottage."

"I'll do it," Gabriel said, holding out a hand.

"No way. I'm going in, too."

"Someone needs to be the lookout."

"I have the microphones," I said, starting up the stairs.

Gabriel came up behind me and said in a quiet voice, "You can't get rid of me that easily."

"Obviously," I mumbled.

The door at the top of the stairs opened silently. It was a heavy door, heavier than the one in the infirmary. Gabriel tugged back on the handle to open it wide. Inside, it was dark, the light from the tunnel only illuminating a few feet in front of us. We stood at the mouth of a hallway. Memories came back as they'd done when I saw the stain on the tunnel floor. I remembered the hallway, tripping over Gabriel, and seeing Juanita passed out next to me. I tamped down the visions of what had happened, and stepped into the hall.

Once we were a few feet inside, Gabriel's breath grew shallow. "Oh, God," he whispered. "This is where they got me."

He pointed to an open doorway. It led to the antechamber I'd entered hesitantly the night of Prayer Circle, well behind Gabriel and Juanita.

"You okay?" I asked him.

"Yeah. Keep going."

We entered the Reverend's living room. It was the same as before, lined with books surrounding a cozy sofa and chairs. It looked as if it were someone else's space, a sweet grandfatherly type. Not the cruel man who planned to kill his Flock. I walked a slow circuit around the room, inspecting the books. I passed two entire bookshelves on preaching. Books like *The Art and Craft of Biblical Preaching*, *Doctrine that Dances*, and *The Burdensome Joy of Preaching*. A floor-to-ceiling shelf was filled with Bibles, and other majestic-looking books titled the Qur'an, Tao Te Ching, and Talmud. On another I saw what looked like novels. I didn't recognize any of the titles, but many were labeled "a novel."

"Just put the microphone somewhere," Gabriel said impatiently.

"What are these?" I asked, pointing to a shelf filled with thin cases. "DVDs?"

Gabriel's brows went up. "Good, Ricci. You recognize obsolete technology. Now, plant the damn microphone and let's go."

I slid a few out. They were the Reverend's sermons, dated before the creation of Edenton. I scanned the titles: Blessed are the Peacemakers,

Joy—Fruit of the Spirit, Building a Caring Church. "He's never preached any of these sermons since I've been in Edenton," I said.

"So he's changed up his program."

"Yeah, but drastically." I held up one DVD. "This one's about the preciousness of human life. Why would he preach this then kill his own Flock?"

"He's grown cranky in his old age." Gabriel glanced over his shoulder. "Now come on."

I put the DVD back. I scrabbled for a microphone in my pocket, then stuck it under the coffee table.

"Thaddeus's cottage next?" I asked once we were back in the tunnel.

"Lead the way."

Thaddeus's wasn't far, and inside it was empty and cold. Even Gabriel took a moment to examine the strange skeletons of animals on display on Thaddeus's shelves.

"Why do you think he has these?" he asked me.

"Maybe he hunts. Maybe he likes dissecting them." I thought about Thaddeus's infamous patience—maybe it was more like controlled malice. "What if he kills them for fun, dissects them while they're still alive—"

"Vivisection," Gabriel said.

"Is that what it's called?"

"Yep. Sick stuff."

"This whole place is sick," I mumbled, affixing a microphone to the underside of Thaddeus's desk. After we descended the steps back into the tunnel, I stopped. "I need to go to the kitchen." I held up my wrist. "I want to check the provisions pantry."

"Cool," he said. "I'm hungry. Will you cook me something?"

"No."

"Come on, Ricci." He slipped his arm over my shoulder and I tensed. He sensed my discomfort. "Mia, about earlier, under the stairs—"

"Stop," I said. "Not now, okay?"

"But—"

"Gabriel, I said stop. I don't want to talk about it."

I unthreaded his arm from my neck and looked around the tunnel, trying to hide my discomfort with fake curiosity. I didn't want an explanation on why he kissed me. I didn't want an apology, either. I thought about Bridgette and how much I envied the happiness on her face ear-lier. I didn't want to envy Bridgette. I didn't want to envy anybody.

"We need to keep moving."

I walked in the direction of the infirmary.

"Is there a tunnel entrance in the kitchen?" Gabriel asked.

"I don't think so," I said. "I've never seen a door or anything that would lead to stairs."

"Hmm. Seems like an obvious place to have an entrance."

"No," I said. "Too many people wandering around. They wouldn't risk having a mystery door in the middle of the kitchen."

"Isn't that what the special provisions pantry is? Just a mysterious door?"

"Wait." I stopped walking and turned to him. "Are you saying the pantry isn't a pantry? It's a door to the tunnel?"

"Maybe."

"Then why would Agatha give Bridgette a key to it?"

"I'm only throwing out ideas, Ricci. We'll head back to the infir-mary, then over to the kitchen."

"Agatha was on her way to the kitchen when I saw her," I said. "What if she's still there?"

"We wait for her to leave."

On our way back to the infirmary, I wondered if Agatha was really cleaning up after Bridgette or if she had other plans in the kitchen. Her making an excuse to me seemed . . . *off*.

"We have to hurry," I said.

"What's the hurry?"

"I think Agatha's up to something in the kitchen that doesn't have anything to do with Bridgette's slacking off. Bridgette wouldn't slack off. She's too holier-than-thou to risk looking bad in front of anyone. Especially me."

"Wait," Gabriel said. He dropped his knee to tie his boot.

Impatiently, I waited in the center of the tunnel, arms folded and foot tapping. I was sure I had a sneer on my face. Just looking at him was making me angry. He wanted to apologize. For whatever happened under the stairs. I wasn't even sure what happened under the stairs.

Gabriel glared at me. "What's wrong with you all of a sudden?"

"Will you just hurry up?"

He straightened. "Look, Mia, if this is about what just happened, I want to talk—"

Down the tunnel, the sound of a motor buzzed—the same sound as the golf cart Freddie drove. It was coming from the opposite direction of the infirmary. We both took off running toward the infirmary, the sound of our pounding feet reverberating through the tunnel. I wondered frantically if we could be heard over the motor. We dashed to the top of the stairs to the infirmary and stopped. Over the sound of the motor, over the sound of everything, we heard shouts. Sharp, angry shouts. The words were muffled from behind the steel door to the infirmary.

The sound of the motor grew closer. Gabriel and I huddled in the small doorframe, as if the darkness could conceal us from what was barreling down the tunnel. With a sudden slam, the yelling on the other side of the door stopped, and the motor barreling down the tunnel gunned louder.

I twisted the door handle and cautiously pushed the door open. Gabriel gave it an impatient shove and dashed inside, tugging me along with him. The door closed behind me, silencing the sound of the cart.

Inside, heavy darkness hung around us, a single lamp over the desk in the exam room throwing a streak of long, dim illumination into the back hall, where we stood motionless, waiting for a clue of what to do next. Was anyone in the infirmary? Were we alone? It was late, probably almost midnight.

I stepped forward first. I felt Gabriel behind me, giving me the confidence to move ahead without having to look back. The exam room was empty. Tables lined either side, each neatly set up for the next patient, much like we'd left it before we'd gone into the tunnels. My raincoat remained where I'd left it. It was an Edenton uniform raincoat, so it could have been anyone's. And I had more to worry about than someone discovering my raincoat in the infirmary.

"What do you think all that yelling was about?" Gabriel whispered in my ear.

I suppressed a shudder. "I don't know."

I trudged to the front door of the infirmary. It was closed, the blinds over the glass shut tight but still swinging slightly, an echo of the door being slammed. I pried open the slats of the blinds.

"Oh, God," I cried at what I saw.

"What is it?" Gabriel came up behind me and looked outside.

In the misting rain, dark figures wrestled on the muddy ground. Punches were thrown. Grunts and pained moans sounded through the glass of the door's window.

"That's Grizz," Gabriel whispered.

"Who is he fighting?"

The other man got to his feet, and flipped back his dreadlocks, water flicking off them into tiny, reflective droplets in the overhead light. I went dizzy at the sight.

"It's Doc Gladstone," I gasped.

Other figures appeared and dragged Doc Gladstone to his knees. Grizz, standing above him, wore an expression of disgust, and worry. He reached down to the side of his belt, where he kept his walkie-talkie, and found it missing, slashing his arm though the air with an angry punch that hit nothing.

"Why you?" he yelled down at Doc Gladstone.

Doc Gladstone did nothing, said nothing. He remained on his knees as one security guard tied his arms behind his back. Another lifted him to his feet, and shoved him toward the door of the infirmary.

"Hide!" I said and we scrambled around for a place to go. I slid into a spot under the desk and Gabriel crouched beside the bookcase.

The door flew open, banging against the wall, blinds jangling in an outraged crash. I jumped at the sound. My mind, blank with distress and fear, couldn't focus on what was happening.

Squeaking and clomping footsteps led to the back hallway. Doc Gladstone, in his lilting accent, said, "You're making a mistake, Grizz. This is a mistake."

"Shut up!" Grizz yelled, sounding angry, but also hurt, as if tears could burst from his eyes at any moment.

High-pitched beeps from the keypad by the door to the tunnel sounded. The men stormed through the door, letting it fall closed with a soft click. Then, silence.

"What the hell?" Gabriel asked in a whisper.

I crawled out from under the desk and stared into the hallway, at the door to the tunnel. The floor leading to it showed a violent pattern of sliding, muddy footsteps.

I turned to Gabriel, who still stood by the bookshelves. Sickening shock hit me. Doc Gladstone's bookcase for his medical journals, the ones that held the secret messages from the network, was completely empty.

# Chapter Thirty

Jittery, I grabbed my raincoat from the exam table and punched my arms into the sleeves. Gabriel, seeing my panicky gestures, unhooked his raincoat from the coatrack and gave me a curious look. I snatched Gabriel's wrist and dragged him toward the door.

"We need to move," I said, blinking back tears.

"Can you at least explain to me what is going on?" Gabriel said, tagging behind with a mystified expression. "What just happened with Gladstone?"

"Walk and talk," I said, peeking out the door.

The rain turned into a hazy mist, blowing through the air like tiny white insects. With a trembling hand, I fished the last microphone from my pocket and headed out of the infirmary with Gabriel in tow.

"Where are we going to plant that one?" he asked.

"We're not," I said, twisting it to turn it on. I wiped my eyes as subtly as I could. I didn't want Gabriel to see I was crying.

I led Gabriel to the path. Before lifting the mic to my mouth, I glanced around. All the security guards seemed to be elsewhere. Maybe they were guarding Doc Gladstone. With a sinking feeling in my chest, I hoped all they were doing was guarding him.

"Hey," I said quietly into the mic. "This is Mia. I'm not sure if you can hear me, but the security guards just took Doc Gladstone away. And all the medical journals are gone. So, they'll know everything soon. Whatever plan you have in place to save the Flock, it needs to happen sooner rather than later." I twisted the microphone off and stuck it in my pocket.

Gabriel maneuvered around a puddle. "Why did Grizz take Doc Gladstone away?" he asked.

"He was . . ." I paused, ". . . is the network's inside source."

His face didn't show any signs of shock at my news. "Well, I think we're the network's inside sources now."

"Gabriel . . . you're right," I said, a little to myself. "I just hope—" I took a breath to keep from sobbing. "I just hope they don't kill him."

"Should we go see if we can find him? Back to the tunnels?"

"No." I took his elbow. "We need to get to the kitchen, find the poison in the pantry, and return the key to Bridgette before she gets up in the morning."

"Then what?"

"We need to figure out how the network can invade Edenton. How they can get in here and get everyone out without anyone being killed."

"And that sounds like a perfectly reasonable, doable plan," Gabriel said under his breath. "Easy as falling off a branch."

"A log."

"Huh?"

"It's 'easy as falling off a log.'"

"For you, maybe. I'm the one who'd never climbed a tree, remember?"

We sloshed along the path. Plants and trees around us dripped with water. Rivulets ran down the paths, pooling into puddles of mud. I tried to ignore the bleakness of our situation and continue forward. Without Doc Gladstone, without the information he had on the inside workings of Edenton, what was I going to do?

"Ah," Gabriel said suddenly. "So that's why the drugs he gave me today didn't work."

"What?"

"Earlier, when I was supposed to 'regain my memories,' that's why the drug he gave me didn't work. Because he's part of the network."

"They were just supposed to make you relaxed, make it seem like the drugs were working for Thaddeus's sake."

"Damn. I'm glad I didn't say anything to screw it up." He stepped over a large mud puddle, then held out his hand for me. "And the journals? Why are they significant?"

I took his hand and he helped me over the puddle. "That's how the network communicated with Doc Gladstone. No doubt Thaddeus is going through all of them now and, before long, he'll find out why I'm back. The last communication between the network and Gladstone was about me coming back to Edenton to help him. I don't think they know about you, though. Although I'm sure they'll figure it out."

Gabriel let go of my hand. "And take us like they did Gladstone."

"Yeah," I said with sickening certainty.

A light was burning in the kitchen window when we approached. I leaned against the door, trying to hear if someone was inside. My nerves buzzed, shredded since watching Doc Gladstone taken down so violently by the guards. I couldn't wait for Agatha to leave. I needed to at least get inside the kitchen and see what she was doing.

"Wait here," I whispered and started for the door handle.

Gabriel grabbed my arm. "No."

"I'm going to find out what Agatha is up to. How am I going to explain why you're with me?" I asked.

He lowered his eyes, as if in thought, then nodded. "Okay, it's fine."

"Oh, so it's fine, is it?" I reached for the door handle again. "I'm so glad to hear you think it's fine," I mumbled.

The door opened silently. Inside it was warm and dry. But it still smelled like bleach, not like there'd been any cooking or baking.

"Agatha?" I called

A crash sounded, pots hitting the ground, then a shadow shot up from the floor and stumbled forward into the light.

"What are you doing here?" Bridgette asked. Her hair was pulled back in a perfect knot. Her uniform was wrinkled in places, but otherwise in order. Her dog-tag necklace was slung around her neck, outside her collar.

"Looking for Agatha." I glanced around. "Is she here?"

"No."

"Why are you here?" I asked.

Her hand clutched her wrist. The wrist where she'd worn the key. "Looking for something."

Before I could hide it behind my back, her eyes shot to my own wrist. "Why do you have my key?" she yelled, lunging forward.

I twisted my arm behind me, covering the coiled yellow plastic with my hand. "I'm borrowing it!" I yelled back.

She slammed into me, knocking me back against the counter.

"It's not yours! Agatha gave it to me!"

The kitchen door swung open and Gabriel sauntered in. "Hi, girls," he said as he walked over to the refrigerator, opened it, and peered in.

Bridgette palmed my shoulder and tried to twist me around, facing the counter. I bracketed my legs in place, but her grip tightened.

Gabriel snatched a Tupperware bowl from the refrigerator, lifted the lid, and sniffed it. "This may have gone bad," he said, wrinkling his nose.

"What are you two doing here?" Bridgette demanded, swiping at my hands.

"I need to look in the provisions pantry," I struggled to say as she grabbed at my arm and scrabbled around for the key.

"It's not your pantry to look in!" she yelled. "Agatha gave me that key! You stole it! I'm in charge of this kitchen!"

Scrambling to stay on my feet, I looked over her head at Gabriel. "Little help?" I asked him.

Gabriel shut the fridge. "I'm going to hold you down while Mia looks through the pantry," he said as he walked over to us. "Although, I was hoping to never have to touch you, Bridgette." He scooped her up and she flailed against him.

"Get off me!" she said, struggling away from him. "I know about you, Gabriel. I know what kind of guy you are. How you used girls before you came to Edenton."

Gabriel's eyes turned hard as stone, but he didn't let go of her. Instead, he ignored her furious cries and pinned her arms back behind her.

Used girls?

I straightened my shirt. The provisions pantry was in the back of the kitchen. As I passed Bridgette to get to it, she swiped a caged-tiger paw at me.

"I'm going to tell Agatha about this!" she cried.

"And I'll tell her how I got the key," I said, sliding the key into the lock. I glanced back over my shoulder. "Do you think Freddie will be embarrassed that I saw him naked? I mean, I've seen you naked plenty of times, so earlier in the guard house really doesn't count."

Bridgette went limp with shock and forced down a visible lump in her throat.

"Mia likes to watch," Gabriel whispered in her ear.

I shot him a squinty scowl and unlocked the pantry. "You're disgusting, Gabriel."

"You're the one who watched through the window." Then he spoke to Bridgette. "I would have had the decency to at least clear my throat. You know, in case you liked being watched."

Bridgette, to her credit, stood stone-faced, sagging in Gabriel's arms like a stringless marionette. I'd expected a tantrum. But, thankfully, she didn't utter a word.

The pantry door creaked open. It was cool inside, not quite as cold as the refrigerator, but much cooler than the other pantry we used to house the canned goods. A little light switched on as the door opened and I peered in. Lining the shelves were various objects that seemed peculiar for Edenton: expensive-looking chocolate in a red velvet box, a jar with flakes of edible gold, three bottles of wine with foreign labels, a couple of cured meats wrapped in thin twists of string hanging from bars along the top, a few small glass jars filled with exotic sauces that we never used in the dishes we served day after day. At the very bottom of the pantry sat large containers of shrink-wrapped powdered Tang.

Out of all the odd things in the pantry, those containers were the strangest. Why such a vast quantity? Is that how the Reverend planned on killing the Flock? With poisoned drinks?

On the top shelf I spotted an unmarked box. I opened the top and saw seven vials of a whitish powder, but there were indented spaces in the Styrofoam lining for ten. Three must have been used for the Bright Night cookies.

"I found it," I said. I was certain that these were what I saw Agatha hiding in her apron that made the clinking noise in her pocket the day we baked the cookies.

"Found what?" Bridgette asked.

Without answering her, I took the box from the shelf, carefully scooped out the remaining vials, and replaced it with the lid securely in place. I held one of the vials up to the light. The powder inside was white, crystalized. It looked a lot like salt or sugar to me.

"I'm kitchen manager, Mia," she said. "What is that?"

"Poison," I said.

"Poison, what for?"

I cast her a meaningful look. "To kill the Flock. Remember the cookies, Bridgette?"

"Oh," she said. "Those greedy fools deserved it. Planning on making another batch?"

Gabriel let her go. "I can't even touch her," he said.

I turned on the water at a prep sink near one of the large cutting boards and poured the poison down the drain.

"Not one word to anyone about this, got it?" I said. "Or I tell Thaddeus about you and Freddie."

She blinked back tears. "We're in love, you know."

"I'm sure you are," Gabriel said flatly.

Bridgette whipped her head toward him. "We are. It's just . . . the Reverend won't let us be together. He said that Freddie isn't going to be courting me. He's been chosen for someone else."

"It's all very interesting, Bridgette," I said, "but I'm trying to concentrate here." I opened the next vial and spilled the crystal powder into the running water.

"Really, Mia?" Bridgette said. "Because Freddie was chosen for you."

I stopped, stunned into silence. Bridgette stood, hands on hips, her glare as sharp as the knives hanging on the magnetic strip behind her.

"Well," Gabriel said to me with a falsely pleasant, strange smile. "At least you know what you're getting now, huh? No surprises."

Before I could say anything, Bridgette lunged for him with her nails out like a cat's claws.

"You bastard!" she cried.

He held up his hands, shielding his face. "I was kidding!"

"Bridgette," I said in the most calming voice I could muster. "Stop or else . . . " It seemed to draw her attention from Gabriel. I picked up another vial and emptied it. "I can guarantee you Freddie is not interested in courting me. From what I—" I stopped for a second. "From what I can tell, he's very interested in you."

A small grin crept up her face. "Good." But then her lip, stretched into that upturned smile, began to tremble. "But we can't be together. The Reverend won't allow it."

"Why not?" I asked.

Bridgette threw her arms out to her sides. "Because he makes the decisions, Mia. He's the one we answer to. We serve him."

"You are so brainwashed," Gabriel said.

"Shut up," Bridgette said. "All you are is a boy slut who was dragged here to Edenton by your parents to cleanse you of your disgusting sins."

Gabriel didn't move, didn't say anything back, only lowered his chin to his chest and glowered at her. After a few seconds of tense silence, he asked, "How do you know about that?"

"Some of us are more privy to information than others, Gabriel. I heard about your ways well before you got here."

I had the sense then not to ask what she meant, even though I had a good clue, considering what he'd said about drugs and tattoos—and what he didn't say about the girls in New York.

I pinned her with a pointed glare. "What happened in our lives before Edenton doesn't matter, Bridgette."

"Yeah, well . . . " Bridgette fiddled with the hem of her skirt. "Look, you have your poison." She waved a hand at the remaining full vials by the sink. "I won't say anything if you don't say anything about Freddie." She shifted her eyes to Gabriel and back to me again. "And if you refuse to court Freddie."

Freddie was a sweet, good guy but I did just see him in a very intimate position with Bridgette. "Of course I'll refuse to court Freddie."

"Won't matter soon anyway," Gabriel said.

"What does that mean?" Bridgette asked.

"Nothing," I said and reached for another vial. As I unscrewed the cap, I heard a sound outside the kitchen door.

"Someone's coming," Gabriel whispered.

Bridgette threw a smirk in my direction. "Might be Agatha," she said.

I shoved all the vials into the pocket of my dress and quickly locked the pantry, throwing the key to Bridgette. She frowned as she slipped it onto her wrist.

The kitchen door swung open. Freddie walked in. Grizz was huge, and Freddie was close to his size. I'd never noticed Freddie's potential menace until we were in the kitchen, after hours, with his . . . girlfriend? I'd seen him naked, and he shouldn't have seemed quite as scary. Shouldn't have.

His dark eyes looked Gabriel and me over with suspicion, then focused on Bridgette. "What's going on?"

"Found my key!" she smiled, holding up her wrist.

"Good." He swung an open palm to us. "What are they doing here?"

"Well, Mia?" Bridgette asked. "What are you doing here?"

No help from her, then. I stood silently, blinking rapidly, trying to think of an excuse. I was growing tired of all the acting—the lying. I wasn't a natural liar.

Gabriel reached up and placed his hand on Freddie's shoulder. Freddie looked down at it as if his hand were made from flesh-eating acid.

"Fred," Gabriel said. "Got some news. Looks like we're going to have to blackmail you."

"Didn't we just blackmail Bridgette?" I asked him.

"You did!" Bridgette said with a perfect pout that made Freddie's eyes cloud with doubt.

Freddie swiped Gabriel's hand away. "Mia, what's this about?"

"Uh." I stuck my hands in my pockets, one touching the vials of poison, the other fingering the microphone. The idea struck, so obvious and clear that I couldn't believe I didn't think of it earlier. "Freddie, you know the back gate? The one through the jungle that leads to the administrative section of Edenton?"

Freddie glanced around uncomfortably. "Yeah."

"You think you can leave that unlocked?"

He tilted his head to the side. "Why, Mia?"

I glanced at Gabriel. He smiled a knowing, crooked smile. I smiled back, because despite it all, his sudden coldness that night on the mountain, the push-pull earlier in the tunnel, he was with me, here in Edenton.

I reached in my pocket and touched the microphone. All the network needed was a location, the code to enter the tunnels, and the invasion could begin.

# Chapter Thirty-One

Dawn approached quickly, the sky lightening over the trees in the East. Bridgette and I rushed back to our cottage to change for breakfast prep before the other girls woke.

The vials clinked together in my pocket. By the time we'd talked to Freddie, it was late and I expected Agatha in the kitchen at any moment. I'd have to figure out a way to get the vials back into the pantry during or after breakfast.

Inside our cottage, Dina and Aliyah were still asleep in their bunks, the thin gray light seeping into the room. I sat on my empty bed, still made from the day before, and unlaced my boots. Bridgette did the same, but with a sour look on her perfectly sculpted face. I glanced up at Lily's bunk, then down at Juanita's, both deserted, tautly made, the blankets flawless and stretched so tight a button could bounce off of them. Their set of bunk beds was like an abandoned ship, a ghost ship, anchored to the floor of our cottage. An everyday reminder of what the Reverend had done.

I scooped a change of uniform from my trunk and headed into the bathroom. Immediately, I poured the rest of the poison into the toilet and flushed it.

"Hurry up," Bridgette said, banging on the door.

I changed, brushed my teeth, pulled my hair back in a ponytail, and placed the empty vials in the pocket of my skirt. I swung the door open with all the energy I had left in me.

I grinned at Bridgette. "Do you think I look pretty?" I asked her.

"No," she said. "You never look pretty."

I held out my hand. "Give me the key back or I'll go ask Freddie if he thinks I look pretty."

"Why are you being so mean?" she asked me, taking the bracelet off and handing it to me.

"Stress."

I dropped it in my pocket as Bridgette slipped past me into the bathroom and slammed the door. I was being mean, and I knew it. But

227

sometimes that's what Bridgette reacted to best: a spoonful of her own bitter medicine.

"You guys are up early," Aliyah said, rubbing her eyes.

"I didn't sleep much," I said.

She looked worried, her skin creasing between her dark, thin brows. I knew what she was thinking. That I couldn't sleep because of my Prayer Circle experience. I had to tell her the truth at some point, about the network. I wouldn't have to blackmail her for help.

Dina hopped out of her bunk, and as she and Aliyah were pulling uniforms from their trunks, we heard a knock at the door. Before I could answer it, the door swung open. He stood in the doorway like a big tree, thick arms branching out on either side, clutching the jamb.

"Girls," Thaddeus said, ignoring Aliyah and Dina in their varying states of undress and staring directly at me. "Would you please make way?"

I stepped back away from the door and Freddie rolled in a wheelchair. Sitting in that wheelchair, a chalk-white sheet tucked up to her chin, was Juanita. My heart slammed into my ribs at the sight of her. Freddie parked the chair next to her bunk.

I whispered her name but kept my distance. Her eyes were open, but they were blank and glassy. Strands of dark hair escaped the elastic tie at the nape of her neck and hung around her drawn face.

Aliyah threaded her arms through her uniform dress and rushed to her side. "What happened to her?" she asked, stroking the skin along Juanita's hand with her fingers, and skimming them along her arm, near the tape that anchored a tube running from her arm to a bag of liquid hanging on the back of the wheelchair.

"Accidental gunshot wound in the village where she was volunteering," Thaddeus said.

Freddie stood behind him with a grim expression. He then escaped the cottage without a word.

"Gunshot?" Dina asked.

I stood staring at Juanita. She was as pale as the sheet draped over her, dark circles like purple bruises beneath her eyes. I could barely believe she was here. What did she remember? From her deadened gaze, it seemed she didn't remember much of anything. Or even heard what we were saying. I blinked out of my daze.

"Why isn't she in the infirmary?" I asked quietly.

Thaddeus was quiet for a moment, his eyes still on me. He said, "We're waiting for the new doctor to arrive."

"New doctor?" Aliyah asked. "Where is Doc Gladstone?"

I said nothing and hoped my blank expression didn't betray the fact that I knew what happened to Doc Gladstone.

"He's unavailable," Thaddeus said. "The Reverend will explain when he is ready."

"If she was shot, shouldn't she be in the hospital?" I asked, finding my voice.

"She was discharged from the hospital in San Sebastian earlier." His dismissive tone sent ice through my veins. "I've asked Nurse Ivy to check on Juanita, but she's held up on an assignment for the Reverend. She'll be here when she's finished up." He inclined his head in our direction. "Until later, ladies."

As soon as he was gone, I joined Aliyah at Juanita's side. I knelt down next to the wheelchair and placed my palm on Juanita's forehead, unsure why. But it seemed like the appropriate thing to do with my shaking hands. She smelled of adhesive and pungent alcohol and something I couldn't place, something lost and foreign. Her eyes remained unfocused, the distance in them frightening me.

Too softly for Aliyah to hear, I whispered, "I'm sorry," into Juanita's ear. "I'm sorry for leaving you alone." She didn't react.

"What is she doing here?" Bridgette asked, standing in the bathroom doorway. She stared at Juanita as if she were laced with writhing maggots.

"She's here to recover," I said.

"From what?"

"A gunshot," Dina said as she blinked back tears. She looked away from Juanita and focused on tying her shoes. "It happened while she was helping the poor."

Images rushed back from that night, the memory raging out of control for a second. I fought the urge to cry.

"A gunshot?" Bridgette asked. She swung a look at me. "I can't believe you left her alone in that village."

"Bridgette!" Aliyah said. "They didn't choose to leave her. They followed the Reverend's orders." She turned to me. "Right Mia?"

"Of course I didn't want to leave her," I said, trying to hide the hitch in my voice. In my mind, all I saw was Juanita, laid out on the black asphalt of that jungle road with black blood seeping through her red dress.

Juanita mumbled something.

"What, Juanita?" Aliyah asked.

Juanita's eyes remained unfocused. "Don't leave me alone," she whispered. "Don't leave me."

Guilt tightened my chest. I rose to my feet and brought my hand to my throat. I heaved a sob I couldn't hold back.

"Of course you didn't want to leave her," Bridgette said to me with a hint of malice. "Come on girls, we have breakfast duty."

"Wait!" I said. "We can't leave Juanita. You just said—"

"We're leaving her in our very safe cottage. Not in the middle of a strange village."

I glanced down at Juanita, then thought of the vials in my pocket. I needed to refill them and get them back into the pantry before anyone noticed they were gone.

"I'll stay," Aliyah said.

"You can't," Bridgette said. "We're short-handed." She gestured at Lily's empty bunk, and at Juanita.

"Get the girls from the laundry to help," Aliyah said and sat on the bunk next to Juanita. "I'm staying here."

"Then Mia," Bridgette said, "you need to work harder to make up for it."

I shrugged. "We'll see."

Bridgette sneered, but said nothing to me. "Let's go, Dina."

Dina gave Juanita a small, encouraging smile and followed Bridgette from the cabin, pulling the door shut quietly.

"Thank you," I said to Aliyah. "For staying with her."

"I want to," Aliyah said, pushing a strand of curly hair from Juanita's face.

"But if Nurse Ivy—"

There was a knock at our cottage door, then, and without waiting for an answer, Mama stepped in. My speeding pulse felt as though it would burst through my veins. I needed to get to the kitchen to replace the poison. And I wasn't ready to face her.

"Mia," Mama said. "We need to talk."

"I—" I started to protest.

"Now," she said in a snippy tone that didn't sound at all motherly. At least not a motherly tone I'd heard from her since I was a young kid, when I'd done something wrong and was ordered into a time out.

"It's all right," Aliyah said. "I'll make sure Juanita is okay. Promise."

"Outside please." Mama motioned behind her.

"Be right there," I said. After Mama left to wait for me outside, I turned to Aliyah. "Thank you," I whispered.

She smiled.

Mama stood outside our cottage. When she saw me, she turned and walked in long, confident steps. Her uniform dress, starched and unwrinkled, was as stiff as her spine. She sat on a bench beside the path. It was still early, so many of the Flock were asleep.

I sat next to her.

She folded her hands in her lap.

I shifted, locking my ankles together.

She tucked a piece of hair behind her ear.

I leaned forward, elbows on my thighs.

She stretched her neck to the left, and to the right.

A soft breeze blew through the frangipani bush next to her; the cloying scent was almost too much for so early in the morning. With no sleep for two nights, I was beginning to feel dizzy.

"How was it?" she asked.

"How do you think it was, Mama?" I asked. "Monsieur Lambert sends his regards."

She half-turned her head toward me, saying nothing, her eyes widening a fraction. Her mouth opened, then closed again, like a landed fish. After long moments of impenetrable silence between us, she said, "Lambert?" in a choked voice.

"You knew what they were sending me into," I said. "And you let it happen anyway."

She wrung her hands in her lap, tension paling the skin of her knuckles and wrists. The sun was rising now, casting a pale pink glow in the sky. Hazy morning shadows stretched across the path, as if deciding to come into sharper focus.

Just like Mama, I thought. Deciding whether she wanted to tell me the truth, or remain fuzzy and indistinct.

Finally, she said, "Mia, I didn't have a choice. The Reverend would have forced you to attend anyway, and if I tried to stop it, we would have been punished."

"We?"

"Your brother and myself," she said. "That's how it works. Threats." She fully turned to me. "You know there are those of us who remember. Practically everything we experienced. Some of what happened to us is murky, but other things we remember. We spend every day hiding our memories of that place, of what they make us do."

"What would they have done to you," I asked, "if you stopped me from going?"

Mama flattened her palm along her skirt, straightening a crease that wasn't there. "Those kind of details you don't need, Mia. If I can't protect you from the Reverend and Las Casitas, I can protect you from knowing things like that, from experiencing things like that."

She peered up into the lightening sky. "I was so afraid when we first arrived. Your father left and all I had was you and the church." Her green eyes swelled with tears. "I couldn't find work. And if I did, I couldn't afford to pay anyone to watch you while I went to work. I found out I was pregnant with Max. It was one thing after the next. Hurdle after hurdle." She wiped her eyes. "Then I heard about Edenton, about the utopian society the Reverend created, how they'd purchased land and built the town.

"It was so beautiful when we first came here. The love, the support. Everyone wanted to take care of us, of each other. And I wanted to take care of them, to contribute to the whole. It was such a loving place to be."

"But it's changed here, Mama," I said.

She glanced around at the perfect flowers, the quaint cottages, the well-kept yards, the pristine white fence that held the jungle at bay.

"Why can't we just leave?" I asked.

"And go where?" Mama raised her voice, and caught herself. "Do what to make money to survive? And do you think he'd let us go? Don't you think I've tried before?"

"You tried before?" I asked in disbelief. "You tried to escape?"

"A few of us did. You and your brother were with us, asleep in the back of the truck. But we were caught . . . and punished." She smoothed her palm along her thigh again. "I don't want you to ever feel pain like that, Mia."

My stomach pitched. "Like what, Mama? What did they do to you?"

"It doesn't matter." Her lips tightened. "Clearly, the memory drugs at Las Casitas didn't work. Just pretend they do. Pretend like the rest of us do. Don't say anything, don't talk to anyone about it. And we'll get through this, okay darling?"

She hadn't called me darling in months. "What is there to get through, Mama? This is all there is. We aren't living. We're existing at the hands of an egotistical madman."

Mama's face crumpled. Her soft brown hair fell from its knot as she tilted her head forward. "This is our life, Mia. We need to accept it. Find joy where you can. Even if it's with that boy Gabriel."

A surge of hope flooded me—fleeting hope. I pictured a normal life with Gabriel that I'd never have. Even something as simple as going on a date. It would never happen in Edenton.

"The Reverend wants me to court Freddie," I said.

She twisted her head toward me. "The security guard?"

I nodded.

She nodded back. "He seems nice enough. Court him then. Just try to find happiness in the little things, in the other people, in the sanctity of ritual and routine, and it will be a fine life here, Mia."

"I don't want a life here. I want to make my own choices, create my own destiny. I don't want to be whored out to old men. Goddammit, Mama, this isn't living!"

Before she could chastise me for taking the Lord's name in vain, the alarm sounded, high and grave and oppressive, through the sweet-smelling morning air.

It was time for a Bright Night.

In the unflinching light of day.

# Chapter Thirty-Two

I rushed back to the cottage. Aliyah was walking out the door like an obedient robot.

"You can't go!" I said, grabbing her shoulders.

She furrowed her brow. "Huh? But I have to go to Bright Night."

"No," I said pushing her back into the cottage. "Please, stay here with Juanita. I'm sure Thaddeus would understand."

Aliyah bit her thumbnail. "But Nurse Ivy—"

"Don't trust her, Aliyah. Don't leave her alone with Juanita."

Aliyah looked away for a moment, memories dancing behind her eyes. Her gaze snapped to mine. "Oh! She was there. That night of Prayer Circle. She . . . " Aliyah skated her palm over her upper arm.

I took her hand. "Please. Stay here. Watch over her. If Nurse Ivy comes—" I stopped, unsure what to say. What could she do if Nurse Ivy showed up and began poking Juanita with needles? Could Aliyah stop her? "Just keep her away from Juanita."

"How?"

I glanced at the door, knowing there was no lock. At least not from the inside. "Hit her."

Aliyah's eyes widened. "Huh?"

"Smack her, kick her, do anything you can to keep her away." I started toward the door.

"Where are you going?" she asked.

"I have to get to the kitchen before Bright Night begins."

She said something, maybe a mumbled prayer, but I ran away too fast to hear it. I dodged Flock members dragging themselves toward the pavilion, which was the opposite direction from the kitchen. Off in the distance, I spotted Agatha, her drawn face the only one visible in a sea of turned heads. She was coming toward the kitchen. Toward me. She hadn't seen me, though, so I hurried into the kitchen.

Inside, it was empty. Items for breakfast preparation were left on the counter, abandoned. Cartons of eggs sat open; slices of bread lay out, slathered with butter, ready for the ovens. Boxes of mangos and papayas were stacked on the floor, a few pieces of fruit half-chopped on cutting boards.

I grabbed a blue box of fine salt off a shelf. Pouring the salt into the small vials was close to impossible at first. My hands shook and salt spilled on the floor. Frantically, I searched for a small funnel I'd had last night. I riffled through a drawer, the clatter of plastic and metal loud to my ears. Finding one, I filled the remaining vials. My tired eyes stung from lack of sleep. Through blurry vision, I screwed on the tops and laid them out carefully on the counter next to the pantry.

My hands still shook as I tried to shove the key in the lock. I dropped the key, picked it up, and tried again. I had to work faster, but my fingers felt thick and clumsy, and slippery with sweat. Sweat ran down my face, into my already blurry eyes. I wiped it away with the shoulder of my sleeve.

"Hurry up, hurry up," I muttered to myself.

Finally the key slid in the lock. It clinked open. The box was still on the top shelf, seemingly untouched. I grabbed it, carefully put the vials back in, and began placing the box back on the shelf.

A click sounded behind me. I pushed the box on the shelf and shut the pantry door. I stepped as far away from the door as I could get before Agatha walked into the kitchen.

"Mia?" she said, wrinkles in her brow deepening with suspicion. "What are you doing here?"

"I—" I glanced down at the salt spilled on the floor. "I made a mess and wanted to clean it up before I went to Bright Night."

"There's no waiting for Bright Night," Agatha said, coming forward. "Go, now. I'll take care of this."

"Of course." I nodded once and headed out the door.

It was then I realized I hadn't locked the pantry.

* * *

As the sun rose over the trees, heat thickened the air and morning fog clouded the depths of the jungle, creeping through the leaves and into shafts of light. Insects swooped through the pavilion. Lazy ceiling fans circled above, barely creating a cool breeze below.

I stood alone at the edge of the pavilion, watching the Flock take their seats. I scanned the crowd for Gabriel, wondering what happened to him after we'd separated and I'd watched him head back to his cottage. After we'd left Bridgette and Freddie in the kitchen, we'd given the network the location of the back gate, as well as the code to enter the tunnels. Had they even gotten the message? We had no way of knowing.

I made my way between bodies, trying to wedge through people to get to my assigned seat with the girls of my cottage. Or those who were left from my cottage. Only Bridgette and Dina sat at our seats, backs erect and eyes alert, staring at the empty stage. I hoped Aliyah would stay behind with Juanita, even if Nurse Ivy showed up. Aliyah had it in her to take care of Nurse Ivy if she needed to, and it gave me a little bit of comfort.

Mama dutifully directed her charges, the children from the schoolhouse, into their seats along the right side of the pavilion. My stomach clenched as I saw Max recognize me. His face brightened. He shot up in his seat, as if he wanted to run over to me, but Mama gently pushed him back down. On her lips, I read the word "after." He gave me a small wave.

I waited silently, stealing glances at the row where Gabriel should have been sitting with his cottage mates, hoping he wasn't doing anything reckless, or stupid. Or overly courageous.

Freddie entered alongside Grizz, and they stood at the front of the two main aisles while the other security guards ushered any stragglers into the pavilion. As usual, their guns were slung across their backs. Freddie's eyes went straight to Bridgette, but she didn't look his way, only kept her gaze fastened on the Reverend's vacant throne.

Slowly, I slipped my hand into my pocket and pulled out the remaining microphone. I didn't know if it was working or not, but I stuck it beneath the bench anyway.

Moments passed. Long moments when nothing happened onstage, and only the murmurs of the Flock could be heard, growing louder as time went on.

I leaned over to Dina. "Never had one of these during the day, huh?" I asked her, mostly for whomever might hear me through the microphone. "Why do you think we're having it?"

She shrugged one dainty shoulder. "Maybe the Reverend has something special he wants to preach to us about. Or maybe—"

"Ssssh!" Bridgette said.

I waved my open palm at the stage. "It hasn't even started yet. No need for shushing."

Dina cracked a very small smile.

"Doesn't matter," Bridgette said, straightening her back and elongating her neck. "We must be respectful of the way."

"What way, Bridgette?" I asked in a low voice. "We wait for the Reverend to preach at us, then he does something horrible to teach us a lesson?"

"What are you—" Bridgette hissed, but she was cut off by a round of gasps.

I glanced at the stage and watched, helplessly, as two security guards I didn't recognize shoved Doc Gladstone to the front of the Reverend's throne. My gut dropped at the sight.

They forced him to his knees. His face, half-covered by dangling dreadlocks, was swollen and ravaged. A trickle of blood ran down his chin from a split in his lip. His left eye was shut, bulging to almost the size of an egg. He lifted his head, but winced in pain, his right shoulder veering off at a funny angle.

The pavilion went silent. No one moved to help him. No one asked what happened. Everyone accepted what they saw before them, without question or doubt.

Long minutes passed as a kneeling Doc Gladstone stared off into the distance without a wince or a word. His posture, although broken, was strong and willful. The collar of his shirt was torn, exposing blotchy, darkening bruises on the dark skin of his chest. With steely eyes, he dared us to say anything, but I knew to offer words of comfort or prayer would be an insult.

"Pride." The word boomed through the speakers in the pavilion.

The Reverend, dressed fully in blue, ambled onstage, stroking his beard thoughtfully. "Pride brings destruction in our kind of life. It casts a shadow over the land in which it walks, a pall over the selfless, tainting the mutual sacrifice and respect we have for each other."

He approached Doc Gladstone, who, despite his determined stance, recoiled. With the tip of a chubby finger, the Reverend stroked one of Doc Gladstone's dreadlocks. Suddenly, he flipped it up into the air, and with a quickness I'd never witnessed from him before, whipped something shiny from the pocket of his shirt. With two quick hacks, he sliced off one of Doc Gladstone's dreadlocks. It danced up through the air like the tail of a kite, then sank to the ground with a thump.

Doc Gladstone remained stoic, expression blank. I hoped that was blank indifference, and not fear. Although I knew he must have been as terrified as I was. More so. Much more.

A wave of panic washed over me, making me light-headed. Not to him. Not Doc Gladstone. To be made a fool of in front of the people he cared for, the people he'd sworn to protect; it sickened me. But something—years of caution, of nervousness, of fear—kept me in my seat.

"What is pride?" the Reverend asked. He skated his gaze over the Flock, all of whom reflected Doc Gladstone's blank expression. "Pride means to act arrogantly, to have a high opinion of one's worth." He picked another dreadlock between his index finger and thumb, examined it with a tilt of his head, and severed it from Doc Gladstone's scalp. "Self conceit." He flicked the dreadlock before Doc Gladstone with disgust, as if it were a poisonous snake.

"How sharp is that knife?" Dina whispered in disbelief.

Maybe it was the only rational thought in her head, because none of this could certainly make sense to her. Doc Gladstone was a pillar of Edenton, not a spy for the network. I squinted at the knife in the Reverend's hand. It wasn't a knife at all.

"It's a scalpel," I whispered back.

With a shot of terror, I recognized it was a much larger version of the one I'd seen in Doc Gladstone's office.

The Reverend picked another dreadlock from Doc Gladstone's head. "Adam and Eve ate from the Tree of Knowledge so that they might elevate themselves, to be like God." He whacked the dreadlock off. "Pride." The Reverend lifted another. "Lucifer's desire to compete with God led to his fall from heaven." And the dreadlock was sliced away. "Pride." Beneath that grizzly red beard, the Reverend's lips twitched into a sadistic smirk. "The Tower of Babel was constructed to reach up to the heavens, to bring people closer to God's level." Slash. Another lock hit the stage floor with a dull thud. "Pride."

My breath caught in my throat.

In a darkening voice, the Reverend continued, "David thought himself so above others that he felt he could sleep with another man's wife and murder him." With a calculated swing, another ropy lock fell away. "Pride."

The Reverend snatched the rest of Doc Gladstone's dreadlocks with a swipe of his hand—the few that were left—and jerked Doc's head up and back. Doc Gladstone winced, obvious pain wracking his body, but he kept his expression stony.

"As we all must learn," the Reverend said as he held the scalpel aloft, "Pride cometh before the fall." With a whip of his thick arm, the Reverend slashed the sharp blade across Doc Gladstone's throat.

Silence.

Everything came into focus with agonizing slowness.

A spray of blood shot through the shafts of golden morning sunlight.

The Reverend released the remaining dreadlocks.

They curtained Doc Gladstone's face for a moment before parting, revealing a look of stunned surprise.

The body fell forward, head tipping back and eyes gazing heavenward.

The Reverend splayed his arms, presenting Doc Gladstone as if he were prized slaughtered cattle.

Doc Gladstone's dark, shocked eyes met mine as he toppled over. And in that moment, I saw it. That flicker of tenacity that never seemed to leave him. Even as his life was stolen away.

He hit the stage with a violent thud. Blood pooled around his head.

The Reverend stepped back to avoid getting a stain on his shiny white shoes.

Then, nothing. Only the creeping blood on the stage moved, widening into a horrifying halo around Doc Gladstone's head. The image would be seared into my memory forever. An image that would visit my nightmares, and be with me every day. An image I'd never forget, no matter what I did or where I went.

But that was exactly the Reverend's cruel intent.

I glanced at Mama. She sat, hands clasped in front of her, mouth tight. The children surrounding her stared with petrified fascination at the stage. Mama blinked multiple times as if she were coming awake and, through the crowd of people between us, found my gaze.

*Get them out*, I wanted to yell across the pavilion. *Get the children out of here.*

But she didn't. Couldn't. The Reverend would never allow her to take them away.

She looked sad, defeated. Accepting her—our—situation.

"Our fine doctor," the Reverend said, now pacing behind Doc Gladstone like a winning prizefighter, "the person we trusted with our health, with the well-being of our physical forms, had decided a different fate for us. A fate that included destroying Edenton. Destroying everything we've created. Allowing the outside world—a world full of cruelty and depravity—to invade our peaceful lives."

My throat constricted. I blinked back tears. How long? I wondered selfishly. How long before the person up onstage, killed at the hands of the Reverend, was me?

A commotion started at the left side of the stage. The two security guards, the two that had dragged Doc Gladstone onto the stage, now shoved another person before the crowd. That person was Gabriel.

# Chapter Thirty-Three

I watched Gabriel's every movement, tears of shock blurring my vision. He stared wide-eyed down at Doc Gladstone's prone body, taking notice of the blood-soaked dreadlocks strewn about the stage. The security guards edged him forward, toward the Reverend, but Gabriel lunged back, only to be shoved again.

Warmth enclosed my hand. I tore my gaze from Gabriel and looked down to find Dina's fingers wrapped around my hand. When I met her eyes, I saw sympathy. Sadness. An urge for acceptance. Gabriel was going to be killed on that stage, like Doc Gladstone, and as a member of the Flock, I should—no must—concede to the Reverend's plan.

Thoughts tangled in my head, but before I could unravel them I heard the Reverend call my name. I jerked my head up to find people staring at me.

"Mia," he repeated, folding his hands in front of him, around the bulk of his belly. "Please come to the stage."

The breath left my lungs. My palm went to my chest. Beneath it, my heart pounded furiously.

"Me?" I asked.

The Reverend laughed, a curdled sound. He opened his arms wide at his sides. "Yes, child. Up on the stage, please."

I rose to my feet as if tugged up by strings and walked to the stage steps, avoiding all the eyes fixed on me. I felt the magnetic pull of Mama's worried stare, heard Max's whispered mumbles, but remained focused straight ahead. My legs jittered. Nerves clawed at my gut. I mounted the stairs, and stepped around Doc Gladstone's sprawled, lifeless legs. The toes of his boots were slick and dark with blood.

I didn't look at Gabriel. I didn't look at the Reverend. I kept my eyes focused on the trees in the distance, sunlight piercing between the leaves. From behind, I felt a presence, looming with an airless heat, and twisted around to see Thaddeus standing very close. Terrifyingly close. Behind him, in the brightening morning sun, Agatha clutched one of the pavilion's columns with anger scored deep in her features.

Thaddeus snagged my arm, holding me utterly immobile. His fingers dug into my skin with bruising pain. I winced.

One of the security guards released Gabriel, leaving him struggling in the other guard's hold. The guard picked up Doc Gladstone's ankles and dragged him off the stage. Blood left a long slick smear trailing from his body. His limp arms trailed the wooden floor, his own shorn dreadlocks catching in his fingers.

I swallowed down bile, and turned my face away.

"No," Thaddeus said in my ear. He breath smelled of peppermint and alcohol. "Watch, Mia. Watch what we do to the traitorous."

"Are you calling me a traitor?" I asked.

"Now, Mia," he said from behind my shoulder. "Why would I say that?"

Doc Gladstone's head banged down the stage steps. The sound echoed through the pavilion, bouncing off the trees, disappearing into the muck of the jungle. Onstage, the blood was already viscid and a blackish crimson, coagulating at the edges of the long smear. The colors were almost beautiful in the sun, like a swatch of watercolor.

"Now, this boy," the Reverend said, swinging his open palm in Gabriel's direction, "is the very definition of prideful."

Gabriel's attention snapped to the Reverend. He blinked around in confusion.

"First there is vanity," the Reverend shouted.

I watched Gabriel steel himself, fists clenching. His eyes shot from one security guard to the next and I could tell he was trying to plan some kind of escape. But how could he get away? What could I do? I couldn't wrench away from Thaddeus's grip.

"Charm is deceitful, and beauty is vain—"

"I'm not vain, you bastard," Gabriel said in a steady, calm voice.

The Reverend's smug smile melted from his face. Behind his wiry, red beard, his mouth tightened. No one spoke back to him during a Bright Night. Let alone call him a name other than the Reverend or Sir.

But Gabriel, eyes ablaze, appeared fearless. "But charming, sure," he said, mouth half-curled in a smile. "I'll go ahead and take that as a compliment."

The Reverend inhaled a deep, calming breath and turned to me. "But where would he be without that pretty face, eh Mia?" The Reverend snarled and twisted back to Gabriel. "A pretty face, a cultivated charisma that lures in victims—hopeless girls who, despite wanting more from him, end up defiled."

My stomach turned over.

"Hopeless?" Gabriel squinted at the Reverend, then at me, and his eyes widened as if he realized what the Reverend had said. "Mia isn't hopeless," Gabriel said through his teeth. "And we never . . . " he paused and flicked a glance at me " . . . defiled."

No one dared to snicker. No one dared to move.

The Reverend gave a thick, hearty laugh. "We know of your wicked ways," he said. "What you did before you came to Edenton. What you've done since you've been here." The Reverend smirked down at Gabriel's mother and father, sitting next to each other, hands clasped together. "The two of you have suffered enough. His past has destroyed the soul within and we are left with nothing but a shell. It may be impossible for me to resurrect what is already spoiled."

A tear trailed down Gabriel's mother's face.

"Other than my sin of vanity," Gabriel asked, "what exactly did I do?" He jerked against the security guard's grip. "Shouldn't you read me my full list of accusations before judgment?"

"Of course, Gabriel," the Reverend said as if he were talking to a young child. He twirled the scalpel between his fingers, grinning. "This boy exhibits the ultimate kind of pride. The pride of a boy who . . . " he pointed the blade at Gabriel " . . . got away with murder."

Gabriel's face went bloodless with mingled horror and confusion. "What did you say?" he asked in a strangled whisper.

The Reverend turned to the Flock. "Those of you who have gotten to know this boy in the short time he's been here may not find this difficult to believe, but Gabriel here killed his own brother." He stamped his foot on the stage. "Killed! Without remorse, without punishment. This murderer walks among us!"

I wanted to reach out, take Gabriel's hand, try to comfort him. Tell him these were only words. Words used by the Reverend to intimidate. But Thaddeus held me back and all I could do was watch as Gabriel's eyes grew vacant. His arms hung stiffly at his sides, even as the guard clung to his bicep.

"He shot his brother at close range!" the Reverend yelled. "Directly in the face."

He shook his head and dropped the bloody scalpel in his hand on the stage. The clank reverberated through the rafters of the pavilion. He held out a hand and the security guard who had dragged Doc Gladstone off the stage placed a handgun in his palm. The Reverend held the gun up. "The murderer among us shot his brother with a gun like this one."

"But you just killed Doc Gladstone!" I yelled, thrashing in Thaddeus's grip.

He tugged me back.

The Reverend pivoted and faced me. "Doc Gladstone was a sinner. What did Gabriel's brother do to deserve to be killed so coldly?" He turned to Gabriel. "Eh, son? What did your brother do?"

As if snapping out of a dream, Gabriel blinked and glanced down at his parents. "What is going on?" he asked them. "Did you plan this?"

Neither of his parents would look up, keeping their focus on their joined hands. Together, as a couple, they silently and willingly abandoned him to the whims of the Reverend.

"Answer me, boy," the Reverend said.

"He did nothing," Gabriel whispered.

"Louder," the Reverend said.

"My brother did nothing to deserve what I did to him."

Gabriel's voice carried through the pavilion, but had lost all its strength. He was surrendering to the intimidation of the Reverend. And, brilliantly, the Reverend knew what chink to wedge open in Gabriel's armor.

"Nothing?" I cried, outraged. "He manipulated you when you were a little kid!" I turned to the Reverend. "Why are you doing this?"

"Doing what, my child?" the Reverend said, speaking to the crowd sitting in awe before him. "Exposing a murderer? A sinner? A prideful creature who duped us all into believing he was one of us?"

"He didn't dupe anyone," I said. "His parents brought him here because they thought it would help. That you could help." I waved a hand at the Flock. "That we all could help him."

The Reverend grew angry, his face reddening. Thaddeus's grip on my arm tightened. I shouldn't have been answering back.

Gabriel stared at me with unfocused eyes. "Stop."

I tried to take a step toward him, but Thaddeus wouldn't let me move an inch. "What?" I asked Gabriel. "Why?"

"Because it's true," Gabriel said. "I should have been punished. I wasn't."

"It wasn't your—"

"Enough!" the Reverend said. "Thaddeus, take her to the side of the stage until I'm ready for her."

*Ready for her?* My limbs went numb. I stumbled back, dragged by Thaddeus, close to where Agatha stood. Her face hadn't lost that snarling anger I'd seen before.

"What did you do?" she whispered to me. "How did you get into the pantry?"

Thaddeus was close enough to hear everything.

"I don't know what you mean," I lied, doing a poor job of it.

"You've changed everything, do you know that?" she said in a seething whisper. "Now, it won't be peaceful. It will be hell."

My stomach dropped. What would be hell?

"Control yourself, Agatha," Thaddeus said.

At the front of the stage, the Reverend folded his arms over his great bulk and glared down at the faces turned up to him in reverence and, what the Reverend considered essential, fear.

"Everyone, come to your feet," he said.

As the Flock did, he motioned for the guards. They swarmed the pavilion, guns flung across their backs, and began moving the benches that had been so carefully aligned. With scrapes and screeches along the wood floor, they arranged the benches in a circle, surrounding the perimeter of the pavilion. Without the rows of benches, the area was a vast, yawning space.

The Flock stood in the center of the pavilion in confusion. Mama huddled the younger schoolchildren around her, a few silently weeping.

"Grizz," the Reverend called down from the stage. "Take the children and Maria to the schoolhouse."

Grizz, who'd just placed a bench down at the edge of the pavilion, seemed confused for a moment and looked to Thaddeus for confirmation. From the corner of my vision, I saw Thaddeus curtly nod once. Grizz lumbered over to the children and herded them out of the pavilion. Mama trailed behind, flashing a concerned glance at me over her shoulder. Max turned from the small pack of children and ran toward the stage, calling my name. Grizz swooped him up in one big arm and carried him off to the schoolhouse. Max didn't utter a word. He reached out one small hand and waved to me.

I hoped it wasn't a wave of goodbye.

What was about to happen that even the Reverend didn't want the children to witness? They'd just witnessed the doctor, who'd treated them for sickness, who'd comforted them after vaccinations, killed brutally before their eyes. What was worse than that?

And what could I do to stop it?

The Reverend approached the end of the stage, picking his way over the trail of Doc Gladstone's blood. He pointed to Sister, standing in the middle of the crowd, her gray hair escaping from her headscarf. Flanking her, Suzanne and Kori, the girls from the sewing cottage, held onto Sister's arms. Her body wobbled and shook. She'd grown more and more feeble during the years I'd known her. I'd never noticed how feeble until that moment.

"Sister!" he called. "You've been here since Edenton was created. How does our accomplishment make you feel?"

Sister straightened with the help of the girls. "Well, Reverend, we've worked mighty hard to make Edenton what it is. And I know I feel like we've achieved something truly wonderful and unique."

"Really?" The Reverend sounded skeptical. "What about you, Freddie?"

Freddie stood at the perimeter of the pavilion and snapped his head up. "Sir?"

"You're new here in Edenton. Only been here a year. How do you feel about what we've created?"

Freddie glanced at Bridgette, whose attention was directed at the stage. He fidgeted with the strap of his gun. "It's a great accomplishment, sir," he said in such a way it almost sounded like a question. "We're a self-sustaining community. Like no other in the world."

"Like no other in the world," the Reverend repeated.

The Flock mumbled in agreement, a few calling out, "It's been God's work," and, "We've done what no other community has done before."

"So, what you folks are telling me," the Reverend said, "is that we've done something different here. Something special. Exceptional." He glanced back at Agatha and dipped his chin to her.

Agatha heaved a sigh. "Know this is your fault," she said to me and dashed down the stage steps.

I twisted to get a look at Thaddeus. He ignored me and kept his gaze fixed on the Flock.

"It seems," the Reverend said, "you've taken an immense amount of pride in your work here in Edenton."

At the word "pride," a wave of dismay swayed the Flock. People glanced at each other, worried.

Agatha appeared again, coming around the stage wheeling a tall plastic box on one of the dollies we used for taking kitchen waste to the heap. She made her way to the center of the Flock and asked people to form a circle in front of the benches that had been pushed back. In the center of the pavilion, she placed the box on the ground with effort. No one helped or offered to help, which was very unlike anyone in Edenton. She ensured the lid was secure, not locked, but sitting firmly on top of the box before stepping away.

Thaddeus shoved me forward. The security guard holding Gabriel did the same, sliding our protesting feet through the blood congealing onstage. We met in the center, facing each other.

Gabriel's eyes met mine. He looked thrown, as confused as I was. But I saw something beyond the confusion. A dark resignation.

"Well, now," the Reverend bellowed. "It seems we can't remain here in Edenton much longer. Doc Gladstone saw to that prior to his passing."

He paced the stage before us, intermittently blocking our view of the Flock. From what I could see, they stood dumbstruck, staring up at him. The box sat ominously in the center of the circle.

"I understand how proud you feel of this place. I do. Truly. How can I punish you for creating this beautiful, loving place?"

"So you will show us mercy?" someone from the Flock asked. "You are a great leader, Reverend."

The Reverend froze. "Mercy?" His voice was suddenly very small.

He looked back at Thaddeus with a look of doubt. I sensed Thaddeus shake his head at the Reverend.

The Reverend turned back to the Flock, cocked his head, and grinned. "No, children. No mercy. Please, Agatha, open the box and pass around the contents."

As she did, I craned to see what she was handing out—difficult to do with Thaddeus holding me so tightly. I saw objects of different shapes and sizes, glinting in the morning sun.

"Children," the Reverend said. "We cannot stay here any longer. People from the outside world will be here shortly to take over control of Edenton! They want to destroy how we live, our way of life! Therefore, I'm leaving Edenton to create a new paradise. A pure place, untouched by the traitors who have betrayed my trust and love. Where no sinners from the evil world outside can ever disturb our paradise." He held his hands out to either side. "Today, I am Noah. Those who come to attack us, to take away what we've created, are our Flood. The Ark awaits. As Noah took the unblemished animals, the ones strong enough to resist the great wickedness and sin, I take the strongest of our Flock." He swept out his hand in a grand gesture.

Thaddeus thrust a length of heavy chain into my hands.

Gabriel was already holding an aluminum bat.

I looked out at the Flock. Agatha was passing out weapons: crowbars, pointed wooden sticks, ropes with weighted metal balls. Bats, like Gabriel's, chains, like mine.

"Let God decide!" the Reverend yelled, arms outstretched to the heavens. "Those of you with God on your side will come with me to the new Eden! The rest of you will die here in Hell."

The Reverend wasn't going to kill us as the network suspected. He was going to make us kill each other.

# Chapter Thirty-Four

The Flock, laden with heavy weapons, stared at the Reverend in confusion and horror.

"What do you want us to do?" someone asked. It sounded like Angél.

"Fight," the Reverend said, voice colored with anger. "Fight each other for the privilege of joining me on my pilgrimage to the new Edenton."

Everyone continued to stare at him, baffled.

"You have thirty seconds to say a prayer for God's blessing," the Reverend said. "At my command, you will begin!"

Time ticked by. Tears welled in eyes, lips trembled, mouths mumbled in prayer. But no one questioned. No one challenged. All remained paralyzed in compliance, like lambs to the slaughter.

"You," Thaddeus said in my ear, "are to fight Gabriel."

He waved a hand at Gabriel, who was spinning the bat around like a top on the stage floor. He looked up then, eyes flicking to mine. He squinted at me, a look I couldn't quite decipher. A calculating look, or perhaps sinister? Fear shot through my nerves.

The chain in my hands was heavy, cold. I wasn't sure if I could entirely lift it, let alone swing it at an opponent.

Thaddeus shoved me forward. I tripped toward Gabriel. His gaze slid from mine, back down to the bat in his hands.

"Fifteen seconds!" the Reverend yelled.

The guard released Gabriel and stepped away, eyeing us warily. I glanced back. Thaddeus now stood some distance behind me.

I heard a fleshy thud. Even before the Reverend called time, the Flock began fighting. Already, a body was down, but I couldn't see who it was or how badly the person was hurt.

The Reverend walked between us to his throne at the back of the stage and lowered himself into the seat. He banged the armrest with a meaty fist. "Everyone . . . fight!" he yelled.

I was close enough to Gabriel to hear his intake of breath. With the tips of his fingers, he lifted his bat in the air and twirled it at his side.

"Swing at me," he whispered.

"What?"

"They were dumb enough to give us weapons, Ricci. Let's use them for the greater good."

A flash of fear tempered by determination. "On three?" I asked.

"No," he said, tightening his grip. "Now!"

We swung at each other, but knew to bow away from the hurtling weapons. We pivoted. I lunged at Thaddeus, swinging the heavy chain at his head. All the muscles in my arms screamed in protest, but I levered back and used my weight to counterweigh the momentum of the chain. It winged through the air with a woosh, hurtling toward Thaddeus's temple.

In a flash, he lifted his arm and the chain whirled around his wrist, wrapping it like a bracelet. He caught the end in his huge hand with an assured, quick grasp. With one tug, I fell on my knees in front of him. Pain exploded through my kneecaps, now sticky with Doc Gladstone's blood. My palm, still caught in the chain, stung. I gasped as my fingers went numb.

He leaned down and through gritted teeth said, "Do you think you can fight me, little girl?"

He jerked me to my feet. Fury burned in his dark eyes. He tried to whip the chain from me, but I wouldn't let go. Despite the dizzying stinging in my legs and hand I held on, tugging at it with as much strength as I could muster.

As if from a distance, I heard the Reverend cackle. "Can't disarm a child, Thaddeus? Maybe you deserve to remain here in Hell when they come."

They. The network. They were coming and the Reverend knew it.

Thaddeus threw the Reverend a frightening expression, eyes hard and mouth tense with anger. It stole the laugh from the Reverend's throat. The Reverend sobered and fidgeted on his throne. He looked away.

Thaddeus lifted me to my feet with what seemed like a mere flex of his bicep. As the pain faded in my legs, sounds around me grew louder and sharper. Fighting. Hits, slaps, crashes, and thuds; cries for mercy and grunts of strength. The sounds of the Flock fighting each other for their lives.

But I couldn't look away from Thaddeus. His face was so close to mine. The whites of his eyes were clear and unblemished. Like the purest marble. But his irises were fathomless, deep with loathing.

"You've caused enough trouble, Mia," he said. "We should have taken care of you when we had the opportunity."

"Oh?" I said and wondered when that opportunity happened. During Prayer Circle? Or sooner? White-hot anger welled inside my chest. I planted my feet firmly, one behind the other and let out a breath. I shot my knee up with enough force to connect with his groin. His eyes grew wide. He buckled over.

With strength in the midst of the pain, Thaddeus backhanded me across the face. I tasted coppery blood as I skidded backward along the stage floor with bruising force, my head hitting hard when I finally came to a halt. The chain chased across the stage after me, clinking frenetically until it crashed into a pile. I crumpled into a ball, gasping with shock and pain.

Thaddeus threw the Reverend a hard look, then glared down. He kicked out at me and his booted foot connected with my ribcage. I cried out as my left side twitched in agony.

"You're not worth any more of my time," he said, and waved someone over. "I have other things to attend to."

I heard the chain again, this time a slow, neat jingle of straightening links. With effort, I glanced up to see Agatha coming toward me, a length of chain dangling from her veiny hand. I struggled to raise myself onto my elbows. The world swayed around me. With my blurred vision, I saw Agatha lunge, swinging the heavy chain at my head.

I rolled out of the way. The chain hit the floor with a wood-breaking thwack. I heaved myself to my feet and crouched low, dodging the wildly swinging chain.

"It could have been a peaceful sleep," she said in a low, dangerous voice. "The profound blackness of sleep. Nothing more. No pain, no violence. The rest would have been absolute and tranquil. There was only enough poison to take out a little over half the Flock. The ones that survived would have gone with us."

"Us?" I asked, wiping blood from my lips.

She swung the chain again and I jumped out of her reach. "The important ones. The ones who make Edenton what it is," she said. Her hair escaped her neat bun and madness swirled in her eyes. "The chosen ones."

The Reverend, nestled on his throne as if in front of a TV, tsked loudly. "Agatha, do you think you are more important than anyone else here?"

Agatha dropped her arm, the end of the chain hitting the floor. Her eyes opened wide with disbelief. "Reverend, you said that we would—"

But before she could finish her sentence, a blur of silver smacked against her ear and she folded into a heap on the floor. Gabriel stood with the bat in his hands. It was coated in blood and I looked past him to see the security guard, gun still in his hands, beaten and unconscious, sprawled out on the floor.

I raised my eyebrows at Gabriel.

He shrugged. "Little League. I could hit a sixty-mile-per-hour ball when I was eight years old."

"Nice," I said. "Messed up, but nice."

I bent to pry the chain from Agatha's fingers, feeling no remorse. She'd killed eleven people on the last Bright Night—who knew what other horrible things she'd done for the Reverend. Her fingers were chilled from the iron, flecks of rust on her skin.

When I stood, pain shot through my back. I winced, squeezing my eyes shut. As I opened my eyes, I saw the Reverend pointing his handgun at Gabriel's temple. I thought, with a detached sense of ludicrousness, that I didn't know such a disgusting lump of a man could move so fast.

"I know a game we can play, Gabriel," the Reverend said. "Deer hunter?"

"That's a little expected, don't you think?" Gabriel asked, his tone mocking. But his brow was wrought with worry. A slow drip of sweat tracked down his face.

"You have a smart mouth, boy," the Reverend said. "It would be a relief to silence it."

"You won't do that," I said to the Reverend.

"Do what, child?" he asked. "Take away what God gave him? His life? It's my every right to take it away."

"No, you wouldn't kill your key moneymaker."

The Reverend's eye ticked.

"You know, your best money-making prostitute," I said, flashing Gabriel a look. "Sorry," I said to him.

"All good," he said. "I've been called worse."

"Do you two think this is some kind of joke?" With a tilt of his quivering second chin he indicated the Flock warring in the pavilion. "Your peers are dying. Killing each other for the privilege of joining me in the new Edenton."

"How are you going to refill your stock?" I asked, stepping closer to the Reverend.

"Stock for what, child?"

"Las Casitas?" I asked. I waited for a reaction. His face was a blank mask. "The members of the Flock you sell to high-paying patrons. Like us. Gabriel's worth a lot, according to Thaddeus. Why would you kill your prized animal?"

"Now you're calling me an animal?" Gabriel asked, acting a little too confident. I could see through it though, down to the panic rippling below the surface of his calm.

"Enough of you," the Reverend said.

I heard him breathe out in a huff. He raised a meaty hand and, with one push, shoved Gabriel toward the edge of the stage. He grasped at the Reverend for balance, knocking the gun from his hand. It skittered off the stage and into the fighting below.

I rushed forward.

"No!" I caught Gabriel by the hem of his shirt, but it slipped from my fingers and he tumbled into the flailing limbs and madness of the Flock.

I dove in after him, hitting the floor with a thud that rattled my teeth. The fighting around me was loud and frantic, flashes of bloody faces dipping into my line of vision. My hand felt weighty, and I realized I still had the length of chain in my grip. Something swung at my head and I ducked, only for it to catch a hank of my hair and drag me to the ground. Tears blurred my eyes. I looked up to see Enrique standing over me with a chain in one hand, crowbar in the other. When he smiled down at me, his teeth were coated with blood.

"I'm sorry, Mia," he said. "But I have to bash in your pretty face." He lifted the crowbar over his head.

I scrambled backward. "You don't have to do this!" I kept moving as he advanced on me. My back hit the edge of the stage. I was cornered. "Do you want to see Ibbie?"

Enrique paused, crowbar over his head. "How do you know about Ibbie?" he asked. His eyes went from dark and haunted to soft.

"I met her the other night," I said, eyeing the crowbar. "She's trying to get to you and Angél. She wants to be with you guys again. She loves you and misses you and wants to get you out of here—"

In a flash, a bat caught him in the stomach. He doubled over and fell to the ground. I looked up. Bridgette, face streaked with tears and dirt, glanced down at me before swinging the bat wildly into the fighting mass of people.

I stared after her for a few seconds, thunderstruck, and scanned the pavilion for Gabriel. I caught sight of him in the far corner on his knees. Someone had him in a choke hold from behind. I scrambled to my feet and ran toward him, dodging people along the way. I skidded to a stop in front of them, breathing heavily and staring at the man choking Gabriel. At first, I didn't recognize him. I blinked, trying to figure out who he was.

I heard Gabriel rasp, "Mia. Help."

I swung the chain at the man's head and he struck the floor like a sack of dirt.

Gabriel fell forward on his hands, gasping for air. I dropped to his side.

"You okay?" My eyes went immediately to the reddening mark around his neck.

He coughed. "Almost." He coughed again. "Who was that guy?"

"Prayer Circle," I said. "He was in the Reverend's cottage serving those pink drinks."

I glanced around the pavilion and realized there were a number of faces I didn't recognize. Had the Reverend let loose the locals he employed to help kill off the Flock?

Onstage, the Reverend was sitting back on his throne watching the mayhem with a shameless grin. I helped Gabriel to his feet and glanced around for the gun that had fallen off stage, worried that if one of the Flock found it, he or she would gun down someone in the pavilion. The fighting had to stop. I flung my arm around Gabriel and dragged him along with me, back to the stage, and ran up the stage steps.

"Make them stop!" I yelled to the Reverend once we reached the top.

He slowly turned his head toward me. "Come here, child, and I will."

"No," I said.

"You want them to stop? Then come here." He reached out a hand, bloated fingers curving to beckon me forward. "You did this, girl. You made all this happen."

"This isn't my fault!" I said.

"Isn't it? If you hadn't interfered, we'd still be living here peacefully. Now come here and see how many lives you save!"

*You've changed everything, do you know that? Now, it won't be peaceful. It will be hell.*

I shuddered at that thought. This was my fault. If I hadn't escaped, if I hadn't come back for the network, hadn't stolen the poison. I stepped forward, but Gabriel held me back.

"Don't," Gabriel gasped, still catching his breath.

I unhooked Gabriel's arm from mine and walked toward the Reverend. At the edge of the stage, I saw the bloodied bat Gabriel had held earlier and swiped it off the ground.

The Reverend laughed at me.

Gabriel called my name, but I kept moving.

"You won't use that, child," the Reverend said as I approached.

"You don't know what I'll do," I said. "Now make them stop fighting."

The Reverend glanced at me with suspicion, and paused briefly before yelling "Stop" over the horrific din of the skirmish below. "Everyone stop!"

Everything went eerily silent. Edenton seemed frozen inside a block of ice. Even the morning sun, reaching down around us in wide golden beams, was still and cold. The wind in the trees stopped. The birds silenced.

I breathed in steadily, deeply, trying to calm myself.

Down on the floor of the pavilion I didn't see a crowd. I saw a jumble of mangled limbs, matted hair, and crumpled forms. A few older, male members of the Flock stood, clothes torn and skin bruising, slashes leaking blood, along with the faces I didn't know. I saw Bridgette and Dina among them. They stood back to back, breathing heavily, each armed with a bloodied weapon. I saw Freddie, standing against a column of the pavilion, gun raised, dark eyes wide with horror.

The other security guards had disappeared.

Sister lay contorted in the back, where she'd stood with the girls from the sewing cottage, her arms and legs twisted in unnatural directions. Suzanne stood next to her, wooden board in hand, the end of it stained dark. Her face was splattered. Eyes bright and expectant, she stared up at the Reverend. At her feet, Kori began crawling away from her as if she were contagious and deadly.

"I want each of you," the Reverend bellowed, taking my arm in a harsh grip, "the survivors, the ones blessed by God Himself, to witness the death of this girl."

In a panic, I tried to wrench my arm away and swing the bat at him at the same time. I connected with his shoulder and he let go of my arm. I swung again wildly, but the bat slipped from my grip and tumbled to the stage. The Reverend's hand hooked onto my arm again, tightening with a wounding force. I cast my alarmed gaze to Gabriel. A security guard now stood next to him, gun pointed at his head.

The Reverend continued, breathing heavily, clearly in pain. "She cast aside our beliefs for her own. And, you know what those beliefs are? She believes in doubting everything! She believes knowledge is freedom! She believes that faith . . . " He paused for effect. "That faith is not wanting to know what's true!"

The quotes from Papa in my sketchbook.

So the Reverend knew everything about us. There were no secrets for the Flock. Only secrets kept from us.

He looked down at me. The Reverend's mouth was a thin pale slash. Belatedly, I realized he was holding the scalpel.

My heart thrummed painfully against my ribs. Maybe one was broken? I glanced around for some kind of weapon, but I couldn't wrestle out of his grip.

"You are a cruel and evil man," I said, voice sounding shaken. But the Flock needed to know. They had to know. "You do nothing in the name of God, you do it for yourself." I looked out over the Flock. "He sold us at Las Casitas like we were slaves!"

In those left standing, flickers of understanding lit their eyes. Maybe they all remembered what happened at Las Casitas.

I glanced back at the Reverend. He glared at me from beneath his sweating brow.

"What happened to the preacher?" I asked him. "The one who preached sermons about joy being the fruit of the spirit and blessing the peacemakers? What happened to that good, devout man? The one you were before . . . before Thaddeus turned you into this monster?"

The Reverend screamed, a rough unadulterated cry of hatred and rage, and swung the knife. I lunged back. My feet slipped out from beneath me, sliding uncontrollably in the blood on the stage. His full weight hit me, knocking me to the ground. I couldn't tell where the scalpel was as he clambered over me. I hadn't heard it fall. Then it was there, above my face, the metallic edge winking beneath the dried blood. Gasping, I struggled, but he pinned my legs with his.

He grinned at me, his teeth a canine mix of dull and sharp. A long line of spit leaked from the corner of his lip and stretched down to collect in my hair. I turned my head away.

"Thaddeus said you all would do as we said. He said that you would obey us without question!" Tears glistening in his bloodshot eyes, he held the scalpel to my neck and leaned down closer. "Now, Mia." His breath was rancid and sour. "Recognize you are a sinner—full of vices and wants—and repent before you step into death."

He was breathing heavily, as if saying the words had stolen his remaining strength. I shifted my weight to my elbows and shoved my shoulder into his, causing him to lean to one side. And the knife's edge to slice along the skin of my throat. Superficial, I thought, so I could keep going. Just a superficial cut.

Ignoring the stinging pain, I tangled my leg around his, pulled, forcing him to tumble with me. We struggled, rolling over and over, a whirlwind of clashing arms and kicking legs. He screamed again, either with pain or determination, so loud it felt as if my finer bones vibrated beneath my skin.

Then he was over me, on his knees, the knife held high above him.

"Be still," he yelled. "And know that I am God: I will be exalted among the heathen, I will be exalted in the earth!"

# Chapter Thirty-Five

The Reverend hovered there, gazing down at me with a gleam of madness in his eyes. I watched paralyzed as the scalpel arced down toward me with unnatural slowness. I squeezed my eyes shut.

A gunshot rang out. My eyes sprung open. Before the knife slashed across my neck, the Reverend's expression was scrubbed blank with shock, and he stilled. The scalpel clattered as it hit the stage floor. Scarlet blood seeped through the blue fabric of his shirt. He tipped back and collapsed, his bloated body contorting awkwardly when he hit the ground.

I couldn't move. Icy fear held me down. Slowly, tears stung my eyes as the disbelief took hold, spilling down my cheeks, searing a cut on my face. I let out a breath or a scream, I couldn't tell which, and forced myself to sit up. I twisted back to see the surviving members of the Flock staring at something in the back of the pavilion.

There, in a beam of morning sunlight, Aliyah stood, holding the Reverend's gun out in front of her, still aimed at the stage. Her face was tracked with tears.

My heart stuttered at the sight. She shot him. She shot him to save me.

When she saw me rise, she gradually lowered the gun and leaned back against the post behind her. Her gaze skirted the pavilion in astonishment, at the battered and the bloody, at the broken and the dead.

Gabriel ran toward me and took me by the shoulders. "Are you all right?"

I stared at him. In those green and blue eyes I saw the sharp outline of my battered face.

"Are you hurt?" he asked.

"No," I said. With shaking fingers I felt for the cut on my neck. They came away with only a small amount of blood. I glanced behind him. "What happened to the guard?"

Gabriel shrugged. "He took off. After . . . " He jutted his chin at the Reverend's body.

I turned and looked out over what was left of the Flock. Beaten bodies laced the ground of the pavilion, limbs twisted in unnatural directions. Blood and dirt stained the wooden floor. The humidity was heavy. The metallic scent of blood, and a smell that wasn't unlike thawed meat, hung in the air. Nausea hit me in a wave and I dropped to my knees, throwing up what little I had in my stomach. I felt a warm hand on my back, then fingers raking the hair away from my face. I wiped my mouth with the back of my forearm and glanced up to see Gabriel.

"Liar," he said. "You're not okay."

"No, I'm not," I said as I got to my feet again. "I don't think I'll ever be okay."

He looked out over the pavilion. "Me neither."

A few men I didn't recognize lay on the floor, injured, but the ones who had survived had fled. Now, from high on the stage, I picked out some of the faces of the dead. Juanita's mother. Mama's cottage mate, Jin Sang. Two children would be motherless. I glanced around. More than two.

I saw Edgar in the distance and a flood of people behind him, rushing toward the pavilion. Each wore green-and-brown camouflage clothing, and they were armed with guns. Some, though, held white boxes with red crosses painted on the side.

They'd come. Too late.

When Edgar reached the entrance of the pavilion, he stopped cold. "Dear God," he said, and I looked out again at the bodies.

Bloodied weapons littered the floor. Bridgette and Dina, shock in their wide eyes, picked their way to Aliyah, who had slid down the post and sat sobbing in her hands. Then members of the network swooped in behind Edgar and immediately began tending to the wounded, as if they'd expected to find the Flock dead or injured.

Edgar made his way around the perimeter of the pavilion and caught sight of us onstage. He climbed the steps.

"We tried to get here sooner," he said as he approached, "but we got lost in the tunnels." He shook his head. "What in God's name happened?"

I couldn't think about it. I didn't want to relive it. Not now, not ever.

"In God's name . . . " Gabriel repeated. He took Edgar aside and explained what he could in a low voice. I tried not to listen.

When a helicopter swooped overhead, I ducked, even though we were covered by the roof of the pavilion. I must have said something because suddenly Gabriel was at my side, Edgar rushing over behind him.

"It's ours," Edgar said. "We're bringing medics in to airlift out the wounded."

Immediately, my thoughts went to Juanita.

"Aliyah!" I called.

She lifted her face from her hands and looked up at me. Dina sat next to her, her arm wrapped around Aliyah's shoulders, rocking gently. Bridgette stood above them, staring down at her own hands as if she'd never seen them before.

"Juanita?" was all I needed to say.

"She's okay," Aliyah said in a shaky voice. "I found Nurse Ivy lying on the ground outside our cottage a few minutes ago." Her haunted gaze drifted around the pavilion. "She looks dead. So I ran here to find you and . . ."

Juanita wasn't dead. But so many others were. I glanced down at the Reverend's body, bloated and still. A sick sense of relief hit me, relief at the lifeless way his arms sprawled out at his sides, how his leg twisted up next to him in a freakish angle. He was dead and couldn't hurt us anymore.

Screams sounded through Edenton. At first, it sounded like the squeals of the children in the play yard, but the screams became piercing. Panicked.

"The schoolhouse," I said to Gabriel, then turned to Edgar. "The schoolhouse! The Reverend sent the children to the schoolhouse."

I bolted down the stage steps two at a time, pain jolting through me with every step. Just as quickly as the screams rose up in the silence, they stopped. When I got to the doors of the schoolhouse, Gabriel was already there. He rammed his shoulder against the double doors, but they were locked. He tried to kick them open, but they held firm.

"Wait," I said to him and listened at the doors for a moment before yelling, "Mama! What's happening?"

No answer.

"Mama!" I said, pounding on the door.

Edgar came up beside me. "Stand back," he said, pulling out his gun. "Get away from the doors," he called loudly. "I have a gun! Get the children away!"

Still, there was no sound on the other side.

Edgar shot the lock at a downward angle. Wood splintered into the air, and the lock dropped away. He pried the doors apart, dashing in first, gun pointed ahead of him. And froze. Gabriel and I followed, and the room came into view.

Grizz stood at the far end of the schoolhouse, holding his gun. The children huddled together in front of him, Mama shielding as many as she could with her body, including Max, but there were too many to protect.

"Eugene!" Edgar called.

Grizz, with a shocked stare, turned and met his brother's eyes. A wave of recognition passed between them. Then Grizz looked back at the children and aimed his gun.

"Eugene, stop," Edgar said. "This isn't you."

"This isn't me?" Grizz asked, eyes glittering with tears. "You don't know me anymore."

"I know you wouldn't do this."

Edgar motioned to the children. Max, arms curled around Mama's leg, silently sobbed. I couldn't stand to watch Max cry.

"I'm going to the nursery after I'm done here," Grizz said, and hiccupped a sad laugh. "The nursery. The Reverend wants me to shoot the babies."

"The Reverend is dead," I said. "He doesn't give orders anymore."

Grizz laughed again, but this time the brimming tears in his eyes spilled down his face. "You think the Reverend gives the orders?" He kept the gun focused on the children.

"Who gives the orders, Eugene?" Edgar asked.

"Will you stop calling me that?" Grizz yelled at his brother.

"Then who?"

"Thaddeus, okay? Thaddeus gives the orders." His eyes flicked to Edgar. "The Reverend is a joke! He's done whatever Thaddeus told him to do for years!" Grizz squeezed his eyes shut and opened them again. "Why are you here? You abandoned me," Grizz said to Edgar.

"They sent us to different foster homes," Edgar said, keeping his gun trained on Grizz. "How could we stay together?"

Grizz began to weep openly, gun still focused on the children. The kids stood motionless, staring at his gun.

"Thaddeus told me I had to kill them," he sobbed, wiping his eyes on the sleeve of his shirt.

Edgar approached him slowly. "Eugene—"

"My name is Grizz!"

"I'll never call you that," Edgar said. "I'd never call you a name not given to you by our mother."

I saw Grizz buckle at that, like he'd been punched in the stomach. But he straightened his back once the emotion faded. And aimed his gun again.

"What the hell is wrong with you?" Gabriel said to Grizz. "Your brother is here. Your brother! He's here in Edenton to take you home. And you're following Thaddeus's orders? What's the point now?"

"It's what I do. Follow orders."

Was that what Grizz had become? Nothing more than an attack dog for Thaddeus, acting at his command?

"When was the last time you saw your brother?" I asked Grizz softly.

Grizz paused, genuinely thinking about the question. "Almost ten years ago."

"Ten years," Gabriel said, coming around to face Grizz and the gun. "I haven't seen my own brother for about that long. But my brother is dead. Yours is alive, well, and right here."

Grizz nodded, once. "Out of the way, Gabriel."

But Gabriel didn't move.

I glanced at the children. Some looked confused and lost. Others wept. And Max, so little for his age, would remember this moment forever. Whether he wanted to or not.

"What about my brother, Grizz?" I asked in a whisper, eyes fixed on Max. "Don't take him away from me."

Max looked up and called my name, as if he'd just realized I was there. Mama mumbled what sounded like a prayer with her eyes squeezed shut. Her arms were stretched wide across the children she protected behind her.

"Dammit, Grizz!" Gabriel yelled. "You have a brother! He's right here. Standing beside you." His eyes flicked to Edgar and back to Grizz. "Granted, he has a gun pointed at you, but still, he's here, because of you. You know what I'd give to have my brother back?"

"Grizz, please," I pleaded. "Please don't take my family away from me. You've protected us for so long. Whenever I saw you, Grizz, I felt safe. Don't turn against us. We've always trusted you. These kids are innocent. They haven't done anything to go against the Reverend—or Thaddeus." I paused a moment, then whispered, "Please."

Very slowly, Grizz lowered the gun.

Gabriel swiped it from his hands.

Seconds later, Mama and Max were in my arms.

# Chapter Thirty-Six

The fading sunlight peeked its way through the frosted window of my room. I traced the glass with my finger, wanting to wipe away the opaque film, but it was permanent. Bitter, icy air seeped through the casement, causing my skin to lift into tiny bumps, even though I wore a fleece sweatshirt. I'd never felt this kind of cold before.

"Hello," Dr. Haarland said in her sharp Eastern European accent. I turned from the window and saw her standing in the doorway. Her unnaturally red hair was pulled away from her face, so unlike the picture on her ID badge hanging from her neck. Below the Elysian Peak Hospital insignia, her photo showed her hair loose and flowing over her shoulders in blond waves.

Her icy eyes flicked to the small, untouched tray of pills next to my bed. "No sleep for you, I see."

"No," I said. "I'm feeling better, though."

I'd been refusing drugs since the network had morphed the pavilion into a makeshift first-aid center. Even when they'd loaded us on busses to transport us to the airstrip near Edenton, I didn't take my meds for the bumpy ride.

"What about sleeping?" she said as she walked into the room. She grazed her finger over the screen in her hand and it flared to life. "Any issues?"

I shook my head, even though I couldn't sleep, and perched on the wide windowsill. A chilly draft hit the back of my neck. I reached back and took my hair out of its ponytail, letting the thick brown strands block the cold air.

"I'd like to take a look at the wound on the side of your neck." She placed her flat computer on my bed. It was like the one Edgar used to control the telescope, only bigger. "May I?"

I said "Yes" and she peeled away the bandage. She gave a curt nod.

"Dinner service is ending soon," she said after replacing the tape on my neck. "Will you be joining the others in the cafeteria or taking it in your room?"

Since arriving two days ago, I'd eaten meals in my room, feeling too jumpy to leave. They'd put me in a small, comfortable room with a soft bed but no view. I couldn't complain. We were all someplace safe, out of Edenton, being taken care of by a devoted team of doctors and nurses.

"I'll go to the cafeteria," I said.

"Very well, I'll let the nurses' station know," Dr. Haarland said.

With a smile on her fuchsia lips she left my room. The door drifted closed behind her.

I washed my face and pulled my hair back. Then I stepped out into a hallway that was long and artificially bright. My soft-soled slippers made no sound on the tiled floor. My room was at the far end of the hall that had become the women's wing. I'd ventured out only once, to find Juanita, but was told she was in another part of the hospital for more critically injured patients. Mama had come to see me, as had Aliyah.

Gabriel hadn't, though.

I found Aliyah's room a few doors down from mine and knocked. There was no answer.

"Aliyah is in therapy," a nurse said as she passed. She looked down at the little device in her hand. "She'll be through in about forty-five minutes if you'd like to come back."

I nodded and thanked her, trying to remember what injuries Aliyah sustained. I couldn't recall any physical ones.

By the time I'd made my way to the cafeteria on the first floor, many people were finished with dinner, draining out through the double swinging doors. It was hard not to spot Freddie, who stood at least a head taller than the others. Bridgette was latched onto his arm, her head leaning on his bicep. Dina, still Bridgette's shadow, smiled at me as I passed and I returned her smile, happy to see someone without a dazed look in her eyes.

Windows lined one side of the cafeteria. The bottom half of the glass was opaque, like the window in my room. An indigo sky was visible through the clear glass top, touched by wispy lavender clouds. Round tables were scattered over the polished concrete floor. Uniformed hospital workers arranged chairs neatly.

Mama sat at one of those tables, with Max. When she saw me, she stood. Despite all we'd been through, the smile that lit her face caused my heart to expand a little in my chest.

"Hi, Mia," Max said, shoveling chocolate pudding into his mouth. Two empty bowls sat next to him on the table, both swirled inside with smudges of chocolate.

Mama took my hand and led me to the seat next to her. "I'm so happy to see you down here," she said.

I was glad to see her, too. My resentment had faded over the past few days, and I was left with a simple, uncomplicated love for Mama. "I needed to get out for a while."

She gave me a small smile and took my hand. "Good. Do you want me to get you some food?"

I said, "I can get it."

"No, no. You sit." Her gaze lifted above my head to the far corner of the cafeteria. "There's someone who has been waiting to talk to you."

I followed her line of sight. Gabriel sat at a table in a darkened corner of the room. His parents sat on the opposite side of the table, his mother smiling fondly at him. The left side of her face was bandaged. I'd heard his parents had survived the Flock's fight by escaping the pavilion, but not before searching the crowd for Gabriel. His mother had been knocked unconscious and Gabriel's dad had dragged her out of the pavilion.

They spoke quietly. Mama raised her hand, catching Gabriel's mom's attention. His mom touched Gabriel's arm and he looked up at her in pleasant confusion. She tilted her head at me. When our eyes met across the room, I watched Gabriel's expression change. The curious smile on his face shifted to something harder.

"Are you sure he wants to talk?" I asked Mama. "He doesn't look very happy to see me."

Mama stood. "I'm sure. Come on, Max." She held out her hand to my little brother. "I'll get you some more pudding."

Max lifted the bowl to his mouth and licked the inside.

With the exception of the workers straightening chairs, we were the only ones in the big room. Gabriel's parents seemed to get some kind of hint from Mama, because they left the cafeteria, too.

Gabriel waved me over. I examined him for a moment. He wore simple clothes like mine: a fleecy dark shirt and jeans. He watched me between strands of hair falling over his forehead. The half-moons of gray beneath his eyes could have been a trick of the light, but I knew he was as exhausted and devastated as me. But that familiar beauty of his was still there. The dark hollows beneath his cheekbones, the smudge of his eyelashes, the way a shadow dented his bottom lip. The emptiness that clouded in my chest since arriving at the hospital started to melt away. Adrenaline sang through my veins. I wanted to run to him, but instead, I waved him over to my table.

"Ricci . . ." he mouthed.

I slapped my hands on the tabletop, the sound causing a hospital employee to turn, and I stood. I took my time making my way around the chairs to the other side of the room. His eyes, lit with a sleepy kind of danger, tracked my progress, causing my skin to heat. He hadn't bothered to come see me during the past few days, but I hadn't bothered to seek him out, either.

"You summoned me?" I asked and folded my arms across my chest.

"If it were only that easy," he said and pulled out the chair next to him. "Will you please sit down? You're making me nervous just standing there."

"I'm making you nervous?"

"Even outside of Edenton miracles happen. Sit."

I plopped down in the chair, my arms still crossed.

"They wouldn't let me come see you," he said. "We can't go into the women's wing of the hospital."

I felt a tiny bit elated. He did try. "Really?"

"Yeah, and if you'd bothered to try to come see me, you'd know you can't come into the men's wing either. Unless you couldn't come see me for some other reason. Are you doing okay?"

"Yeah," I whispered. "It's just weird being here. And not in Edenton."

"Better, though, right? Not being in Edenton?"

I smiled. "Yeah, better." I shifted in my seat, a little closer to him. "Are you okay?"

He waved me off. "Sure, you know, still emotionally rattled but no one knows trauma like me. I layer traumatic event over traumatic event, and they start canceling each other out."

"Mia!" Max called and ran up to the table. "I got you chocolate pudding."

He slid a bowl in front of me. He held a second bowl in his hand, spoon shoved into the pudding, ready to eat. I thanked him, but he'd already started shoveling pudding in his face. Mama approached with a tray. She moved the pudding aside and placed the bowl on the table.

"Gabriel." She smiled in greeting.

"Hi," Gabriel said with uncharacteristic shyness.

"Mia, please eat. Max and I are going to the recreation room to play some games. Join us there after—" She flicked her gaze between Gabriel and me. "After the two of you talk."

"Sure," I said.

Mama kissed me on the top of my head and left with Max in tow, pudding and all.

Gabriel glanced over his shoulder. "My dad said the network didn't find Thaddeus."

A familiar fear chilled my spine. "Of course he had an escape planned. He seemed to have everything planned."

"Except you kneeing him in the nuts. He didn't see that coming." Gabriel reached a finger out and stroked the skin on my hand. "You were incredible. Through all of it, you know that?"

I watched his finger trace a pattern of little circles, shocked by the feel of it, and said, "You were, too. I didn't expect you to come back to Edenton after we escaped."

"I didn't expect to, either. But I had a lot to come back for."

"Your parents?"

"Yeah, them, too." His hand gently squeezed mine and then he drew it away. He took in a big breath. "So."

I poked at the salad on my plate. "I guess you're headed back to New York after they release us." My heart felt as small as a stone in my chest.

A tiny line appeared between his brows. "Um, maybe."

"You said that's where you belong."

"I have to tell you . . . " He stopped, shook his head once. "No, I *want* to tell you something. Something I've never told anyone."

I leaned in a bit closer, throwing a glance over my shoulder at the cafeteria workers cleaning up the dinner tables. "Okay," I said.

"A few years after Griffin died, I found a note he left for me."

"A few years after he died?"

"Yeah. He died when I was eight, and I found it when I was thirteen. I'm sure it was kind of a joke on me, too." He shrugged. "He hid it in a book on the bookshelves in my room, and I wasn't the most voracious reader."

I tilted my head. "Was it hidden in the Bible?"

"Jesus Christ, no. Why would I have a Bible in my room?" He lowered his chin and stared at me. "You know me better than that, Ricci."

"I was kidding. I do know you better than that."

Gabriel's lips curved up. "Good. Well, it was hidden in *The Stand*, by Stephen King. Ever heard of it?"

"No," I said, a little embarrassed. "We weren't allowed to have secular books in the house when I was young."

"Oh," he said, and looked like he wanted to say *I'm sorry*. "My dad," he continued, "used to get me entire series of books. I had hundreds in my room, even though all the books I read for school were on my phone. I think he hoped they would keep me company because he couldn't—or wouldn't. Spine after spine of titles stared at me, begging me to read them. I would pull them down and look at the covers. Decide if I wanted to read them on my phone."

"Wait," I said. "You actually judged books by their covers?"

"Idioms are idioms for a reason," he said with a shrug. "That's what I was doing when the note fell out. Staring at the two figures on the cover—one in white with a sword, the other in darker colors with a sickle." He paused and studied a scratch on the wooden surface of the table. "I remember wondering *why a sickle?* when the note slipped out from between the pages."

I asked the question cautiously and slowly. "Was it a suicide note?"

"Not really. A message maybe? It was dated the day Griffin died and scrawled in his twisted handwriting, like his fingers were all cramped."

"Are you sure it was from him?"

"Yeah. I'm sure. The handwriting was his but it was just a little . . . different. Rushed, maybe? I sat on the floor of my room right in front of the bookshelves and read it over and over until I'd memorized it."

He intertwined his fingers in front of him on the table, not looking at me but at some spot alongside the table. Quietly, almost reverently, he recited the words:

> *Gabe, their indifference is our legacy. And now, it's our nature to hurt—to hurt ourselves, to hurt others. My blood*

*is on your hands like yours is on mine. Remember the*
*blood. It will keep you from destroying everyone you love.*

He paused and smiled again, but this time it was only a facsimile of
a smile. "Not as cheery as, say, a Hallmark card," he said, "or a bomb
threat."

I felt a slow burn of anger in my chest. How could someone do that
to a little kid? Then I thought of the Reverend, of Thaddeus, and what
they'd done to two hundred people.

"Their indifference? Does that mean your parents?" I asked.

"Yeah."

"Griffin had, you know, problems." I pointed to my temple. "He
wasn't right in the head."

"We can say that, sure. But I ended up hurting everyone I cared
about, everyone I loved, because of him." He leaned against the wall.
"Mia, I know it was because of him, but I can't just forget what that note
said. It fucking scarred me. I'd suffered this unbelievable trauma. I went
through a trial, hours and hours of therapy, lost all my friends, occasionally lost my parents—even Miss Beverly didn't come back to take care
of me after that. We couldn't get a nanny for months after Griffin died
because none of them wanted to be near me. They were all afraid."

He dragged his fingers through his hair. "Right before I found the
note, things were getting a little better, you know? My parents tried to
be with me, as much as they could. I was back in school. I was making
friends. I started playing baseball again . . . " He took in a deep breath.
"Then I found it. And I realized he was right—"

"No—"

"Let me talk, Mia." He sounded terse, impatient.

I tucked myself back into my chair, folding my arms over my chest
protectively. "Okay."

Gabriel squeezed his eyes shut, wincing. "I'm sorry," he said. "You
need to know—" He stopped. "Let me talk for a minute. If I don't say
it now, I never will."

I nodded.

"I like it when you obey, Ricci."

I gave him a squinty scowl.

"Teasing. Sorry." He shifted in his seat and his face drifted closer to mine. "I believed what he told me in that note, that if I cared for someone, I'd be responsible for the bad things that happened to that person. Like what happened to Griffin, like what happened to my parents' relationship—before and after he died. Griffin told me that when I was born they began drifting apart, living separate lives."

I felt my face redden with exasperation. "How could you believe anything he told you?"

"How could anyone in Edenton believe anything the Reverend told them? You believe the people you love and trust—blind love is still love."

I couldn't disagree.

Gabriel said, "After I found the note I said screw it and gave up on the therapy and became what Griffin was—a player, a guy I hated being, but I wouldn't let myself care about anyone or anything. Because I believed every word of that note. I believed for years. I believed it when I came to Edenton. I believed it until—"

He stopped and glanced around the cafeteria. I followed his gaze and saw one of the workers watching us intently. Her hands were stacked on the top of her broom handle, and she let out an impatient sigh.

"Come on." Gabriel seized my hand and yanked me to my feet.

At the end of the room was a small door. He tugged me to it and we snuck through. I didn't notice if anyone saw us. I didn't really care. Outside was a hallway, dark and barely lit with brass wall sconces. It was different here than in the parts of the hospital I'd seen before. It smelled of lemon wax and dust. The tiled floor led away in a series of black-and-white patterned diamonds.

Gabriel scanned up and down the long corridor.

"Where are we going?" I asked.

"Don't know." He craned his neck and spotted something down the hall. "This way," he said, dragging me along.

I shot a quick look over my shoulder. There was no one around. No one had followed us from the cafeteria. The hallway was eerily quiet, only hollow knocking sounds came from the radiators interspersed down the corridor.

Gabriel pushed open a folding door. Above the door a sign read "Telephone" in blue letters. He shoved me inside the narrow wooden box. The backs of my knees met with a little corner bench. Gabriel stepped in front of me, so close our bodies touched from chest to legs. He closed the door behind him. A small, dim light above us popped on.

"What are you doing?" I asked him. My insides fluttered.

"I came back for you," he said.

"You came back for me? When?"

"Remember when you were standing in that torn green dress and Veronica was prepping you to go back into Edenton?"

I nodded.

"I stood in the doorway of that room and thought, *she's goddamn fearless.*"

I laughed. "I was scared to death!"

"Fearless, and strong. I came back into Edenton because I hoped you were fearless enough to be with me."

"Be with you?"

Gently, he took my face in his hands. "You know what, Mia Ricci?"

I smiled up at him, surprised. But I couldn't blot out the bubbling happiness in my chest. "What?"

A mischievous light lit his eyes, reminding me of that first night I'd met him in the kitchen, the night he stole my knife. The night he changed everything.

He brought his lips to mine and whispered, "I'm so happy you're not my sister." And he kissed me.